The Maids of Havana

THE MAIDS OF HAVANA

Pedro Pérez Sarduy

authorHOUSE®

AuthorHouse™
1663 Liberty Drive
Bloomington, IN 47403
www.authorhouse.com
Phone: 1-800-839-8640

First published by AuthorHouse   3/16/2010

ISBN: 978-1-4490-7070-0 (sc)

Printed in the United States of America
Bloomington, Indiana

This book is printed on acid-free paper.
Translation from the Spanish: Jonathan Curry-Machado

Edition: Jean Stubbs

© *Cover design: Ilmi Pérez Stubbs*

Front cover photo: The Floral Dance, Sociedad Bella Unión, Santa Clara, Cuba, 1949 (Family collection, courtesy of the author)

First published in French by Ibis Rouge Editions, Matoury, 2007
First published in Spanish by Editorial Plaza Mayor, San Juan, 2001 [2004]
Second edition in Spanish by Editorial Letras Cubanas, Havana, 2002

BY WAY OF PREFACE

I didn't think I would be the one to have the exceptional pleasure of presenting to Cuban readers *Las criadas de La Habana* (The Maids of Havana), a first incursion into the genre of the novel by the poet Pedro Pérez Sarduy. I was both very pleased and very enthusiastic about accepting the invitation from the Puerto Rican publisher, Plaza Mayor, to present a book by one who is part of my literary family.

In the Cuban narrative tradition, it is not common for poets to write short stories and novels. However, around the middle of the twentieth century major Cuban poets did begin to publish narrative genres, and I would like to begin this presentation by noting all the narrative of the sixties owes to one writer, the poet Pablo Armando Fernández. Pablo Armando's narrative – a lesser known area of his work – is what made possible the birth of the novel I have the honor of presenting to you all, The Maids of Havana.

As I said before, Pedro is part of my literary family. He was born in Santa Clara in 1943. He studied French Language and Literature at the University of Havana, where we were both students. Literature was not his sole interest. For a number of reasons, he followed in that Caribbean tradition whereby we writers are rarely professionals in the literary field – we may be veterinarians, photographers, or sailors. He himself had many occupations, but one in particular was journalism, from which we now know comes the freshness of his approach to fiction.

I believe in the power of the word, and, while this is the novel of a poet, I must again say that The Maids of Havana is born of literary experience grounded in Pablo Armando's *Los niños se despiden* (The

Children Bid Farewell, awarded 1968 Casa de las Américas Prize), and at the same time grafted on the literary phenomenon of the time we know as the testimonial novel.

I think the poet who wrote *Surrealidad* is able to move in and out of the literary conventions of this technique, and, above all, the ethic of authors regarding their chosen characters and spaces, while still respecting the advances in fiction in the Spanish-speaking world and certain forms of the novel, conceived as open, so open as for its lightness of touch to draw on contemporary female discourse.

In this, we have much to thank him for, and not only for the theme of a Black Cuban woman as exceptional as Marta, who, naturally, bears close relation to his mother, born and raised in the city of Santa Clara. In her youth, she went to Havana as a maid, shaped by values that in turn shaped this young writer.

I believe that in this novel there are elements that are fundamental, because it remains literary while at the same time registering the popular voice of certain women's worlds that at times seem closed and far apart from the world of men.

This is an extraordinary contribution because it is a chronicle of an un-chronicled social psychology whose complexity of racial and gender relations is of a richness yet to be appreciated. I truly believe it's going to be very hard to classify this novel.

What is important is that it is sheer joy to read, and with a boldness of expression in taking on the conflicts of Cuban society today, of Cuban culture, the experience of migrations and the existence of such diverse poles of that culture which is to be found disseminated throughout the universe in the knowledge that, today, there is only one Cuban culture.

Don't miss out on *The Maids of Havana*. Forget all you've read and written about maids around the world, especially in this Third World. Forget Jean Genet and read Pedro Pérez Sarduy.

Nancy Morejón, Winner of Cuba's 2001 National Literature Prize
Presenting the Cuban edition of Las criadas de la Habana *at the 2002 Havana International Book Fair*
Translation: Solimar Otero

ACKNOWLEDGEMENTS

I wish first and foremost to thank the Center for Latin American Studies and Center for African Studies at the University of Florida, Gainesville, USA, for hosting me in the Fall Semester of 1993 as a Scholar on their joint Rockefeller Foundation program. During my time there I conducted archival and library research in the University's invaluable Cuban collection housed in the Smathers Library. I was also able to visit and conduct interviews in various urban areas of the state of Florida, home to the vast majority of Cubans who have emigrated from the Island - the first of many visits and interviews to follow, not only in Florida but also other parts of the United States, including Washington D.C. I would like to thank in particular the then Center directors, Professors Helen Safa and Olabiyi Yai, who have remained close and followed the various iterations of the book, as I worked on first the Spanish, then French and now English editions. Many others have journeyed with me, reading the manuscript and offering linguistic and literary criticism, and my gratitude extends to them all, but I wish in particular to thank Jonathan Curry-Machado for his painstaking work in seeking to render into English my *cubanismos*, on which we have compiled a glossary; David Akbar Gilliam for his helpful suggestions on the translation; and my partner in life and implacable critic

Jean Stubbs for her meticulous English-language revision and edition. The book, of course, is dedicated to the memory of my mother Marta, and also Julia, my aunt 'Tona', and all those women who apparently have no history...

Pedro Pérez Sarduy
London, January 2010

Contents

The Floral Dance

We were crossing Vidal Square in Santa Clara that Sunday in the middle of May when my brother-in-law Rey, Antonia, Orlando and I decided to have breakfast at the Café Parisién. Curiously, though we'd been drinking a lot, we were only tipsy, and having fun talking about the dance and singing some of the songs everyone knew by heart, since Isolina Carrillo had made them all the rage again. My sister-in-law and I threw each other a look and began singing together:

> *Two gardenias for you,*
> *With them I am saying,*
> *I love you, I adore you, my darling.*
> *Take good care of them I beg,*
> *For they'll be your heart and mine.*
> *Two gardenias for you,*
> *They come with all the warmth of a kiss,*
> *Like those kisses that I gave you and never*
> *Will you find in another love's embrace.*

We loved singing, especially after a couple of good drinks. Orlando and Rey provided backup, one imitating piano and the other whistling the melody, laughing as they listened to Antonia singing the second verse:

> *By your side they'll live and talk to you*
> *Just like when you are with me*
> *And have you believe that they say I love you.*

> *But if at dusk one day*
> *The gardenias of my love should wither,*
> *It's because they can see*
> *That your heart has betrayed me*
> *And you've found another love...*

I looked up at the big clock on the town hall. It would soon chime six in the morning.

The Floral Dance was the one all the young, especially young married couples, looked forward to each year. Girls spent months preparing their outfits, as if they were getting married. I remember that was the year my husband Orlando's brother married Antonia, who worked in the Trimiño household. They were very well known. Five of them were classical pianists and violinists, and they owned the best fabric stores in Santa Clara, Cienfuegos and Sagua la Grande. Antonia was slim like me, but taller, and we'd always go shopping together, especially to look for fabric to make our gowns. We already had several from previous dances, but there was absolutely no way we were going to that year's dance in the same clothes as the year before, let alone what we wore to the Christmas Eve dance in Placetas, where Beny Moré played.

My mother Alberta somehow always managed to keep all her dancing daughters happy. She used to make our gowns herself, and often had to chaperone us while we were still single. But that was all in the past now, at least as far as I was concerned, since I'd been married for over seven years and was lucky Orlando was a great dancer, like his brother Rey. That day, the two of us went to Trimiño's store round the corner from Vidal Square. There was an amazing sale of good cloth, and we were able to buy what we wanted. I was thinking of making myself an organza gown with some pink and white taffeta, but Antonia still hadn't decided what to do for hers. She knew she wanted it strapless, but she'd chosen a white satin that was very difficult to sew and needed stays to hold up the bust without letting the stitching show. But there was time and she did it. On the night, when she arrived at our house in the carriage, dressed for the big occasion, I was really taken by how beautifully fitted her ball gown had turned out, leaving her shoulders bare, and with a light hand-crocheted black stole around her arms and back.

'What do you think, Marta? How do I look?'

'Girl, you look gorgeous!'

The two brothers, my husband and hers, loved it when we dressed up, and we worked all year to please them. They were also something to see. My Orlando, all in white like his brother, didn't like clothes made from drill cloth, preferring to wear pinstripes in winter and gabardine in summer. That year he had a new double-breasted suit and everyone was commenting how well it was cut. He had all his best clothes made by Cordero, a very good tailor married to Florinda, and both were good friends of ours. Since Orlando was a shoemaker, he'd made himself a pair of white patent-leather shoes that were every bit as good as the best *Florisén*, those American shoes everyone wanted. They really stood out. Rey, wearing a really expensive, high-quality white 100% cotton drill suit, as usual was teasing his brother, telling him he looked thinner than a rake.

They both liked to party and would spend everything they had on occasions like this – the great Floral Dance at the Sociedad Bella Unión, for us people of color. That day there were dances all over Santa Clara: at the Sociedad El Gran Maceo, for mulattos and well-to-do blacks; the Casino Español, for the white middle class; and the Santa Clara Tennis Club and the Liceo, on Vidal Square, which was where the wealthy whites gathered to celebrate in their own way. But we didn't give a damn about their dances, because we members of Bella Unión did all we could to make sure ours were the best organized and always had the best bands. Some of the most sought after and hardest to get were Aragón, Beny, Fajardo, Arsenio Rodríguez and Orquesta América. That year Bella Unión had signed up Orquesta Aragón, from Cienfuegos, which was all the rage throughout the country.

Rey had said they would pick us up with the carriage at nine o'clock, and the two of them were there on the dot, impeccably dressed in white. Antonia looked a real beauty, and I must have as well. We cracked up laughing at my brother-in-law's flirting.

'Hey, sis-in-law, why don't you leave that old boy and come with me? Can't you see that's a walking-stick he's got there?'

Rey, who worked as a driver for a well-known architect, was five years younger than Orlando and was always joking about their age… who was born first, who was shorter, who fatter, who drank more, and that kind of thing; and we'd fall about ourselves every time with his loud infectious laugh that would single him out wherever he was. We'd hire a carriage to take us round the city center for an hour or so, throwing streamers, shaking noisemakers, and blowing cardboard horns. The whole city was partying and everyone was heading for their dances in convertibles, hired cars or open carriages, the horses trotting through the cobbled streets, which would explode at midnight with fireworks set off from the tallest buildings. The carriage dropped us at the corner of Plácido and Independencia, and we made our triumphal entrance into Bella Unión watched by everyone. There was always a huge crowd outside waiting to see the clothes of the dancers – particularly the women's gowns. It was unforgettable, especially when you knew what you were wearing was well worth the efforts of a whole year's work. Sometimes the gowns cost as much as a hundred pesos, and there were three or four dances a year. But, as I said, there was no way you'd go twice to a dance in the same dress, least of all the great Floral Dance, where we celebrated the coming of spring and opening of the summer season. It used to coincide with Independence Day celebrations, on the 20th of May, but Bella Unión wanted it dedicated to flowers, and so it remained. It sometimes coincided with Mothers' Day, which is the second Sunday in May, or my birthday, as it did that year, or our first son's birthday, the 13th. Ramoncito, who had just turned six, stayed at his grandmother's and aunts' house, which was close to ours. We knew he was happy we were out enjoying ourselves – as long as we brought him candy next morning. My mother-in-law and sisters-in-law all spoiled him so much that we didn't need worry – in fact, quite the opposite.

As we entered the Bella Unión ballroom, we greeted our friends and then went up to the second floor where tables had been reserved. We sat down while our men took care of the drinks: El Gaitero cider and Pedro Domecq brandy for our special cocktail, Spain in Flames. Antonia didn't drink much, but now and then she did like a glass of good cider. She didn't have time to taste even the first sip before the theme tune of the band was to be heard throughout Bella Union:

> *Aragón, Aragón...*
> *If you hear a sassy* son
> *You can be sure it's Aragón.*

It had been years since we'd danced to the band live, because, so Bella Unión members said, they were really expensive to hire, especially since now they were making records and had been on many tours in Cuba and abroad. But the young management was determined to put on a good dance, and Orquesta Aragón was due reward for all the members' hard work.

We were very happy as we took to our feet and went down the stairs on the arms of our partners to enjoy a truly unforgettable night, which – according to the reckoning of my gynecologist Dr Celestino Chang – turned out to be my first day of pregnancy with our daughter Teresita.

The first number was the danzón *The Magic Flute*, in which the flute soloist Richard Egües did a fantastic solo in competition with the violins and the dancers to see who could bring off the most daring and at the same time smoothest pirouettes. It isn't easy to dance danzón well. Not everyone can do it. You can't be moving your body too much, as you would for a mambo, because it's about gentle turns, pauses, graceful steps and the like. That's why they played the number that goes:

No, negrita, *no...*
Stop dancing the conga like that...
No, negrita, *no, I'm in the* Sociedad...
And if they see me
Dancing like they do in the slums
My reputation as a classy Negro
Will come crashing down...
No...

When Aragón played that number, people went crazy. Everyone was singing. A perfect dance partner was the best thing you could have at a dance like that, and my Orlando and his brother were simply two of a kind on the dance floor. Orlando took me by the waist and led me in a way that made me feel I was on air. Tall and slim as he was, no one would have guessed how firmly he would spin all around the dance floor.

I remember it was at a dance where we met. I can't deny I was dying to dance with him from the minute I first saw him. At the time, my mother was chaperoning three of us, the ones who most liked to party and weren't yet engaged. It was at a dance in Ranchuelo, with the Orquesta Arsenio Rodríguez. We'd gone on an excursion in a bus Bella Unión laid on for the young women who were also members. Ranchuelo was famous for its dances during the days of carnival and had its own little Sociedad that was very well organized. People in the town had money, because almost everyone worked at the Trinidad y Hermanos cigarette factory. They had a Liceo, Casino Español, and Sociedad for coloreds that was the envy of the whole of Las Villas province.

The night I saw Orlando dance and couldn't take my eyes off him, my mother pinched my arm more than ten times for me to calm down. And the inevitable happened. Our eyes met when my mother was paying attention to Yolanda, my younger sister, and Orlando came over and asked my mother's permission to dance with me. She had to agree, for all that she grumbled, though not before allowing herself to be flattered by a phrase that today still rings so hollow coming from Orlando:

'Ma'am, I would be pleased if you were to grant me a dance, but first I would like to dance with one of your daughters,' he said to my mother, motioning towards me.

'And who told you I dance?' my mother responded.

'These danzones make even the tiredest feet in this ballroom move.'

My sisters and I looked at each other from behind the chairs, giggling, though our mother wasn't at all amused, because I'd never seen her dance. She was always chanting old, old, songs for the santos, but I'd never ever seen her move a foot to dance, let alone in a dance hall. She did like taking us to all the dances we wanted, because, after all, they were the best places to meet a good man, and I know our mother had that idea fixated in her head. So that was how my relationship with Orlando began, four years later ending in marriage, after many dance halls, always with our mother as chaperone, right up until the final moment we got married, on the 15th of February 1942, when I was almost 19 and Orlando 25.

The clock in Santa Clara's Vidal Square began to chime, and I looked at the watch Orlando had given me for my birthday. It was six in the morning, and the birds in the trees, which had been frightened all night by rockets and other fireworks going off, were preparing for their journey to the savanna, until their pilgrimage back at dusk, just as they did every day of the year.

María la Sagüera

Maricusa had come late afternoon to have her hair straightened. I'd only done a couple that day, and when she let me know on Sunday that she would come on Monday before it went dark, after she finished her work cleaning doña Pepilla's house, I accepted with the permission of Elegguá. That Monday I'd lit a couple of good five-cent candles for him, and even cleaned his corner. I only worked Mondays once in a blue moon, but I really needed to, because things hadn't been going too well. Besides, Maricusa was one of my best clients, and though I would have preferred her to come in the morning like the other two, I didn't put her off, hurried the housework, sorted the kids out, and prepared the meal so when Orlando arrived he'd find everything ready.

'Marta, sorry, girl, but I thought I should tell you…'
'What now, woman?'
'Look, *Martona*, you know before I was with the doña I worked for Celedonio, the santero in La Vigía, cleaning his house behind the Provincial Hospital. Well, just round the corner lives an old friend of mine, who knows you by sight and who I went to visit a couple of nights ago. When I was leaving I saw something that left me cold. On the corner I saw a couple of lovers who looked as if they were fondling each other goodbye, and a shiver went through me, girl, when I realized the man was your husband. I commented on it to my friend Goyita, and she said she knew the woman by sight and knew she was a *palera*, she told me she was known in the barrio as 'María *la Sagüera*', and I tell you, girl, she's deep into it! Goyita said for some months now that husband of yours comes several times a week on his bike, always at night, and the *chow* is repeated.

For an hour they're making out there in the doorway of the house where she's the nanny for the son of a woman who works in La Eneida toystore. They pay her really well and...'

'So that's why you came today, damn you — to screw up my damned Monday? What was I thinking of, working today!'

I slammed the hot comb down on the burner and went to the kitchen. Perhaps I shouldn't have, but her crowing made me sick. I warmed up some of the second brew of coffee and held back a couple of tears that were welling up.

'Mari, do you want a drop of coffee?'

So as not to wake my baby girl, who was soundly asleep, I only half shouted from the kitchen, which was right next to the only bedroom in the small house.

In the yard, Ramoncito was playing with the new toy cars his Aunt Lilia had brought the day before. She was always spoiling him, bringing him little things from Pedro's bric-a-brac place, opposite Don Lirón's furniture store. Lilia was the youngest of my sisters-in-law, and, like Orlando's other three sisters, worked in the tobacco stemming plant but was also a *bolita* runner for Guayabú, who was the big fat *jabao* with the biggest lottery in Santa Clara. Since there were so many tobacco stemmers and everyone knew Guayabú's *bolita*, drawn Thursday afternoons, could be relied on to pay out, everyone wanted to be his runner there. Although even the smallest gambling houses were banned, people trusted Guayabú's because he'd never had any trouble with the police and was seen as kind of official. My three sisters-in-law were all runners in the stemming plant, though Niña, the eldest, was a runner for old Ernestina. People said she was a communist, though no one really knew her, but hers had a good reputation, too, and the police never bothered her. Those little side jobs earned them some extra money, and so on the weekend they were always bringing things for their favorite nephew, whether for the Day of the Kings or his birthday in May, or on some other pretext. When Teresita was born, it was her aunts who paid for her layette piece by piece. As she began to grow and one or other of them won the *bolita*, they might bring her a new set of clothes. I never had any complaints about them, they were always very good and considerate with me. When they figured things were tight in our house, they'd come to me to have their hair done, leaving up to four or five pesos as a tip, which was the equivalent of three or four jobs.

After re-warming the coffee and tasting a few sips, I poured some in a small pewter mug for Maricusa and went back to the living room.

'Didn't you hear me, damn you? I asked whether you wanted some of this brew.'

'Damn it, *negra*, seeing how you reacted I didn't know what to say! You know I'm not playing around. I care about you and respect you too much for you not to take me seriously. This isn't gossip, but for you to wake up to what's going on.'

I undid one of her buns and, after wiping one of the hot combs with a cloth, started straightening her hair from the scalp down. The grease was cooking with a rich scent of lavender. It was a strong pomade recommended to me by the Sarrá drugstore, which I mixed with rosemary and other medicinal plants, and was a success with my customers because their hair would grow thick, clean and strong. They also really liked the elaborate hair styles I did, which were so much the fashion in those years. They came from the United States, where black women always styled their hair so beautifully.

'That's life, I suppose. I've seen it coming for some time. And if I hadn't found out from you, I would have from someone else. To tell you the truth, I'm grateful to you, since this confirms what I already suspected. But I don't want to talk about it any more now. I don't want the boy to see I'm upset.'

In the living room all you could hear were the noises from outside. Ramoncito, in the yard, making the sound of car engines, was engrossed with his new toys. He always loved playing alone. I don't know if it was out of habit, since I didn't often let him visit Pepe, the little white kid next door, Doraluisa's son, because I was punishing him after catching the two of them hiding in the yard house measuring their willies with a ruler. They froze when I caught them. José Julio, Doraluisa's husband, was a salesman for a wholesale company buying and selling rice and beans from a farm belonging to his family in Calabazar de Sagua. They always had sacks of beans and rice and tins of lard, and sometimes, when she knew things were difficult, she would give me a couple of pounds of red or black beans or a tin of lard. I never asked, mind, even if I was starving.

On the corner by the house they were putting up the city's first set of traffic lights, and the traffic was so heavy that all the time trucks and cars were sounding their horns. That corner of Martí and Luis Estévez was very dangerous. A week didn't go by without there being an accident. I was terrified of the long cobbled street, running from the main road to Manicaragua, crossing the Central Highway and then Vidal Square, and ending up at the train station. Everything going to the north coast had to go down Luis Estévez, which, as well as being very narrow, was one way. But right now the noises didn't bother me, they were more calming as I don't know how many things passed through my head. So many that I didn't even realize when I said to Maricusa:

'Look in the mirror. See if you like it.'

'Yes, dear. That's perfect. Forgive me for making you feel bad, but...'

'I told you it doesn't matter, girl. It doesn't matter.'

She gave me a peso and told me to keep the change. I put out the burner and closed the front door. I went into the bathroom, which was between the kitchen-cum-dining room and the bedroom, shut the door, and, so no one would hear me sobbing, pulled hard on the long chain of the water cistern two or three times, flushing furiously.

'*Mami, Mami*... give me a piece of stale bread. Perico's coming!'

I really don't know how long I'd been in there, but I was suddenly returned to this other reality. Perico was the most popular character in Santa Clara. He was the most revered animal people had ever seen grace that city. Day after day, at the same time, Perico the donkey knocked on the same doors of the same houses in Carmen, our barrio, and children would stop whatever they were doing to stand in the doorway to wait for him, to feed him. He'd take it right out of the little ones' hands. Ramoncito liked to stand on a chair and lean out of the *postigo* top part the door, holding out his hand, and Perico the donkey would take the piece of stale bread he'd asked for by knocking on the door with one of his hooves. Nobody knew where he'd come from, or how old he was, but everyone loved him, and the city practically came to a standstill as his slow donkey trot stopped the traffic wherever he happened to be at the time. When Perico died of old age, as happens, all Santa Clara was in mourning. The city council paid for the funeral in a paddock near Capiro Hill, where they buried him with full honors. Even the municipal band played funeral music, and Eutanasio – one of the two men who would best proclaim funeral eulogies from the Bridge of the Good for all the deceased being taken to the cemetery – also improvised a little speech for the occasion, praising the civic qualities and human virtues of beloved Perico the donkey. To this day he is remembered, not just throughout the city but also in some of the surrounding towns not lucky enough to have such a venerable citizen, by a life-size bronze monument of the animal, which, if truth be told, was nobler than many human beings.

Yes, I knew what she'd said was true and maybe I wished it wasn't, but it was all to be confirmed two or three days later. One night that very week, late, Orlando arrived home on his bike ringing the bell, which he always did from when he turned the corner, going against the traffic, by Don Lirón's furniture store, but making more noise than usual. He was generally very considerate and didn't make a racket so as not to wake the children, especially Teresita, who had just turned three. I got up to prepare water for him to bathe and serve him his food, all without saying a word, waiting for him to to be the one to say what he had to say. It was three in the morning and the children were fast asleep, the girl in her cradle opposite our bed, and the boy in his cot, a bit closer to the living room.

'What are you doing awake at this hour, woman?'

That was the first thing he said to me after bringing in his Niagara bike and leaving it in the yard.

'Have you been working till now in the shop?'

'No.'

I sat down on one of the stools on the earth floor of the kitchen. Quietly, so only he could hear, and making a great effort not to sob, I somehow found the strength for the question to come out as clearly as possible:

'What's going on, Orlando?'

'Nothing. It's over, right now. You don't turn me on any more.'

Alms for the Virgen de Regla

This time it wasn't the rooster crowing that woke me round four in the morning. You could still hear the heavy drops of the first of the May rains that the wind was shaking off the mango tree, dripping incessantly on the zinc roof of the boys' room my brother-in-law had added, next to the one for the girls. The whole roof of the house was made of palm thatch, except for that one room. It had pouring down since nightfall and was easing off. Though there'd been thunder and lightning – which made my sister draw an ash cross on the porch and another on the kitchen floor, to ward off the devil – the rain had been a blessing after almost three years of drought. The water pump on the corner where Cundito lived was drying up, and those who had wells in their yards weren't very happy that the little they had left for watering their vegetables was running dry, especially when it didn't cost them anything. Not everyone could pay the five cents for someone to fetch a couple of cans of water and the three cents to get it from the well. In the last two years old Pastora had made a nice bit of money through this, because her well was deep and tapped directly into the main underground stream from Corralillo spring. But now people had put out their large cans and earthenware jars to collect the rainwater.

Francisco, my brother-in-law, had been very good, after all was said and done, taking me and the two children in, practically without a cent in our pocket, especially after the last two sugar harvests which had been really bad because there'd been no rain.

Before putting away my folding bed, I went to look out of the dining room *postigo* and saw it really was clearing and the day dawning. The rabbit run was quiet and the henhouse was steaming something awful, because despite the rain it hadn't cooled off much.

Only the pigs in their pen were having a good time at this god-awful hour.

'G'morning, daughter. Rain f'yer head.'

It was Belarmino, who was coming down the street squelching through the mud as only he would. Always with his same greeting for everyone: 'Rain f'yer head.' Though nobody knew what he meant by that 'rain f'yer head', neither did anybody bother to ask. We accepted it as his way of greeting, that of an old man, but it must have had to do with the drought of the last few years in that part of north Las Villas province. Belarmino was no more an early riser than everyone else in Pueblo Nuevo, up with the first crow of the rooster, sugar harvest time or not. When the 'dead season' came, he would go to the market where he had a stall for root vegetables and fresh fish that were brought to him on the weekends from the port of Isabela de Sagua. Everyone in that small town knew him, just as they knew about everyone's problems, which really got on my nerves.

'Good day to you, Belarmino. It's good to have rain, isn't it?'

'A blessing, child. A blessing.'

He went on his way without raising his head, which was covered by an enormous jute sack, one of those for 250 lbs of sugar, used a lot in those parts for protection from the rain. I shut the *postigo* and went into the kitchen to make something warm before going out.

My children were sleeping soundly. When I opened the door to the boys' room, which gave on to the kitchen, only Pire, the youngest child of Nena, the eldest of my eight sisters, was making any sound, with his usual snoring. They were all soaked in sweat. The two brothers slept in the same big old iron bed, and my son was in another folding bed. The girl slept with me in the living room. That day I decided not to go as far as I had the week before, when I'd spent the whole morning and part of the afternoon in Sierra Morena. At least the roads would be wet, but not waterlogged, and I might even be able to enjoy the long walk. I could only cover my head with a white scrap of a kerchief, so when the midday sun again began to beat down on the stones I showed that what I was doing was truly from the heart, walking the barrios begging for alms from door to door. I'd never before thought of making a vow like that, but to this day I've never regretted it.

Things in the countryside were going from bad to worse, and we didn't have anywhere we could call our own. One day I went to the kitchen and

told my sister Nena that I'd made a vow to the *Virgen de Regla*, and I was
going to go begging for alms, barefoot and dressed in sackcloth, so as to
get a bit of money, leave some for my children, and buy a one-way ticket to
Havana. Nena looked at me just like our mother used to, may she rest in
peace, and more out of compassion than sadness, she dried her hands on
the apron she wore the day long, and she didn't say a single word.

The day I decided to go to Corralillo was the seventh day of my vow,
and I had five more to go. Country people respect those customs, and
in Quemado de Güines itself they helped me a lot, though no one knew
exactly why I was doing it. But I'd been born in the town, and everyone
had known Matildo, my father, and my mother Alberta, who, when she
was alive, had raised us almost singlehanded, as best she could, taking in
washing, which was all she could do.

People knew if I was fulfilling a vow it was for something really
necessary, not because I was a tramp, since none of my four brothers and
eight sisters was without a trade – except perhaps Miguelito, who since he
was a child had wanted to be a musician.

I couldn't feel ashamed or embarrassed about what I was doing. Quite
the opposite. I had to show great humility, and so I walked with my head
held high.

'Alms for the *Virgen de Regla*.'

And people gave me what they could, a peseta, a dime… or a few
cents.

When the bus stopped at the gravel path by the cemetery, on the edge
of town, the driver opened the door and looked at me as if to weigh up
whether I was a fulfilling a vow or brazenly begging as many were those
days.

'Aren't you Martica, one of Matildo Vargas's girls?'

'Yes, sir.'

I answered the driver, without giving any sign I was going to pay for
the journey.

'Get in and sit down. Come on.'

'May the Virgin repay you, sir, but I cannot sit down.'

That was all I said. I didn't know him, but his face was familiar, as
we'd been living in Santa Clara for so many years. It was round, Chinese-
like, pitted as if it was pox-marked. It wasn't that noticeable, because he
was very black and it looked natural, but I knew it was from the pox, a
bad pox which marks you for life. In the rural areas there were many like

that, especially older people, like this driver, who would have been sixty-something, but strong, as if he'd been a sugar stevedore.

I went to the back of the bus, which wasn't that full, and held on as best I could with one hand, while with the other I held tight my plaster statue of the *Virgen de Regla* and tried to dry some of the drops of water mixed with the sweat running down my forehead.

Without having intended to beg for alms on the bus, during the journey from the edge of town to Corralillo, which was just over an hour with all the stops on the way, I was given something like five pesos. It all started when a small nun, dressed in white from head to toe, looked at me, made the sign of the cross, and gave me a forty-cent coin.

'May the Virgin be with you, sister.'

'Thank you, my child. She's my patron as well, and she's very good.'

Almost immediately after, another white lady who was behind me gave me a handful of *kilos prietos*. A gentleman who looked as if he was a local gave me two quarters, and people in the front seats even called me over to give me more coins. The day had started really well and I didn't feel it on my feet, they felt so fresh, all coated in mud. It had been a true gift from heaven, because the first days, before the rains, had been torture, a test, I thought, because the unpaved roads were so hot they brought tears to my eyes as I walked, and by the end of the week I hadn't even managed to collect the four pesos that was a bit more than the cost of the one-way ticket to Havana.

The driver called out the Corralillo stop, and I said my goodbye without looking him in the face:

'May you have a good journey, and may the Virgin be with you!'

When the bus had moved off and disappeared out of sight round the end of Main Street, I opened my kerchief and quickly counted what I'd collected. Almost seven pesos!

The church bell pealed several times before announcing it was seven in the morning.

In Ofelia's House

If you found a position through an agency, your first three days' wages were for the agency, and from then on the rest was for you. Luckily I rarely had to use one.

The first time I found a position in Havana was through an agency on the corner of 23rd and J, in Vedado. I'd walked all over that week with no luck at all. But, at last, the agency sent me to an address close by, on J Street, on the corner of 9th. I knocked on the door, and it was opened by a woman in her thirties, in pretty good shape. I introduced myself and, without asking me in, the woman, evidently the señora of the house, told me she'd already accepted a girl who had come that same morning. She was explaining this, much to my despair, when an older gentleman came to the door, a bit strange in his ways, who I later discovered was her bachelor uncle. He'd heard me telling the señora I'd just come up from the country and I needed work, and that I knew how to look after a house well.

'I didn't like the one your agency sent, Ofe,' the uncle said, going on to ask, with a tone of indifference, but showing that he was also concerned with whatever decision was taken about the domestic organization of the house:

'Why don't you hire her, she looks decent enough.'

Ofelia, which was really what the señora was called, looked me up and down, and from the corner of her eye she exchanged glances with her uncle, who was leaning his heavy body against the ample frame that divided the hall and reception, trying to focus his eyes on me over the top of his spectacles. Several seconds went by, in complete silence, which seemed to me like minutes.

I was holding a small embroidered handkerchief in my hand, and I don't know how many knots I made in it. She started looking at my head, my hair-do, which that Saturday I'd styled myself. Then she fixed on a couple of drops of sweat that were running down my right temple. She slowly looked over my beige soft cotton blouse that I'd bought in installments from the Turk's shop behind Market Square in Quemado de Güines. Then she examined the arabesques on my clean, well-starched and well-ironed, loose cream linen skirt. Finally, she took note of my half-platform sandals, the best pair of shoes I had, and almost my last, because bit by bit I'd sold the rest. When she'd finished the X-ray, I was relieved when señora Ofelia said all right, that I should come back the next day.

'When the other one comes, I'll tell her the girl I had before has come back.'

Without letting her finish, I repeated what I'd said about arriving from Las Villas, that I was having to stay at my sister's house and... Perhaps they liked me, because a little smile from the lady's uncle and a light sigh from her were, it seemed, signs of mutual agreement for señora Ofelia to tell me to collect my things and return before nine that night.

'Thank you so much, señora. Thank you so much, señor.'

As I walked down Línea, passed by the Hotel Nacional and continued all along the Malecón, the cool of that March midday felt different. I hurried because I wanted to break the news to my sister, who had been so good to me in the two weeks since I'd arrived in Havana. I climbed the three enormous stairways of the old apartment block, Concordia No 356, and when she opened the door she realized right away from the look of happiness on my face that I'd finally struck lucky.

'Give thanks to the Virgin, that she may always be with you!'

I told Mercedes all that had happened. I felt sorry for her, because a year ago her husband had had a terrible accident. He was almost killed when he fell from the scaffolding where he was working on a new building in Vedado, and the compensation had already run out. He'd lost a leg, from above the knee, and what they finally gave him was really a miserable sum. Mercedes, the second of my sisters, worked nights looking after a sick, elderly woman in the house of some rich people in Nuevo Vedado.

That afternoon we talked a lot, rocking on the balcony chairs, watching people go by in the street below. I didn't feel as defeated as when I arrived from the country and with tears streaming down my face hugged her, telling her in detail about the break-up of my home. This time I was talking about my plans for when I was paid my first wage.

Daydreaming, I packed my cardboard suitcase, though I didn't really have many things. Mercedes left for work around five, and I made dinner for Conrado, her husband. He was a really nice and affectionate person, one of those people who are always smiling and joking about everything.

'I bet that damned white uncle of Ofelia took a shine to you.'

That was his response when I told him the good news, because he'd been taking a siesta in the other bedroom when I'd arrived.

'Oh, Conra! You're always the same! I'm not up for that!'

He laughed, showing his four gold teeth among the rest of the yellow-stained ones, I imagine from the way he smoked cigars, passing them constantly from one side of his mouth to the other, savouring that brown thing as if he were enjoying chewing a piece of old rope. Every time he gave off his loud, hoarse laugh, which he did a lot, I was always intrigued about how he'd come by those four gold teeth – two up, two down. They must have cost a fortune.

At eight o'clock I was ready to leave and went to the No 20 bus stop in Neptuno, near Primos y Hermanos furniture store. This time I had no excuse for saving the eight cents the journey cost. I happily paid the conductor without trying to slip past. My mind drifted off again, so far that before I even realized what I was thinking about, I asked to be dropped at the next stop.

Before nine I was already in the house on J and 9th, which was to be the first secure roof over my head for the next few years. That night I fell sound asleep, on a good mattress, with real springs. The next day I woke earlier than usual and set about laying the table and preparing a good breakfast with what there was in the pantry. I brought in the two liters left by the milkman, made toast and took out the packet of cornflakes, but I was worried because I couldn't find anything to make the coffee – until señora Ofelia's uncle came in.

The 'good mornings' were brief and shy that first morning. The little boy and girl, the children of señora Ofelia and señor Alberto, just said 'hello.' Señora Ofelia had warned them not to ask me questions or make comments, as I discovered months later when they opened up to me and little Tico (short for Albertico) started to call me *Tata*. But that first day I got no more than a 'hello' in response to my 'good morning.'

The children left for school in their father's car. Tico was in fourth grade with the Salesians, and Cuqui in sixth with the French Dominicans: one with the priests and the other with the nuns. Julián, the bachelor uncle, came out of his bedroom again, throwing me a complicitous glance, as if reminding me of the difficulty he had got me out of. Again in silence, I tidied away the breakfast service and a little later señora Ofelia reappeared in the kitchen, totally transformed. She was wearing a simple pink gingham dress and looked much better than she had at breakfast. It was around those months she had lost her mother, who she had loved dearly, as I imagine all childen do.

'You seem to be a trustworthy person, Marta.'

'Thank you, señora.'

'Look, I don't know how to do anything. My mother died nine months ago. She was very old. Just do as you would if this were your own home. I don't know how to cook, I don't know how to clean, I don't know how to do anything useful in this house, and anyone who doesn't know how to do anything has no right to give orders.'

Señora Ofelia went to pour herself some coffee, but I told her there was none left and made her one with the Italian coffee maker – God alone knows how I managed to work out how to use it. If it hadn't been for her uncle Julián, they wouldn't have had any coffee that first morning. Señora Ofelia burst out laughing when I explained that I thought you had to put the sugar in the water mixed with the coffee.

'At least you learned how to do it. Every day I understand less about these gadgets.'

I served her coffee and put the rest in a baby food jar I'd washed.

'As you must have realized, there are five of us in this family. Uncle Julián, who's always been good to us, spends six months here and the other six in Manzanillo, where we have a farm my grandmother left us. Alicia, the girl in the big photo on the wall, is Alberto's daughter from his first marriage. She lives with her mother, but spends a lot of time with us. You'll meet her. She's a real doll. And that's all you need to know.'

Except that wasn't all. As she was getting ready to leave the house, she instructed me to answer the telephone and just take messages, without saying anything about where she was.

'I'll be back after two.'

With that she left. The first thing I had to face that morning was a whole lot of electrical gadgets I'd only seen in magazines. As the days went by, and I talked to other maids on the block, I was able to bring myself up to date. I was lucky to make friends straight away with a very respected and educated maid known as Maité, short for María Teresa. She was blacker than soot. The Tarabella family had adopted her when she was a child, because her mother, who had died back then, had worked for a long time for the parents of Anselmo Tarabella, judge of the Fourth Police District.

Halfway through the morning, Maité would pop over. She was well trusted by the Menéndez family, where I worked, and señora Ofelia was very happy I'd got to know Maité, since she was highly thought of among all the maids in that part of Vedado.

'Look, that *Guéstinjaus* mixer is one of the best. To work it all you have to do is move this button to the right, to the speed you want, depending on whether you want to chop or liquefy... Like this.'

Then she gave me demonstrations of how to use a cream whipper, a lemon squeezer, and finally an electric frying pan. Those early days in the Menéndez house were a real apprenticeship for me, and Maité couldn't have been more helpful.

Bit by bit, I began to make friends with some of the other maids in the neighborhood. Often, at night after we'd finished our chores, four or five of us would meet at one or other corner building and talk about our work, our lives, and of course our sweet and bitter loves.

That night, Edelia, a very likeable *jabaíta* from Santiago, introduced me to the rest of the girls who already formed quite a close-knit group.

'So, you work in the Menéndez house?'

That was how one of the girls greeted me.

'Well, be careful. Make sure she pays you. She's very nice, but she doesn't like paying her maids.'

Another of the girls, Maritza, who later told me she'd had a lot of problems when she worked for señora Ofelia, finished for her:

'That's why her maids leave her. She doesn't like to pay.'

Now it was my turn, and I had to do it in the best possible way. I sat down slowly, taking care with the pleats of my blue muslin skirt. I asked Edelia for a cigarette. I think it was the first time I smoked a whole one. I lit it and inhaled the first puff of smoke, thinking all American cigarettes were mild, like 'Kool'; but that 'Camellito', as Edelia called Camels, was much stronger than any I'd ever had before.

'You must be joking, girl. She may not have paid others, but she'll pay me. I came from the country to work because I've got two children to support.'

Three days hadn't gone by since that conversation when one mid-morning señora Ofelia came into the kitchen for a cup of coffee, as she was in the habit of doing. I warmed it and served it to her straight away. I was about to go out to the store, but had time for a brief conversation. She was very pleased with my work, and, she told me, although she hadn't received any references for me, she liked the way I went about things.

'What a coincidence, señora, talking about references, just the other day I wasn't given very good ones for you!'

I knew saying it like that would take her aback. I'm sure she wasn't expecting it. She froze, like a piece of ice, fearing the worst, I imagine.

'What?'

That was all she managed to say, leaving her little black china coffee cup under the sink tap. It was the only one left of a set of six that had been a wedding present. I didn't give her time to recompose herself.

'Yes, you see some of the "*criaditas*" round here, as you all like to call us, have told me you don't like paying your maids. I said maybe you'd kept someone else's money, but there was no way you would do that to me, because I came to work in Havana to support my children.'

This time I did give her chance to regain her self-control. Of course, I didn't tell her the other things they'd said about her, since all I was really interested in was my work.

I made to serve her more coffee, but her mind was somewhere else. She lit up another cigarette. The coffee was still warm. The small pewter mug in which I usually reheated the coffee, letting it sit in *bain-marie*, kept warm for a long time. Not a morning went by that señora Ofelia, when she was home, didn't drink a couple of good cups of coffee. I washed the black cup, dried it very carefully, even trying to bring out its shine, and poured just a bit. At last she said:

'Oh, *Martucha*! What they've told you is a lie, because the only one I didn't pay *was* a girl called Ela and that was because she left for the country without warning.'

'She let you down?'

'Yes, and how!'

'Well, señora, I don't see why you should think that. When you people don't need us any more, you just fire us without much of an explanation, without asking whether our children, or our own food depends on the few pesos we earn serving you. It's enough to say, "Look, so-and-so, I don't need you any more," and that's it.'

I went about my work in the kitchen, and I have to say it was gleaming, as I liked to see it. I washed the little black porcelain cup again, and this time put it on the pink rubber drainer. I waited to see what her next reaction would be, without rushing her. Her response began with a half-complicitous smile, and perhaps a certain irony. She drew on the 'Chester' she was smoking, exhaled a thick puff like women of the world do in those Argentinian films, and began to speak much more softly this time:

'You know... I like you a lot... I like your manner, because you're very frank. I think we'll get along just fine.'

'I hope so, señora.'

My luck was such that, instead of paying me at the end of the month, as was customary, she'd pay me in advance and sometimes with a bonus.

***

Señora Ofelia, it has to be said, could be penny-pinching. She was always buying a little bit of this and a little bit of that. It was a household that lived day-to-day where food was concerned. Ah, but when it came to the house and clothes, she always wanted the best. She'd say:

'*Martucha*, what's left over from yesterday?'

And I'd reply that yesterday's half-pound of lard made yesterday's lunch and dinner.

'Half a pound of lard has gone so quickly?'

She'd ask me, shocked.

I'd explain to her the dishes that had been made and that she knew perfectly well that half a pound of lard was not enough for all the frying that needed to be done in that house. But I wasn't sure she really did know. When I'd go to the store, she'd tell me to buy twenty-five cents of good ham, and, taking me gently by the arm, she'd say, as if to make sure I was in agreement with her:

'Let's get through the day on that. You can do some of those croquettes that you know how to make out of almost nothing, some yellow rice, some root vegetables and that'll do, because we have to save. As you know, the holidays are coming and after that Alicita's *Quince*, and you know how that is.'

Señora Ofelia used to shop in Fin de Siglo, La Moda, and even in El Encanto, the most expensive store in Cuba. According to what Maité told me, she did this to give herself the air of being one of the other great *señoronas* like the Cartas, the Calataleiros, the Torres-Peñas, or even señora Tarabella herself, with whom she secretly competed to keep up appearances.

On occasion, when she returned from one of her dinners, señora Ofelia would be euphoric about the different dishes she had tasted, and she'd describe them to me down to the last detail, asking me if I couldn't prepare them for her someday.

'Delighted, señora, but what you're asking for takes a pound of top-quality ground beef, half a pound of Spanish ham, olives, capers, olive oil, and...'

She'd interrupt me:

'I think a pound of mince and half of ham is too much. Couldn't it be made with a quarter of mince and two or three slices of pressed ham – don't you think, *Martucha*?'

That's how it always was. When I went to Paquito el Curro's bodega to buy groceries, the old man – who wasn't really old but rather middle-aged, a very dapper man who was still looking good – would call me by the family's surname, as he did with all of us, and say in his strong Spanish accent:

'Tell her, Menéndez, tell your señora not to smoke so many Chesterfields and to pay her account, or I'll have to suspend her credit.'

'And what did you say to him?' asked señora Ofelia when I returned with the groceries, but not the carton of cigarettes.

'I told him you hadn't given me a cent and were waiting for the money to arrive from Manzanillo.'

What really happened was that señora Ofelia played a lot of canasta with the money her husband gave her each month, and between gambling and buying in the best stores in Havana, she spent more than she had. The heirs of the farm were her and her uncle Julián, but another brother, who I never got to meet, a half-brother on the father's side, sent some money every month when señor Julián was in the house – but she spent this, too.

It was a day waiting to happen, that morning when señora Ofelia needed some things for a special meal she wanted to make for some guests. I told her what had happened and she turned red as a ripe tomato.

What had happened was that Paquito called me to one side, at the corner of the counter, and gave me this message:

'Listen, gorgeous, tell your señora that from today I can't give her any more credit, that I know every Saturday she goes to her club to spend her money in style, yet doesn't pay me what she owes. If things go on like this, the account will never be closed. Go on home, *morena*, and tell her that from me!'

Señora Ofelia had gone out that morning. When she returned, she greeted me as usual before taking a shower. She asked me what was for lunch, and if I was preparing dinner.

'For lunch I prepared what was left over from last night, señora. But for the evening, I don't know what to do.'

When she came out of the bathroom I told her everything that Paquito el Curro had told me to tell her, down to the last detail. He wasn't actually *gallego*, as the other maids called him, but gypsy, from Andalusia. He'd told me that himself, with great pride. It's just that many people affectionately call all the Spanish '*gallego*' even if they weren't born in Galicia. Anyway, Paquito El Curro's message was that he couldn't go on serving me until she had paid off the outstanding bills. I don't known if señora Ofelia had recently won something gambling, because to my surprise she gave me five pesos and sent me to the EKLO supermarket, on the corner of 17th and K, to buy whatever I needed for the meal. The Minimax had become fashionable among the wealthy in Havana, who liked doing their shopping American style. 'Minimum prices, maximum quality' had gone down well with the señoras and their maids.

Señora Ofelia owed money to a lot of people: Cuza the washerwoman, Felito the butcher, who had the hots for her. On top of not paying them, she'd run up 50 and 70 pesos worth of groceries a month from Paquito el Curro, who was always claiming there was no comparison between his yellow cheeses, hams, olives and oils, and those of the supermarkets. But that wasn't quite true, because, though they weren't the same brand, those from the Minimax were also from Spain and a lot cheaper. But then it wasn't my money. Anyway, for us maids it felt really elegant going to the Minimax. I'd hang on to my trolley and go up and down the aisles between shelves full of everything imaginable, and I felt great, especially when I went in the car with caballero Alberto to do the monthly shopping, or sometimes alone, as on this occasion. You could select whatever you wanted, compare prices, and even amuse yourself gossiping a bit with the other maids. However, some families still didn't trust these supermarkets and preferred to go on buying in the bodegas, above all those that had a lot of Spanish products.

Well, as I was saying, señora Ofelia bought a lot on credit, something she couldn't do in the Minimax – not only her, no one – but she could in other stores. In El Encanto, for example, she bought the most expensive French perfumes and a lot of clothes for the children. She did everything possible, and impossible as well, for her family to be on a par with the children of her women friends who went to the Comodoro, the Yacht Club, the racecourse, and the other places for white folks. She went crazy buying things in installments. One day she bought a beautiful bracelet and matching pair of earrings, which, according to what she told me, were almost diamonds, and cost her two hundred pesos in Kraimentz & Shultz, a really high-class jewellers on Aguila Street. When Elías, the debt collector, came, she hid, or else she'd leave me the same message:

'*Martucha*, if he comes, tell that Elías that the money still hasn't arrived from Manzanillo.'

'Tell your señora I damn well know she's there. Tell her to come out and pay me, because I'm very tired of coming here twice a week and she's never in at a time when a señora really should be at home. And tell her also that she shouldn't go buying things she can't pay for.'

I never knew where to turn in embarrassment, and it wasn't even my embarrassment, but I did my best to convince him, difficult though it was, and in the end he'd leave, cursing as he went.

Of the many different debt collectors who came knocking and who she never paid, it was this Elías, the wrong side of middle-aged, who one fine day found out where her husband's little shop was and went to get the money there. Caballero Alberto was very polite and friendly, but not one to smile much. As with so many other things, he wasn't aware of his wife's problems, and of course I was the last person who would want to open his eyes. In that sense, I was as silent as the grave. I always remembered my grandfather's advice that 'flies can't enter a closed mouth'. Caballero Alberto always left early for his babywear shop on Muralla Street and returned almost always after seven-thirty at night. When the debt collectors came, of course he was never at home. But that day Elías appeared in the store.

'Are you señor Alberto Menéndez?'

'The same. How can I help you?'

'Listen, I'm very sorry, but… I came to talk with you about a personal matter.'

'With me? What's it about? Come through to my office.'

'It concerns your wife… I want first to say that I feel really embarrassed, but I felt I had no choice. You're a businessman and know this better than me. Your wife, señora Ofelia Menéndez, bought some items from our jewelry store. The total amount of credit, with interest, comes to over five hundred pesos in arrears. Each time I go to collect the monthly installment, she tells me she'll pay later or has the maid tell me the money hasn't arrived yet from Manzanillo, or that she's gone to the bank – always some excuse or other, and now six months have gone by since the first purchase, and she hasn't paid more than the fifty pesos deposit, and the credit was to be paid in six installments, precisely because the interest is low and the jewelry was on sale.

Caballero Alberto listened to the debt collector, Elías, in his usual friendly and courteous way, and very calm, above all calm, since he was a man of refined and natural patience. For his part, Elías, who wasn't expecting this kind of behavior, was left stupified after his brief speech, which he appeared to have learned by heart.

Seeing how calmly caballero Alberto took it, he adopted an equally professional stance and waited for the other's response.

'So, you've come to get the money from me, since I'm her husband. When you sold the things to her, you didn't think of consulting me.'

Elías didn't know what else to say. It was as if he'd had a bucket of crushed ice thrown down his back. He wasn't expecting such a reaction. Not knowing how to explain himself better, he went on to say that since he was her husband, and since she had put him off so often without paying him a penny...

'I would like...I ask this favor of you, señor Menéndez, that you... Look, sir, I'm going to lose my job over this...'

Caballero Alberto stopped him right there, without getting angry, but a little more forceful.

'This has absolutely nothing to do with me. As I've already told you, when you sold those things to Ofelia, nobody expected my signature or verbal authorization, and nobody asked me for it. So, go to señora Ofelia, in whatever way you choose, and get her to pay you.'

That same day, Elías returned the way he had come and managed to surprise señora Ofelia at home, at the very moment she was opening the door, and he told her about the conversation he'd had with her husband.

'Oh, Elías, you'll be my ruin! How could you do such a thing? You should have spoken to me first.'

Señora Ofelia was all tears. Even though she knew how to turn on the tears, this time I really felt sorry for her, and even pity. Elías also softened a little, but only a little.

'But, señora Menéndez, you have to see things from where I stand. I have no other way of getting you to pay me. And it's not me, señora. They send me from the store to collect the money from you, and I no longer know what excuse to give the accountant, who on top of everything else is one of the owners. The commission I earn from collecting from home isn't even enough for a pair of decent shoes. Look at the ones I'm wearing!'

None of this went any further than fresh promises from señora Ofelia to pay off the account in the next few days, and with a glass of ice-cold water, a hot coffee, and a handshake, they sealed a truce. Elías left the house, thinking, no doubt, that perhaps he had gone too far, and that his decision to involve the husband was going to lose his employers a client, and perhaps there'd even be a serious admonishment for him from the managers of the company he represented.

Yet, the best part of the whole story was when caballero Alberto came home that evening, earlier than usual. After reproaching Elías for what he had done, I'm not too sure whether for having gone to the store or having returned to the house, and on the point of starting to cry again, señora Ofelia listened to her husband's response.

'Not again, Ofelia! You're always chasing after all those people, in clubs and *parti*s, who have a lot more than you... you're going to be the ruin of yourself one day, and the worst of it is you're going to be the ruin of me, too.'

Caballero Alberto was on the point of exploding. I'd never seen him so angry. After coming back from the store, he had a habit of stretching out on the divan for a while, waiting for me to take him a glass of Tres Toneles, his favorite brandy, and sometimes a drop of really hot coffee. But on this occasion I didn't think of it. Señora Ofelia had given her word to Elías that when her brother sent her the money from Manzanillo she'd pay him, and that was precisely what she repeated to her husband, who, tired of listening to excuses, went to his room and spent nearly an hour in the shower.

In truth, I'd grown fond of caballero Alberto and had a lot of respect for him, compassion even, seeing as how he was such a good man, and knowing the things that señora Ofelia did to him, how she never paid any attention to him, and how they lived like a couple of strangers.

MERY LA ISLEÑITA

In that block of four large apartment-homes, there was a young maid who'd come to Cuba from Tenerife, in the Canary Islands, with her mother when she was little. They called her Mery *la Isleñita*, and she was only fifteen. Her mother, Serafina, was very submissive, and they both worked in the home of the owner of La Botija, a famous silverware store. They were the kind of maid who ruined things for the little work there was to be had. They didn't care about the rest of us and would work for next to nothing.

One morning I met Serafina on the bottom steps and I can't for the life of me remember how the conversation began. I think it had to do with work, which was really the only thing we could talk about. Out of the blue, just like that, she said to me:

'I told Mery you're very good, very clean, but you're a really uppity black.'

I couldn't believe what I was hearing! And right to my face, too!

'Caramba! So being uppity means I don't put up with any uppityness from people like you?'

Acting offended and playing the *señorona* with me, the *isleña* retorted: 'Say that again!'

'I'll say it again loud and clear: what I meant to say, in case you didn't understand, is that you are way more uppity than me, if you must know!'

After that, she began to spread it around the block and among the other maids that I had a lot of nerve and that Mery had told her I'd said that she, Serafina, her own mother, was a submissive maid, because she'd work on Sundays when even the oxen rest. Which was true, but all the fuss she made was for nothing, it just rebounded back on her. All of us had some kind of break, good or bad, each week, and we knew it was true. The *isleñas* had an unenviable reputation in Havana with that widespread attitude of theirs, and I wasn't one to hold back from saying so. Deep down, I was fond of Mery and felt sorry for her, because her own mother was exploiting her like a Cinderella. I sometimes doubted she could really be her mother.

Mery worked two floors above mine, and her mother on the floor above that, in an apartment belonging to the same family. Since all the balconies at the back looked out on the same area, we'd sometimes greet each other while working.

'*Negrita*, what are you up to?' she'd shout down to me.

'I've just finished, my dear. I'm going to shower and get dressed. Today's my day off.'

Mery answered from the balcony above, sounding genuinely sad: 'Look at me, still mopping the floor!'

One day we met out on the street and I said:

'You know, Mery, I like you, and I'm going to help you to see if we can get you out of having to work on Sunday.'

'How are you going to do that, *negrita*?'

'You'll see.'

We planned it between us. Early the following Sunday, I hung the clothes out to dry and went for my shower. I'd almost forgotten all about it, and even thought that the poor isleñita had lost her nerve, when I heard more water come down from the balcony than normal. When I went out, I acted like I was stunned, and Mery began to apologize, saying she hadn't seen my clothes... but I didn't give her a chance to continue.

'Hey, you, *isleñita!* Look what you've done.'

'Ay, *negrita*, I'm sorry!'

'Enough of the *negrita*. Don't you ever say *negrita* to me again, I've got a first and last name, and today least of all when I'm furious. Just look what you've gone and done! You've soaked all the clothes I had here, and all because you're as docile as your mother. You come from that damned island of canaries to work on Sunday here in Havana. Look around you! How many buildings round here do you see throwing water on Sundays? In this country, Sunday is for rest, going out and partying, not mopping floors.'

At that point, as part of my performance, I gave her time to respond:

'But my señora tells me to clean today as well.'

I hadn't realized just how like Cubans these *isleños* talked. That tiny, plaintive voice was heartbreaking, all the more because Mery was white as milk and skinny as they come. She was so skinny she looked like a macaroni, with an untidy mop of blond ringlets down to her shoulders, almost covering her sharp, bony face. Her voice was shrill but clear, and all the neighbors in the building came out to see what had happened. They must have thought someone had fallen. I returned to the attack:

'That señora of yours is inconsiderate, because my señora doesn't make me work on Sundays. They're off at the beach today, and I'm heading out at midday as well.'

It was then that the señora, who I'd seen from time to time, came out on the balcony. She was still in her housedress and with rollers in her hair. I didn't wait for her to ask what was going on.

'Look, señora, all because of you, look what your Mery's done. She's soaked the children's clothes, señora Ofelia's underwear, and even what I was going to wear today to go out. I'm telling you, from now on, and as long as I'm working here, there'll be no more mopping of floors in this building on Sundays.'

Before the two of them could go in from the balcony, I went into my room, making out I was blazing with anger, leaving them with the words in their mouths, especially that *señorona* of Mery's.

About an hour later, pretending she wanted to make the peace, I heard Mery calling me from the airshaft behind the maid's room. I looked out and she made signs that everything was going according to plan and that she'd explain later. Then she said, for anyone who cared to hear:

'Listen, *negrita*. Don't be angry with me. What time are you going out?'

I behaved like a spoiled child and answered rudely, though I was still pretending.

'I don't know what time I'm going, and don't you speak to me, girl, I've got the Congo raging in me now!'

But Mery continued.

'Have you fixed your nails yet?'

Still angry, I answered through clenched teeth:

'Yes, as of yesterday I fixed my nails.'

Then I returned to the attack, as we'd agreed.

'Don't you see that when I leave here I don't go talking about the "señora of the house", or that I'm a maid, because I don't care to. But everywhere you go you're always saying, "the señora where I work is like this, or like that." When I leave here and have to speak of my señora, I refer to her as the woman, Ofelia… that's all.'

'*Negrita*, you do that?'

That was her best yet. She was a better actress than I thought. She listened to all the afternoon soaps, and talked just like Minín Bujones – a really good actress in the two o'clock soap, starring as a well-preserved spinster of Havana high society who put on a really false-sounding affected voice.

'Of course I do, I'm a señora, too, and she doesn't say to me "señora Marta".'

It wasn't quite like that. Out of respect, and as long as she respected me, I said 'señora Ofelia' to her, but not meekly. Anyway, the Monday after, I met Mery on the street and she told me what had happened in her place.

'Ay, *negrita*! Listen, you don't mind, do you, if I keep calling you *negrita*? Well, you can imagine how the señora carried on. She spent the whole of that damned Sunday carrying on something awful. And she took it out on me! Just imagine, señora Rosalía kept telling me: "Just look at that *negra*, she dresses better than the señora of the house and she's nothing more than a maid." I answered her as straight as I could and said: "But, señora, let her be. Why should it bother you if she works as a maid and dresses as she likes? Let her be, because what she says is that you have money but no morals, and she has morals and has to dress the best she can, because that's what she has to work for." *Negrita*, I swear by all the candles lit for the Holy Virgin, she let rip! "Don't you be telling me that *negra* dared say we have money but no morals!" Afterwards I tried to mend things, but I think I just made it worse: "Señora Rosalía, I don't know what it all means, but she's always saying those things… that most of the people living in this building are up to all kinds of things."'

Mery said no more because at that moment someone from the family was getting out of a car and we stopped our conversation abruptly, so they wouldn't see us talking with such familiarity and go running with the tale to señora Rosalía. But our bit of theater had done the trick, like a holy cure. For the rest of my time there, no more floors were mopped on Sundays.

Once my son came to Havana. It was the first time he'd made the trip alone. His father had taken him to Santa Clara, where he was going to High School. The boy had told his father that he wasn't happy where he was and wanted to go on studying rather than start work. He lived with his father's family, his grandmother and aunts. Teresita, my daughter who was only seven, was with my older sister in the country. I was really happy Ramoncito would be with me for a few days. It had been a year since I'd seen him, though we talked on the phone now and then. He was going to stay with Mirta, another of my sisters, who lived in La Sierra neighborhood, over in Marianao. When I took him to the house where I was working, I first introduced him to caballero Alberto.

'Very pleased to meet you, señor,' my young son said, holding out his hand. Then señora Ofelia and Cuqui, their eldest daughter, arrived.

'You see, this youngster, or, as you say, "the cook's boy", has definite promise,' caballero Alberto began to say, out loud. My Ramoncito was turning fourteen at the time, and was quite shy compared to most boys his age. He much preferred to read a book than play ball or hang out on street corners with the other kids. He enjoyed skating and running, but wasn't very forward when it came to girls.

Caballero Alberto carried on making his comments, and of course this began to make the girl, Cuqui, jealous. She was more or less the same age as my Ramoncito, who could already speak a bit of English, since his father had him attending a small school belonging to the family of his godfather Victor Morrell.

Señora Ofelia's only comment was:

'How charming and polite he is!'

With so much attention on him, and like a lump of ice, my Ramoncito stood there with a faint smile barely drawn on his face, looking right back at whoever was looking at him. It was Cuqui's turn to speak:

'Well, he might be polite and all that, but he's in a state school and I go to the French Dominicans.'

Her school was on the corner of Avenida de los Presidentes and 15th Street, and was one of the most expensive girls' schools in Havana. Then it was my turn:

'Maybe so, but bad things go on there, too.'

'What do you mean?' Cuqui responded, way before either of her parents. I knew what I had to say and didn't hesitate.

'Just that. Sometimes I sit on Avenida de los Presidentes and I see and hear many of the things the schoolgirls get up to there. Since they think I'm just a nanny, in her blue and white uniform, they don't stop and think what they're saying. I don't mean those of your age, but I've seen other girls a bit older than you get up to many things.'

Not much older, not that I said that, but the daughter of a maid friend of mine, who worked on 17th Street, told me some shocking things about Amelita, the girl of the house, who wasn't yet fourteen.

When señora Ofelia realized what I was talking about, she tried to change the subject, but caballero Alberto continued in the same vein.

'Yes, what Marta says is true,' he began to say, looking steadily at me. He paused and made himself comfortable, leaning back in one of the big armchairs, before speaking:

'Those people think that just because you're poor, you have no right to education, while they, who – God only knows why – have some ancestry, believe themselves to be above all the weaknesses and vices to which all of us as human beings are exposed. I'm from the barrio of Cayo Hueso, as you well know, Ofelia, since I never denied it, and your mother never forgave you for marrying me. I grew up with Chano Pozo and Miguelito Valdés, two famous artists who came out of the slums, where they were always into absolutely everything. Chano was black. He died knifed in New York. Miguelito, almost white, and look at me, today I'm caballero Alberto Menéndez, though sometimes I'd sooner still be the one who used to throw stones in fights in Trillo Square.'

And looking at his own daughter he said, in a disapproving tone:

'Who can say whether or not this young boy who today is in a state school, as you say, tomorrow won't succeed in becoming far more than you, because deep down you're plain dumb.'

'Alberto! How dare you speak like that to your own daughter in front of the maid!'

It was then I realized just how out of place my son and I were in that drawing room, and I asked for permission to leave.

Caballero Alberto was like that: down-to-earth, impulsive even. He always called a spade a spade, and he said all that to his own daughter. Señora Ofelia jumped to the girl's defense, but the tone of her voice rang so false that even Cuqui felt uncomfortable.

'Oh, Alberto! Why do you say such things to our little girl? Fine... you can't deny the boy seems intelligent and is very polite, but...'

But what? She didn't finish what she was saying, possibly because we still hadn't left the room. But I spoke for her, controlling my rage:

'Yes, señora Ofelia, you can't deny it. He is very intelligent, but he's the son of a maid, as caballero Alberto said.'

The matter went no further, but it was the beginning of the end. Before he returned to Santa Clara the following week, I again took Ramoncito to the house so he could say goodbye to the family. Despite everything, they'd been very good to me. But not everyone was home. Luckily, it was caballero Alberto who said goodbye, wishing him every success in his studies and even giving him a five-peso note.

The next day, on Saturday afternoon, after I'd taken my boy to the bus station and had returned a little sadly to the house, caballero Alberto and I happened to be in the kitchen at the same time. He'd always come to see me, because he liked to stick his nose into what was going on the house and would generally like to say something nice to me. He knew I was upset. He sat down on one of the stools in that big kitchen to drink a cup of coffee.

'Marta, your son is really well brought up. Look, I come from the streets, from the streets, but you never know what life has in store. Life has so many twists and turns.'

Sipping his coffee, he began to tell me about his life, as he'd never done before, at least not with me. I'll always be grateful to him for raising my spirits, which had been really low.

'You know, Marta, they don't only discriminate against you here for your skin color. After all, this country is blacker than it would like to be. The thing is, we don't want to admit it because it doesn't suit us to. For example, the Casino Español, where that señor judge Carabela, who lives opposite, goes, I can't get in there, let alone aspire to be a member like his family.'

We broke out laughing like children, because Judge Tarabella was spindlier than a stalk of cane.

'I'm only the owner of a small baby clothes store, and for more than ten years I've been struggling to expand, but haven't been able to. Where the bank manager's wife goes, my wife can't; or rather, if she does, it's only because she's out of line. The problem with Ofelia is that with the story of that damned farm, she's getting herself into debt all over the place, and she's been getting worse since the day her grandmother died, which was long enough ago. And then what with her mother, that... well, I'd better not say. She thinks she can let herself have whatever takes her fancy. If there was anyone on this earth as like Ofelia as one drop of water to another, that has to be Isabelina, her late mother. Lord Almighty, what a woman!'

He paused to help himself to more coffee, which was still warm, then continued:

'But Ofelia really is the limit. The last thing was that grand Christian Dior fashion show, over in the Country Club. I don't know if you know –

or if it's even worth knowing – who Dior is, but suffice it to say he's a very famous French fashion designer... The thing is, Ofelia kept on at me about going, because her friends were going... Do you know how much one of his dresses costs? Thousands and thousands of pesos! And her friends? Can you imagine Ofelia being a friend of all those millionaires, the Bacardís, the Gómez Menas, the Aspurus? No, girl. No way. I told her to get the idea out of her head, or I'd get it out for her.'

I'd only been with the Menéndez for a few months when señora Ofelia hired a cook, because the work was now too much, what with the children and the house. Señora Ofelia realized this herself. I can't deny I was pleased, because I kept my thirty-five pesos a month, looked after the house and children, and had one Thursday and two Sundays a month free.

When I'd go out on a Sunday, it would be between two and three in the afternoon and I'd get back around nine at night. The week I had to stay in the house, I'd take the children to the beach. I'd get up early, as usual, and tidy their bedrooms. Then I'd get their beach bags and everything else ready. I was like their governess, but Cuqui told me she was too old for me to be her nanny.

'Just get my clothes ready and don't meddle in anything else, understand?'

Then we'd head for the Country Club, the Yacht Club, Barlovento or the Comodoro, or else we'd go on to a party at the house of one of their friends. We'd return late afternoon, but I couldn't go out because it wasn't my day. I was patient with them, while also having to satisfy señora Ofelia's whims, down to the last drop of water. If she wanted a cigarette, I'd have to go and fetch a cigarette from on top of the chest of drawers, because she was incapable of moving. If she wanted a whiskey and ginger ale, I'd have to go over to the little drinks bar to prepare it for her. And so it went on: whether the bath was ready, or a snack. Then the others would say: 'I'm hungry, *Tata*', because I'd still be preparing the food for the children, and if I'd cooked a steak or some roast beef just as they liked it, at the last moment they'd say, 'Ay, *Tatín*, couldn't you make me some fried chicken, with that great sauce you do?' So I'd have to drop what I was doing, and make the chicken, which I'd have marinated. Then, the girl would also want something else.

One day we went to El Carmelo, on Calzada, and I was the only colored maid in the whole damned café. Cuqui went to a table, and I sat down with her. She greeted some of her friends, one of whom said to the other:

'That's why we don't like coloreds looking after us. They might be really good, but they can't come into all these places and not stand out.'

Those last words hit me in the gut. We were very close, and everyone knew what they said concerned me. I excused myself and stood up, making out I was going for some fresh air, and I started watching some ballet classes that were taking place opposite, in the Auditorium. I'd always had a passion for ballet, but what chance had I ever had?

On the way home we didn't speak, but when we got to the house Cuqui began telling me off as though I were a chick of a girl like her:

'Listen, Marta, why did you get up from the table and go to watch the ballet practice? Since when do you know anything about that?'

To be honest, I'd thought it strange she hadn't asked me sooner. The silence between the two of us from the café to the house was a foreboding that she was going to react badly.

'Perhaps I looked out of place among the rest of you, like that little friend of yours said... for all to hear'

'Well, even so, what you should have done was...'

She was searching for the exact words I knew she wanted to say, but perhaps didn't dare, or couldn't recall what I imagine she'd heard her little friends about how to treat the maids. It was too much. I calmly waited, which infuriated her even more. With the other maid, Morbila, she did as she pleased, constantly wiping the floor with her, and her mother either didn't know or didn't want to know. But with me it was different. Agitated, the young lady turned sharply towards me.

'You're Cuqui's maid, and you'd no right to go anywhere without me telling you to, whatever you hear. It was bad of you to get up from the table like that.'

It was then that I moved closer to her, and, speaking more quietly than she had, said:

'Take good note of what I'm going to say, Cuqui. I don't like spoiled children. Make no mistake, I'm not Morbila. If she and your mother have come to blows, I'm not like that. You can't mess me about, because you know perfectly well that I know where I stand.'

It was the first time I spoke to her like that, and the last, because it worked like a dream. She was so taken aback that she left the room and went sniveling to señora Ofelia.

'See, Mami, that's why I can't get to like her. She's always answering back.'

So señora Ofelia came to me, all authoritarian, to protest.

'What happened between you and the child, Marta?'

'Nothing. She asked me why I'd left the café when I heard her friends trying to offend me with their comments about colored maids like us shouldn't be there, and things like that. It made me feel bad, naturally, so I left and when we arrived here she told me off. I told her not to get the wrong idea about me, because I'm not Morbila... the new cook.'

'What do you mean that you're not Morbila?'

'Oh, nothing. I understand the two of you have fights. But that can't happen with me, because you have to respect me, just as I respect you.'

Nobody liked that. We'd been having our differences over little things, but this time our words were more serious. Señora Ofelia looked me up and down, and shook her head from side to side, over and over again. I looked at her, too, uncomfortable and impatient. I felt so uncomfortable I wanted to get out of there before my blood began to boil.

'Attitude, attitude, Marta! Ever since I've known you, you've had a very strong character, and I don't like that kind of people working for me.'

It was the third time she'd said that to me in the past two weeks, and I was already preparing to leave. I didn't reply. I just excused myself and went back to my chores.

Happy Twentysomething, Martucha

One fine day, just before my birthday, we decided to celebrate the occasion at the big place where Maité worked, taking advantage of the family being away at their holiday chalet at Jaimanitas beach. It was Maité herself who decided to give me a *surprais-parti*. All the girls from around Vedado and others who now worked at the Biltmore and Santos Suárez appeared with some kind of gift.

Maité made me an enormous cake, which not even the best bakers at La Gran Vía could have outdone, with three layers of Libby's canned fruit and homemade jam. It was beautifully decorated, and with lettering, somewhat ironic it has to be said, which read:

HAPPY TWENTYSOMETHING, MARTUCHA

Mery *la Isleñita* gave me a bra and knicker set with really pretty pink lace; Edelia brought me another set of underwear; Maritza, a flask of Crusella 'Rhum Quinquina' cologne, which was very fashionable in that never ending hot season; and well, what can I say. Even Irdoína, who had given up working some time before to look after her husband, turned up with a lovely amethyst pendant necklace and a matching brooch in the shape of a scorpion, which I put on right away – everyone knew how much I liked those creatures. In all I collected some twenty or so gifts, including a crate of Coca Cola that Inesita brought from her house.

So as not to make too much noise and be out of sight of the neighbors, we agreed to get together in the dining room of the apartment, which was huge. Maité trusted us, since we nearly all worked in good places and she knew we would behave well, not dirtying the furniture, leaving a mess, and definitely not breaking anything.

'Girls, behave like white folk. Mery, you especially!'

We all burst out laughing, looking at Mery, the only white one in the group. She joined in with us, but she'd gone redder than a ripe tomato. We all knew how to move around those big places full of so many glass knick-knacks that you never knew what use they'd be – big fat ashtrays, candelabras like geese, and a whole host of silly little things, many of which, judging by the store catalogues, were quite expensive. However, the furniture of Maité's family didn't seem to me to be as sumptuous as that of caballero Alberto, who had everything specially made by Orbay & Cerrato.

I was the one who made the seafood salad, with dried prawns, chicken and diced boiled potatoes in a mayonnaise sauce. I also made a sandwich paste from the same ingredients, and between snippets of gossip served daiquiris in some cheap glasses I'd brought from my place, since my people were away for the weekend too.

'Girls, did you hear what happened to the famous Romelia?'

We were caught in suspense. Silvia was always into everything and went on without even giving us time to ask:

'Always acting so high and mighty, and they caught her with her finger in the pie, and in El Encanto of all places!'

'You mean stealing?'

Mery asked, in her little Lilí doll voice.

'And what need does that woman have to go taking what isn't hers, with all the money she seems to have?'

I let the question drop, not wanting to take it further, while I went about preparing another round of daiquiris.

'None, *negra*, it's just people are saying – listen good, I don't want any mix-ups afterwards with you all saying I said this or that... people say, don't take my word for it... she has an illness that makes her take things from places on impulse.'

'Hah! If it was one of us they'd call us thieves and send us straight to lockup, while they call her *cleopatría* and say it's an illness... While we get a headache, they get a migraine... and when they faint, they go running to the psychologist, while we go straight to a santero. That's life, my dear!'

Caridad burst out laughing at her own words, and we all followed suit. It was so contagious that Maité had to raise her voice to tell us to keep quiet, though she was also enjoying herself laughing.

'Damn it, girls, don't make so much noise! And you, see if you can't learn how to talk properly – after all, that's what they pay you for.'

We always took stock of being told off by the oldest among us, and Maité was known for playing the adoptive matron to us all. The only difference between her and Mamá Dolores in the soap *El Derecho de Nacer* was that she wasn't fat and was well spoken. You had to take note of whatever Maité said, because her influence wasn't to be taken lightly; and Caridad – who was very black and worked for a radio scriptwriter who lived in the Retiro Radial building, on Línea avenue – felt very embarrassed. But I managed to animate things again.

'Come on, Silvana, tell us what happened?'

I said this, and she flamboyantly got up from the arm of one of the four black, imitation leather armchairs in the corners of the spacious dining room. Standing was how we all liked Silvia to tell her stories and how she enjoyed telling them. She was more of an actress than Raquel Revuelta.

'What happened? Well, you know how things are, my dear... I found out because her aunt came from Sancti Spiritus to put out the fire that was threatening to spread, because as you know she was giving herself airs and graces long before she inherited her father's tobacco farms over in Cabaiguán.'

Romelia Heredia was a pretty, dyed blonde, tall and with a great body, who'd been Palmolive Beauty Queen some two or three years back, and of all the men after her she chose one that seemed a good match and married José Lorenzo Urquiala – a famous baseball player with the Almendares team, who earned big money playing seasons in the United States. Urquiala was the godson of Don Emiliano, one of the brothers of the countess where Silvia worked, a laid-back guy, and a notorious womanizer, with shares in La Tropical distillery, which wasn't Cuban but was the most popular beer in Cuba, not Hatuey like many people thought. From the start Don Emiliano, who was born in Florida, but whose parents were Spanish, had counselled Urquiala not to marry Romelia, because, as he openly said: 'Son, food today spells hunger tomorrow.' But Urquiala, who was also famous for his macho womanizing, answered right back that for 'a body like that', whatever! He was set on marrying one of the most sought-after white girls in Havana, and I never knew whether the 'body like that' was because of her long legs or her height, because she was up to his shoulders, which was saying something.

Silvia worked as housekeeper in the residence of the Countess of Sabadel – a woman cloaked in mystery who gave a lot of money to the leagues against cancer and for helping the blind, because she was rolling in it – and she kept us up to date with all the scandals that were never published in *Carteles*, *Vanidades* or even the 'Behind the Scenes' section of *Bohemia*, let alone the society pages of *Diario de la Marina* or *El Crisol*, two of the newspapers read by people with money. Romelia's latest adventure wasn't her worst. The big scandal came a year after they'd been married, when Urquiala returned from another season up North and the rumor going round was that his beautiful wife had been cheating on him with, of all people, Eulalio Santacruz, who, it has to be said, was one of the best, and it should be said few, colored baseball players around, who played for Marianao. Everyone knew Eulalio fancied himself as good-looking, and he had every right to. With those long eyelashes and thick black eyebrows of his, and that famous smile showing off his even, white teeth, he was like a mulatto Liberace, because he wasn't really black, or at least not my color. It was a tremendous scandal, though again it didn't come out in the papers, I think for fear that what was gossip would become real, or maybe it would give the baseball player a bad name, and he had good and influential friends among the journalists. In that tragedy, blood wasn't spilled, seemingly because of the strength '*Mandarria*' had in his arm, which is what had led his fans to give him that Sledgehammer nickname. He was the best pitcher of all the baseball teams, and tough as they come. I think Urquiala thought better of it all. You'd hear all this on *Radio Bemba*, which spread the news like wildfire all over Havana, down to the last detail, including the black eye Romelia got from the punch that bully Urquiala gave her. Because that's what he was, a tremendous bully. Sylvia went on:

'Well, girls, who believes theft gets discovered by accident... because I think that if the store assistant... Anyway, it seems Romelia put on a little perfume in the cosmetics department, tried the lipsticks and all that, but next to it was the jewelry department. Everyone is always out to look after her well wherever she goes, since everyone, or almost everyone knows who Romelia is, and, you know what men are like, always wanting to ingratiate themselves with women, and one of the male assistants was all over her, because it seems Romelia would always buy something. But, as the woman turned to one of the mirrors, the assistant was distracted by another customer who had come in person to collect a Champion Swiss quartz watch as a gift for her future daughter-in-law, and he called over a new girl to look after Romelia, and purely by chance she saw the Palmolive star drop down her cleavage a cultured pearl solitaire, which had been in a special display cabinet, on top of the counter, along with other jewels. Romelia took advantage of the distraction, and quickly said goodbye to the store assistant as he was giving the other *señorona* a gallant kiss on the hand.'

Silvia paused to light a cigarette. She didn't chain smoke like many of us, but after a couple of drinks she couldn't stop talking, and every now and then would take a cigarette from one of us. This time she took a Chesterfield offered to her by Maité, who was next to her, and she lit it with a lighter embedded in a glass case, that looked like an Aladdin's lamp and was like an ornament on top of a small table next to the empty and almost empty glasses of the cocktail I'd prepared.

'It seems the new store assistant tried everything to let the other assistant who was flirting with his customer know of the crime she'd witnessed. Meanwhile, Romelia took the escalator down to the street. Finally, the poor assistant called the floor supervisor, but Romelia was by then almost leaving the store through the Galiano Street door, on her way to the nearby parking lot where her red and white Chevy convertible, one of her beauty queen prizes, was being looked after, when one of the top floor security guards shouted to the one at the door, 'Stop her! Stop the woman in the navy blue dress!'

Here Silvia fell silent, and cast her eyes on each of us in turn to know we were hanging on the outcome of the story. Seconds seemed like minutes, and after protests from several of us, Silvia gave us one of her cheeky, girlish smiles, blowing the last puff of smoke from her cigarette, which she put out in one of the cut glass ashtrays. Her performance over, she said as if we were a group of kids:

'Thats enough, the rest you can imagine.'

'Wow!' exclaimed Inesita, who had been following all the performance and detail of *La Guantanamera*, Sylvia-style. The story of the theft wasn't especially important for the value of the ring she had taken, since, it has to be said, we never knew for certain exactly what it was, and, if it had been the solitaire everyone talked about, whether it was real or just some costume jewelry. Although Silvia swore 'by the remains of my great grandmother' that it was a very expensive ring, to tell the truth we never found out, because in all this Silvia was prone to exaggerate a lot. The main thing wasn't what was stolen, as I said, but how the affair was hushed up, because Romelia's aunt arranged for her niece to be whisked away to the countryside, and that was that. The affair was never spoken of again, except amongst us maids.

ALICIA IN SIGUARAYA LAND

Alicia, caballero Alberto's daughter from his first marriage, had a boyfriend called Tony. He was barely twenty, but looked older, since he was burly and played for the American football team of the Vedado Tennis Club. In terms of looks, everything about him was ugly, but the family had money.

Ali, as everyone called her, was a very nice, simple soul and very studious. She'd really taken to me, and I had to her. Her father loved her to distraction, and so did señora Ofelia. She spent virtually every weekend at her father's place, and her boyfriend would come to see her there.

One night, when I returned from visiting one of my sisters, I caught them at it on the almost totally dark stairwell, giving Ali a real fright.

'Ay, *Tata*, where are you coming from at such an hour... so late?' was all she could think of saying.

'I was out,' I responded dryly and stopped for the boy to let me pass.

'And you, what are you doing on the stairwell at such a late hour with your boyfriend?'

Ali wanted to express her authority as the young lady of the house, though she was never suited to the role. Then again, she was with her boyfriend. Señora Ofelia insisted that Tony, whose father was a cattle rancher, would marry Alicia one day, and I'm sure the girl had come down to say goodbye to him with señora Ofelia's consent.

The next morning, which was a Sunday, Alicia told me her boyfriend had said I'd had a cheek, to which she'd said that if anything she'd been the cheeky one, because she'd no business asking me where I'd been at that hour.

'Then, *Tata*, he told me that he couldn't stand you, and that if you were to go as the maid to his house, he'd throw you out himself.'

'Well, don't let him worry about that. Don't let him waste his time thinking about it. I wouldn't go to his house even to visit, because he's very rude, and parents who allow their children to behave like that are just as bad as, or worse than their children.'

He was so rude and vulgar that even in his girlfriend's house he'd take off his cowboy boots and shirt because he was so hot. He was always throwing it in the poor girl's face that he went to Miami two or three times a month to visit relatives who lived in a neighborhood with a name like an American movie actor. For now I can't remember which. But anyway, Ali couldn't afford such a luxury, although her parents were planning on giving her a surprise.

On one occasion caballero Alberto told Alicia that if she continued to follow the example of her stepmother he didn't know what would become of her, and that her boyfriend, Tony, couldn't continue coming to the house, and he didn't care a jot how many cows his father had.

'Because we aren't rich, though Ofelia likes to believe otherwise. She goes around saying that your boyfriend is the son of landowner señor so-and-so, and puts up with whatever that spoiled oaf does.'

That was the start of things taking a turn for the worse, and by the end of the week Ali and Tony had a fight that left her sobbing inconsolably.

Señora Ofelia wasn't about to give all up for lost, consoled the girl with promises of reconciliation, and went to great lengths to meet with Tony herself – though she never said a thing about what they said.

Two weeks hadn't gone by when Alicia saw Tony in a Biltmore club and suffered another heartbreak.

'Just imagine,' she told me after. 'There he was with another girlfriend, and he told all the other girls that I couldn't be going out with him because I was very poor.'

The next week the family went to the Country Club, to a *Quince*, and there was Tony again. He went over to Ali, grabbed her by the arm, and pulled her roughly to him, saying, 'Make sure I don't see you dancing with any of those *pepillos*, you hear?'

Ali was very pretty, probably one of the prettiest white girls in Havana. She had a doll's body, but, in comparison with her friends, or rather those friends that señora Ofelia tried to force on her, she was poor. Ali's mother had a good job as supervisor of long-distance operators with the Cuban Telephone Company. Her parents had divorced when Ali had barely turned three. Caballero Alberto never mentioned her by name, always saying, 'Ali's mother'. She was a beautiful woman, too, quite young and good looking, so far as I could tell from the photograph Ali took out only when she was there and put on the dressing table in her room. Anyway, going back to the girl: Ali was very charming, and was quite the envy, such that people would say, 'What a shame. So pretty, and yet so poor.' Others would throw it in her face: 'Yes, you may be very pretty, but you can't show off a new dress every week like me!' Ali cried a lot because of this, and I'd console her:

'Don't be silly, girl! Calm down! How can you spill precious tears just because you can't wear a new dress every week? Look, they may have a new dress every day, but they don't have your natural good manners, and they don't have your education and your morals.'

'Tata, I'd like to know why you always say they have no morals.'

'Look, my girl, it's really none of my business one way or another, but if you'd done what Tony wanted, he wouldn't have left you like he did. But because you took care of yourself, and I know full well what he wanted from you… that's why he slapped you, because I know that's what happened. You don't realize because you're a child still, even if you're almost fifteen. Besides, I'm older than you and as the saying goes, "the she-devil knows more because she's old than because she's a devil."'

Alicia didn't know how beautiful she was; and if she did, she wasn't vain like her little friends.

When she at last celebrated her fifteenth birthday, it was really something. For weeks there'd been rowing, with arguments and disagreements, and caballero Alberto, who for the first time was happy to make the effort to throw his daughter an amazing *Quince*, had reasoned with Ali's mother for her not to be there. I don't know how, but she didn't so much as show at any point.

The party even made the social pages of *Diario de la Marina*. The orchestra alone, which played the waltz and four or five other pieces, cost him two hundred and fifty pesos. Afterwards, the Riverside Orchestra, with Tito Gómez, came on stage for an hour, and finally a group began to play *rockanrrol* until the party ended.

The boys were all dressed in dinner jackets, and the fifteen girls in long taffeta gowns in different colors, some yellow, others green, bright red and turquoise blue, adorned with orchids from Goyanes Garden – so expensive! Even we maids who were helping with the service all had new uniforms, which señora Ofelia had ordered to be made expressly for the occasion.

There were thirty-five of us, almost all maids serving with families known to the Menéndezes, who had offered their services by way of a gift for the *quinceañera*, which had pleased señora Ofelia enormously.

When the girl appeared dressed in pink on the arms of her father at the top of the main stairs of the Miramar Yacht Club and came down to the strains of *japi-beidi-tuyu* and the fanfare of the orchestra, the many exclamations are still etched on my brain.

'What a doll...!' said the most sincere. 'Just imagine who they must have borrowed it all from!' said others, those who were always scheming yet called themselves señora Ofelia's friends.

The party was marvelous, and I was in charge of all the service... coordinating the champagne, the beer, the liquor, the cocktails for the special guests. Even the owner himself of Sylvain, the French patisserie, made a four-tier cake, and all the sweets and pastries you could think of. And three pink Cadillacs were hired that afternoon to transport the girls for the waltz! There were cars coming and going! They paid for it all on credit, 'and for what?' I asked myself as well. To socialise with those people of the Country, Vedado Tennis and Yacht Club, the Casino Español, Centro Gallego, and such... all those whites who after all had far more than they did.

But señora Ofelia achieved what she'd set out to achieve. Ali's *Quince* was being talked about for ages after, because when I left them and the years went by, almost always my best reference when I went looking for a new position was that I'd been in charge of the service at the *Quince* of the Menéndez' daughter. People's comments when they wanted to make some kind of comparison, were: 'Ah... yes... it was good, but not like the Menéndez girl's *Quince*!' That's to say, everything was before or after Ali's *Quince*. With this, señora Ofelia won the forgiveness of caballero Alberto for all her wrongdoings up till then.

It was around the same time that señora Ofelia took the children's godfather as her lover. He was one of the owners of Los Amigos car business near Infanta and 23rd. She was one of those señoras – and there were many of them – who acted so very fine but were in fact more unfaithful than a bitch in heat. They put on an air of morals that most of them didn't have.

Señora Ofelia and that man spoke on the phone in English. She would keep me away from the phone, thinking me stupid enough to fall for it.

'*Martucha*, if anyone phones, don't answer it, I will, understand?'

Of course I understood! So, if I was near the phone cleaning and it rang, she would hurry to it saying: 'No, don't go, *Martucha*, I'll get it!' It was totally out of character, since she was usually so lazy that even if she wanted a drink of water she'd have me fetch her one. And now the phone was ringing, she wouldn't let me get it, after she'd instructed me from the start that this was one of my household duties. When she'd finished talking, and the phone rang again shortly after, then of course I did have to answer it.

'Oh, *Martucha*, get the phone, will you please!'

One day I made a comment and she realized I suspected something. Acting as if I couldn't hurt a fly, I said, smiling:

'Ay, señora, you seem to have some kind of problem, because until you've spoken in English on the phone you won't let me answer it.'

She just looked at me all serious and left the room. Months later, on Valentine's Day, she said: '

'We'll give the place a good clean.'

I looked at her and burst out laughing:

'Ay, *seño*, you're a sly one! What you really mean to say is that I should fix the place up special. Isn't that it?'

'That's right. I want you to fix the place really nice, as though you were expecting your boyfriend.'

'But I don't have a boyfriend, señora.'

'No, but in a manner of speaking, so you make a special effort and leave it really nice for me.'

Señora Ofelia and Cabellero Alberto's two children, Tico and Cuqui, often went out with their godfather, who in truth looked more like their great-grandfather, though from a distance he looked good for his age. I'd get them ready and he would come in his big car and take them around Havana and to the stores, and they'd come back laden with gifts. Señora Ofelia referred to the man as 'the children's godfather', but just that once, because from then on, not even that.

That was the day señora Ofelia called me and said:

'*Martucha*, when you've finished in the kitchen, close the door.'

I'd known he was coming that day, even if for just an hour. I'd no reason for it to be any concern of mine. Caballero Alberto was about his business, the children were at school, and when I finished my work at around two in the afternoon I shut the door to the kitchen and went to rest in my room without bothering myself with what was happening on the other side.

Quite a bit later – it must have been about two hours, since I slept a siesta – señora Ofelia and I met in the corridor outside my room, and I saw she looked really bad and out of sorts. Later I learned they'd had a fight on that Valentine's Day. She realized I'd guessed something. Woman's intuition told me the relationship would fall apart, whether for good or for bad – though as far as I was concerned, I couldn't care less. After all, that was white folks' business.

Sure enough, what had to happen, happened. Towards the end of that February, she called me to tell me that I couldn't continue working for her, because the situation was getting very bad. The thing was that caballero Alberto had discovered everything, which was not surprising since the whole neighborhood knew, and everyone was gossiping. But what's more, he was almost bankrupt and they were going to separate. But she said nothing of all this to me.

'You know, *Martucha*, I can't go on paying you the forty pesos a month. As you know, last year we fired Ela, and now I can't offer you more than twenty-five pesos.'

She was putting me on the spot, because she knew full well that my work was worth much more than that and also I couldn't afford to earn so little.

Without so much as a by your leave, I collected my things and went to my sister Mercedes' place, which is where I always went for refuge, whether or not I had work. But not too many days went by before I had found another position, this time without the help of the agency but through the recommendation of a friend who was also in the same line of work.

BERTICA AND C. CONTE

Bertica and C. Conte got divorced as well. One day the señora called me and told me I could stay there as long as I wanted, but I should start thinking about finding another job, 'because I can't go on paying you what you need.'

She was very good, as far as things go.

'I like you, Martica. The only thing against you is that you have to serve to earn a living, but you have a lot going for you.'

She really liked how I always had my hair and hands done.

'Take this peso, Martica, and go for a manicure. I like taking pride in having a maid like you.'

One day, the señora called me and showed me an address in Nuevo Vedado, where they were looking for a maid.

'If you need any references, tell them to call me, I'll be home all day.'

So one Saturday afternoon I got dressed up and walked the length of 23rd Street as far as 26th Avenue, and from there headed towards a street opposite the Acapulco cinema. With a little difficulty I found the address, which was on 35th Street. It was the señora herself who received me. She seemed very nice and explained everything:

'Look, here you cook and clean. There are three of us in the house, and when you've finished on Saturdays, you can have the rest of the weekend to do whatever you like.'

The señora very much liked my appearance, until she glanced down and saw my hands, and, without making any pretence of it, looked at her own and asked me if I was working. 'Of course, señora,' I answered, and almost without letting me finish she asked me where.

'For the C. Conte family, on Línea.'

'And if you're so good, why are you leaving... have they fired you?'

'No, señora, on the contrary, but I can't tell you the reason I'm leaving.'

Then the señora looked at her own hands and again at mine.

'And how is it that, though you are a maid, you manage to have such a pretty hair style?'

'Because the señora where I work is a considerate woman and says I am as much a woman as any other and want to look as good as any other, the only difference being that unfortunately I have to serve as a maid to earn my living.'

That brief explanation, as the two of us stood in the hall, didn't convince her much. She looked again at her own hands, and this time she was so embarassed it immediately dawned on me she didn't know how to go about telling me what she felt she had to say.

'Look, no... let's leave it... I can't imagine those hands of yours being able to work well.'

And I left, without putting up any argument. I'd already left her the telephone number where I was working and, sure enough, she phoned señora Bertica.

'Good afternoon. This is señora Orfila y Basset speaking. You don't know me, but a colored girl gave me your telephone number and said she worked for you.'

'Ah... yes, that would be my girl. Her name's Marta. Did you arrange to take her on in the end?'

'Well, not exactly. That's why I'm phoning. So it's true she works for you.'

'Yes, she's my maid, and so you know I'm not making it up, I invite you to visit me and we can talk some more over a cup of coffee, if you like, because if you haven't taken her on, you've let slip a great maid. What's more, see how discreet she is, because the reason she can't continue working here is that my husband and I are separating, and I can't afford to go on paying what she was earning. She has two children, one of whom I know. She was so discreet she didn't tell you that is why she cannot continue with us.'

On the other end of the phone line there was a long pause, as if señora Bertica had something else to say, or to speak more slowly than she usually did.

'Would you mind telling her to phone me when she arrives?'

'She'll have to call you tomorrow night or Monday, because today is her day off and she's gone to her sister's place.'

On Sunday that weekend I had a wonderful day at Guanabo beach with Norma, my eldest niece, her boyfriend Carlitos and Guillermo, one of their friends. I got on really well with Guillermo, but at the time didn't have the faintest idea of what was in store and that we'd be together for many years. Anyway, that was why I didn't get back to the house until a little before nine, and señora Bertica happily told me, in full detail, what had happened, and stressed she had promised I would call señora Orfila y Basset. So, first thing Monday, I did just that.

'Yes? Who's speaking?'

'Good morning, señora, it's me, Marta, the girl who came to see you on Saturday for the position.'

'Ah, yes! I'm glad you called. Listen, I've spoken with your employer, and we're in agreement. I wanted you to call to see whether you can start work with us as soon as possible.'

My answer was quick, far quicker than she was expecting. 'No, señora, thank you all the same. The thing is, I'm not really interested in working for you. I'm a very good housekeeper, and can find work anywhere. I don't need recommendations.'

It was then that señora Orfila y Basset tried to come up with some explanation, but I cut her off, saying I knew what had happened, she'd had a complex about her hands and comparing them with mine, but I had no such hang-ups.

'You didn't agree with a maid having hands like mine,' I said in the end, and said goodbye as softly as I could. Without waiting for her answer to my 'thank you for everything, and goodbye señora, I'm very busy at the moment,' I hung up.

It wasn't the first time my hands had been cause for envious comments. They really were lovely, and not because I say so – I don't have a single vain hair on my head – but I do remember that the caballero where I once worked told me one of the two things María Félix needed to complete her beauty were my hands. 'Those long smooth fingers and fine nails. Those hands so soft, I don't know how the hell you keep them that way, doing this awful work. They're the hands the Félix woman needs; the other is the voice.' Santillana was, is, the name of that señor, who wrote poetry and novels and seemingly was quite famous, because he was often on radio. Caballero Santillana was always flirting with me and even confessed, out of the blue, that he was madly in love with María Félix, the famous Mexican actress who had at the time been in Havana for a few days. Those were the years when everyone wanted to look like her, married as she was to one of my favorite composers, old Agustín Lara. Well, I never knew whether he was single or divorced, and didn't have time to find out. I quickly invented some reason for finding another position closer to where I was staying, saying I had to leave. I don't know if he realized it was because I'd become scared to be alone with him and his craziness, but anyway he was very courteous in letting me go with a twenty-peso bill and a parody of one of the most famous songs Agustín Lara had written for María Félix:

> *"Do you remember, Pretty Marta*
> *Pretty Marta, Marta of my soul*
> *Remember the flowers..."*

And so he went on until I said goodbye, with a light handshake. Very romantic and all that, but I wasn't up for those little games, and anyway he wasn't my type.

Señora Bertica and her husband were very good to me. One day my son, who'd passed his exams with flying colors in Santa Clara, called me because he wanted to give me the news and know how I was. He called me very often. When I answered the phone I told him that he'd given me a fright. 'Besides, son, you already called me once this week.'

From the other end of the line his voice sounded sad. All he could say at that moment was that he'd wanted to hear my voice. 'Yes, me too, son, but I don't earn that much, I don't have enough to pay for the calls with what I earn, you know it's only thirty five pesos a month.' Cleaning, cooking and washing what they call smalls.

Not hearing any reply to what I was saying, I said it again and asked: 'Did you hear me, son?'

Almost sobbing he said yes, he was listening. He was choking on his tears. The conversation had finished, once he'd quickly calmed down and could tell me how well he'd done in all his exams and how he wanted to prepare for the baccalaureate.

When I'd hung up, not noticing the señor had been listening, I dried a few tears and as I was about to get on with my chores, I suddenly saw him looking at me. It made me jump.

'Marta, I was listening, not because the topic of your conversation interests me, but because I need to know what's being said in my place on my telephone. But when your son calls, however often, don't say he can't, and when you've finished talking tell the operator to charge the call to me, and tell your son to call whenever he likes.'

I tried to explain to him that I hadn't reacted like that to be mean, but because I was worried about what I earned and what it would cost me to pay for various long-distance calls.

'Don't worry about it. You know what it is, having that little angel of yours so far away and having to deprive him of hearing his mother's voice, all for a few pesos. That's terrible! Look, take this. When you send him the little things you send him every now and then, tell him this is a gift from me for being a good student. It's a very famous American boxer. In the United States they've just made this little toy figure, which sticks to any smooth surface with this suction pad and looks as if it's boxing. Take it, I know he's going to like it.'

I took the toy of that blond American and thanked him. I really didn't know if my son would like it, because the last thing he was interested in was boxing. I smiled as I dried my eyes and the caballero patted me on the shoulder before going back to his office. I looked again at the little toy, which had the name Joe Palooka written on the base. I hit it lightly with my finger and it swung in all directions.

Caballero C. Conte's work had something to do with boxing matches and boxers, and he received many good gifts from beer, rum and sports clothes factories; he spoke a lot on the telephone with New York and was always off to one place or another. People were always calling him from all parts of the world: Mexico, Venezuela, Puerto Rico… Buenos Aires even. I'll never forget the names of many of them – Kid Chocolate, Kid Gavilán, Pupi García, Niño Valdés – and sometimes I'd be the one who opened the door and served them – not just the boxers, who were really friendly, but also the radio and television sports commentators. I sometimes think that if I'd earned money by knowing famous people, I'd be very rich by now. But I was never under any illusion, so as not to die of the disappointment.

The moment he disappeared into his office, señora Bertica came into the dining room, where the scene had taken place, and I went across to tell her.

'I'm very happy because I heard my son's voice again, but I felt he was sad.'

And I told her everything up to the moment when the caballero had left, then started crying, this time, for real.

'Oh, Martica! What are we going to do with you? If you hear from them, you cry, and if you don't, you cry too.'

I hadn't felt this good in a position for some time and it wasn't only because of the work, but because by the end I felt a certain bond with señora Bertica.

They didn't have children, and I think it was because the señora couldn't get pregnant. They'd been together for many years and she was from quite a wealthy family, although it was the caballero who made the money. Señora Bertica's sister and mother lived on the first floor of the same building, of six big apartments, including the señora's and the one belonging to the family. It was there I met Cusi, who was the maid of Lalita, señora Bertica's older sister, and their elderly mother, who everyone called doña Gertrudis. Lalita didn't like anyone calling her señora. She was very likeable, although she didn't like men. 'They're all hypocrites, liars and frauds, and after they've done with you what they want, they leave,' she told me once, when I had gone down to their apartment to take her a pumpkin flan I'd made for her and the doña.

Cusi was my shoulder to cry on when things were difficult, and we'd talk a lot. One cool February night, we went walking along Línea, towards the Malecón, and we met Silvia. Being a friend of Silvia's could really open doors for you. She didn't talk about her work, and didn't like to be asked much, though she was always happy to chat for a while, gossiping about all the grand *señoronas*, without mentioning names, and accompanying her stories with loud bursts of laughter.

'You know what, girl, you-know-who said to me, "Hey, *mulata*, tell the Countess's driver to take me home," and you know what I can be like. I stopped her dead in her tracks, took out my fan from down my blouse, and after fanning myself a couple of times, just like Lola Flores, I told her that not even in her dreams would the Countess think of talking to me like that, and I suggested she walk the few blocks to her place, if she wanted to stop having to wear a brassiere one day. You should have been there! She turned as green as marjoram. "How dare you! How dare you!" She just kept repeating: 'How dare you! How dare you!" And she set off walking. What a nerve, can you imagine, speaking that way to Silvia, Tatica's youngest daughter?'

Barely twenty years old, Silvia was the mulatta with the most admirers in the whole of Havana. Few people knew that she was also a maid. She had hair down to below her waist, thick, shiny hair, like a horse's mane, tied into two enormous braids that bounced across her hips to the rhythm of her gait, which, judging by the looks she got from the men, was something not to be missed. It wasn't that Silvia liked to be provocative or anything like that. It's just that from birth she had one leg slightly longer than the other, and instead of limping she looked as if she was shimmying her hips when walking. They called her father Tatica, he was well known in the tobacco workers' struggles, and not just in Havana. He'd worked for a long time with the big leaders of the cigar rollers, and for that he was very well known to the BRAC. Tatica was almost always in prison. I never knew how it was that Silvia managed to be working for the Countess of Sabadel all those years. It was one of those things you just didn't ask, because you'd never get the answer you wanted, and besides, it was none of my business. In the distance, over by El Morro, the sound of the nine o'clock cannon fire rang out.

'Well, folks, I'm off. I don't want to get caught in a real explosion. You know, things aren't looking too good.'

And with that, she walked off down Línea towards where she lived, on 15th Street, almost at Paseo. Cusi and I said goodbye to her and slowly walked up to 21st Street, along the side of the Hotel Capri; 19th Street was closed for the construction work on the skyscraper of luxury apartments taking up the whole of the block formed by 17th, 19th, M and N Streets.

Heart of my Hill

I'd been anxiously waiting for December to come. I'd a few pesos saved for when I went to Quemado de Güines to see the children. Ramoncito would travel there from his aunts' house in Santa Clara, for I'd written to him some time before telling him to be prepared for when I sent word that I was about to leave for Quemado de Güines, where we would all meet up. I'd been in Havana for almost three years by then and it seemed like an eternity, especially being so distant from my daughter at such a tender age when a mother's warmth is most needed. But I couldn't complain. After all, life hadn't been so hard on me that I felt defeated or anything like that; and though it had been years since I'd worked for others, I hadn't forgotten all the chores of a real house.

I bought a ticket for the 'Special' that left at midnight, run by the Ranchuelera bus company that had only recently started up services from the capital to Sagua la Grande, and had a stop in Quemado de Güines. The new bus station, which was on Rancho Boyeros Avenue, had been opened halfway through 1951. I'd never been there before, because when I came to the capital, the stop was in Old Havana.

The air conditioning in the building competed with the cool December night air outside. In spite of it being close to the festive season, the bus station wasn't full, probably because the only companies that ended journey there were those running interprovincial buses, like Santiago-Havana, or those going to Camagüey, Holguín, Bayamo and all those places where I'd never been. I'd had my fill of the countryside with what I already knew.

When I got out of the cab that I'd booked by phone to come from the Hotel Nacional, an older man, who looked a lot like my brother Tito – half bald, with a mischievous boyish face – took care of my two suitcases full of things for my children and relatives, and all the clothes I planned to wear for the first time while I was there. After buying myself some candies and drinking a cup of chocolate, I went through to the passenger waiting room, where I decided I'd smoke a cigarette and wait for them to announce the departure of the bus.

*****

The first time I'd done some work as a maid had been in the house of Colonel Begerano, who lived on the outskirts of town, on the road that goes from Quemado de Güines to Sagua la Grande. That man was bad, real bad. He'd give anyone a whipping who dared say a word against General Machado. My mother washed clothes for him to support us all, and always used to warn us not to open our mouths except to say 'Good day', how much the laundry would cost, 'Thank you', and be gone from there. That was back around 1930, when I was ten or eleven.

Matildo, my father, worked the harvest as a canecutter in the fields belonging to Ulacia sugar mill. He worked like an animal, sometimes up to fifteen hours a day, not counting the journey to the fields and back on foot, and only to earn a few pesos in tokens – barely enough to buy cornmeal and lard for his growing family in the store that also, it seemed, belonged to the mill owner.

Back then, there were already thirteen of us, and my mother was pregnant for one last time with Millito, who died of typhoid before she was six, the only one of the fourteen children my mother gave birth to who was to die young. I helped my mother with the clothes which, with my brother Miguelito, a year younger than me, I'd take to Colonel Begerano's place. His was one of the lovelier houses around town, with paddocks and horses, and even a deep well, with a windmill, which never seemed to run dry. Just one of that man's army fatigues was worth all he paid my mother. They were khaki, really hard to scrub, to get off all that saffron-colored soil peculiar to the area, which got into every pore. The trousers were made of a dark beige material, and had to be left very clean, of course, and starched, and with borax even, so they'd be as shiny as his tall, dark brown leather boots. What a man that was! Miguelito and I would set off together from our house, which in those years was close to the cemetery, between the railway line and the power plant, and walk that dusty track barefoot with the bundles of clothes neatly placed in one of those lovely wicker baskets my father used to make – and which sometimes we even sold.

It was a good way, nearly five miles, but we liked going a lot, because on the way back the two of us would enjoy collecting eggs from the hens' nests under the thorny hedgerows round the big houses belonging to Fina, Mauricio and Ermenegildo, as well as Pordió's smallholding. Pordió was a fat, bowlegged black man, quick-tongued and in-your-face, who worked in the slaughter house and lived with his two sons, one of them not quite right in the head, about the same age as me, and the only family of color living in that part of town. People were very afraid of Pordió and said some really ugly things about him, that he was Haitian and a voodoo man, that he'd maybe cut up his wife with the same machete that was always on his belt and buried her in the yard under the bottle gourd tree because he'd caught her with another man, that he'd maybe shut her up in a room, and things like that. But no one dared look inside Pordió's house, nor even stop outside, because he had a pair of big black dogs that were really fierce. What's more, you could hardly see anything from the outside for all the trees and creepers all over the place. That house was really scary. To get to it you had to go down a long narrow track, which was impossible on foot when it rained because it would be deep in mud. It was down there that the cane wagons, pulled by oxen, came and went from the nearby cane fields, headed for the two sugar mills in the area – San Isidro and Ulacia, because they couldn't go through town – and had no reason to anyway. *Pie-dra-fiii-na!..... Me-dia-luuuu-na*! were the names given those unfortunate beasts, who looked more worn out than you could imagine. I don't know why they'd been given names that were so musical... and rhythmic. Miguelito made fun of the Colonel, calling him names, making sure I was the only one who could hear, because my mother could never get to hear we knew such things: "Be-ge-raaa-no!...Peeeople-kiiii-ller!.... Son-of-a-biiiiitche!" ...!' And lowing like oxen, we'd fall about laughing.

Many people didn't dare go down there on foot. Only mischievous kids like us, who weren't afraid of the *brujerías* that people put under the silk cotton and palm trees, nor of the savage dogs, nor snakes, or anything, would think of going down Hangman's Alley, as people called it. The story was that from one of the branches of a mango tree they'd lynched a black who had been a slave and led an uprising in the area at the time of *La Guerrita del Negro*, in 1912, in which my father had been involved, though he'd never wanted to talk to us about it. But also, only my brother and I knew where the hens laid, and sometimes we collected as many as ten or twelve eggs, which we'd sell three for five cents. All of this without saying anything to my mother, who was always trying to find out what we were up to.

I remember one day she discovered Miguelito with a really pretty reddish brown egg, still warm, and until he told her where he'd got it from she wouldn't lift his punishment, which was making him kneel on a fistful of dried grains of corn. I felt sorry for my brother, because he didn't say a word or shed a single tear. My mother sent me and another of my brothers out to play so we wouldn't see Miguelito's punishment against the wall, next to the altar for the santos. He didn't want to tell on me, because I'd been the first to find the egg in the cow's tongue hedge of Generosa, an old gypsy who read cards and who my mother didn't get on at all well with. She didn't forgive him until he told her what she wanted to know, and that was over an hour later. However, the saddest thing of all wasn't that, but sending the two of us to old Generosa's house with the egg wrapped in a white kitchen cloth, to give it back to her and tell her where we'd got it from, and that our mother had told us to apologize. I can't bear to remember it! But though we did, because we had to – not before begging our mother not to punish us like that, promising we'd never do it again – Miguelito and I still carried on looking for nests with eggs, only this time taking greater care and making ourselves our own '*huaquita*', as we kids called hiding places in those days.

Miguelito and I went everywhere together and laughed a lot, teasing all the time because he was quick off the mark and quite naughty. But he didn't like to work and did all he could to avoid doing anything in the house. I think that's why he became interested in music ever since he was little. Though it wasn't only him. All four boys played guitar, but Miguelito was the only one to make himself one out of two spinning-top cords. It looked nothing like a guitar, though he kept insisting that it was, getting angry with anyone who argued with him, playing it for sound, though it didn't at all sound like a guitar. Years later, when he'd become a real guitarist, he always reminded people who listened to him singing, in bars and parties, how he'd made his first guitar, and he was quite famous for inventing stories about those years. Although he exaggerated everything, there was a lot of truth in what he told, but people don't want to know about the hunger of those years of the Machado dictatorship, especially poor folk, who had nothing to their name. My older brother would go to the slaughter house and, if he was in luck, would come back with some bones that had been picked real clean, that he'd somehow got hold of, and that my mother would boil and boil for hours and hours, putting in a few root vegetables she'd come across, and with that we filled our bellies, because we didn't even have bread. There were so many of us, and there was no work or money to buy rice, cornmeal or lard... Those were the days when if there was a dime in the house, we were rich, because we could buy things to eat.

Miguelito liked to sit under the plum tree at the end of the yard, away from the latrine, and he'd start singing something that to another's ear would seem a totally incomprehensible phrase, over and over again... 'Heart of my hill.' Then he'd strum the guitar a couple of times saying '*riquitín, riquitín...*' and then again 'Heart of my hill', repeating this litany until my mother came out into the yard and gave him a piece of boiled sweet potato, and then he'd go quiet, because if truth be told he was simply hungry.

For those people who don't know what a latrine is, I'll describe it. As you may have imagined, the latrine is the little room where you do your necessities, but don't necessarily wash yourself. Generally, country families make it out of wooden boards, in the yard, as far as possible from the house, although anyone who can makes it with bricks, but that was a luxury. They came in different forms, bigger, smaller, more ventilated, with a light bulb if you had electricity, with a bolt on the door or just a piece of wood to ensure privacy while you were in there tending to your bodily needs. The floor was made of boards as well, covering an enormous hole. In the center was a box, two or three feet high, with a round hole in the middle. There were stories of heavy people falling halfway through and even drowning in shit. I never had any proof, but people were always talking about things like that, especially at wakes, when you heard all kinds of strange tales. I hated those latrines with all my heart, not just because it was so uncomfortable to get up on the box and in the right position so as not to miss the target when it came to pass. For me the latrine was the most degrading invention ever invented for defecating. That's why I nearly always used the chamber pot, rather than climb onto one of those boxes. The only effective way of controlling the stench was to be continually throwing in lime and creosote, until you finally had to give it up for lost and fill in the latrine with earth and cement, but not before first having the next one ready. That's why you could often see yards with two or three filled-in latrines, which the children never liked to play near.

We couldn't even contemplate going to school. Neither my mother Alberta, nor my father Matildo could read or write, and they didn't seem to have time to worry about us learning. So, of the nine girls and four boys, only seven of us reached sixth grade – not counting Millito, who was always so ill while she was alive and didn't make it to school. I'd had to repeat third grade twice, since was I always missing classes, partly because of chores in the house and because I didn't want to go to school barefoot and with no knickers. That's why I thought by accepting the job doña Emelina, Colonel Begerano's wife, had asked my mother for me to do, I'd be able to get some money together to buy myself a pair of shoes, even if they were only canvas.

When we returned with the peso and one *real,* which was the money for the clothes, and I gave my mother the news, she didn't answer straight away, but that was nothing new, because she'd always do the same when it suited. Before sitting on the stool in the big kitchen-dining room with its earth floor – which I had to clean with cold ash and water – my mother went over to the fire and, with some tongs my father had made from the hoop of a lard barrel, got one of the burning logs that were boiling a pot of water to cook cornmeal, and lit her inseparable butt-end of a cigar. She'd buy the tobacco leaves from a seller, hang them from one of the thin wooden beams holding up the zinc roof of the kitchen, and later roll a cigar for herself with the dried leaves. It smelled liked hell, but there was no way that anyone could make a face. My mother was very strict, and had a strong temper. You had to call her by her name, and no one addressed her in a familiar way, except my father, but that didn't bother her, because anyway they didn't talk much. With her tortoiseshell hair comb she pinned back her two long grey braids and at last sat down on the old wooden stool, next to the larder, where she always stored those puddings she made which I loved so much. I adored the *majaretes* made from freshly ground cornmeal, the *boniatillos* made from sweet potatoes, and the *buñuelos* made from cassava, but sometimes there wasn't any sugar to put in them. Besides, they weren't always for us, because she'd put them out for the santos; and she threatened us when she imagined Miguelito or I had put our finger in the dish of *majarete,* or if one of the puddings was missing.

'So, doña Emelina wants you to clean that big house three or four times a week, and she'll sort it out with me. She didn't tell you how much, did she?'

'No, ma'am.'

She sucked again on her cigar butt, and through the space between her only two yellow upper teeth, she spat out a dark gob so fast only she knew where it landed. At the same time she got up from her seat and went to throw on it a couple of spoonfuls of ash from the fire, and spread it two or three times with one of the old, heavy slippers made out of a tire that she always wore. She put a pound of cornmeal in the pot and, after returning to her position on the stool, blew out a puff of smoke that escaped through the kitchen window, while from afar kept an eye on the bubbling that was now starting, like fireworks exploding to celebrate the big meal of the day. The food might have been poor, but my mother was able to cook cornmeal full of flavour and dignity. It always smelled delicious, because of the tomatoes and seasoning, and more so on this occasion since she'd thrown in the two pieces of pork crackling that were left in the tin of lard. I couldn't hide the anxiety that came over me, and fidgeted with a doll that I'd made for myself out of a dry corncob. If what doña Emelina paid my mother was good, I'd ask her to give me some to save up and buy shoes for school. I didn't look her in the eyes, but rather at her lap wrapped around with the apron made from sackcloth of white wheat flour. She paused, and finally said:

'Fine, I'll sort things out with her. Now, get going, feed the sow and see if she's finally given birth.'

***

When the bus taking me from Havana to Quemado de Güines passed down the almost empty road through the town of Corralillo, my heart was beating so fast I put both hands on my chest to keep it in. Everything had begun here, or rather, the beginning of another ending.

The kids were going to be so happy to see me again, as would be my older brothers and sisters, when many of them hadn't really given their consent for me going to Havana in search of a new life. 'What's all this? A woman of your age, on your own, going about Havana?' That was the only reaction from Cucho, my eldest brother. But when it came down to it, he and the others knew that there was nothing else I could do. The work situation was terrible all over, as well they knew. Things were worse than ever in the sugar factory, what with that 'sugar differential' after the great harvest and now the 'dead season' was worse than ever. If I'd stayed, no one would have taken care of me and my children.

The Havana-Sagua interprovincial bus had left the Central Highway after passing along the Matanzas seafront, headed for the main towns along the north coast of Matanzas and Las Villas provinces. It was a long, boring journey, except for the half-hour stop in Jovellanos. All the passengers had to get off, since they had to refuel with petrol, and there was time to drink a small coffee, straighten out my crumpled clothes, buy some of that delicious Madeira cake, and go to the toilet – though when I travelled I always avoided the public toilets because they were so disgusting. I never understand why women have to be so inconsiderate, and throw away even their used sanitary towels where everyone can see them.

'Señora, señora, we're in Jovellanos. You have to get off.'

The woman sitting right next to me had fallen asleep as soon as the conductor had punched her ticket and the driver had switched off the lights as we left Cotorro, leaving behind the noise of the capital and the twinkling new lights of its streets and avenues. Little by little we were deeper into the narrow, poorly repaired Central Highway, with its potholes out of nowhere softly rocking the corpulent body of the woman, who'd started snoring, competing interminably with the bus engine. It was said the new motorway would be opening soon, which would begin the other side of the Via Blanca tunnel and join Havana with Matanzas along the north coast, and from there go on to Varadero, and continue after to Cárdenas, saving more than an hour on the journey.

I'd tapped her lightly with my elbow, which made her jump in her seat, looking for an explanation for what had disturbed her deep sleep.

'Oh, thank you, my dear! Where are we, did you say?'

'In Jovellanos.'

'Ah! Excuse me for not introducing myself, dear. Luisa Evangelina Tejera, at No 13 Martí Street in Sagua la Grande you're most welcome.'

I answered her very courteously and gave her the address of where I worked in Vedado, though I then made it clear that it wasn't actually my house, which she understood without further comment. We got up right away and were the last to leave, before the bus went to the garage to refuel the tank. Luisa Evangelina Tejera went straight to the toilet, and I whiled away the time buying a few little things, including two Madeira cakes. Then I drank a cup of coffee with milk. Given the time, there was quite a lot going on at the Ranchuelera stop. There was even a woman selling lottery tickets, calling out her numbers in such a low voice that it was easily lost between the noise of one or other passing bus and people's voices. I stopped a few minutes when I passed by her to see what numbers she had. The number I liked the most that always brought me luck was one ending in 513. The little old woman looked like my grandmother, with her grey braids tied in a couple of buns on either side of her ears and a red kerchief covering her forehead and tied in a knot at the back of her neck.

She didn't seem at all taken by my presence when I asked for two tickets of 023513, she didn't even raise her head. She cut them out with her long, yellowed nails, and with the same hand with which she held them out to me, waited for the two quarters I gave her, and something more, judging by how insistently she left her hand open and still held out towards me. I took a *real* out of my purse, which she accepted very gratefully with a smile that was more like a toothless grimace.

'That's a good number, my dear. May *Santa Bárbara* guide you always.'

'Thank you, señora. I need it.'

With that I returned to the bus, which was once again revving its engine full throttle. When I was back in my seat, the conductor began to count the passengers. Only two people had ended their journey in Jovellanos, but there were another ten waiting for empty seats. It was December, and people were like a swarm of ants everywhere, preparing for the Christmas and New Year festivities.

'Only two, as far as Sagua la Grande,' the conductor was emphatic when he shouted to the ticket seller, who looked like a postman with his dark Prussian-blue gabardine trousers and combination bus worker's cap and grey khaki shirt.

'Two for Sagua!' the ticket seller repeated, even louder, lighting up his cigar butt with an old-fashioned mesh lighter, for a few seconds lighting up his tar-black face, typical of the blacks of Jovellanos and this part of Matanzas, which was also known for its red clay soils. He looks Congo, I thought to myself.

'Two here!'

A hoarse voice rang out from the group of people pushing and shoving outside the bus door, because they all wanted to be lucky enough to be the first. La Ranchuelera only took passengers for their own destination points, not to leave people along the route, and although the next stop was Quemado de Güines, they preferred to take those going to Sagua first, which was where the bus from Havana terminated. Two tired-looking men came forward. By the light of the single fluorescent tube that was hanging from the roof of the wooden doorway of what was one enormous café and restaurant, I could see through my window that one of them was furiously chewing the remains of a cigar and his companion was eating what might have been the last piece of roast pork on bread. One of the two – peasant farmers from way out in the country, judging by their boots, straw hat and two cages with a dozen turkeys and guinea fowl, which miraculously were not making any noise at all – paid the ticket seller – who was standing on the first step of the bus, savoring his butt end, too – for single tickets as far as Sagua. The same ticket seller with the jet-black face stored the two cages in the luggage hold, watched by the two fortunate newcomers, waiting for the hold to be shut before getting on the bus, not in much of a hurry, and going to the back of the bus to take the two empty seats, next to the compartment with the air-conditioning motor, leaving a wake of smells which, as luck would have it, I could easily identify, from the dew following a drought, to those of rabbit and goat dung, through the penetrating smell of the smoke from cigars rolled from fresh leaves by their own hands. The driver closed the door and started up the bus, which slowly edged its way along the empty, half-dark, dusty streets of Jovellanos enveloped in thick mist. The church clock on the main street struck three forty-five in the morning. According to my watch, it was three thirty, which was almost the same.

***

The *Quemadense Ausente* festivities were the best of the year. Long before I was born, they were held on the 26th of December, I suppose to coincide with the traditional Christmas and New Year festivities. They weren't like carnival in Havana or Santiago. They were more like the *parrandas* of Camajuaní, Ranchuelo, Remedios or Placetas. When we lived in Santa Clara I never missed those festivals, but since I left for Havana, this was the first time I'd been, and it all seemed different now, coming as I was on my own from a city as important as the capital of the country. It wasn't the same, the two-and-a-half- or three-hour journey from Santa Clara to Quemado de Güines in a taxi, as the almost seven hours from Havana in one of those new, air-conditioned buses.

I hadn't been able to shut my eyes during the whole journey. While the bus crossed the dark countryside on the highway, I could barely stand the emotion as we drew closer to arriving, and I passed the time remembering the controversies there were surrounding those festivities, because the two principal barrios of Quemado de Güines – La Puya and El Perejil – competed every year, always in the most closely guarded secrecy, in how they made the floats, the themes and colors, as well as the songs and congas, and how they were going to prepare the fireworks, and how many rockets they were going to let off. Great care was also taken decorating the barrio, houses and streets, many of them paved with stone, known as *mocorrero*, or *pelonas* in other parts, brought from the cays of the north coast of the province to cover some of the dirt streets of town. People liked to decorate the street corners with palm fronds and reeds or bamboo, which many of the kids used to make bazookas, to fire with carbide – a stone that really stinks, and could be used for many different things, such as for ripening avocados and lighting lamps.

My mother was born in La Puya, and for a long time the whole family lived and grew up there, until, when she separated from my father, she went with her unmarried daughters to live in Dobarganes, a poor barrio next to the railway line, on the outskirts of the city of Santa Clara. My mother, Alberta, never saw my father, Matildo, again – and she didn't want to know anything about him. I never knew what he did, but she didn't want to even hear his name. During the New Year festivities, people were always looking for Papá to slaughter their pigs. He was an expert in cleaning out the guts and viscera with leaves and twigs from guava trees, because not everyone wanted or liked to clean all that muck and you really did have to know how to select the guava twig and make it absolutely smooth so no splinter would get caught in the chitterlings while cleaning them well with a lot of the juice of bitter oranges and the guava leaves. I liked to watch, but I didn't dare do it myself. Then he'd prepare the pig's blood to make black pudding. He was an artist at butchering pigs, goats and sheep. Then, many people would recommend him to roast the pig on the spit, filling the air with the rich smell of pork crackling, and I'd have me and my brother, Miguelito, watch how the pig's skin toasted. Papá continued roasting pigs in what was left of the second house that had once belonged to the family, at least for a while, but he lost it, I don't know whether it had been through gambling, or he stopped paying what he should have, in money and in kind, with root vegetables, pigs and other livestock. The owner had leased him a small plot of land to grow crops and pay him that way little by little. That's why he kept the big patio to continue tending the crops, and in a corner behind the big gate onto the street was his little room that he'd built himself from the bark of the royal palm, at the back of another family's house. He kept the patio well sown with eddo, sweet potato and cassava, and it was surrounded by many trees of sweetsop, mango, custard apple, soursop, coconut, guava, orange and grapefruit, both sweet and the large sour ones that could only be used to make *torrejas,* or skins in syrup.

That's why in December Papá always earned some money, because, old though he was, he spent the rest of the year tending the plot. There he had sown lettuce, radish, beetroot, carrot, tomato, coriander, parsley... and I don't know how many other sorts of green vegetables, which people bought a lot, especially in the cool months between November and January, which also coincided with the sugar harvest.

The plot was everything to Papá. He kept it well looked after and clean, and he liked to sit on a wooden bench that he'd made himself out of two palm trunks, where he'd smoke the cigars he rolled himself, as was the custom among humble country folk. There he would silently contemplate the colors of his patio, which was no longer really his, and he seemed to drift far away, looking over the trumpet tree which sometimes, when there was a breeze, shed one of its large dry leaves, making a light noise, as if it was scatching the back of its trunk. It wasn't like the racket that was caused when a leaf separated from a palm tree, or when the *palmicheros*, who sold the palm kernels for fattening pigs, knocked one down with a blow from a machete. So there Papá stayed, resting out his years, until my son arrived with a plate of food and cold water with ice from old Pastora's house. Pastora was one of the few people in the barrio who had a fridge, and had started up her own business selling five-cent blocks of ice and delicious *durofríos* of melon or even chocolate, three for a nickel, because she said she wouldn't open her fridge for less than five cents. When it came to making money, there was old Pastora. She was the first in the whole town to have a television, and in those years there were only three in the whole of Pueblo Nuevo, or La Puya as its biggest fans called it. One of the other two was in the house of O'Reilly, a mulatto doctor who had also been the town's mayor, and another had just been bought by Pagosá, a fair-skinned mulatto, who ran a taxi among the nearby villages. At night, after seven, having eaten and washed up, old Pastora would switch hers on, and the older people would bring their stools to sit, while the youngsters sat on the floor of the big porch, watching the programs from Havana, without a sound apart from the sucking and crunching of *durofríos*. Of course you had to pay for that tiny cinema, which stayed open until eleven, but no one minded, since it was the only entertainment there was after dark. Only a few older people, friends of old Pastora, could occupy the best seats, which were some chairs and a sofa in the living room, because the rocking chairs and armchairs were reserved for the family.

Nena, the eldest of my sisters, had taken upon herself the responsibility of looking after Papá, although, to tell the truth, my other three brothers worried a lot about him and would come to visit. Tito came from Camajuaní, Monguito from Santa Clara, and Jesús came on his enormous, scandalous American motorbike from San Germán, in Oriente, to see the old man, at least once a year. Papá loved boiled root vegetables and cornmeal with avocado, which was known as 'Blonde with Green Eyes', because of its combination of colors. When there was anything else, like cod or bonefish, which is dry with lots of bones, but bigger and cheaper than cod, everyone was really happy. Now and then people ate ground meat, and a chicken would only be killed when someone was ill and there was no alternative, because generally they were for selling.

'Ramoncito, take Papá his food and tell him to send me over a few radishes for the salad.'

Sometimes my son would go into the plot and get the freshest radishes and other green vegetables himself. On occasions, Papá had already prepared a bundle of the best lettuce and hung it from a big iron sleeper nail that someone, I don't know who, had buried in the palm tree, and was waiting for his grandson to come with the food in a bowl and the tin can of cold water or lemonade. The two of them got on really well together, they loved and cared for each other, although always in silence. Papá had invented a little job for him, which involved preparing the bunches of lettuce from the plot and the cress that he brought from Moon Gully – not far from there, but where not many people in the town dared go, let alone in the early hours of the morning, because that's when they say the dead and the *güijes* come out in those parts. Papá didn't care for that talk of the dead, nor little shaven-headed black creatures, nor anything else like that. He'd sharpen his short machete like a knife for the slaughter, and with his jute sack would head out for Moon Gully in the cool early hours of Friday or Saturday, long before dawn, accompanied by his kerosene lamp – the same one he used for lighting his little room made of royal palm and its dirt floor, where he always went barefoot to rest his tired feet. There was a period when he used carbide stone, but for a time they were hard to get hold of, since it seems that the Rural Guard didn't like it much that the youngsters made explosions with bamboo bazookas during the New Year festivities, and the bomb sound seemed to be for real. Papá wouldn't for the world let his grandson touch that machete, which he'd fought with in the last war of independence. He did take great pride, however, in showing him his veteran's medal, and even a very old photo of the Association of Colored Veterans, with him in a white frock coat buttoned to the neck, with his machete in his belt, and he talked about how he went up into the hills to fight when he was only fifteen, things the boy loved to listen to. It was thanks to the veteran's pension they gave him that he was able to sharecrop a piece of land, and there built the little house where many of us were born,

including me. Papá was a great walker, and he'd mend his own boots. He'd
be back before midday, sweating heavily. Then he'd pass by my sister Nena's
house and pick up his lunch through the kitchen window. Before washing
himself with water from the pump, he would let himself cool down a bit,
because he said if he didn't he'd catch a chill and come down with a cold.
Afterwards, he'd eat his lunch and lie down on his cot to take a siesta
for a couple of hours, but never before soaking the sack filled with cress
and leaving it in the shade or covered with banana leaves. When the sun
went down a bit behind the mango trees, Papá would sort out the cress,
cleaning off the snails and other bits from the stream, and then separate it
into bundles that Ramoncito laid out and tied with palm-bark fibre that
had been soaking to make it softer. He'd go out to sell his merchandise
around five in the afternoon, just before eating, since in the countryside
people eat a lot earlier than in the city. Three bundles of lettuce for a dime
and seven cents a bundle of cress. Sometimes what my son earned in a day
was between ten and fifteen cents, sometimes twenty, after walking and
walking barefoot, or in worn-out tennis shoes, around the town, hawking
his grandfather's lettuce and cress, which people always bought because
they knew Papá's would be clean and good quality. So much was it so, that
the only seller of greens who could go from one barrio to another without
any problem was Ramoncito. Maybe it helped that many of his uncles,
aunts and cousins lived in that other part of town. That's why he nearly
always came back to Papá's plot of land with the money from having sold
everything. The two of them would count the money together and even
argue at times about the little tip the housewives sometimes gave him. But
there were times, when he was in a good mood, he'd give the boy five cents
extra, which he'd put in a gourd moneybox he had buried at the other side
of the patio so his cousins wouldn't find it.

Three of my sister Nena's children went to school: Daisy, the youngest,
and her two brothers, who were coming up for twenty. The only money that
came into the house was from my brother-in-law during the sugar harvest,
since he had one of the best jobs in the mill, as the sugar tester, keeping
watch over the molasses before they crystallized into sugar. More than
anything else, he wanted his two sons to enter the mill before he retired,
but neither of them was thinking of following in his father's footsteps – and
anyway, what they'd be paid as apprentices was a pittance. For my part, I
gave thanks from the bottom of my heart that my sister and her husband
looked after my children for me, especially the girl, who I'd been very sad
to leave, and who was now there alone, without her brother, since their

father had come to take him away. He'd wanted to take the girl as well, but I stood my ground and wouldn't let him. Later I found out that neither of them had much of a good time there, but at least they never went to bed with empty stomachs and I have to thank my sister and brother-in-law for that. Then, many years later, Ramoncito told me my eldest niece hid the packages I sent every other month from Havana to alleviate the situation, and would sell off some of the little gifts that were specially for my two children – like the Milo chocolate powder they liked, or the boxes of La Estrella chocolate biscuits and other sweet snacks that they loved.

Ramoncito told me he'd had to go to school in worn-out boots because my brother-in-law sold the shoes I sent, or bartered them with the peasant farmers during the dead season. I never imagined such a thing could happen, and the poor boy was afraid to send word to me, though he complained to his father every time he went from Santa Clara to Quemado de Güines to see them. He also had to carry bucket after bucket of water to put on my brother-in-law's plot, which he jealously watched over and cared for. The plot of land was much smaller, and had more delicate, harder to grow vegetables, like cucumbers, bay, spinach, coriander, and such, though some years he liked to plant iceberg lettuce. In reality, what he planted he didn't want to sell – he was way too proud and dignified to go out selling things, unless someone came expressly to buy something. He had also reared a lot of rabbits, hens, roosters and even fine ones for cockfighting, ducks, and he was always fattening three pigs, which he'd slaughter in December: one for the family's consumption, another to sell, and the third he roasted himself and sold at the festivities on the 26th of the town's *Sociedad* for coloreds, which was facing the park, on the opposite side from the white people's *Liceo*. Ramoncito went to school in the morning, and when he came home in the afternoon, before resting, he'd go off to the pump to fetch buckets of water for my brother-in-law to water his vegetables. He didn't send his own sons, because Walfrido was apprentice to a baker and came home from the bakery around seven in the morning and slept until gone two in the afternoon, and Juancito worked in a carpentry shop, though he was almost about ready to leave for Havana as well, and escape his father's whims. Sometimes my son earned a few more cents when some neighbor or other asked him to fetch them a couple of buckets of water, which weighed a lot, especially, I imagine, for a twelve-year-old boy as skinny as him.

Now, looking out of the window, in the distance you could see the first light of another clear December morning, and the bus slowed down as though expressly for me to appreciate, in all its splendour, the blue sign painted on a sheet of grey metal, rising out of the ditch at the side of the road, welcoming me to Quemado de Güines. Just before the railway line that went from Sagua la Grande to the sugar mills, where two of my nephews and a brother worked, the bus stopped for a few seconds, watching for the signal at the crossing, and set off again slowly across the rails. Further on was the cemetery, its walls uniquely decorated with enormous encrusted crosses. One of the few times I'd gone into the cemetery had been when Eduviges, my grandmother on my mother's side, died aged almost a hundred years old. I remember she always dressed in blue gingham with a white jute-sack apron. She chewed a cigar butt the whole damn day, and with the help of an ebony stick that was as old as she was, if not older, walked in espadrilles through the country where her services as a midwife were much in demand. People who knew about these things said she was the best midwife in the whole area, because long before the seventh month, she took charge of the pregnancy and could tell whether it was a boy, a girl, or even twins. There wasn't a newborn belly button that didn't heal in seven days using the ointment she secretly made herself with snake fat. And best of all was that no child had ever died on her. I loved my grandmother a lot. She was all the time saying that people had to respect her because she was a black from Africa. I'll never forget those words of hers. She'd repeat them with much authority, with an accent in her voice that wasn't like ours. We all knew from her that she'd been a slave and that they'd brought her to Cuba without her mother when she was less than ten years old, but she never wanted to talk much about that, and even less so with me, because she really loved me. When something or someone annoyed her, she would raise her stick, and with her other hand on her waist loudly say: 'Don't mess with me, I'm a black *gangá* from Africa, you hear?' I never knew when it was that my grandmother became pregnant with her only daughter, my mother Alberta, who never knew her father, because, according to my grandmother, he'd been a 'brave rebel of '68'. Grandmother Eduviges had made herself a remedy so she'd not give birth again after my mother, because she told me she'd had to work hard to pay the 'free belly'. My mother knew about these things, but she never liked to talk at all about slavery. That's why I took it so hard when my granny died, and I spent the whole night at the wake, where they beat the drums without stopping in her palm fibre hut out in the scrub, out near the swamp, and I wasn't afraid to accompany her to the cemetery, which wasn't far from where we then lived.

We were now passing by the baseball stadium, which seemed to have been recently painted, with a blue and white wash. Then the Market Place, where you could buy everything, from a saddle to fresh fronds of royal palm that peasant farmers also used for the tobacco barns. The bus slowed down again, to turn a corner, on which happened to be the school where my son and some of my younger nephews went. La Ranchuelera was too big for the town's narrow streets – accustomed to the traffic of cars, empty carts, carriages, horses and bicycles, but not made for a bus this size. People stopped to stare with curiosity and surprise, and children ran behind to see who was arriving from the city, and if anyone needed their luggage carried on foot to their house, if it was nearby; or, if they wanted the luxury of hiring a cab from those parked around the square, they would take charge of finding one for a few coins you might be prepared to hand out to them, because you'd just arrived from Havana. Passing the only cinema in town, the driver sounded the horn to warn a man on horseback not to dare try to cross. Along one side of the square stood the only church in all Quemado de Güines, at the top of the new boulevard that the townsfolk called La Avenida. On the other side of the square, next to the drugstore owned by Cunduna, a relative of the first and only *Batistiano* mulatto mayor of Quemado de Güines, the post and telegraph office could just about be made out, painted blue, white, and grey, with the only public telephone in the whole territory opposite the long-awaited interprovincial bus station of that town which was decked out for festivities only once a year, at the very same hour.

Señora, no! Madam!

One September 1st, I started work in the house of a family that was half foreign, quite close to my previous position in Ofelia's house, also on Línea. Everyone in the building knew her as '*la Polaca*'. When I say, 'everyone', I mean us, the maids, of course. I don't know why they called her that, since she was actually French, but we called every woman who was foreign, or foreign-looking – pale, blonde and blue-eyed – 'the Polish woman', or 'the little Polish woman', if she was rather short.

Señora Evelyne owned a very famous jeweler's on Galiano Street. I was only with her a month and a bit. She paid me a good wage, it's true, but she was also very inconsiderate. She gambled a lot. They'd begin their canasta party at eleven at night, and at five or sometimes six in the morning there I was, still serving drinks, food, changing ashtrays full of cigarette butts, and sometimes at the end, if señora Evelyne won, I had to prepare a succulent supper with wine and, on some special occasions, even a breakfast with French champagne, caviar and all that. Of course, afterwards she gave me a few pesos, and the same when one of the guests won, they'd always give me a good tip. But they couldn't pay for the exhaustion I felt, because this was two or three times a week, not counting Saturday nights running into Sunday.

Evelyne and her husband had a daughter called Monique, a real pretty little white girl she was, quite well developed for eleven. I never spoke more than two words with the husband. He seemed French too, but I didn't have the chance to find out, since he spent most of his time traveling abroad, buying and reselling diamonds and other precious stones.

Evelyne was the most elegant woman I'd ever seen. She was a natural blonde, of regular height, and very attractive. You could tell her from a mile off by the perfumes she wore. I learned something from what she told me once, though why I can't recall:

'If there are two things in this world that are unmistakable, one of them is French perfume.'

The other thing was champagne, because, so she said, the best grapes in the world for making that drink could only be found in the province of the same name, which was precisely where she was born. Anyway, she was always repeating what she said about perfume, and when she really wanted to impress, she'd add the champagne.

She also didn't like to be called 'señora', but it was because she said it wasn't as elegant as her own 'Madam'. Since she was the one paying me, I gave her the pleasure of calling her Madam Evelyne.

Right from the start Madam Evelyne liked me, so much so that she even gave me a flask of Rochas perfume after the first week I was with her. Seemingly, she saw something different in me. One day she said in that husky voice of hers, rolling her r's like mad:

'What would have been your future if you'd been rich like me?'

Not just rich, Madam, I thought to myself. I knew what she was trying to say, because, although I was a maid, black and divorced with two children and with my own ways, I was blessed with a good figure, and by my attitude she could tell I wasn't one of those who allowed themselves to be subjugated, or anything like it. I told her there was no need to let yourself be trampled on just because you're a maid.

'Of all those who have been here, you're the one who has given me the best service.'

She liked to say that, with her slow and deliberate way of talking, as if counting exactly the words she wanted to use, and no more. But she was too finicky. One day she called me:

'Marta, please, after you've taken Monique out, do wash all the dresses, even if it takes you an hour. There are so many germs in this city.'

Very well, Madam! I didn't say so to her this time, though I was thinking how tired I was of her being such a nuisance, bothering me all the time. Didn't she know what it was to hand wash those dresses, with all those lace frills? I nodded in agreement. In reality, I was fed up with her impositions and constant lack of consideration.

Monique was incredible for an eleven-year-old.

'Don't tell me little girl stories. I may be the size of a girl, but I want to know about grown up things.'

Whenever we went out, that forward girl wanted me to tell her love stories and would ask when she was going to have her period, and whether after that she could get pregnant, and this, that and the other. I didn't lie to her, because soon enough she'd be a young woman, but I'd have preferred it to be her mother tell her what, after all, it should be her own mother telling her.

One afternoon, the girl came down in a lovely pink dress, and I took her to a birthday party not far from the house. We went walking this time, as far as Paseo, where it crosses Línea. I don't know why Madam Evelyne thought of letting me take her there on foot, because even to go three blocks she'd get her French car out of the garage. I went in my maid's uniform, of course – well pressed and all. On the way the girl said:

'Are you crazy, Tica? I don't want you to tell me the stories from books. Tell me the stories about things you've done as a woman.'

The nerve of the girl! That Saturday afternoon we arrived at the children's party in El Potin, on the corner of Línea and Paseo. All the nannies I knew were there in their smart uniforms. Many were surprised to see me in the neighborhood again, since I'd disappeared from there two months before.

'Girl, you look good! How's your white lady treating you?'

It was Basilia who asked me, a maid who was a mulatta *jabá*, with really bad nappy hair, who worked down by the Malecón in the house of a doctor who'd become rich and famous giving abortions to wealthy women, especially American women who came from the United States with the express purpose of seeing this gynecologist. There were many others doing the same, but he was the best.

'Who are you with now, my dear?'

It was the obligatory question asked of anyone who had been absent for a while, because when you have contacts in a particular area, it's difficult to leave. There were many maids who specialized in Miramar, in the Country Club, others in Nautico and Siboney. There were those who had under their belt Santos Suárez, Casino and other southeasterly neighborhoods. But Vedado was Vedado and fast growing with all the new buildings going up. It wasn't the same with Nuevo Vedado, where, although they had money, people lacked social standing. Families in Vedado customarily employed maids in their homes, and we were more likely to be accepted if you knocked on their door with a letter of recommendation – if there was a vacancy, that is. My friends, or my acquaintances I should say, for I had few real friends, but, well, I always called them that... so, anyway, my friends knew that I was doing well, and was in a good place. You could tell the class of employer by the quality and elegance of the uniform. But not everyone who lived in Vedado had money. Many people would give their right arm to live in Vedado.

My uniform was lovely. The skirt was semi-fitted, made of dark blue fine cotton linen, like a pinafore, with straps crossed at the back tied in a big bow behind the waist. The blouse was white, with a lace half collar and a small pocket on one side, out of which protruded a small mock handkerchief made from the same cloth as the skirt. Oh, yes! A little cap that I wore on my head, like nurses, though different from theirs.

The two hours the party lasted passed quickly and I had a great time chatting. I said goodbye to all my friends and left it that I'd spend a free evening in the barrio talking with them. The 'barrio' was what we always called the area where we worked and would meet up.

I looked for Monique, and this time we left in the car, because Madam Evelyne had promised that she'd come to pick us up, and at six on the dot we were ready. When we arrived at the house, I told Monique to take off her dress and give it to me. Although I knew the dress was one of those Madam Evelyne sent to Chantres, the dry cleaners on Calzada, when Monique brought it to me, I put it to soak, prepared something simple for dinner, vegetable soup and a ham omelet with fried potatoes, and then popped over to Maité's place, to be back before nine. At that hour of the night I set about washing the dresses and hanging them out, well protected from the damp night air. The following day, really early, Madam Evelyne went to church and came back at around nine-thirty. She passed through the kitchen just as I was coming in from the patio with the five dresses, including the pink one Monique had worn for the party.

'Marta! What have you done?'

I knew exactly what she was referring to, but I acted as though I didn't understand, and asked her why she was so taken aback.

'That dress! Why did you wash it?'

'Madam Evelyne, you told me that whenever I went out anywhere with the girl in one of her dresses I should wash it, and that you should not have to repeat this to me. I've carried out your orders. I didn't know whether this dress should or shouldn't be sent to the dry cleaners.'

After that outburst, slowly and softly looking me in the eyes, she said, tripping over her words, because when she got angry, her Spanish didn't come out well, despite speaking so haltingly:

'I wouldn't dare like to think you did this on purpose, because I think you are clear-headed enough not to have thought that this dress was for washing at home. But, all right, I forgot to clarify things, and didn't take into consideration your temperament.'

'Well, Madam Evelyne, all I can say is that you said not for you to have to repeat it to me.'

Just then, Monique appeared and tried to meddle in the conversation.

'Mamá, isn't it what I told you, I don't like this nanny. She doesn't tell me the kind of stories I like, or anything. She tells me I'm a girl, still, that's why I don't like her. When I'm out on the street, she holds my hand, because she says she has to look after me, and I don't want her to hold my hand.'

Her mother told her to be quiet, in French, and the girl quickly understood, since she went to the Alliance Française, a very selective school on Avenida de los Presidentes and 17th Street – although she'd been born in Cuba, she seemed to speak French very well.

Monique left, complaining a bit, half in French, half in Spanish. With a final reprimand of 'speak correctly, Monique!', the girl obeyed her mother at once, as always. Everything the kid had said about my responsible behavior with her on the street was all true, but it seems the problem with the dress was what complicated things in the end.

Monique was like that. She would let out things like that wherever she was, suddenly and without warning, never bothered about what she was saying, like the child she still was, after all. I said nothing more to them. It just came to my mind what that girl said to me one day when we were going out to the Rodi Cinema, on Línea:

'Don't think you're going out dressed like that, in that skirt, as if you were going out yourself. Put your uniform on, because if you don't, you're not going with me.'

'Listen, girl! Even if I don't put it on, everyone will know I'm your nanny. Whether or not I go in uniform, it's obvious I'm no relation of yours. I'm your maid, your nanny. And anyway, this is going to end right here. I'm going to speak to your mother for her to pay me what I'm owed.'

On that occasion I didn't do it, because the girl had two end-of-course parties and I'd promised Madam Evelyne I would take her. But this time, giving her notice, so she wasn't caught out, I did do it, and, astounded though Madam Evelyne was, I left.

María's Cemetery

After that, I was in another house where there were seventeen in the family, and seven servants. Of the seven, the only one who earned thirty-five pesos was me. All the others earned between fifteen and twenty a month. The señora of the house had brought them with her from Camagüey, where she had land planted with sugar cane and orange trees. One fine day, one of them, Roxana, said to me:

'How come you earn thirty-five pesos?'
'Ah – because I'm not docile like the rest of you.'
'Listen to her! Don't you know that if María hears us speaking like that, she'll give us a good dressing-down. We sometimes earn as much as twenty pesos, but no more than that.'
'That's your problem. I'm not docile. I give good service, and if she needs me, she has to pay me for it.'

One day this same Roxana came panting into the kitchen, as if her heart was about to burst.

'Ay, *negra*! María's arrived!'
'So what? And who is María? It's not as if María's going to eat anyone!'

I don't know if it was the same Roxana, an impudent white girl, or the nanny, who was at that moment preparing the baby bottles for the two twin grandchildren, but the fact is that one of them went and told María that I'd said that she, María, wasn't going to eat anyone. The next day, as usual, I prepared her breakfast, and Roxana took it to the dining table. I didn't see her taking breakfast, because I was doing other chores, but when she went back to her rooms, she called me through the intercom, and I went straight away up to the first floor of the residence.

'So you're Marta,' she said, slowly looking me over from head to foot, and I, of course, observed her as well.

'The very same in the flesh, señora.'

'You know the whole family has told me you cook very well, give very good service, and have a very good attitude, but you are also very strong-willed.'

I knew where this was going and was on my guard.

'Señora María, do you believe that being strong-willed means someone who has their own way of working?'

'No, of course not. I only say this because... I don't remember who... one of them... told me that you'd said had I eaten anyone... did I have some cemetery of my own... things like that.'

'No, señora, it wasn't exactly like that. One of them, as you say, came into the kitchen as if she'd seen the devil incarnate, saying over and over 'María's arrived... María's here...' with such fear and trepidation that I asked her whether you had eaten anyone, or had a cemetery of your own, and it came out that way because it really bugged me.'

I held her gaze, and saw a slight smile form. Next thing she told me she very much liked how I was and didn't like being served by people who fawned. I also smiled. Saying this, she wiped the smile off her face, or what attempted to be a smile but was more like making a face, and asked dryly:

'What do you have for dinner tonight?'

'Well, señora, I'm used to people seeing what they're going to eat when it's on the table, unless you ask for something special, and even so I'd ask you wait until the dishes are on the table.'

In fact, I didn't know what I would cook, since I had various special diets to cater for, including two of the older brothers who were vegetarian for religious reasons. I was quite happy to indulge them and invented a lot, and must have done well seeing as how they always ate up everything. But María continued the way she was, quite bitter underneath.

One Saturday afternoon I finished my work and went up to my room, at the end of the patio, in a little two-storey house for the servants. The apple mango tree was laden; it would only take one good downpour for them to be ready to be picked, before the birds ate them or they smashed on the flagstone floor.

I dressed, went downstairs and went out, leaving everything ready. At about six in the evening, María told one of the other maids to call the cook. That was me, and the one who answered was Lourdes, a *mulatica* who loved to dance, and it so happened we'd become really good friends:

'Cook left before lunch, señora, because Sunday is her day off.'

'What do you mean, she left before lunch, without me knowing?'

'Yes, señora. When she finished, she went to her room and I saw her come down very smartly dressed, carrying her bag.'

Lourdes was from a small town near Vertientes, south of Camagüey. I'd never been that way, but from what she told me, it was very much like my hometown. She'd been born and raised in the country home of María's family, where her mother had been in charge of the servants for more than thirty years.

In the few weeks I'd been there, Lourdes and I had talked a lot and come to be fond of each other. In other words, we understood each other well.

When I returned on Monday, really early, around six in the morning, Lourdes was waiting for me on the iron staircase leading onto the garden and from behind the railings said:

'Listen, *negra*, don't say I told you, but María is going to fire you because you left without telling her.'

'Don't worry, mulatta, I know what I'll do.'

We went up and I told Lourdes to come into my room and explain what had happened. When I heard the story and I told her I'd be leaving, and thanks for everything, she was left speechless. Right there and then I packed my bags and went down to the kitchen, where I left my suitcase and bag, prepared María's breakfast and took it myself to the dining table. I said my good morning and immediately asked for what was owed me.

'What do you mean, what is owed?'

'Yes, señora. Look, to be frank, it's not in my interest to work for you. I can't continue being watched. This is your house, and I respect that, which is why I prefer to leave before it's too late. You need a cook to suit your whims, and I can't work like that, and on top of that, there are too many people giving orders around here.'

That's how it really was. The niece would arrive and say, 'this goes here', then the daughter-in-law would come, 'no, that goes over there', then the nephew would follow and change everything again. There was no order in the house.

María looked at me again, but, like someone who doesn't like it or didn't exactly understand what was being said, barely turned her head and said:

'So, you want to leave?'

'Yes. I'm leaving. I'm not happy working in your house.'

Now I was the angry one. All the other servants were going about their business as if nothing was happening, when really they all wanted to know how it would end. Even Rebolico, the old gardener who was always joking with me, heard what was going on and started to sniff around to see what was going to happen. Without looking at me this time, she said:

'And if I were to raise your wage, would you stay?'

'No, señora, it's not the money that interests me now. What's more important to me is the house where I work and the señores I serve, and, as I said before, I don't like the way things are around here.'

It was then that things changed brusquely, and her conciliatory tone of voice turned authoritarian.

'Well, you'll know you'll have to come back tomorrow to get your money, because I don't have any cash to pay you right now.'

'That doesn't matter. I don't need the money right now. I'll be back tomorrow for it.'

And I left, with a conventional 'See you later' to everyone. The next day I dressed the best I could and in the afternoon rang the brass bell of the front door of the residence. When one of the other maids answered, her head appearing through the *postigo*, she told me to go round by the garden gate.

'No way, darling,' I told her. 'I'm not a maid of this house any more. Tell María that I've come to collect my money.'

I doubt that she, Marisela, expected an answer like that. She was too disconcerted to do anything but open the door and show me into the reception, no further, but enough to know I was inside the residence and through the front door.

That morning señora María appeared in her red Chinese taffeta dress, decorated with butterflies and flowers in many colors. She always said that dress really suited her, since you couldn't see the extra pounds she had put on. I still don't understand why she liked it so much, because it didn't suit her at all. And she said to me, all smiles, which was rare to see coming from her:

'Listen to me, *negra*, if you must know I don't want you to leave here. I like how you are. You may not like working in my house, but I really like how you are. Tell me how much would you like to earn?'

'No, señora, thank you. Yesterday I told you no, and I'm sticking to that today. Let me say it again, I'm not interested in working for you. There's too little order here, and that's not going to end by paying me four or five pesos more. A maid I may be, but I don't like working that way.'

In the end she paid me my money and I got ready to leave. When one of the maids accompanied me to the big porchway, she said goodbye with a little smile of complicity, and I just said by way of a farewell, half in jest, half-serious:

'Didn't I tell you I don't grovel like the rest of you?'

The Doctor in Languages and
Zoraida from La Puntilla

Not long after leaving María's house, I went to work for a señora who had several titles in languages who had to be addressed as 'doctor'. She had a whole litter of cats, which ate better than the servants.

One day, one of the cats had kittens, and she called me to clean her.
'Are you crazy, doctor?'
'What did you say? Everybody I've had here has done it.'
'That may be, doctor, but I'm not one of those "everybodies", and if that's what it comes down to, just give me the little you owe me, and I'll leave now.'
When she realized what I was saying was true, she tried to hold me back, and told me I was very impulsive.
'Not impulsive! Who told you that for twenty-five pesos a month I'd look after your cats? If I've never washed "that" for a person, I'm certainly not going to wash it for an animal, least of all a cat.'
Dr Elvira lived alone, but the house had to be cleaned every day.
'Look, doctor, let's not argue. Pay me my money and I'll go.'
'No, no. Wait. We can reach an agreement...'
'No, doctor, we aren't going to reach an agreement, of that I'm sure, because you need someone to wash your cats' nappies, and that person isn't me.'
It was then I brought up the fact that she didn't like the maid to use the telephone if she had a cold.
'Look, if there's one thing I don't like it's that if you have a lover he's calling you at all hours. It's all right for your close family... or to know

how your children are, but nobody else. Ah, and if you have a cold, don't speak on the phone or I'll catch it.'

Those warnings came on the first day. As luck would have it, shortly after she caught a bad cold, and one of my sisters called me.

'Marta. It's your sister on the phone.'

'Doctor, please tell her I'll phone her later from a phone outside, because you have a cold and I don't want to catch it.'

For her that was really something. All she said to my sister was that I would call her later. A while later she came into the kitchen where I was, and I realized she was watching me, but I didn't meet her eye. I knew what she wanted and why she was there, standing at the entrance to the dining room. But I decided to look at her, like so, in the way of not wanting to, and say:

'Were you wanting something, doctor?'

'No. I'm just watching and analyzing you.'

'Ah… It's to do with the telephone. Oh, doctor, you're more intelligent than I am, because I'm just a maid. Your maid… and black… like you said… we're not very smart. I reckon that infections don't recognize age, or color, or economic position. If I can pass my cold to you, then you can also give me yours.'

'You know it all, Marta.'

'Oh, no, doctor… just enough to defend myself!'

From there I went to work in the neighborhood of La Puntilla. It was the first time I'd ever worked in Miramar. It was in the house of Dr Ramiro Bejart, who lived in an enormous newly built chalet, some three blocks from the Hotel Residencial Rosita de Hornedo. The family consisted of the married couple and Mocha, a little dog that was a mongrel before she went to live in that fine neighborhood. Nobody lasted long with that family, because Zoraida, the señora of the house, was a tyrant.

She was badly traumatized because they'd had to operate on her goiter and she said she'd been left with an ugly scar… She was also always talking about an accident she'd had driving her convertible, and after the crash they'd had to amputate her mother's leg. But, quite apart from this, nobody mixed with that family, largely because of señora Zoraida. Dr Ramiro was a good person, but even his mother couldn't get on with his wife Zoraida.

And so this woman crossed with me and my character, both a lot stronger than hers.

I began to work one April 7th and was with them until August 30th the next year. I stayed so long because they paid me a very good wage to put up with her bad manners. Dr Ramiro gave me seventy pesos a month, and they were only two of them. I cooked, cleaned, did the laundry and took the dry cleaning, plus some other chores. I knew my work, and there wasn't much furniture – it was big but there wasn't much of it. Everything was very spacious and cool, and not much dust came in. So the work wasn't killing. The doctor liked how I was, and I think she did, too, despite everything, but she was very domineering and the doctor was happy for me to treat her firmly. She would say to me:

'You impudent black woman.'

And I would answer her in a similar tone:

'You're the impudent one.'

'You think you own this house,' she would say, modifying her language a bit.

'No, I don't, señora, I don't think I own any house, I'm the maid and I know my place, but I'll never humiliate myself for you or anybody else.'

'So brazen,' she'd say.

'More brazen are you,' I'd reply.

Each time we exchanged words like this, she'd start snivelling, and if her husband was home would say:

'Ramiro, Ramiro! Don't you see how this hussy treats me!'

But he'd make me signs to continue. It was in that house I first heard any talk of the politics of the day and that they called President Fulgencio Batista *El Indio*.

'I guess *El Indio* will be with us for a while.'

'Do you think so?' I replied. 'You know, there's nothing bad lasts 100 years...'

'... nor body that can withstand it. And what exactly do you mean by that?'

But I didn't give her any more explanation than a shrug of my shoulders and continued with my work. Señora Zoraida talked a lot with me.

'*Negra*, did you know I've become a member of the Havana Hilton?'

'What's that?'

'Something you'll never know, even if you win the lottery. Just think, it cost me a thousand pesos to join. It only opened last week, and I've already spent a whole day in the swimming pool.'

'Ay, señora, the world is always turning. Maybe one day it will be me going to the swimming pool and nobody will have the faintest idea where you are.'

This made her frantic...

'Listen to that! How outspoken! Next I'll be thinking you're with Fidel.'

'I'm not with any Fidel, but I do know that something or someone has to make things change so that one day what we're going through you'll have to go through, too, for you to know what life is like.'

'No way! *El Indio* will be here for a while yet,' was the only consolation in her reply.

It was unusual for there not to be three or four different people eating there every day. I don't know what they were involved in, but I do know they had more money than you'd think. One day a police officer arrived, apparently an old friend of the couple. My duties, of course, consisted in serving in whatever way any visitor might want. The policeman was in uniform, with his car parked at the entrance to the garage with his driver outside. He wasn't that old but had a lot of grey hair, and wore semi-dark glasses. They never mentioned his name, but if I saw him again I'd recognize him.

I went to the little table made of thick, opaque glass and served them ice-cold Hatuey beer, the only beer they ever bought, with a plate of olives, slices of ham and cheese, and crackers. They talked freely, as if they were locked away in their own world, but since I wasn't very far away, I listened to bits of what they were saying.

'... and you know, Ramiro, the fucking bastard fell to the ground, and I grabbed him by the neck of his shirt and let go of him again, like they do in the movies, and I kicked him a couple of times and stuck my boot up his ass... and the guy said: "Officer, for your mother's sake, don't hit me any more, have done with it and kill me." And I told him, "Don't bring my mother into it, you fucker, I've got no fucking mother"...'

At that point I took more beers over to the table. I wiped the glass with a cloth and changed the ashtray for one that was a bigger and I liked more, because it was made of a heavy transparent glass, instead of the other with the ugly letters spelling Cinzano. As I left, I gave him a look of such hatred that everyone must have noticed. I didn't mean to, but I couldn't help myself, and he was looking at me, not understanding why I held his look, while señora Zoraida, enjoying the story, let out one of those loud laughs of hers, and with great exaggeration said:

'Ay, but how can that be...!'

And the policeman continued with his story. That was towards the end of 1957. When they thought I'd gone again, the policeman told the couple, in as low a voice as possible:

'Shit, between ourselves... things aren't going at all well... After we finished off "*Manzanita*", we've had to tighten the screw. Things have been getting pretty ugly, especially up in the hills...'

'*Manzanita*' was the nickname of a student leader, said to be very courageous, and whose real name was José Antonio Echevarría. I think he was known as 'Apple' because he was quite plump and so white that he'd go red in the sun. Well, they killed *Manzanita* around the middle of March 1957, in an ambush they'd set up down the side of Havana University, after the assault on Radio Reloj, while others fired on the Presidential Palace in an attempt to wipe out Batista; but it failed, I don't exactly know why, but it failed and they were hunted down. The following day, early Sunday morning, señora Zoraida said to me:

'Listen to me, Marta, you know you've a bit of a nerve. Last night, while the Captain and Ramiro were talking and you went to serve them, you gave him such a look, I saw you, and you may not think so, but I was watching you, and they also were aware of it.'

'Why should that bother me? Don't you see he's the kind of man who if it wasn't for the uniform and pistol he wears wouldn't dare slap a Chinaman? Yes, it's true, I heard what he said about how he mistreated that boy, and God knows whether he's dead or alive. Do you think I could look at him nicely? No!'

'Well, look, I don't know whether you could or should have looked at him nicely, but don't you ever forget you are in my house, that you are my maid, and that you have no business to look at anyone who comes to this house – at least not that way. He noticed, though he acted as if he didn't, and just so you know, he could have you killed in the short space between here and the Kasalta café.'

'I don't doubt it, señora. But it's true. Do you think a man handcuffed, defenseless, being beaten by another... is right?'

Señora Zoraida didn't look straight at me, but she didn't stay quiet.

'You say you don't know anything, but you do know who Fidel is.'

'I've told you already, that I'm not with any Fidel, and I don't understand politics, but I do have a niece who once told me that all these abuses will stop when the *barbudos* come down from the hills.'

'You have a niece who said that?'

'Yes, I do! I don't understand anything about politics. What with my children not being here, I can't worry about anything else, and I don't have time to analyze what's going on, but my niece does, she's more intelligent than me, and has studied.'

In time, whenever that police captain returned, or any other, they minded what they said, and señora Zoraida read out exactly how I should behave. Even so, I told señora Zoraida that since I still didn't like the military or the police, I would go on looking at them as I pleased.

'Look, *negra*, keep quiet, because if I were to tell the captain that you told me he makes you sick and about your niece... things wouldn't go so well for you.'

'Of course things won't go well for me, if he doesn't have a mother, like he said, and with that night butcher's face of his.'

Dr Ramiro had come into the dining room on hearing how heated the conversation was getting, and he asked his wife not to argue with me any more and let me work, thinking that it had to do with some of her foolishness, as it usually did.

'Don't you realize this woman has put up with you more than I put up with you?'

'That's the last thing I needed, that because of this *negra* you go throwing my behavior in my face.'

'Anyway, for the time I have left here...'

My thoughts betrayed me in words. My reaction had been totally unwitting, but I didn't regret the words that came out. The two looked at each other, and it was señora Zoraida who spoke first, while I started to wash the dishes.

'I can't believe you're going to leave.'

'I've lasted long enough, señora.'

And she began to cry again, disappearing into her rooms on the upper floor of the house.

'You're not going to leave, are you, Marta?' the doctor slowly began to say.

'Yes, Doctor, any day now.'

'Happiness is short-lived! You've been the only person able to keep Zoraida in check for me.'

Señora Zoraida felt at a loss, and I thought I'd overdone it a bit, but I was sure she wouldn't threaten me again with that police captain. It wasn't as if I was having a bad time, after all. But I didn't like the friends the couple kept.

One Saturday afternoon, I'd finished early and was smoking a cigarette in the kitchen, as always letting my mind wander, thinking about my children. My thoughts were far, far away when señora Zoraida came in and said:

'Come here, *negra*. Sit down. I'm going to show you some pictures.'

She pulled me by my arm, and we sat at the big glass table in the middle of the dining room.

'Eh…and what's this? It looks like a brothel.'

That was what came to my lips when she showed me the first of the photos that she had hidden away in a box of fine chocolates. It looked just like a big country house that an aunt of my mother had near Sitiecito… with those enormous porches with beautiful mosaic floors and verandas with wrought-iron arabesques.

'Be quiet, don't say things like that, because I trust you.'

'And you tell me you're a decent woman? So that's why you went to Florida, to do business.'

At that time, señora Zoraida would have been about thirty, and you could see that in her youth she'd been beautiful and strong. Dark, with thick hair, quite curly… dark-skinned and eyes emerald color. In the countryside I'd seen peasants with blond hair and green or blue eyes, but naturally dark with those eyes and in Havana was rare. It seems that after the accident and all the medicines Dr Ramiro made her take, señora Zoraida had aged some, because the photos were only two or three years old, yet the difference was marked, though I didn't say so, out of discretion.

'Sometimes I take them out and look at them, and it doesn't seem possible that was me. These were taken about four years ago, in the summer of 1953, in a summer house on one of the small islands near Key West. I keep them well hidden, because if Ramiro sees them, he'd tell me off, because he thinks I burned them. I think my own mother did some kind of witchcraft so I'd marry that old man. The thing is that now he's got a lot of money, even if he's almost twice my age.'

I looked at her and began to laugh.

'You know a lot, *negra*. I can talk to you and you might look stupid, but you catch on to everything.'

I didn't reply, and she continued turning the pages of the first album, describing the photos to me.

'When I married Ramiro, the family didn't want the wedding, because they said I was colored… Can you believe that? Me colored!'

I looked at her, and threw myself back exaggeratedly, as though something new and surprising was suddenly before my eyes.

'Señora, to be black you don't have to be that dark. So his family said...?'

Señora Zoraida's surprise was even more exaggerated than mine:

'You don't mean to tell me that with these eyes and this hair I could be black?'

'No, no, no. No way. You're not black like me!'

She didn't answer me and turned another page in the album.

'Well, they really didn't want me to marry Ramiro, but he was crazy about me, and you know that I like mature men, because they're devoted to you and don't go chasing women. You know, one day my mother took me to one of those hairdressers – the sort you might go to – and they put a hot comb through my hair like you do, but no way, once was enough, and it was to kill the lice I'd caught. I don't know how you people can bear it!'

'Ay, señora! If they used the hot comb on you, then it's because you needed it.'

'Well, I don't know about that. What I do know is that Ramiro's family didn't like me, and still don't, but they have to put up with me because what I've got down here is worth a million pesos.'

And she put a hand between her legs. Señora Zoraida would tell me things about herself, and deep down I was sorry for her. She always told me the same story about when her father had bought her a European car called an MG, and it was MG this and MG that, and it was the prettiest in all Havana, a convertible, with two black leather seats. Only it crashed on a famous curve on the road to Managua, and they had to amputate her poor mother's leg, and she was lucky to escape with her life. She always told me the same story, and I listened.

That day she decided to talk about her husband, Dr Ramiro Bejart.

'He was so poor, the bastard, he only had one suit, and had to really work to become a doctor... And now his mother goes giving herself airs.'

Dr Bejart had two sisters, but they married Americans and now lived in the United States, and his mother had taken in a lot of washing for her children to have a career.

'Just imagine, *Martona*, Ramiro's father drove tanker trucks for Shell/ICA and lost his life in a terrible accident. Didn't you hear, Marta, about a truck that overturned some years ago and the driver was trapped? Well, it was my mother-in-law's husband, Ramiro's father. He was burned to a cinder, poor thing. Since then, all the life went out of the old girl.'

Señora Zoraida continued turning the pages of the album, barely looking. Sometimes she stopped just to point at some detail in the beachwear she had on, or to identify the people with her. They were all young, and looked like Americans, because they were nearly all blond.

The doctor's mother was quite an old woman, but very strong. She was a blue-eyed mulatta, and I imagine she'd been very beautiful in her youth. That's why señora Zoraida went back to repeating:

'Such airs and graces she puts on now whether I'm mulatta, or I'm this or that… and after all, what's he? If he has a good position and a clinic now, it's because my father helped him so much. Without that, he'd never have been able to raise himself up. I'll never forget that old suit of his… it had turned yellow from so much use, and I never knew what color it had been.'

I had to laugh at the things she said. The day señora Zoraida's father came to lunch he really liked the roast chicken that I'd made him without his daughter knowing. He knew and always had a good word for me, as on this occasion, when he added:

'So Marta's leaving us… What an excellent person and what a wonderful cook she is!'

I thanked him, but my words were lost under señora Zoraida coming out with:

'Yes, Papá, she's very efficient in everything, but she can't keep quiet about anything you say to her. She's a black barrister. Pity she's so black!'

'Zoraida! Don't be so rude, damn it!'

Señora Zoraida was taken aback by her father shouting at her. I took it in my stride, as always. But to annoy her, and reaffirming what señora Zoraida had said about me, I touched the end of my hair, near my ear, and then stroked my right index finger down my left arm, alluding to the skin color. She was the only one who noticed.

'See, Papá, can't you see what I'm telling you? Look what she's saying, that you're colored, that I should see your kinky hair.'

It wasn't true, since her father wasn't mulatto, not even Cuban by birth, but Lebanese, owner of a tannery. I knew this because I heard the doctor say so, though I didn't know where that country was. Sometimes señora Zoraida was more ignorant than I was. Anyway, I was in the dining room and señora Zoraida's father hadn't paid her any attention and was enjoying the fresh *buñuelos* I'd made with grapefruit shells in syrup.

After I'd washed up, the doctor came over to me in the kitchen, smoking his cigar, as he did when he'd eaten well and wasn't hurried. He wanted to confirm whether I was leaving.

'Since last April when you came to work in this house, I've been the happiest man in the world, because you're the only person who has been able to cope with Zoraida.'

Of course, that really moved me. Then he put his hand on my shoulder, gently, like good doctors do, and said:

'Marta, do you need to earn more?'

I could have cried. No, no, it wasn't possible.

'No, Doctor, it isn't that I need more money.'

I did need it, but that wasn't it.

'It's just that I think I'm in love and I want to be with a really good man, and I want to stop working so that I can look after him.'

'Well, start thinking about what our present should be for this union, because you deserve it.'

'Thank you, Doctor! I don't know how to thank you!'

We didn't talk about it again. They both understood the reasons, and señora Zoraida was the first to understand, despite everything. So my final week in that house went by, between family lamentations and señora Zoraida's extravagances and madness.

But I couldn't keep it up any longer. I was tired of all that and didn't know how things would end, nor whether my decision would turn out for the best. I promised them I'd find a replacement, and sure enough, Charito, my niece, agreed to go there. But she only lasted twelve days, because she and Zoraida couldn't stand each another. All Zoraida said to her was: 'With that angel face of yours, you can't deny you're very much your aunt's niece.'

Time Will Tell

This Revolution had turned all jobs upside down, including positions for maids. There were monied families leaving the country, including the few doctors who would see you, and those who couldn't leave right away were sending their children on their own, like sacks of potatoes, up North. At the time a rumor was going round that Fidel had signed a contract to send the children to Russia, and that the Russians – who didn't believe in the *santos* or in anything, since they were communists – were putting the children to work in a concentration camp they called Siberia, where it was freezing, and where they did all kinds of terrible things to them. At least, that would be the spoiled children of well-to-do families, because even the little white kids of the barrio were still hanging about the streets as usual, and my children and my nephews and nieces, and all the kids around were having a better time than ever before, because they even received gifts for the Day of the Kings.

Amidst all the gossip going at the time, it was said there'd be no more servants, which left us all up in the air, since we didn't know how to do anything else. Nor did we know what would become of all those señoras who were accustomed to have us do everything for them, though there were some of them who didn't want to leave the country, and that was when the scrapping began over who would go first, the grown-ups without the children, or the children first and parents after, because they had to stay to look after the old folk. It was criminal to see all those little children boarding planes on their own – well, actually they were accompanied by a priest or some nuns – and going off to a strange land, all on their own, which I imagine was even worse than really being sent to Russia. But, to be honest, none of it left me either hot or cold. I'd already suffered a lot being separated from my children all that time, and I'll never forget it. Well, there was such a lot of fuss up and down the country, what with the nationalizations and the sabotage in the cane fields and the cities, and the proclamations against the revolutionary government and Fidel's long speeches on radio and television, and the journeys made by leaders to foreign countries, and the threats of invasion that had everybody's nerves on edge, not just mine. All this had the country in turmoil, and people were very nervous, on tranquillizers, what with the militias and the marching. I was too old for all that nonsense of 'one-two-three-four', and many people made fun of the four steps adding 'wearing out shoes and eating no more'. But things were serious, because they were also saying that at any moment the Americans were going to straighten things out, especially after Fidel went to the United States and told them a thing or two, because he didn't see eye to eye with them and they didn't see eye to eye with him. But the Americans didn't come. Instead the bastards sent Cuban mercenaries as cannon fodder in the Bay of Pigs in the early hours of an April morning, just after Fidel had declared that we were socialist. Then there was this chant:

We're all socialist, onwards we toil
and if you don't like it, go drink castor oil.

At least the invasion was over in seventy-two hours, and the Americans realized that Fidel and the people weren't playing around, because they even swapped the mercenaries who were captured for baby food. I remember it was on television when Fidel reviewed the prisoners and there were all kinds there: spoiled rich kids, priests, and even a few blacks. Fidel stopped in front of one of them – I think there was only one – and asked, 'And you, what are you doing here?' I was embarrassed – not for myself, but for that boy – because it was true. Poor Fidel, struggling to solve racism in Cuba, and there was a fly in the glass of buttermilk. You had to see it to believe it! Ramoncito was barely eighteen then and was in the student militia in Santa Clara – and if the war hadn't stopped in time, he would have found himself in battle. But since he was a student, they gave him and his *compañeros* other tasks, leaving them in the city to control those the government knew were backing the invasion, while the fighting was in the south of Las Villas province.

As if that wasn't enough, the following year, when he came to Havana to study, he was caught up in the Missile Crisis and had to join the militia again. But since he was still a student, he stayed in Havana in the reserves and didn't have to go back to Santa Clara, but he did have to stay in the barracks. That time it was worse still, because it was to do with the atomic bomb and all that, between the Russians and the Americans, and us in the middle. Just imagine, an atomic bomb in Havana! In less than four years of Revolution, the commotion caused by the Americans on the one hand and the counter-revolutionaries on the other was never-ending. Nobody could think what would be coming next. And then those damned Russian missiles came, and those spy planes flying over head until Fidel in his beard got heated and he ordered them to be shot down. Kill the dog, and cure the rabies. They only needed one.

Guillermo was mobilized in an anti-aircraft battery for a month and a half. There was no way to make up for all the scares we were going through. It's just as well things were straightened out when the Americans promised they wouldn't invade Cuba and the Russians took away their missiles, under protest from Fidel, but they took them all the same. Those cold, grey days will be with me all my life. I think that was when I started suffering from high blood pressure.

To be honest, I didn't really understand much about politics, but, well, the poorest people were the happiest, especially us, blacks, because we had a lot of faith and hope in things finally turning out as God ordained, without having to hunt for some politician to get us a hospital bed or a dentist, and not how those rich folks wanted things to be. So we could have decent jobs and our children could have a little more education, because all the best schools were for people with money. Even the half-decent schools were for the white kids, like the Antolín González del Valle school in Santa Clara, where the kids went dressed in the smartest of uniforms, looking like the Silesians. Because even at that school they wouldn't accept coloreds. If they didn't say no, they'd tell you there were no places left for that year, and then it would be the same story next time round. Ramoncito really liked that little school, which was near my mother-in-law's house, because his uncle Humberto was the dry cleaner who did the family's clothes, and my son delivered the clothes and was infatuated by the school, but there wasn't the money to send him there, and no way would they take in my little black kid. At least he could go to the school run by the family of Víctor Morrell, his godfather, because that was for colored folk. Everyone in that family had a profession, mostly in teaching or in music. They lived in a beautiful big house to one side of the Buen Viaje Church, near the Maristas school, in a neighborhood near Vidal Square, that was a bit mixed, where some three or four mulatto and black families of good position lived. Most were people of considerable standing, like doctors, lawyers, dentists, and teachers, and there was even a Masonic Lodge on that street. Every Saturday morning, and three times a week during the holidays, we sent him to that private school so he could learn a bit more. It was a little supplementary school, not like the other public or private schools where pupils passed from one grade to the next. It all started because we were concerned that Ramoncito should learn as much as possible, and his godfather, a cabinetmaker who was well known in Santa Clara, agreed and insisted that the boy must study. But we didn't have money for that. So he did what he could to help us, since, when it came down to it, the school wasn't for everybody; you had to be from a family with resources – colored, but with money. Víctor spoke with his sister Carmelina, who had retired from the Escuela Normal teacher training college, and whose school it was, for her to place the boy because, he said, he was intelligent and he, Víctor, would take care of paying for his godson's studies as a gift, and as his duty. We were, of course, very moved by this.

But, well, returning to the present. Here I was in Havana, and after eagerly signing up for the night school on Calzada del Cerro, I realized after two or three months that, however much I wanted to, I wouldn't be able to complete all the schoolwork, housework, and three or four days a week working as a maid. After thinking about it a lot, I went to speak to the teacher and told her that I honestly couldn't, that I simply couldn't continue. Marilú, as the teacher was called, was very sorry but not surprised. I made up a story, which she pretended to believe. I told her I had problems with my eyesight, that it was tiring, and, although I liked the little school and had learned a lot, it was torture after more or less thirty years to find myself sitting at a desk again. She liked how studious I was, above all in Reading and Composition, History and Geography. But the teacher knew better than me that the realities of life were much stronger than my desire to learn. Even so, to give myself a boost, I promised her that as soon as I had sorted out my situation I would return to study. That night – I remember it as though it was yesterday – I walked home alone, really downcast. For the first time in ages I felt as if the world was crashing down on me.

***

'Well, yes, Martica, with all this *revolú*, you know, Cora left me, and since I trust you I sent for you to see if you could spend a few months with us until I can find someone else, because I know you have to look after your husband. I've even got calluses on my hands from carrying buckets of water and mopping the balcony, and I think I've even strained my wrist, because you know I'm not used to these domestic chores, and I'm beside myself.'

The fact is I didn't have the luxury of only looking after Guillermo, and so, after working for señora Patricia, where I went after leaving the house of that crazy señora Zoraida and Dr Ramiro, I took on some outside jobs, a few here and there, not like before.

Señora Patricia was very different. She had two children who studied in La Salle, another private school, and her husband was a lawyer with Eagle Life Insurance. She looked after things in the house, and also a building of eight modern apartments opposite the Arenal Cinema, out in Verbena, in the Sierra neighborhood, between Miramar on one side and Almendares on the other. It was an enormous, very comfortable, old house, with a red tiled roof, three big bedrooms, a separate garage, front porch, terrace, and quite a large back patio and small garden. Behind the kitchen was an iron staircase that went up to the maid's room, which was quite airy and had its own bathroom. Her children were no bother, off at their regattas and tennis, and such, with no time to be flitting around the house; and when they weren't studying or doing sports, they were out hunting, so the place they'd least likely to be found was in the house, and the señora in her office doing the accounts and things. They paid very well and left me to do what I wanted in the house.

I didn't have time to find out what her husband did, other than what señora Patricia told me the time I answered the phone when she called me at Bebo's store, on the corner of the *solar* were we lived in Cerro.

'Caballero Teodoro went up North with the oldest boy, to see to some business there, because it seems we're thinking of establishing ourselves there, until the waters settle back down to normal here.'

The morning I'd agreed to go to see her at her house to talk about the position, she behaved as always: treating me very politely and very friendly. According to what señora Patricia told me, the girl who'd been working there had left because a relative had sent for her to go to Santiago de Cuba, where he was going to find her work. Then, as I drank a coffee she herself made for me, she said:

'Ay, Marta! I'm so happy to see you again! You've no idea! The girl who was here was very good, but she spent the whole time saying how that guy with the beard is going to find work for all the maids, and that everyone has to be equal. Can you imagine, Marta! You maids working in banks, hotels and up-market stores! At least it won't be in El Encanto any more, because, even if they rebuild it, it could never be like it was before it was set on fire. Say what you like, he's to blame such things happen.'

I just looked at her, and smiled now and then, because even I, knowing little or hardly anything about politics, knew that at least something had to happen, or was already happening, and that things would not be the same again.

'Well, yes, Martica. Cora left me, and since I trust you, I sent for you to see if you could be with me a few months until I can find someone else – these days maids want to work less and less.'

Everything was very confused, and Guillermo had been left without work. Anyway, with what he was earning, which was only twenty-five or thirty pesos a fortnight as a construction worker, and then only if he could find work, it wasn't enough for us to be able to keep the house – or room, I should say, which is all we had – at least until they reduced the rents, a measure that suited us down to the ground. On top of this, I'd decided to bring my daughter from my sister's house, which meant spending a lot more time with her, since she'd suffered so much from the separation and she was showing it by rejecting me. Well, that's why I decided to start work again, little by little at first, only after midday for a few months, until Guillermo could get settled again and start work and I could get back to night school, because I didn't feel as old as some, who didn't want to learn. But, damn it, if that was the only way to stop being a maid and start doing something else in life – like my dream of opening a good hairdressing salon like Delia Montalvo's on Reina Street.

So these so-called señoras would meet in the Minimax and say to each other:

'What are you doing in the supermarket, girl?'

'Don't say anything, my friend. My maid left me this week!'

'Oh, girl! That seems to be the fashion these days. Mine left too, and she was really excited! Now they've got it into their heads to go and study – I don't know what. But anyway, this is bound to be nothing more than *Reina por un día...*'

'Let them dream on, and we'll wait and see what happens when they wake up!'

'Can you imagine? Now they're believing what *that* crazy degenerate still reeking of the bush is saying: that he's going to turn all the maids into secretaries, teachers and doctors. And they believe him! They're all carried away!'

'That they are. He's just filling the poor dears' heads.'

One day señora Patricia asked me whether I had any opinion, or anything to say, about what was going on. I told her no, that only time would tell.

'Woman, what do you mean by that?'

'Oh, nothing, *seño*. Time will tell!'

Don't Mess with the Santos

When Guillermo returned from work that night, he confirmed all the rumors I'd been hearing all day from the neighbors. Since he'd joined the Party some four years back, they'd been sending him all over the place. First to Angola, then to the United Nations Cuban Mission in New York, then to Montreal for the same… off here, off there, and for the last year or two he'd been head of the maintenance brigade at the new convention Center, out in Cubanacán. Every day he was picked up by the construction truck and dropped off, along with the rest of the workers, on their way back from the site, down Fifth Avenue, then along 42nd Street to Almendares Bridge. From there they'd go down 26th Avenue to the Vía Blanca. The truck always dropped him at the fruit market, before turning down Calzada de Dolores, heading for the barrios of Víbora, Luyanó and Lawton. After saying goodbye to his compaños, he'd cross the highway and continue home on foot.'

'*Vieja*, you don't know how complicated things are out there, with diversions and the militia and police all over the place, with what's going on at the embassy.'

When he arrived home from work, I'd always give Guillermo a drop of coffee. We both sipped from the same little blue and white pewter mug we'd won on one of our first dates, years ago, from Coney Island Park.

'What's that you're saying, *viejo*?'

I sat down on the only wing chair in the room, which was also where my clients sat when I straightened their hair with the hot comb. Friday and Saturday were an exception, for during the week I'd try to finish around five in the afternoon to be ready for him when he arrived tired from work,

107

since he'd be up every day at four-thirty, while it was still dark, to catch the truck between five and a quarter after.

Guillermo took one of the two cigarettes I lit together, taking care not to breath in the smoke from the strong one, which was for him. I knew he liked that kind of gesture, and I always tried to please him.

What with all my chores and problems with my eyesight, I hardly ever picked up a newspaper, but some days before it had been on the news on television that a mob had forced their way into the Peruvian Embassy. They'd killed one of the guards, a young man new to the job, and Fidel had ordered guards to leave their posts at all the embassies, and people had been free to start going in.

'Things are getting ugly, because the place is full to overflowing. All the scum of Havana is piling in there. The area's been cordoned off, and they've left only 70th Street open as far as Fifth Avenue, which is where all the antisocials are getting into the embassy.'

That same day, at noon, Manuela, my neighbor who lived at the entrance to the *solar*, had woken up really worried – or so Julia, who was always talking to her, told me – because it seems one of her two sons, the one everyone knew as Pimpinela, had gone into the embassy, to force the government to let him leave to go up North.

Pimpi, as I called him, was delightfully effeminate. He was more delicate than a fifteen-year-old girl in the bloom of youth... though he was no younger than eighteen. His mother and I didn't talk much, since Guillermo and I had argued over him flirting with that long-haired hussy. I can't stand that. Who did she think she was, enticing another's husband like that? But Pimpi was something else. He'd come noisily flip-flopping up the passage into the *solar*, wearing a brightly colored shirt and denim shorts so tight you could see his crack. He'd sit on the stool by my plants and start talking without waiting for anyone to start up a conversation, until someone did pay him some attention and get him going, because his language could be foul. Eneida, Baba's woman, would get him talking trash, like a parrot, but, when I was in a good mood, he'd talk to me about other things. To tell the truth, everyone in the *solar* liked him a lot – well, almost everyone. Guillermo spoke with him occasionally, my son too, and even Baba, who was a lieutenant in the army. The only one who couldn't bear the sight of him was Filiberto, who never missed a chance to say things to the poor boy, like if they hadn't shut the UMAP camps, he'd never have been let out until they'd made a man out of him, one way or another. I think the vultures would have eaten him long before then. Filiberto was brutal the way he talked. In my book he was born to be a pimp. He spent his whole time making up stories and complaining about there not being this or the other. When all's said and done, he'd never in his life had anything. He was always inventing shady schemes, saying bad things about the government all the time, and whenever he played dominoes in the yard he'd constantly tell everyone how he intended to send his daughter up North before she was fifteen, so that she could have a cake and eat ham and cheese sandwiches – so she'd know about the good things in life – but he never made a bean. For him, everything was Fidel's fault. Everyone in the *solar* knew what Filiberto was up to: how he was a runner for the *bolita* (which was illegal), bought beer in the Mercado Unico to resell at a really high price, and things like that, taking advantage of people's needs. He was lucky no one had ever turned him in, and even Baba, who was his neighbor, would sometimes play dominoes with him at the same table, but never as his partner, even though he knew he was so disaffected and even had some marijuana plants in a couple of pots hanging outside the window of the shower room he'd built onto an empty patch of land. If there was one good thing about that *solar*, it's that no one was a stool pidgeon, and when it came down to it everyone got on well, having been living together in the same situation for years. But to go back to what I was saying, when UMAP happened, Pimpi was just three or four years old, luckily for him, because it was terrible what the government did. They rounded up not only queers, but also television entertainers, like that handsome Albertico Insua, apparently for living the good life, enjoying the 'dolce vita' as in the movie; those religious people in white who went round proclaiming worship of Jehovah as the only true God, in Heaven and on Earth and under the sea, and who refused to salute the flag, give blood or do military service; and even all those spoiled kids, who never in their lives had had to work. So the task of the UMAP was to make real men of all those people through agricultural work.

Pimpi was very pretty, a high brown like his mother, with very good thick, curly 'Indian' hair. That day, he saw me going about my business in the kitchen, and it was my turn again to be his shoulder to cry on.

'Ay, Marta, if I only had your hands, how happy I'd be. Look how frightful mine are!'

'Ay, Pimpi! What the hell do you want my hands for...?'

It was the kind of comment he'd make when he wanted to start up a conversation though the *postigo* opening of the kitchen, right next to what was the only shower for all ten families in the *solar*. On the other side of that was the *excusao*, the only toilet for almost twenty people, including Fela and Gumersindo, the two old people who lived in the rooms next to each other at the end of the passage. Every time one of them emptied their chamber pot, covered with a piece of card, you had to shut the door or go out to the street until the stench disappeared, and every time they went right past the *postigo* of my damned kitchen. I gave Guillermo a really hard time about it, because for all he had a Party card and all I did to hide my santos and my glasses of water for the spirits so his *compañeros* wouldn't see them and know I was a believer, and all for nothing. None of the apartments in the microbrigade where he did voluntary work was allocated to him when the time came; it was always wait and wait, and sacrifice yet one more year, and another year, all for nothing. Oh yes, they gave him medals, but when there was housing, there he was, the very first to raise his hand for it to go to someone else with less merit than him, who hadn't sacrificed so much or so often as he had. When there was an old house that needed repairing, there he was getting hold of the materials for his friends – or those who claimed to be his friends, because every time they came around on a Saturday, to drink until they could drink no more, it was to ask him to get them some cement, bricks or iron rods. And the stupid fool always did. On top of everything, he'd put the construction materials in the same truck from his work, to give to his friends in the name of *sociolismo*, running the risk he might be found out some day. And here I was, stuck in the same tiny room as always, with or without the Party card, because as the saying goes, there's no way out of skid row. It really embarrassed me, but more than anything made me angry. What the hell! Even he, who was *abakuá*, had to renounce his beliefs to be accepted into the Party, and there we were still living in the same pigsty we'd been in since we first got together twenty-five years ago.

I remember the night of 31st December 1958. We were bringing in the New Year at the home of Guillermo's brother Nené. It was a great party, which went on right through to the middle of New Year's Day, and we hugged and kissed each other, and even cried, cheering because at last we saw some light at the end of the tunnel. I remember, as if it were now, how Clotilde, his mother, who had been initiated as a daughter of *Changó* for forty years, became possessed by her santo just after midnight, in the midst of everyone celebrating the fact that Batista had fled. We were all partying, except her former husband, the father of some of Guillermo's brothers and sisters. People called him 'Maniguela', but his real name was Leovigildo. Maniguela had been a big Batista supporter, and even had permission to carry weapons. He went round with a revolver hidden in the back of his belt. Since he and Clotilde had been separated for many years, Maniguela only went to the house, which was his and he'd left to the family, once or twice a year, when he knew several of his children would be together for some special occasion. That New Year's Eve, it seemed he was the only one who wasn't up for that kind of party, for in the middle of all the fun he disappeared and didn't reappear for a long time to come. It made no difference to his children, since they hardly ever saw him anyway. Well, Clotilde was calmly in her rocking chair, happy drinking her *aguardiente*, joking at the adulation of her children, grandchildren, sons- and daughters-in-law, and smoking her cigar, when Carmita, Guillermo's youngest half-sister, called to let us know that *la Vieja*, as we all called her, had been possessed by *Changó* and was calling to talk to us all, and so over we went. Since Guillermo was the only one of the six brothers who was *abakuá*, according to him his beliefs wouldn't let him accept what the *la Vieja*'s santo might tell him to do. It was under protest that he listened to what his mother's santo told him in front of us all, that he had to settle down, stop drinking so much, which had always done him a lot of harm, and that he also find time for her 'horse', his mother's 'horse', (meaning *Changó*), and that if he didn't he'd be left out in the bush, because 'my son, you don't mess with the santos', and beware if you do, as the Miguelito Cuní song goes. I'll never forget what her santo told him. One by one, the brothers and sisters, brothers-in-law and sisters-in-law, nephews and nieces, grandchildren, and all those who were there that New Year's Eve, filed past the altar and through the arms of the santo of *la Vieja*, who had become immensely strong, despite being almost eighty years old, and she held us to her ample breast and shook us hard from head to toe, while turning us round on our feet. Then she cleansed us with a bunch of herbs, *Rompe Saragüey* and basil prepared for the occasion with Paradise leaves, which *Changó* likes most and is very sacred because it protects, brings luck and is the best for cleansing the house and removing evil from every nook and cranny. All this and more was prepared in advance, since it was to be expected that sooner or later *La Vieja*'s santo would make an appearance, and woe betide any member of the family who wasn't there at that moment! All that lasted around a couple of hours, and after she was as if nothing had happened and was partying along with us, drinking good *aguardiente* that we'd had to search high and low for, and asking me what her own *Changó* had told me. Because I was special for *la Vieja*. When she'd had a couple of drinks and the party was at its height, a guitar appeared, which the youngest of my brothers-in-law played really well, and I didn't need much encouragement, though I did wait for everyone to quieten down and listen, to sing one of those Vicentico Valdés boleros, which will never go out of fashion and I always dedicated to Guillermo:

> *You have a strange*
> *kind of loving.*
> *I can't get used*
> *to your ways.*
> *I can't bear knowing*
> *you'll carry on as you are.*
> *You have to get on with your life*
> *but it's all the same to me.*
> *You'll do just what you want,*
> *I know that now.*
> *I'll leave you alone,*
> *my sweetheart,*
> *and never again, my love,*
> *will I think of you.*
> *You have a strange*
> *kind of loving,*
> *that's why I don't trust you.*

***

I don't want to boast, but I loved singing so much that when I was at my best, my voice came out just as I wanted, and everyone loved it, telling me I sang really well. Guillermo and I got to know each other listening to songs in bars and at the cabaret. The first time we went out together, we were with my niece, who was the girlfriend of a friend of his. Even though I really fancied Guillermo, I didn't want to make any advances, because I had my own problems with the kids and, though I was the same age as him but looked much younger, I had my doubts because I was divorced – not legally, but separated and with two children. But he insisted over and over again until finally my niece and Carlitos agreed to invite us out with them one Valentine's Day, to the Alí Bar, where Beny Moré would be singing that night. Even though Beny turned up really late, almost two in the morning, it was well worth the wait because after a few drinks too many he sang better than ever, and I even sang a duet with him that I don't think anyone will forget, least of all me. The owner of the Alí Bar came over specially to our table to tell us that everything we had from that moment on was on the house. Beny, all dressed in white, with his familiar wide-brimmed hat and cane, put his all into it when he started to sing – still off stage, and with the spotlights searching him out behind the curtains, among the audience, then… that song I love, which goes:

> *How did it happen?*
> *I can't say how,*
> *Can't explain what happened,*
> *But I fell in love with you.*

Such emotion! The whole room full of people started clapping. Beny was simply always larger than life. That night my voice was better than ever, and although a few other people had dared to sing along, and Beny's voice rose above all the rest, mine stood out when he began the following verse:

> *It was a light*
> *that lit up my whole being;*
> *your laughter like a spring*
> *filled my life with unease.*

It was in the orchestral chords that followed this verse that Beny came over to our table, which was right at the front, on the dance floor. Although he didn't seem to be surprised by my voice, because he was so professional and knew better than anyone that nobody could surpass the ring of his, he gave me that roguish look, as only he knew how, but without giving offence to my partner, and with the microphone in his hand, he came towards us and stood very close. After a charming bow to Guillermo, by way of asking his permission for me to accompany him, a courteous gesture on his part, Beny led me back to the band. People began to clap again, more politely this time, eager to know what role I was about to play. Perhaps they thought I was some unknown artist, or that we were friends of Beny, I don't know. But in that moment I was more of an artist than anyone and the drinks didn't let me down, but rather helped as they always do, above all when they're dry, like that matured Bacardí rum. Guillermo couldn't contain himself, he was so happy. We were all dressed to the nines, in fine clothes. I was looking so elegant that night. I wore a fitted white dress of raw silk that showed off my waist, which has always been small, following the contours of my body, though not overly so. It suited me beautifully. Though I never went to the theater or anything like that, I paid a lot of attention to how television artists looked, and there was a black singer, with a powerful soprano voice, Xiomara Alfaro, who was very elegant when she moved. She didn't sing boleros or anything like that, and the poor woman didn't have much luck because that face of hers and being so black didn't help, and she was always traveling between Acapulco, Buenos Aires and Caracas. But I noticed that Xiomara Alfaro looked great on stage, not like some artists who would make a mess of it, and that night I imitated her a bit. I don't know if people realized or not, but towards the end of the song Beny looked at me – he'd never left my side throughout, as if ready to help me if I fell or something – and I suddenly forgot the ending. I don't know if it was because I was so overwhelmed or because of the strong scent of the good eau de cologne he was wearing. Whatever, he looked at me and gave me a little signal that we would go out singing together on a high note. I imagine Beny thought I knew something about music, but I didn't. I knew nothing, although I knew how to sing and to sing accompanied, because of all the times my brother Miguelito and I had done duets. Anyway, Beny gave a signal to his big band to drop the accompaniment, and in unison we threw ourselves into the last line that goes, *'But I fell in love with yooouuu'*. Turning back to his big band, he closed with a flourish, while the audience applauded like crazy, and Beny took off his wide-brimmed hat that you could spot a mile away, and, giving me his other hand, directed the audience recognition to me. People were still clapping as Beny took me back to our table and from there lifted his famous cane to signal to the brass section, who began to play a wonderful *son*. I think it was the one where the chorus goes, *'Castellano, what a band you've got... Beny Moré, what an amazing big band you've got!'*

We stayed at the table savouring that moment, and Guillermo gave me a long kiss, tasting of rum. Those were the days! That night was truly unforgettable, one of those things that I would never want to be repeated, because I know it could never be anywhere near the same again. But, well, that was some years back.

***

I remember that when Guillermo came back from Angola in 1979, he told me stories of when he was in the trenches on the outskirts of a town called Santa Clara, on the border with South Africa. He spent the whole time they were under siege there thinking about what his mother, or rather his mother's santo, had told him that night, many years before, and he swore that if he got out alive he would start looking after his *Changó*. Twelve days and twelve nights trapped in the ambush sprung on them by soldiers of that evil black man they call Savimbi, stuck in that trench and with the body of one of his *compañeros* in combat rotting right there beside him, unable to bury him. This affected him for a long time after, I think always, since he was never the same after the two years he was in Angola. And that was despite not having gone there to fight, but to do the same job, building schools, hospitals and the like. Being a Party member, he couldn't refuse to do anything. But I know full well that he wasn't looking after his *Changó*, because he should have been becoming an initiate of *Changó*, but he kept putting it off and putting it off with the excuse of being busy, and one day the chickens would come home to roost. And when all's said and done, the communists' rag is as red as *Changó*'s! Then one day one of my brothers-in-law came to tell me that Clotilde had died, and he, Guillermo, was now on another internationalist mission in New York, working on the building that was Cuba's UN diplomatic mission. This time it was better, a kind of reward for having served in Angola, and it was worth the sacrifice because he was able to bring back some suitcases of things we needed and all that, but he couldn't travel to Havana to see his dead mother before they buried her, although he knew she was ill with diabetes and her heart could fail at any moment. It affected him a lot. I don't know why I was thinking about it, but the fact is that I knew there were things he didn't like but felt half obliged to say yes to everything, and I was really angry with him for having made me take down the santos from on top of the wardrobe and hide them in a corner, since everything can be seen from outside, from the passage. I think that's why we never got anywhere, because we weren't looking after the santos as we ought and every damn thing had to be hidden.

Anyway, going back to Pimpi, those were his comments when he came looking for me to chat. I always answered the boy, always paying him attention and always with respect. With his defect and all, he was a good boy, though nobody understood him.

'Ay, Marta, I don't know why I like chatting with you so much!'

He said this, clicking his tongue, sounding for all the world as if he was frying eggs.

But now we were all concerned about Pimpi and all the things we were hearing about what had been going on in the Peruvian Embassy: how the people there were going hungry and thirsty, and red under the sun, that the Red Cross had been called on and a port was going to be opened to go up North, as they did with Camarioca in 1965, and that there were many bad people mixed in with others who didn't agree with *el proceso*, and even the poor effeminates had gone in, and among them Pimpi, who, the damsel he was, was bound to be trampled on. I understood him, because he was always telling me:

'Ay, Marta, I don't know what I'm going to do with so much macho stench in this country, he himself for one...'

And with the fingers of his right hand he would touch his shoulder, alluding to the stripes of the Commander in Chief.

'They're everywhere, that's why I never go out. They never leave you alone. So if they don't give me permission to leave, darling, I'm sure I'll grow wings and fly straight to Miami.' That's what Pimpi's fears were like.

After that conversation with Guillermo, things got really ugly, and the whole of Havana was again in turmoil. From my block alone some fifteen people had gone into the embassy, and Pimpi was there.

'Do me a favor, old girl, heat me some water to bathe.'

'The bucket's ready, dear.... and the towel and soap are already there.'

In early April, after they'd killed Pedro Ortiz Cabrera, one of the soldiers guarding the building, it was reported in *Granma* that those who'd gone into the Peruvian Embassy without resorting to violence wouldn't be blamed for it and would be allowed to return home until the question of their leaving the country was sorted out, but those who had used force to get in would not be given such permission. The thing was, Guillermo explained to me, that it was very political, since it seems the Peruvian Ambassador, who was held in high regard by the Cuban government, had spoken with the antisocials who had gone into the embassy and convinced them to return to their homes, and avoid problems, and he promised they would receive authorization to leave the country to go to Peru or the United States – which is what they did. But his government didn't like the persuasive attitude he'd taken and ordered him to make the asylum seekers return to the embassy. The diplomat lost his post after doing that kind of work for many years. For its part, the Cuban government was very angry, especially, as they reminded the Peruvians, when after the 1970 earthquake, the Cubans had sent a hundred thousand blood donations for the victims, but weren't prepared to see Cuban bloodshed for a handful of criminals. When the place filled up, the Cuban government decided to guarantee food and sanitation, including milk for the many children that were in there.

One morning very early, shortly after Guillermo left for work, I heard a terrible commotion outside, and it turned out to be Pimpi, who had taken the government at its word and had asked for a pass to remain at home until all was arranged for going up North. Unfortunately for him, that same morning Alejandrito, the dental technician who lived on Calzada del Cerro, and was always dressed as though he was fulfilling a religious vow, had spent the night in the room with Manuela, Pimpi's mother, and an ugly argument broke out, which could be heard all over their little yard that gave on to our passage.

'You're nothin' but a fuckin' queer, d'you hear? You'd no business goin' in there. This is all 'cos you such a fu-fu-fu-fuckin' qu-qu-qu-queer. They should've cut your arse, so'd you'd not be such a fuckin' queer....'

And 'fuckin' queer' this and 'fuckin' queer' that, because Alejandrito, apart from having a bit of a stutter, had a problem pronouncing words, and pulled a lot of faces, blinking all the time, when he got mad, and was often made fun of behind his back. Although he was very good at his job, he'd grown up in the barrio ever since he was a kid, first in a wooden rooming house down by the canal, and then, after the room burned down, in a good stone house he managed to get on Calzada. But he was as stupid as they come when he talked, even though he was white, on the outside, because he always went round with colored people, and every day wore his promise to San Lázaro, with his beads and all, something few people did in those days: jute sacking trousers and short yellow-orange gingham shirt known as a *guapita,* the colors of Babalú-Ayé, the Yoruba-Lucumí santo of illness and disease. While all this cursing could be heard in the passage, poor Pimpi just kept repeating:

'That's why I'm going, shit, even if I die trying, so as never to see any of you ever again.'

For her part, Manuela, who seemed to be in deep with Alejandrito, raised her voice still higher, and almost screaming asked why life had treated her so badly, what the hell had she done to deserve such suffering, and that if this was God's punishment, why didn't he get it over and done with... Well, the scene lasted about an hour, and nobody wanted to intervene, until Alejandrito slammed the front door and left, but not before shouting from the street:

'Don't expect me back 'till that fuckin' queer of a son of yours has left with all the rest of the scum.'

The sobbing continued and Julia went over. She was always up early, because ever since Miguelito, my brother, had been living with her, the room had become impossibly small. Chiqui – one of her three sons by another man – also slept there, as did Luisa and my nine-year-old niece Machucha. Miguelito had at last managed to find work as a cook on a ship in the Gulf Prawn Fleet, and spent a good part of the year on the high seas. He also had two children in Santa Clara and was still very close to his woman there. But Julia, who was eternally patient, did not seem to mind, and whenever he came home she never shut the door in his face, quite the contrary. That morning I called to her through the little kitchen *postigo* and gave her some good coffee, not the kind mixed with chicory, that was hot and just brewed, and we began to comment on what was going on, because it was such a racket that it had woken up the entire barrio. When she came out into the yard, she told me she was going to see Manuela, now that Alejandrito had left.

Then I got down to the household chores. Half an hour had barely passed, when Pimpi himself appeared at my door. His head was shaved, he had a black eye that was swelling up, and half of his right arm was in a splint. His greeting was much less festive than usual. He sat down in his favorite corner and, without saying a single word, put both his hands on his bare and badly shaven head, and a couple of big tears began to well up. Then Eneida, Baba's woman, came out into the yard with two of her sons, Pompo and Ulises, and some of the children from the back who were getting ready to go to school. They all gathered round Pimpi, who, in the face of such curiosity, could only say:

'You can all leave me alone as well, I'm tired of everyone, *coño!*'

I signalled them to leave and, taking on the role of nursemaid, led him by his good arm into my room, lowered the curtain and left the door half ajar, so people would know not to be bothering me this early.

I made him a cup of lime tree tea from a small sprig I always had in the kitchen, and without asking him anything I spread a little mentholated balm where he had the mark of what appeared to have been a massive punch, and covered it with a sage leaf. All this was in silence, with tears welling up now and then. Later I turned on the radio to know what time it was. I didn't find out, because just as the newsreader said, 'Radio Reloj, the time is…', and the pips sounded, old Fela appeared at the half-open door.

'What happened this time, Martica?'

'Ay, Fela! Things are looking bad!'

Fela always brought me a little something. With her long, bony hands, that woman, who had more years on her than Methuselah, held out to me a box of mild cigarettes she'd put away in one of the pockets of her big dark grey cardigan. She usually shared things with me from her rations. Since she didn't smoke or drink coffee, and I sometimes prepared a puree of root vegetables for her, or seasoned the steak she got with her special diet ration, she gave me things in return, as well as the cigarettes and sometimes cigars that she got on her ration book as an adult, and her quota of coffee. She knew my temper, as did everyone, but she was never angry over my responses, which were never rude, because I know I'm not rude, at least not to anyone who isn't rude to me. That's why she didn't take it seriously when I said:

'Can't you see, Fela, what they've done to Pimpi for having gone into the embassy with those crooks? Don't you listen to the news?'

Fela assimilated this summary of events with an answer suited to her years:

'Poor boy! God bless him!'

And she went away silently, leaving behind the stench of her waste in the air, even though before stopping at my door she'd taken care to rinse out her chamber pot and throw the remains down the toilet bowl, and not in the same place where everyone has to wash their dishes and fetch water to wash and drink. In reality, she did do that when she thought no one was looking. But, well, at her age what more can you ask? It was enough that she was alive and managing to live alone.

'Thank you, Marta!', Pimpi said, having drunk all the infusion in two or three gulps.

'You're welcome, son. You can stay here as long as you want. Nobody's coming to have their hair done until midday, and in a little while I'll be going to fetch the vegetables from the store, they say there are bananas for those with a special diet.'

'No, Marta. Don't go yet. I need to talk with you.'

The serious tone in which he asked me to stay left me no alternative. Besides, going to the store was only an excuse to leave him alone for a while. But he wanted to talk, or, I should say, talk to me.

119

'Wait while I get some cigarettes and something to eat and drink, I feel terrible, all weak.'

I opened the solid old Frigidaire, whose motor I'd had fixed, so I could start selling the *durofríos* again, knowing Guillermo didn't like me selling things because he said his *compañeros* in the Party would criticize him for suffering from that illness they call 'ideological deviationism', but even so I sold them discreetly when he wasn't home, so as not to cause him any trouble. The thing is, that the Frigidaire worked just as good as the first day, as I once again proved, because the tray I'd prepared really early with strawberry and orange syrup was ready. I served myself a little cola and a piece of bread pudding I'd made the previous day. I offered a piece to Pimpi, but he didn't want any. He just accepted a little of the drink, which was a bit too syrupy. When I took him the glass, he drank it in one gulp, and then I sat down on the edge of the bed, and I was all ears.

'Listen, Marta, my dear, I'm going to talk to you frankly, and what I have to say is for your ears alone, and you have to swear on those santos you have hidden over there.'

I laughed and told him that yes, I swore on all the santos.

'As you'll have realized, everyone hates me because I am how I am, and not how people want me to be. They've hated me since I was born. All my relatives wanted to see me, if not dead, at least to forget I was family, because ever since I was little I'm not how they would have wanted me to be. All my *compañeritos* at school, or when we went to the fields to work, hated me, the State hates me and this government hates me, since they can't tolerate queers because they aren't ready for it, and on top of everything, my mother deep in her soul hates me because, simply, she can't hate me... No, don't interrupt me. I'm only going to say this once. Let me finish.'

Outside someone was asking for Pimpi. It was his mother who had come in with Julia, but she was saying he was with me, that's why neither Pimpi nor I answered.

'Why can't she just leave me in peace, as well! What the hell should I do? Well, sort things out as best I can, and do whatever I want. At the same time as hating me, because this society doesn't know how to deal with people like us, and there are a lot of us, they pity us because they believe we've been sick from birth. Listen, not long ago the police rounded up a whole lot of us by the Hotel Capri. The whole of Havana heard about it. What for? Nobody knows. We were doing the only thing we can do these days in Havana, flirting among ourselves, from the Coppelia ice-cream parlor to the Hotel Nacional. But, no, we can't even do that, because there are foreigners there. As if foreigners don't know what queers are! They might have another name, but there are queers wherever you go. Ever since I could reason, I've had to put up with my mother, that wretched woman out there, with her guilt complex because my father abandoned her when he realized she'd given birth to a queer. Yes, queer – that's what I am, and very queer, too! My two brothers would commit 'brothercide' if they could, because they like to act real macho. And now this latest man my mother's got, Alejandrito, who gives the impression of having bigger balls than anyone else, lets loose his machismo on me. So, tell me if you understand what I'm saying.'

Until that moment I'd been eating the little breakfast I'd made for myself, but suddenly a knot formed in my throat, and I choked on the piece of pudding I was swallowing. I got up and went to the kitchen to warm some coffee. What was I going to say to him? I went back to the chair and lit another cigarette. As I was about to say something, Pimpi interrupted me:

'No, you don't have to answer. You least of all need to give me an answer. I understand you, because I know that you know I'm more mature than many people think. I act the goat to survive. Marta, I have no future here. I'm tired of being humiliated. I'm tired of being seen as something defective. When it occurred to me to go into that damned embassy, it was my decision alone and it's nobody's business, do you hear, nobody's. Anyway, a lot of my people are there. Some because they want to be, others because they had no alternative, which is the same thing. There's everything under the sun in there, darling. But we had to stick together because many of those fucking bastards in there just want to take advantage. You won't guess who's in there. I don't know if she's come out or not... well, Yeya, that fat slut from round the corner, who thinks she's white because she dyes her hair blonde – Yeya, and her husband, that fag Tuti, are in there. It was Tuti who from the moment he saw me had it in for me, and started to insult me along with others, because my group got together in one of the best rooms on the upper floor, which had air conditioning until they switched off the electricity, and he wanted it, not just him, but for a group of people for whom he acted as if he were the boss along with that butch of a wife of his. Many of us wanted to leave once MININT guaranteed that nothing would happen to us and they gave us a card saying that we'd be among the first to leave for abroad. What more can I say? The thing is that since we didn't let ourselves be messed with, Tuti took it out on me, and along with others they trapped me in a corner and shaved off my hair with a razor blade and scissors that they found in one of the embassy rooms. In the struggle other people got involved, and I was the one they beat really badly and they broke my arm, and one of those to blame was Tuti. He and his woman stayed inside, but I got out because I couldn't stand it any longer, and the Red Cross looked after me. Too many people on top of each other and talking all the time, and scared and shitting themselves all over the place, and kids screaming, and the shouting and fighting, and all the people who kept arriving in droves. Even from Las Tunas, darling! I don't know how it's all going to end, but there's no going back, not even to build up some momentum. I'm getting the hell out of this country!'

And that's exactly what happened. One day Pimpi was gone without a trace, not even a goodbye. Throughout April and May, the newspapers gave the number of people who'd left for Peru, and above all those who'd been picked up by boat to go to Florida from the port of Mariel. It was like a movie. Everyone was agitated, with rallies repudiating all those who up till then made out they were revolutionaries and, when the opportunity presented itself, came forward to leave the country. And what riled people most was that they were tho ones who'd had the best life here, like Felito, a man who had worked all his life for the Housing Reform, and who people knew was always on the take with the house swaps, and who made life impossible for the poor unfortunate people who needed to change their housing. You had to go see that lousy bastard in person, and he arranged the swap according to his whim, so long as you greased him up well with some money. Well, all the front of that man's house, which was at the start of Santos Suárez, where the No 83 bus goes, was plastered with eggs, and ugly graffiti was painted on the wall of the porch. Nobody cared so much that the criminals left, because Havana had definitely become more dangerous than ever before, what with robberies and all, from the food stores to the little underwear that, after so much sacrifice to get hold of it, you hung out to dry on the lines in the yard. But well, when it was known that someone who'd done so much damage was leaving, people took it out on that person, as was the case with Laberinto, the butcher on Cerezo Street, who had even bought two American cars with the money he'd taken through cheating with the meat. Everyone in that part of Cerro knew full well that Laberinto was in with the truck drivers who distributed the meat every other week, and even with the people in the slaughterhouse. What they did was to weigh the fat and gristle as if it were lean meat, and then they'd also take half an ounce off every pound of the ration they were supposed to give you. And all this was to resell the meat at exorbitant prices to those who could allow themselves the luxury of paying. When people found out that Laberinto had left consumers high and dry and had gone into the embassy as well, they painted a massive sign on the butcher's shop, which read:

Laberinto, Slaughterer, Good Riddance

And they held his well-deserved repudiation rally at the very butcher's store, even though he was no longer there. It was symbolic, more than anything. Most entertaining of all was when a woman, who everyone knew was his mistress, was the first to ask to speak to denounce Laberinto, even though, of course, she had taken full advantage of his cheating. People weren't at all taken in by what she said and hissed so much she had to leave running.

From our barrio, many of my friends knew people who had left, but, thank God, nobody from my family, except for my sister Yolanda – though she'd left for up North with her husband and two of her three children some five or six years before, and the only contact I had with her was through the photographs that Rolandito, one of her sons who hadn't been able to go with them because he was of an age to do Military Service, occasionally brought round to show me. The photographs were nearly all the same, always showing somebody's birthday cake, with everyone very elegantly dressed, showing off their new patent-leather shoes, in couples or as a family, next to a car of the latest model, holding a can of Coca-Cola, because they knew that to find a soft drink in Havana was nothing short of winning the lottery, but then for years there'd been no lottery either. My poor nephew, who wasn't able to speak well and was a little backward at school, sat down to contemplate the photographs of his parents and brothers living in a place called Jersey City, where there were many Cubans. But, well, among the people I knew well, who I dealt with every day, few had gone into the Peruvian Embassy or were trying to go up North, until that Sunday at the end of May, when at a little after ten in the morning Inesita, my old friend from my time as a maid, appeared. As soon as she saw me, she fell into my arms crying, and told me that Gracielita, her only daughter, had left the previous day with her boyfriend, who had a brother living in Miami who had come for them in a boat to the port of Mariel.

For many years Inesita worked for the Robledos, a family that left shortly after the triumph of the Revolution, going first to Puerto Rico.

Señor Robledo, who had relatives in that country, had been the manager of one of the Coca Cola bottling plants, and not long after the nationalization of all the American businesses, the company offered him a good job in their central office in some city in the south of the United States, but, before settling permanently there, he wanted to be sure of things, and so decided to leave his family in Puerto Rico until he could establish himself. When señora Robledo y Albemar, as she liked to be called, because she said her own surname was also of good lineage, asked Inesita if she would go with her, Inesita said no, because she was with a man who was very revolutionary and wanted to set up home. The señora understood and after giving her a number of good gifts, such as two sets of bed covers, tablecloths, lots of clothes and even cutlery and kitchen utensils, told her that she would keep in touch, in case she needed her help one day, if things hadn't changed before then and they'd returned.

But that was all a story, because my friend never really lived with Octavio, who was much older than she was and had got her pregnant, which señora Robledo y Albemar never knew, which is just as well since she wouldn't have approved, being a strict Catholic, one who never missed going to Sunday mass with a rosary and mantilla; and although some members of the family knew him by sight, señora Robledo y Albemar didn't know Octavio was married. Although I loved and still love Inesita, just as if she were my own sister, she also knew that because of my own experience in my marriage, I didn't support her letting herself get pregnant by a married man. But Inesita, who'd been a real firebrand when she was younger, was the simple soul and good woman she'd always been. In fact, some of her friends used to call her 'Goodwoman'.

'Ay, Marta, that Octavio drove me crazy! He's so nice and so affectionate, and one day we just couldn't contain ourselves, and without putting on that little rubber cap we were all over each other in my room the whole Sunday my white folk were in Varadero. I didn't have time for anything... When he put his tongue in my ear, I was away.'

That was how she'd given me the news almost twenty years ago. Because Inesita's stories were always like that, her language was so dirty you had to be careful who was around. I was fond of her, and still am, and I let her entertain me with her stories of her love affair with Octavio. To tell the truth, that mulatto was something else, and didn't at all look sixty. I guess the work he had as a line repairer for the Electric Company was what kept him strong and handsome as a racehorse. But I never let her have an inkling of what I was thinking. Inesita felt no remorse for what Octavio's poor wife must have been feeling, but I put myself in her place. When at times I'd make some reference to this, the first thing she'd say was:

'Let her examine her conscience, since she's the one who can't hold on to him. Anyway, my friend, as the saying goes, "What the eye doesn't see, the heart doesn't grieve over."'

'Yes, all very well for you to say that, Inesita, but I can remember when I was the one who was desperate, having bad dreams thinking that Orlando was enjoying himself in the arms of another woman, and there I was alone, suffering, with no appetite to eat.'

'Yes, Martina, my sister, you're right, he is married... but, what about me? I'm the one they call the other woman in his life, the lost woman. But let me tell you something, I'm human too, made of flesh and blood, just as she is. I'm the other woman people talk about, the one they curse, the home-wrecker, like Enrique Santiesteban says in his program *Divorciadas*. I'm "the other woman", maltreated by life, who people insult, like you, who claims to be my friend, are doing now. Everyone only worries about her life, but nobody worries about mine. I'm tired of being lonely and needing a bit of love. No one thinks about that. I have no tears left to cry and I'm heart-broken, if you must know.'

And with that we remained silent for a while, before finally hugging each other, one crying and the other comforting, with no ill feeling, because deep down we've always loved each other a lot.

When her daughter was born mid-January 1960, I went to visit her in the Maternidad Obrera Hospital, out in Marianao – which was where she had a room she was living in. Inesita was really happy that beautiful winter's day, because she'd succeeded in getting what she had wanted so much, a little girl.

'Don't worry, sister,' she said as soon as she saw me. 'I'm not planning to force the child on him. Now I've got what I wanted, the rest is up to me. I'm going to bring her up as I've always wanted, and I'm going to give her everything that I never had.'

And that's exactly what she did. Long after the Robledos had left the country, Inesita began to work as a maid in the house of some foreign diplomats, because although positions were prohibited in the old way, you could sign up in a government office, and if you had good references saying you were revolutionary, you could get work in diplomats' houses and receive a very good wage, and even some gifts every now and then. That was how she managed to educate Gracielita, who was first in one of the best nurseries in Havana, the MINREXITOS, which is on Rampa and was attended by the children of officials and some employees of the Ministry of Foreign Affairs, MINREX. Inesita took great care in looking after her: she made all the girl's clothes herself, taking her and picking her up from the nursery, where she was the center of attention of many parents, because her daughter was so well looked after, always well dressed, with a couple of big bows in her long hair that Inesita took great trouble over brushing, with a lot of grease, torturing the little one early in the morning, and at night before putting her to bed when she loosened the two long braids. Her obsession with the brush was to make her natural curls disappear, without recourse to the hot comb – which on more than one occasion she was tempted to use. In the end it was all in vain, and as the girl grew she gave up trying. After finishing secondary school with good grades, she won first a scholarship to the Lenin Vocational School, and then another, for being good at science and math, and she graduated in the GDR in Genetic Engineering, a rare field not many knew anything about at that time. When she returned she got a good job in the National Center for Scientific Research, with a good salary and benefits. But it seems Gracielita had the same luck as her mother, and, I think, all of us. While she was still a pretty young thing, and because that's what she was, the girl fell madly in love with a young man slightly older than her. He was an engineer, too, and it appears held views opposed to the government, although he seemed discreet about it. Inesita didn't like the man at all, and I think it wasn't so much because he was white as because he wasn't very integrated into the Revolution, despite working in that special government center. It seems events proved her right, because the two of them also went into the Peruvian Embassy and wound up leaving for Florida, and that's what the poor woman had come to tell me that Sunday morning, a cool and beautiful day in early June 1980.

'Oh, sister, I'm ruined, ruined. I just want to die.'

Inesita was a lot thinner than the last time I'd seen her, at the start of the year, when she came to offload with me about how little she liked Gracielita's relationship with Jorge, her sweetheart.

'I knew he wasn't revolutionary, but I never imagined it would come to this. I feel so ashamed, Marta, my daughter caught up in all this! What did I do to deserve this? I did everything for her, gave up my life to give her an education and look how she repays me.'

Gracielita was pretty and very well educated; she even spoke perfect German and Russian. And it was true what Inesita said. She had given the girl whatever she wanted. She did what she liked with her mother, to the extent that, although Inesita didn't want her to go to the GDR, the girl convinced her, and at just fifteen years of age she went to the other side of the world to study. Now, having calmed down a bit, she began to tell me the story.

'As you know, Marta, I never liked Jorge, because of the way he talked and the influence he was having on Gracielita, who had very good relations in the Youth and who everyone thought highly of. But that Jorge, that Jorge, he just couldn't keep to himself! One night, some time after the trouble began with the embassy, Gracielita came home and told me she was going to spend a few days in the Escambray, for work. Like an idiot I didn't ask her anything except how many days she'd be there, and whether she was going alone, and whether she needed to take any clothes with her so I could iron them for her. But she said no, she was in a hurry, since they were waiting for her, and it was going to be a special experimental station up in the hills; she'd be fine with a pair of jeans and other bits of underwear and T-shirts, and yes, she was going with her damned Jorge. Of course, I said no more than that she should take care and should call me at the phone in the corner store, where you know they take messages for me, to know when she'd be coming back, and so on. But days and days went by, and I began to get worried, until early one morning, there was a knock on the door. I got up excited, thinking it was Gracielita, but no, it was the president of the CDR Zone Committee with a notification from the Ministry of the Interior informing me that my daughter had sought asylum in the Peruvian Embassy, and they wanted to talk with me. Marta, girl, I swear I was speechless. I couldn't believe it. Can you imagine, my Gracielita caught up in the embassy with all those wretched people? I took such a bad turn that Georgina, the president of the Committee, who'd given me such a good reference when I began working for the Diplomatic Corps, took pity on me and broke the news more gently, because she realized I didn't know anything, and wasn't an accomplice or anything to Gracielita being in there. From that day on, I had no peace or respite with myself until one morning Gracielita appeared, all disheveled, with big bags under her eyes and a face like I'd never seen before, and told me firmly, and without faltering, that she was very sorry but yes, it was true, she'd gone into the embassy with Jorge and, despite them both being technicians, they'd given them permission to leave with the "scum". What I didn't know, because Gracielita never told me, was that Jorge's father was in the United States and that he and his sister had been brought up by relatives, because his mother had died many years before in a road accident.

The father and brother had now reclaimed him. Jorge had a sister I didn't know, but who was well integrated in the revolution. The thing is that at that moment I began to reproach her and insult her as never before, asking what on earth she was going to do in the United States, saying they would kill her because in that country they don't like blacks, but all she kept repeating was that I should stop saying that because she wasn't black, she was mulatta, and very mulatta. But I didn't care, and I didn't listen to her, and in an impulse I still regret, I threw a bundle of clothes in her face and told her to get out, if that was how she was going to repay me for everything I'd done for her. Then she looked at me, and then my Gracielita burst into tears. Ay, Marta, it broke my heart! And I hugged her and held her tight to my breast, holding on to her to see if she'd change her mind. I couldn't stop crying and tearing at my hair, and I kept asking her a thousand and one times why, why she was doing this to me... The last words she spoke to me were to ask me again to forgive her, but that I was never going to understand. She hugged me, and left forever, and my heart left with her as well. Ay, Marta, I lost my Gracielita, my only child!'

And she cried as I'd never seen her cry before, cursing herself a thousand and one times, pouring blame on herself for sins that she herself had invented. I don't know how long she was like this, but when my son Ramoncito, his wife and the two grandchildren arrived, as they used to every Sunday, I realized it was one o'clock in the afternoon and that Inesita was stretched out on the bed getting over her crisis, and that I hadn't done anything in the kitchen. Guillermo had left early that morning for San Agustín, to do voluntary work on a new microbrigade building for technicians from the Soviet Union.

Lord! What a fate! Why do all these things have to come my way? Give me strength to listen to another's cries, to take on the suffering of others!

After thinking this in front of a glass of water I took from behind the frame with our wedding photo, on top of the wardrobe, I wet my fingers and passed them first across my forehead, then over my neck and chest, and I shook my hands strongly, to shake off all the evil that might take hold of me. I put a sprig of basil behind my ear, and made ready to welcome my grandchildren and the rest of Sunday.

GRACIELITA IN THE NORTH

During the year following all that Mariel hullabaloo, many things happened. Just over twelve months had gone by since I had last seen Inesita. A couple of weeks before that hot Saturday in June, my old maid friend sent word she was going to drop by, for me to fix her hair and to chat a little. And so she did. I remember it as if it were now, when she arrived at midday and the room was full of clients, but we greeted each other as if we'd never stopped seeing each other, with affectionate hugs and kisses on the cheek.

'*Negra*, you look good!'
'And so do you, dear!'
I replied, trying to sound sincere, but it was a lie, and she knew it. She looked as if all the woes of the world had befallen her, and it showed most in her face, her cheeks looking bonier and with dark bags under her eyes. When I told her to take off her pretty headscarf, with its multicolored rose print, and undo her hair, as it tumbled out – in those days Inesita still had a lot of hair – it was speckled with many grey hairs. And then the way she was dressed just didn't suit her at all, a light blue Chinese cotton skirt to below the knee and a plain, short-sleeved schoolgirl-type blouse, and a pair of cheap hand-crocheted pumps. She was looking a lot older than her forty-something years.

'No, I don't, woman! Even the blind would realize what a mess I am.'

That day there were three or four of my regular clients together in the room, along with some new ones I'd been recommended, who were sitting outside in the yard, sheltering from the sun, on some stools the

129

neighbors would put out for me when I need them. I'd been up early, shortly after Guillermo had left for the *micro*, so as to leave the day's meal ready before beginning with Beba, who had started a little cleaning job two days a week in the home of a French woman with the same name as that famous ballet, Gisela, who lived in the FOCSA building, because she was a foreign technician who worked for Radio Havana Cuba, a station that only transmitted abroad.

'You know, she pays me with cans of food and pork, and whatever else I fancy from the foreign technicians' store, up to my salary of 70 pesos – 'cos what would I do with the pesos, my dear! She knows the Russian women in the FOCSA are all the time dealing, and my Gisela has learned a lot, though she isn't into as much as the *bolos*.'

Beba was good to me, because it would seem her job was really good and she'd always bring me a little something: if it wasn't a jar of Bulgarian jam, it was a chorizo or sausage of some kind, and even at times a packet of good, mild cigarettes – not those that came on the ration book, which were more dust than leaf, and which people still sold on the black market for up to 20 pesos a pack.

'Ay, Marta, they're smart, these white folk, especially the foreign ones! Nothing slips past them. Gisela might be French, my friend, but she's too much. She smokes like crazy, she's like a chain smoker, one after the other, like the Crusellas chimney in its time... but she met an even more hardened smoker over in Buenavista, you know, and I found out that she's done some tremendous deals with her. It turns out that the woman is very old and has smoked all her life up to three packs of American cigarettes a day, but now can't get American cigarettes and makes do with the mild, but what she gets on the ration isn't nearly enough. To make a long story short, I don't know how she met up with Gisela, but I think that a niece of hers works in the National Bank, where the foreigners change their money, and one day when Gisela went to the bank and was chatting with the woman who was serving her, it came out that her aunt, who had traveled a lot and had even been in Paris, was a heavy smoker, things like that, and as time went by they started up a great trade. Because the old lady comes from a monied family and didn't want to leave the country, and the widow of a famous surgeon who died before the Revolution, and she's alone, well almost alone, since she lives with her mother who is even older than she is, and she's old enough... Well, anyway, the thing is, Gisela, who smokes one after the other, would give the old lady mild cigarettes, because Gisela smokes the strong ones, in return for little baccarat glasses, porcelain ornaments, fine tablecloths, and even some beautiful lamps, colored stained-glass ones, which are just lovely. I know, because I heard her say so one afternoon, that they're really good quality and expensive, because a friend of hers, also foreign, once visited wanting to buy some old French furniture from the old lady, and asked where she'd got hold of the three *tifani* or *estifani* lamps, or something like that 'cos they're very famous; and Gisela told her friend straight up, what I'm telling you. She was careful not to give her the address, but I know, because I'm in on the deal, running there and back, and since the old lady lives near my neighborhood, it's much easier for me to drop by, hand over her quota of mild cigarettes, and then some other time Gisela goes by in her car to pick up her new acquisition.'

Beba never stopped talking, and it was just as well that at that hour of the morning she was the first, and I could still put up with all her jabber.

'And do you know, her husband, who teaches at the university, doesn't smoke. Gisela has ashtrays all over and the place stinks to high heaven. I don't know how he puts up with her...'

'Girl, that's a bit over the top! Bad habits are bad habits, after all!'

Most of my clients worked as maids in the homes of foreigners, though not Russians, Hungarians and Czechs and all those people from the socialist countries. They rarely employed anybody, because most of the men from those places came with their wives, who accompanied them to look after them while they worked, and the children went to a special school out on 31st Avenue, between 18th and 20th Streets, in Miramar, which in its day had been the Convent of Las Ursulinas, who were really good little nuns. But what my people wanted was to earn their food, so they worked for the real foreigners, those from capitalist countries, who understood the situation and sorted things out for you without so much haggling. Anyone who could did it, although my people didn't like those Russians, who weren't used to deodorant and would be sweating heavily in those nylon shirts of theirs, and in the heat we have in this country! They had more gold in their teeth than a pawnshop. For that, yes, if you wanted to find someone who loved gold, find a Russian. They couldn't put more gold on their teeth if they tried, but they were always looking for it! I remember in the first years of the Revolution the government opened a shop on the corner of Calzada and E Street, in Vedado, where confiscated goods, especially jewelry that had belonged to rich families that had left Cuba, were sold off cheaply to anyone who came. And there were the Russian women, lining up from the early hours of the morning for when the shop opened sometime after midday, to buy gold jewelry, which you just knew they'd take back to their own country to sell on. There weren't just gold Swiss watches, rings and chains, but even diamond necklaces and chokers... Those were crazy years, when money came to have practically no value. They also sold a lot of good porcelain, and I know good things when I see them; and pearl necklaces, mother-of-pearl fans, gold and silver embroidered dresses, religious objects, and, well, what can I say. You'd find them at the head of the line, all fat and well fed, the *compañeras* from those fraternal countries. That went on until 1967... I never learned why they closed that little store, but I imagine they'd cleaned it out. So I don't doubt that those little lamps Beba spoke of were also worth a fortune, since the families who lived in those good neighborhoods over there had lots of luxury odds and ends.

Before I'd finished Beba's hair, around nine-thirty in the morning, Irma and Olguita had already arrived. Irma was a stern spinster, who was always cagey about her age, and gave herself airs as a señorita. Can you imagine, señorita in those days! She worked for the CTC, the Trade Union Congress, and was one of those *'Patria o Muerte'* revolutionaries. Olguita was just the opposite, black with some Chinese, big-assed and sassy, with 'good hair', thick and curly, but she liked to wear it long and well-straightened. She'd come to Havana five or six years back from Gibara, a little town in the north of Oriente province, wanting to study, anything, and she did, because she became a Russian translator in the Makarenko language school near La Copa, in Miramar. But she was also working as a maid – without the people at the school hearing about it, of course, because she was in the Youth, and I think they were even considering her for the Party. She worked in the home of a North-American woman who was said to be doing research with the Ministry of Public Health on the child vaccination campaigns and women's healthcare.

'You know, darling, the bits and bobs those white folk give you go further than the 164 pesos I earn, wearing myself out with my students six hours a day, Monday to Friday, trying to teach them Russian. When all's said and done, there's nothing to buy anyway. I get along just fine with her apartment, which even has hot water in the shower, and I only have to go two mornings a week, Mondays and Fridays, or sometimes on Saturdays when I do a big general cleaning, and that's it. What she gives me from the Diplostore is worth three times more than I could buy on my salary. And she lets me do what I like in the place, because Rebecca doesn't get het up about a thing, not even her lover who's up to I don't know what, except that whenever I'm there, he spends the whole time staring at my backside and drinking all the beer he can, because he knows he won't find that beer she buys, that comes in a green can, anywhere except in that apartment. She's a good person, but up to all kinds of tricks – she's no spring chicken, though she's aged well, because of the exercise she gets in the swimming pool of the Sierra Maestra, the big apartment building for foreigners that before was called Rosita de Hornedo, and he's one of those new-wave white boys who do nothing except screw around, hustling foreigners, and that's why I...'

'I don't think it's right to be talking like that in public, without knowing who you are talking in front of.'

I knew it. It was the first time the two of them had come at the same time, and I knew the two of them would be like oil and vinegar. Since I knew Olguita better, I'd been quietly tugging her hair for some time in the hope she'd change the subject or stop talking, but either she didn't understand me or she pretended not to. You couldn't be saying those kinds of things in front of Irma, who didn't understand Olguita's ways.

'I'm sorry, señora.... just who do you think you are talking to...?'

'Caballero, I don't want any political arguments here!'

It was all I hit on saying, but just as Irma began to say her piece:

'No, Marta, nobody's arguing, but I don't think it's right for her to speak that way, let alone in front of strangers. In the first place, because the Revolution has been very generous to those of us who are working women from humble backgrounds. How can you overlook the benefits achieved in education, health and housing? The government is making a sacrifice, depriving us of some things, so that foreign technicians – especially those from the fraternal socialist countries – come to Cuba and collaborate with us. But for them, we wouldn't be here today.'

'Hold on, hold on... if you're really serious... I don't know what sacrifice you're talking about, other than what we're doing in this country... not just to get hold of food and clothes, but everything, and we blacks, yes, blacks, are doing just the same or worse than before, especially us women, because at least before we could get sepia-colored things for the likes of us. But now? Ha! Just ask Marta, who knows about such things and is older than both of us. Isn't that right, Marta?'

Without waiting for more of an answer than a tug of her hair, she continued, and I let her, at least for the time being:

'Do you know what I make face powder for my skin color with? Red brick, that's what with. Don't you know that what stockings there are in this country are for whites, because we black women don't exist, so do you

133

know how we get by? By using coffee ground to dye them with… Don't you know that in this country there's no pomade to straighten hair… or alcohol to light the burners? Don't you know that the skin cream in this country is all designed for white people, girl? What country have you been living in? I don't know why you got me started.'

'I'm not talking about that. You young people have no sense of history, you've no memory of things and want to solve everything with life's trivia, you've no perspective. Tell me, how many countries have completely free education, from nursery to university, not to mention health care? And that has to come from somewhere, doesn't it?'

'That's exactly why we're as screwed up as we are! How can you be talking about sacrifice and sacrifice, and when anyone manages to get a little something some other way, then the criticisms start, the discord, scaring you with all that "I'll tell on you", and things shouldn't be like that, and this and that and the other, and I'm just tired of it! And so what, if I'm just as much of a *compañera* as you are? But I won't keep quiet about the thousand and one outrages of a whole line of crooks in the government, at the expense of those who are revolutionaries.'

That was where I had to interrupt. I stopped untangling her hair and stood in the middle of the room between Irma, who was in the rocking chair, and Olguita, in the wing chair, and who could now lift her head, since she'd had her chin on her breast while I was untangling the hair:

'Listen to me, what do you think this is? My house isn't a CDR Zone Committee or anything like that. Here nobody can insult anyone else, because I won't allow it, and I don't want any political speeches, not from either side, since I'm not mixed up in anything, and I don't want to be. D'you hear?'

And so the argument, or rather what was about to become an argument, ended right there and then. Any other time I wouldn't have got involved, but with Irma there I couldn't let my place be turned into what she wanted, because whenever she came to have her hair done, she'd fall into the same talk about politics, and Fidel's last speech, and I don't listen to speeches from anybody, but then again I didn't want to lose a client. In any case, I was closer to Olguita than Irma, and it was the third time she'd come, and she always left a good tip. Anyway, it was my home, and they should respect it. So, to cool things down, I began to talk, for whoever cared to listen, about the times before, when I arrived in Havana looking for a position as a maid. Those times were definitely different. What wouldn't I have done do to have a position like that, like Olguita's or Beba's, and have time to do my own thing. But those were different times.

When I finally finished Olguita's hair, the room had filled up and nobody remembered the incident any more. While the hot combs heated, I went to the kitchen to make myself a coffee with condensed milk and a piece of bread with oil and garlic, which is what I always fancied eating when I had a lot of work on. And that was when I heard the unmistakable voice of Inesita calling through the *postigo*:

'*Negrona*, you're such a pain, damn it – you never call me!'

Inesita's greetings were always like that, in good times and bad, going on about how it was more than twenty years since we'd seen each other, that we didn't do things together like we used to, and so on. After we'd made a great fuss of greeting one another, and she'd left her bag and umbrella in a corner, she went over to Julia's room to unburden her woes, talking all the time, about the cross she had to bear for the rest of her life, about her darling daughter Gracielita, and all the girl must be going through.

'Ay, Julia, I've been so afraid all these months, words can't explain. At least after all these months I received the first news from Gracielita. She sent me photos, and is doing as well as can be expected, so I'm a bit more resigned.'

Julia had all the patience in the world when it came to other people's sufferings, and no one knew more than her about suffering. With her slow deliberate walk, tilting her head from side to side, always smoking strong cigarettes and even cigar butts, no one could have known how much Julia knew. She didn't bother anybody, and nobody bothered her. The only bit of money she had coming in was from the clothes she washed and ironed, and the few *pesitos* her eldest son, who was one of those traffic cops who go round on a motorbike, brought her from time to time, because my brother was never capable of anything other than not taking life seriously, since he didn't even like good jobs. Nothing seemed to go right for her, day in, day out, putting up with one blow after another, even from her two daughters, because both got pregnant one after the other before they were fifteen years old. Though I shouldn't talk, because my daughter Teresita also got pregnant when she was off doing her teacher training in Topes de Collantes, and if it hadn't been for my son and my daughter-in-law I don't know how I could have stood what that girl made me go through. She even got married in a wedding dress and everything – though not white, of course – when she was four months gone. But Julia wasn't bothered, because she'd also given birth for the first time when very young, and had never got married. So you couldn't say she set a very good example! Her only consolation was the *espiritista* sessions, which I also attended from time to time. They were in Clarita's house, on Calzada de San Salvador. You had to see it to believe how Julia worked the dead! After lighting nine candles on the altar, making the sign of the cross and all that, the *espiritista* sessions began with the reading of several prayers, always by Clarita, the host and director of the temple. When the regulars of the center, and the novices, found out that Julia was going to be there, the room would fill up, because she generally worked very well – very clean and natural. First Clarita would explain what was going to happen that night, which might be a request from one of those present, to invoke the spirit of a deceased family member, or sometimes to find out about a relative suffering from some illness and living outside the country. Then the strongest medium would begin to sing softly, lulling almost, and all the other mediums, none of them as strong as Julia, would form a chorus. Sometimes, as happened with her, you couldn't make head or tail of what she was saying and suddenly her spirit would appear, who was Mahatma Ghandi, an Indian patriot who fought for peace and dressed like a saint, covered in a piece of linen, and walked with his stick doing charity among the poor, and that's why they killed him. Julia even had some photographs of the old man, who she was completely devoted to, so much so that if anything good ever happened to her, like the day she won a hundred pesos in the *bolita*, instead of giving thanks to God, or at least to the santos, she'd say thanks to Mahatma Gandhi, and make the sign of the cross. Well, when this spirit possessed her, she spoke as if she really was Hindu, with the weirdest accent, although you could understand what she was saying, and she'd begin to talk and answer through Clarita, who helped her with everything. *Epiritismo* is very nice and clean, and at the end of a session you came out fortified. So the neighbors liked Julia a lot, and people would go to talk with her, especially my clients, and she would always have a comforting phrase or remedy for the ailments of body and soul, even if only a word of encouragement from a woman who had practically nothing material to her name, nor wanted it, for good or for bad. And so, without being asked about her daughter, Inesita opened up her heart; and Julia, who had her own way of answering through old black proverbs and sayings, moving her head from side to side and tying the impeccably white scarf that she always tied tightly on her head, like a turban, said:

'Ay, Inesita, don't get so heated! You're not seeing the wood for the trees.'

'Look at this, Julia, read this letter that came last week, the very first, after so many months.'

Nobody knew that Julia couldn't read, not because of her eyesight, but because she was semi-illiterate. Very few people knew it, because I remember that when they took the census for the literacy campaign, she hid in Fela's room so as not to have to answer what at that moment only I knew. Sometimes she could be seen sitting for hours on end by the door of her room, leafing for the hundredth time through an old magazine, from before the Revolution, or one from Spain, one of those with shiny pages and lots of photos in color that Ismael, who was the boyfriend of Katia, the eldest daughter of Eneida and Baba, would bring her from abroad, because he was a merchant seaman and was always going around with things nobody else had, and since he's a good person was always giving things away, as if it was his mission. It looked as if Julia was reading and rereading and reading over and over again, but no, she wasn't reading, she was just leafing through the pages, looking at the photos, as though trying to recapture something from a past she didn't know, transporting herself to another world, far away across the sea and the desert; but not reading, because she didn't know how.

'You read it. My glasses are broken, and while you begin I'm going to make some coffee, since this week's ration came yesterday.'

Not needing to be asked twice, Inesita opened the long, white, bulky envelope and began to read the first of five long sheets, typewritten by her daughter Gracielita.

San Agustín, 18th November, 1980

Mi querida Mima,

I would so much have liked to write to you sooner, but to be honest I couldn't, and when you read what follows in this letter you'll understand why. I'm writing from the town where Javier, Jorge's brother, lives with his North-American wife Bessie, and their nine-year-old son. The town's called San Agustín, and it turns out to be the first in this country to be founded by the Spanish, in 1565. The main source of work here is tourism, and Javier and his wife make their living from a prosperous little shop, or boutique, down in the old part of the city, selling pieces of craft jewelry made by the Indians, and from a couple of apartments that they own in Fernandina Beach. As it happens, this is a historic place, because it's where José Martí organized an expedition in January 1895, which was discovered before it could set off for Cuba. I felt very emotional when I found out; those are things they teach us at school and I never thought I'd see for myself. San Agustín isn't very big, but it is very pretty, and looks a lot like many Cuban towns. There's even a river on the outskirts of the town called Matanzas, and every time I cross the bridge I remember those two rivers, the Yumurí and the San Juan that cross the city of Matanzas. Can you believe such a coincidence? The population is about 20,000, more or less, depending on the season of the year. I tell you this, so you don't go thinking I'm in San Agustín, in Lisa, near our house.

First of all, I hope that when you receive this you're as well as can be expected along with all the others. Though you may not believe it, I've been thinking a lot about you since that sad goodbye. We're well, at least for now, although Jorge's family was mourning the death of his father at the beginning of the year. His brother hadn't told him about his heart condition, because the old man didn't want to mess up whatever plan his son might have for reuniting the family – he was still thinking that his daughter would also come in her time. But, well, that's life.

Mima, it wasn't easy for me to make this decision, but I have no regrets. The year that's just ending has been very hard for me, and only I know how hard. Although I hadn't spoken to you about my work for a long time, things weren't going well for me, and I was creating problems for myself because of the way things were, and how the scientific research in the Center was being done. In the end I became very disillusioned. It's hard to explain this to you, because I don't think you'll understand, and besides, it can't change anything now. Anyway, there was no way of changing anything. In the end, my relationship with Jorge decided everything, for better or worse, because the Party people knew he wasn't in agreement with many things to do with the country's politics; and although he was, and still is, a good economist, he was, as they say, 'burnt out'. It wasn't enough for him to have his own opinions, he just couldn't keep quiet about them.

When it occurred to us to go into the embassy, we didn't think things would turn out as they did, with thousands and thousands of people clamouring to leave the country. That was one of the reasons why we took the government's guarantees, because we were going to be reclaimed by family in the United States. Contrary to what's been said all this time, inside there weren't just counter-revolutionaries and scum. There was something of everything, 'like in a drug store'. To begin with, Jorge was totally against leaving the embassy, because he said that if his compañeros from work got hold of him they'd throw him in prison, but the people from the Ministry of the Interior kept their word, and there weren't any big problems with me either. I think that, in the end, our colleagues in the Center were happy to be rid of us. You never know.

That morning we left Mariel early, in a yacht with forty other people on board, including the captain of the boat who was a Cuban who was regularly making the return journey to and from Key West. Jorge's brother was very happy, and they spent the whole journey hugging each other and even crying. They got very emotional. I don't know if it was because of their joy at

seeing each other again, or because of the news
of the death of the old man, or both things
at the same time. It had been thirteen years
since they'd seen one another. As you know, his
father had to leave Jorge behind because he had
to do his Military Service, although I think
what the old man wanted was to get rid of his
wife and daughter, who didn't want to go – the
old woman went mad in the end and never came
to her senses.

After arriving at Key West, they took down
our details, and the next day we were taken
by road to the concentration point in Miami,
where they began to process us – that's to say,
they took down more details and such things.
The journey is really lovely, along a beautiful
causeway across the sea, over bridges between
the small islands. Javier helped us a lot, and
left us in good hands, but we had to wait about
two weeks before meeting up with him again, in
San Agustín, which is as far as Camagüey from
Havana. Since we said that we were educated
professionals, during those two weeks they had
us helping in one of the offices dealing with
the refugees, to process other Cubans who were
arriving, and who really were scum, like those
that piled into the embassy in the first few
days. We made friends there with other Cubans
who'd been living in the United States for quite
a long time.

Mima, North-American bureaucracy is worse than
ours, I swear, though at least it works. The
papers you have to fill in, and the amount of
detail you have to give is overwhelming. Things
are less complicated for us Cubans, however it
might seem, at least for qualified people like
us. The forms you have to fill in make you tell
your entire life story: whether you have family
in the United States, whether or not you were
in the Party, whether your parents or close
relations were in the military. They ask you

what race you belong to – for example, just so that you know, here I'm not mulatta, or mixed race, or Hispanic, although we speak Spanish. Just 'Black', negra. That's one of the reasons we've decided to leave and sort things out for ourselves without Javier's family, because I've noticed – they try not to show it in my presence, mind – but I've come to realize that I'm not very well accepted among them, and Jorge doesn't want to face up to it.

Here in San Agustín, people who are more or less my shade of skin are like that because of taking the sun on the beach, because here there are very few people of color. But can you imagine, saying I'm black! When they saw on my form, in the box for Ethnic Origin, I'd written 'Cuban', with a capital 'C', they quickly asked me to put what I was supposed to put. And to avoid complications I put 'mixed', and they asked me to add what indigenous group I belonged to, and since I didn't understand very well at first what they wanted me to put, a very nice Cuban girl, who spoke English like the North-Americans and did voluntary work finding places for Cuban refugees to stay, recommended that I put 'Black Hispanic', which is like saying 'afroespañola', and so everyone was happy, but on two occasions I wrote 'Cuban'.

Over here there aren't many mixed race couples, like in Cuba, and even in Europe, where it's in fashion. In fact, I haven't seen any. The few times we've gone out for a walk around the old part of the town, near the 'Castillo de la Fuerza' of San Agustín – we call it that, because the Morro de San Marco, which is its real name, looks just like the one facing the Plaza de Armas, in Old Havana – we've noticed how people look at us, or seem to, because you can tell we're not from around here, I don't know whether because of the way we dress or talk; and I've realized that Javier and his wife *(who have adapted very well to the way of life here) don't feel altogether comfortable when they're with us.*

Although Jorge's brother and his wife are well connected economically, and have been very good to us, as far as they could, we've received enough from them, and they're starting to feel the costs of having us, despite the fact that for the time being we get help in cash from the government. That's why, using the little money that Jorge has earned doing odd jobs, plus a little loan, we're going to go to Miami off our own backs, though with a little help up from Jorge's brother. Jorge has it in his head to start studying in a university up here, because, according to Javier, people like him can easily get a grant to study for a qualification, or validate an existing one. I have other plans to pave my way in my scientific career, which cost me so much to achieve, and for that I need to sort myself out first. For now, we're trying to see how we arrange our personal affairs. But, well, we're better off than many other people who are still caught up in the paperwork of finding where to live, because they don't have family over here.

The newspapers and television have been doing reports all these months about the 'Marielitos'. I don't know if over there they've given the news of the protests in the camps where they're temporarily housing the Cubans. I imagine they are, because it makes good propaganda for the Cuban government. But the bad publicity over here for those of us who came through Mariel hasn't done us any favors, when we're not all the same, which is one of the things I've always had problems with. Together, but not mixed up, as the saying goes. There's a bad element in this whole process, and an especially bad element where there are lots of blacks and

tough guys together, causing problems over
anything, as they did last June in a military
camp in the state of Arkansas, where they'd
relocated several hundred Cubans who didn't
have good records.

I don't blame them entirely, but that isn't the
way to go about things. They'd spent weeks and
weeks waiting for their papers to be sorted out,
so as to be able to begin their new lives here
in the United States, which is what everyone
wants, but they just couldn't get their situation
settled. Things got so violent that they had to
send in the soldiers, because those bad guys
were rioting and had begun to set fire to things
and throw stones. And so, after filling the pot,
it was ready to bubble over.

In the camps where they sent the people during
the process there were fights one after the
other; there were disputes over the slightest
thing. They'd escape from the camp, break up
the seats and tables in the dining halls, and
dirty the floors so much that the place was
like a pigsty. The men's dorms and some of
the women's weren't looked after. Some of the
women seem to have carried on as prostitutes,
as they had in Cuba, and there were pimps all
over the place. If it hadn't been for the job
that we managed to get, and people knowing and
respecting us a little, we'd have had problems
too, because through all this, there weren't
enough guards and other people there to look
after us, and the North-Americans didn't speak
a word of Spanish and you can't tell what the
hell they're talking about, they speak so fast
and unintelligibly – most of them, at least.
The young ones were abused so much they had to
be separated from the rest after a very ugly
incident that took place in broad daylight,
when one of the toughest groups beat up and

then raped an effeminate young mulatto boy and a girl who was also quite young. I think if I'd spent another week in that hostel, I'd have gone mad.

Now the just are having to pay for the wicked, and I think it will be years before we can be clean of all this. But even though you don't want to, when you're asked, you have to say who you are, and when people here find out you came through Mariel, they throw you all in the same sack.

I don't think I have much more to tell you for now. Next week we're going to Miami, a big, beautiful city which we didn't have time to enjoy, because the day Javier picked us up at the camp, it took a while to sort out the papers with Immigration there, so when we left Miami it was already night-time, and we had to make it fast on the freeway, since the journey takes about ten hours, what with one thing and another. I'm going to photocopy this letter and send it by two separate routes: first through my friend Helga, whose mother's address in Dresden I know by heart, and the other through a Cuban señora, an old neighbor and friend of Javier and Bessie who's going to visit family in December. She's lived in the United States since the start of the Revolution, and works as a laboratory assistant in the Veterinary School at the University of Gainesville, which is where Jorge would like to go, though not just yet. I don't know which letter will get to you first, or if they'll reach you at all, but always remember I love you very much and I'll do everything I can so that one day you can come here to be with me. Since communication is so difficult between Cuba and the United States, I don't know when you'll get another letter from me. As soon as I have a fixed address in Miami, I'll send it to you. Though it's still a few weeks away, I hope you have a happy New Year, so far as you're able. Don't feel bitter towards me, Mima, and don't forget that I'm still, and always will be, your Gracielita. A big kiss and an even bigger hug. Goodbye, from your darling daughter,

Gracielita

Inesita knew this first letter from her daughter almost by heart, and each time she read those four typewritten sheets of paper that had reached her from the GDR, long after they'd been sent, she told me she'd spent the whole day crying. When she'd finished reading the letter to Julia, she carefully folded the pages, almost caressing them one by one, finally putting them back in the envelope. Repeating over and over again her darling daughter's name, Inesita gradually gave up all pretence and burst into tears again, though not for long, because Julia spoke sternly to her, telling her that while Gracielita was getting by as best she could up North, she was wrecking her own life, and that wasn't right, and her daughter wouldn't like it. It was pitiful to see her suffering like this!

I left her in Julia's house all afternoon, without disturbing her, because I knew that what she needed was a good shaking, and I couldn't do that like only Julia could. I would have been rougher and more direct with her, because I wasn't going to put up with her weeping over a spoiled girl, when Inesita was the one who had always agreed to everything she wanted ever since she was a baby. But, well, love is blind, and a mother's love more than any other, because there's no halfway measure, something only a mother knows.

It was towards the end of the afternoon when I called Inesita, to start doing her hair, and I was surprised by the peace and tranquility reflected in her eyes. Her smile, which in the good times was always on her lips, with no concern for her two protruding front teeth, now reappeared, though softer than before. Later I learned that Julia had not only spoken to her in her special way, but when the time came sat down with her in front of a glass of clean water, and said the Prayer for *Santa Clara* three times – the one that goes:

Holy Mother Santa Clara, mirror of purity, firm foundation and living faith, charity and host of virtue – cleanse our hearts of all stains and blame, I beg

you, for the peace and order of my soul, because I have trust in your infinite
goodness and through your merits reach for the glory of your name. Amen.

Then she cleansed her with some sprigs of basil she had taken from one of
the plants I have in the passage. After silently asking her spirits what only
she knew she'd asked, she was able to pass on to Inesita, who was a good
soul, all the spiritual harmony that Julia almost always harboured, even
in the worst of times.

ON CALLE OCHO

Meantime, while all the frenzy over Mariel in Cuba, especially Havana, melted away like a *durofrío* in summer – which always lasted all year – in the United States there was continuing discord caused by the latest invasion of Cubans, and this had had its repercussions for Gracielita, as for the great majority of Cubans in exile.

Every now and then, attention returned to the *escoriados tapaditos*, as people ironically called those who had had good jobs and even responsible positions in the political and mass movements, yet joined the rest of the scum, having kept *tapaíto* what they really were: disaffected and two-faced. So for the rest of the year, the repudiation rallies against those kind of people continued, sometimes outside their homes, or if they were still at work on the day they were discovered, the rally would accompany them down the street, where others would join in, even if they didn't know who the person was, because there are always those who are ready for that kind of scandal. I felt ashamed by it all, and didn't know why there had to be such a spectacle. Along with that little word *antisociales*, so also *escoriados* entered into people's talk, along with *gusanos* whenever anyone referred to those who'd left the country and were classed as counterrevolutionaries. I found it a bit confusing at times, though I never said anything, so as not to appear ignorant. But I never really understood what or who a counterrevolutionary was, whether it was someone who carried out sabotage and put people's lives at risk, like that criminal act in a Miramar daycare center that caused so much indignation throughout the country, or anyone, like my own sister, who'd decided to accompany her husband and her children, never having so much as thrown a stone at a dog, because deep down she was quite a coward, and just didn't like it here. As for me, I never liked any of those words, and never let my clients use them in my home, whatever they might think, because we all have our problems, and it's my home.

As time went by, Gracielita's letters became more frequent, almost always through the same friends in the GDR, and as a result, Inesita visited more often, and when she did both Julia and I would get to know in great detail Gracielita's situation up North. She would drop round in the evening, to accompany Julia to the spiritualist sessions, where she'd become one more in the group. But while she sought and found good therapy in her visits to Clarita's house-temple, the main pretext was to tell us about what was happening with her darling Gracielita in the almost five years she'd been in the United States.

It seems the girl had been jinxed with a spirit curse ever since she arrived in Miami, because from the start nothing had gone right for her. Provisionally settling with Jorge in a tiny apartment in a Miami neighborhood called Little Havana, the couple's happiness didn't last long. Their very different interests were rapidly pushing them apart. As he'd said he would, Jorge enrolled at a local night school for foreigners, and within two years had validated his studies and went off to the university his brother had recommended. He had the good fortune, good for him, but bad for Gracielita, to finish his studies with a kind of scholarship the American government was giving to the Cubans who left through Mariel, who behaved and wanted to better themselves. And they say they're not socialist?

According to Gracielita's description in her first letters from Miami, Little Havana was to her like a jigsaw with different pieces that were bits of many Havana neighborhoods all mixed up in the heart of a very big city. It was full of Cubans and, of course, *cubaneo* was the main language there, as in other neighborhoods Gracielita began to get to know, like Hialeah – where Yamila had her little house and which is full of Cubans who are a bit better off. The places can be spotted a mile away because they're so like other Havana neighborhoods, such as Casino Deportivo, Alturas de Luyanó, Buena Vista and even Miramar, but especially that part of Marianao.

The fact that the neighborhood was called Little Havana didn't mean it had always been inhabited by Cubans, or that those who owned property there were Cuban, but rather American. The area was a big stretch of land that many years ago had been called Riverside, like that Cuban band that almost always played for the whites here in Cuba. According to Gracielita, in the early 1900s the owners had divided the land into small lots for families on modest incomes to build their homes. Of course, for whites, because the one for blacks was very separate. But that was long before the Cubans appeared, at least until after 1959 when the first of those affected by the Revolution found it was the cheapest area to rent, and little by little they were able to buy and build their own homes, and even open small businesses similar to those they'd had in Cuba at the time. All along the main streets and avenues, lots of stores began to appear with names very familiar to Cubans, like La Marquesina, La Esquina de Tejas, Fin de Siglo, El Corte Inglés, La Isabela de Sagua, and so on. From then on, Riverside stopped being Riverside to become what it is today: Little Havana, with an unmistakably Cuban flavour. Although most of the houses remained as they had always been, the new tenants began to give it a creole taste, with a whole series of adaptations that made them like those in Cuba, or at least where they'd been living before they left, or they'd aspired to have. When they succeeded in building or adapting a house with a porch, the dream of every Cuban family, they'd take out their rocking-chairs to enjoy the fresh air and contemplate people passing by the palmitos, arecas and crotons and even paradise trees they'd planted in the well-tended beds. They began to work at whatever they could, never looking back. They became doormen, cab drivers, bus drivers, anything, even when in Cuba they'd been employees in a clothing store or a public notary. That way they managed to save their money and buy their own little house, and, giving thanks to the *Virgen de la Caridad del Cobre* for all they'd achieved, they began to fill the neighborhood with shrines – something never before seen in the area – and they supplied themselves with all manner of santeria artifacts in little stores which many of them began to open and they called '*botánica*' because of all the herbs and other things they sold there to do their *brujería* – for good or evil, but witchcraft all the same. And then they go talking about how the blacks...! Because after all it was white Cubans who were mixed up in all this... until Mariel, when the blacks, who really knew the rules of the religion, managed to get in. But the '*botánica*' was still owned by them. Then there were the corner sugar-cane juice and Cuban coffee kiosks and the Cuban food, with fritters, guava pastries, mamee apple milk shakes, and all that gave Little Havana a different and distinct touch, like the Great Havana of its day, with all those Cuban airs and extravagances the majority of us, who never do things by halves, are used to. The murals and decorations on the front of the houses and stores made it impossible to mistake the area for anything but a real Cuban neighborhood, as we could see from the magazine photos and clippings Gracielita sent from time to time, and which she described as being 'too tacky for me to dare live in this environment for long', all the anguish of exile that engulfs the Cubans who live in Miami waiting for the 'liberation of the *Patria*'. From glass shrines at the entrances to the houses, with statues of *San Lázaro*, the *Virgen de Santa Bárbara*, the *Virgen de Regla*, and much more often the *Virgen de la Caridad del Cobre*, with the little boats and its three shipwrecked seafarers and all, floating on water above a fountain with tiny lights spraying little jets of water, and even the murals that Gracielita described so well, where a group of men can be seen playing dominoes, under the flattering gaze of what is taken to be a typical Cuban woman, white of course, dressed in national costume, surrounded by red, white and blue balloons, the colors of the Cuban flag, or the little corner stores announcing:

CREOLE FOOD   DAILY SPECIALS
DELIVERY OF MEDICINES TO CUBA
MIAMI MEATS   BUTCHER'S #1
SLAUGHTERHOUSE PRICES
SANDWICHES   CAFÉ CUBANO

with a steaming cup on the side, and

LECHONES TO GO 89¢ POUND   ORDERS TAKEN

beside an artistic portrait of an antiseptic little pig; or the one that seemed to be trying to copy the neighborhood cafes:

CANTINAS JULIETA   HOME DELIVERY

This enterprising way of life was summed up by those signs, beside which people would have their photos taken to very affectionately send back to the hapless family members who had stayed on the island, at least to make them envious when they knew what they were eating. It was all a way of bringing that little piece of land a bit closer for those who didn't know when, or if, they'd ever be able to return. I suppose the Americans have no reason for having the same tastes as us, and the transformation was made little by little by the different waves of Cubans who arrived on the Florida coasts, above all in Miami, which for many had already become the other leg of Cuba, the roasted one.

***

After renting the tiny apartment on the corner of 5th Street and 14th Avenue and reregistering at the Immigration Office to receive the stipend they were still entitled to, the first thing Gracielita and Jorge did was to go out and explore a bit of Miami. Mixing with the Cuban crowd strolling around the neighborhood, the two had an air about them of the newly arrived, and they'd long realized this was how they were perceived – aside from the combination of Jorge's white skin, dark hair and blue eyes with the splendid mulatta Gracielita, which had always caused a stir in Havana, where even at school she'd been nicknamed *La Piola*, for her marked preference for white boys. Gracielita had never seen anything out of the ordinary in that, but now she sadly began to notice the similarity between that part of Miami and the city of her birth, Great Havana. But she was conscious of who she was, she felt proud of the cinnamon color of her skin and showed it with all the dignity she could muster, because she would hear the catcalls from Cubans whenever she ventured out alone to the supermarket El Oso Blanco, which was a few blocks further up.

'Yes, but this isn't the real Havana, and the United States isn't Cuba! Here, the worst thing that can happen to you in this country is to be black. Everything else has a solution, but not being black!'

That was Yamila's response as she served herself yet another helping of freshly fried green plantains to go with the two slices of *lechón*, her favorite roast pork.

Walking down Miami's famous Calle Ocho on Saturday afternoon was for the new arrivals to discover a whole world that was unknown to them yet was at the same time quite familiar. That day, they'd agreed to meet another Cuban couple they'd got to know in the Transit Home in Miami, where Gracielita had spent her first days in the United States. Contact with Yamila was kept up by phone between San Agustín and Miami. Gracielita had realised that Yamila and Reinerio had been in the United States for a long time and had volunteered to participate in

Operation Refuge, organized around the time the Cubans were arriving from the port of Mariel.

They'd agreed to meet at Casablanca restaurant, on the corner of Calle Ocho and 23rd Avenue, in South-West Miami, better known as *'sagüesera'* – nobody knew whether because of the number of people that had arrived there from the port of Isabela de Sagua, coming from the nearby town of Sagua la Grande, or because that's how 'South-West' in English sounded to the Cubans. The same thing happened with Cayo Hueso, because that's what the Spaniards called it, but when the Americans came they understood 'West' for *Hueso* and translated *Cayo* to Key, and so changed it to Key West, though you don't need to know much about geography to realize that the key isn't to the 'west' of anything but rather at the southern tip of Florida, and more to the east than the west of the United States. But Yamila, according to Gracielita's description, was as slim and mulatta as she was, but with natural chestnut blonde hair. Gracielita didn't describe Reinerio much at first, because she didn't seem to care for that mulatto *indio*, with his naturally straight hair and 'pretty walk', who worked as an accountant for an insurance firm.

'Welcome to the Heart of Cuban Exile!'

That was Yamila's greeting, directed more to Gracielita, who was looking radiantly young that day in her white pants, white canvas pumps and loose pink cotton blouse with three-quarter-length sleeves. After going into the restaurant, and ordering various meat dishes, including chicken of course, as well as black beans and white rice with fried ripe plantains, the traditional fried green *tachinos,* fresh salad and all that kind of food we Cubans die for, the two couples downed a jug of beer and another of fresh lemonade, while each of them in their own way shared their frustrations and hopes of past, present, and above all future.

'Listen, guys... Let's just stop all this talk about race, as we say "he who has in him no Congo, has Carabalí". We're all Cubans, and we're here for the same reason. Let's enjoy the food and have a good time without talking about politics – at least for today.'

After his little sermon, Jorge served more beer. At that point one of the two waitresses who were serving the twelve tables in the place, which were almost all full, came towards the group and put on a fabricated friendly smile to ask Yamila, in half-Mexican Spanish, if they were happy with the service. They all praised Guadalupe, which was how she had introduced herself when the two couples were seated at one of the four tables at the back of the room. It was well situated on a kind of platform with a view of the Avenue, and the men's compliments went accompanied with rather too many smiles, looks and an unnecessary comment or two. When the waitress went on to the next table, where two men were devouring a plate of roast pork, Reinerio took up the thread of the apparent disagreement of a few minutes before and supported Jorge's proposal, throwing a look at Yamila and a sign by winking with his right eye to try to tell her to change the subject. But there wasn't time, because Gracielita had already begun to respond, and the atmosphere became as heated as the Miami climate.

'I don't believe that one thing has anything to do with the other, Yamila. I understand how this country is, and I'm going to adapt to the circumstances and realities here, but I won't for that deny what I am or what we are.'

'Just wait till you come up against the real world. Hopefully everything will turn out well, but don't be fooled by appearances and don't forget I've been here longer than you. And let me tell you something else...'

Yamila couldn't finish replying to Gracielita, before having to pay attention to Reinerio responding in a loud voice:

'Listen, guys, you're going to give me indigestion, and the food's cost us enough! How long are we going to go on about this? We met up less than an hour ago, and we haven't stopped talking about the same thing. Let people live their life how they want. That's enough!'

In the end, the lunch finished peacefully, as might have been expected, because nobody was in a fighting mood. Between the custard and crème caramel, and several cups of Cuban coffee and a cigarette or two, the subject didn't come up again, at least not in the presence of the two men. When Yamila had taken care of the bill, paying with one of her credit cards, the four of them got into the car that Yamila skillfully drove down the wide *sagüesera* streets, looking for the first exit from the city, onto one of many routes that crossed the wide channels between Greater Miami and Miami Beach, where they were headed. They spoke little during the journey, except for Yamila's brief comments to explain some detail or other of the imposing landscape. Silent the whole journey, Gracielita gazed into the distance, somewhat indifferently, at three gigantic cruise ships that took up the whole dock, some pleasure boats, and three black men and a black woman fishing off the side of the road, and in the background the enormous building where they make the city's main newspaper, the *Miami Herald* in English, with its Spanish version, *El Nuevo Herald* – which, despite making much of it being Hispanic, in truth answered to the whims of the Cuban community, for apart from the obvious differences it was very like *Granma*, but with advertisements. When they entered Miami Beach, well to the south, over one of the first bridges, Yamila looked for a place to park. She put several coins in the parking meter, enough to last up to the period when it was free to park, and the two women began to walk arm in arm at a prudent distance from Jorge and Reinerio, who followed, down Ocean Drive, which ran parallel to a portion of the beach. A thousand and one thoughts went through their heads as they enjoyed the innocently festive atmosphere of South Beach, quite amazed by the memories of many Cuban cities this part of Miami Beach brought back. The apartment blocks, hotels and stores, painted in soft, bright colors, were so similar in architecture to those in Cuba that it was difficult to say who had copied whom first. The afternoon light, the people and the heat contributed greatly to making that mirror image seem real.

'I'm really grateful for your concern about me.'

Yamila lightly squeezed her left forearm and said there was no need.

'Look, Gracielita, I don't want to discourage you, but things here are very different from what you might imagine, as you'll find out for yourself in time. Just when you were disembarking at Cayo Hueso, there were serious riots of black Americans in Overtown, which used to be called Colored Town, before becoming the black capital of Miami, about the time I was born – the poor Afro-North-Americans, of course. The others keep out of it and anyway don't live down here but up in the northeast, out of the crowded city. They don't even go to the beach. Those that can vacation in the Bahamas, the Virgin Islands or any of the other Caribbean islands, but not Miami Beach, or any of the beaches on this Florida coast. Anyway, it was something awful! The worst part is that the blacks set fire to their own neighborhoods. They always do the same. They never cross the line to where the people with money live, or the middle-class suburbs, but keep it among themselves. And they're the ones who lose out. That's what I'll never understand. As I told you once, being "Cuban" isn't a race but a nationality, yet for the North-Americans, or "Anglos" for short, which is what they're called these days, there's no difference, because you're "black", we're "black", even if we think of ourselves as mulatta, or *jabao*, or quadroon. It doesn't matter which of these sick classifications we Cubans believe in, it means nothing to anyone here; it simply doesn't feature in the system's computer, it doesn't figure on any of this country's forms. Either you are or you aren't! If you're middle-class, you don't pretend to be anything else, and vice versa. That's to say, either you adapt or you don't adapt, like it or not. This is the country of assimilation. Within your own four walls you can do what you like, but out in the world, you have to behave according to the rules of the game. This is a country made up of immigrants who don't like foreigners; here, with the exception of the native Indians, we're all immigrants. On the other hand, the things that go on in this city are worse than what happens in the American movies. Not long after your arrival, which couldn't have been at a worse moment, the Afro-North-Americans in Liberty City ran wild, hunting down Anglos to cut their throats – I mean really, it's no lie. It all began in March, when a 38-year-old black American, who was riding a motorbike, took a red light and the police went after him when, according to the police report, the motorcyclist gave them the finger. You can't do that here, they consider it to be a real obscenity, and sufficient motive for them to put a bullet in your head. For example, when you want to ask for two of anything with your fingers, don't do like the Cubans, leaving the middle and index fingers standing while hiding the other three in the palm of the hand. You mustn't do that... Well, the Anglo policeman chased the black American and after a few minutes more police rounded on him and beat him up so badly the poor man died in hospital. A bit later, the case appeared in court, and the four policemen implicated in the affair were acquitted. Well, that's what ignited the riots in Liberty City. The black Americans, above all the young ones, were thirsting for revenge and hunted down several Anglos, even though they didn't have anything to do with anything, only they were white and found themselves in the wrong place at the wrong time. They did terrible things to them, even cutting off the tongue and ears of one of them, and well... These things happen here, and not just in Miami. All the big American cities are sick with the violence that reflects the ill that afflicts all of us human beings, and the state of Florida comes top in the statistics for violent deaths, that is, with firearms. When they talk about Cubans or Cuban-Americans, the blacks don't exist. And I find that very insulting, because you see North-American women whose skin is lighter than yours or mine, and they feel proud to say they're "black", not mulatta. Even in Tampa, I met mulatto Cuban families who've been here for generations, and they consider themselves "black", because that's how things are in this country. And for better or worse, the Cubans haven't been able to reach agreement on this. I tell you this so you don't have a bad time It isn't easy. During my last days in the Refuge, I remember that my boss, pure Anglo Saxon, told me that there was no hope for the *Marielitos*, because they didn't know the rules of the game here, because they didn't understand competition. As an example, she told me she'd sent an engineer for an interview, but he didn't get the job. She couldn't understand why, until she saw him in person. He'd gone poorly dressed to the appointment, unshaven, looking like he'd been dragged through a hedge backwards. Things are very different here, although there are many freedoms and choices. They complain about the cold, here in Miami; they can't find the food they're used to and don't know how to find substitutes. The ones who arrived with you don't know these things, and neither do the ones who came after. You have to make a decision, set a goal, and not waste time.'

By the time Yamila had finished her little speel to Gracielita, who had been quiet the whole time, the heat was getting to them, and the two couples were ready for a cooler, which didn't mean they wanted a dip in the water, since none of them had come prepared to swim. Despite the summery winter, October was never the ideal season for the people of the area, least of all the Cubans. At the end of Ocean Drive, they found a restaurant bar that served different types of drinks. They'd walked several kilometers, and all needed a rest. On the pavement opposite, tourists and residents of South Beach Miami were mixed in amongst some young people showing off their bodies, skating pirouettes in the fresh of the evening.

Such an unforgettable day out was not to be repeated ever again in quite the same way. Gracielita tried to bring what she'd learned chatting with Yamila to bear on her own experience, but not very positively. Gracielita was set in her ways, and bit by bit began to make concessions.

After a couple of months of arguing, neither of them giving any ground, Jorge packed up his few belongings and left Gracielita, who found some consolation in Yamila, who by then had become her best friend – in fact, her only one. Towards the end of her second year in Miami, Gracielita successfully completed an intensive English course, and another in information technology, which she passed with flying colors. To celebrate that night, Yamila invited her to eat out in a very good restaurant on the other side of the 'Bahía del Vizcaíno', as Gracielita called Biscayne Bay. They had a great time. Gracielita dominated the first part of the conversation, telling anecdotes about the school, while Yamila kept joking about whether she had forgotten Jorge. This was something Gracielita had no intention of commenting on, other than what had been said on the phone from time to time, as friends, just that they didn't bear a grudge about the past. The two women went up to the bar on the second floor, where they had a panoramic view of the bay, and could see the silhouettes of the city's tall buildings. Gracielita didn't have the slightest inkling that Yamila was about to tell her things she didn't know about her life. When the waitress approached, she told the two of them her name and from memory recited all the bar-restaurant cocktails. Yamila was quick to recommend one of the specialties, which Gracielita was happy to accept.

'Two pina coladas, please. One with little rum.'

Although the order had been made in English, Gracielita made fun of how Yamila had changed the 'ñ' of '*piña*' for the 'n of 'pina'.

'You almost made it sound rude,' Gracielita said, holding back a laugh.

'The problem is that there are many young people of Hispanic origin working here who speak Spanish but are used to it being asked for like that, except for the Cubans, who say it in a loud voice, as if to insult the waiters for not saying '*piña colada*' as it should be, and not pina colada. Anyway, what I was going to say is... I bet you didn't know I was North-American!'

Gracielita's incredulity was taken by them both as a joke.

'I had wondered, but since you never told me anything, I didn't want to ask you. Besides, we haven't had many opportunities to be quietly on our own.'

'It's a long story, but I'll tell you briefly, so that you at least know the truth. My father was born in Tampa. My grandparents, who I never knew, worked in the tobacco industry in Ybor City. My parents met there in 1955, although my mother, who was born in Cuba, was originally sent to Tampa by a half-American aunt, who had opened a little school for the children of Cuban émigrés and wanted my mother to help her out. The aunt died shortly after, and my mother gave up that work, almost immediately starting as an auxiliary nurse in a small hospital. To cut a long story short, so as not to bore you, my parents lived together, even after my mother's only, and somewhat late, pregnancy, and they didn't get married until I was three years old, and she was thirty-four. Unfortunately, I don't have many memories of my father, since he died in the United States in early 1962, and shortly after my mother and I returned to Cuba. I know that he was mulatto, with hazel eyes like mine, but very conscious that he did not belong to the white race, although his mother did. However, my father's circle of friends was principally among his own people. In photos he looks very elegant, and with good dress sense. My mother reminisces about him a lot, and is always saying how that time of her life was the happiest. And she never remarried. It was not long after that she made the arrangements to claim her American residency, because she couldn't adapt to the situation in Cuba. Besides, we no longer had any close family. Since I'm the daughter of a North-American and she never lost her residency status, there were no complications and we came on the Camarioca airlift in 1965. I was almost five.'

By the time the two glasses came with the refreshing cocktail, Gracielita had a better idea about Yamila's world, something she'd only had a very patchy and confused picture about until then, though she'd never admitted that because she felt deeply about her relationship with Yamila. The two of them, who had both been born in 1960, with almost nine months between them, got on very well, as if they'd known each other all their lives.

'According to my mother, my Dad wasn't a man who liked to get mixed up in politics, but was more inclined to business, though he was very patriotically Cuban, from the old mold, with a strict sense of civic duty. I think he was even a freemason, and also a member of the executive committee of a society for Cubans of color, founded at the turn of the century, when racial segregation in this country was at its worst. Out of necessity, people had to group together among their own, in order to survive, and even then it wasn't easy. Despite everything, he spoke Spanish with difficulty, and with a very funny accent, according to my mother, who always did everything possible for me to learn both English and Spanish correctly. I know my accent isn't completely like a Cuban-Cuban from Cuba, but I don't speak Anglo either, with an accent that shows you're not from here or there, making a mess of the language. Luckily, my mother was able to claim some money from my father's estate, which she didn't even know about. That's how she bought a little house, studied to become a social worker, and was employed for a good number of years by the state of Florida, until she took early retirement. Now she looks after some elderly people in Fort Lauderdale, a pretty city on the coast to the North of Miami, where many Anglos have settled together, leaving the blacks and the Hispanics behind. She also lives there, but not for the same reason. Those who have remained down here took refuge, as you must know by now, in the residential areas of Coral Gables, on the edge of the black ghetto; Coconut Grove and those condos, or buildings of Key Biscayne and the Northeast, among other places that those who have no money don't even ask about. You do realize you have to be very careful you don't end up in the wrong place? I imagine it's the same in Cuba, isn't it?'

Then there was a silence, that neither of them knew exactly how to fill. Gracielita was infinitely grateful for the friendship that had developed in such a disinterested way between them. Almost unconsciously and uncontrollably, they couldn't stop their eyes from glistening. They were both equally enraptured, gazing at the irregular harmony of colors reflecting on the waters of the bay, from the sun filtering between the tall buildings of the city. Gracielita thought they could be in the Habana Libre Hotel's Polinesio restaurant, as she commented to Yamila, but she also thought of the foliage of the Tropicana Cabaret. All that was missing, she told her friend, was for them to be sitting on the other side of Havana Bay, looking back over the city. What an illusion! The atmosphere inside was almost tropically Cuban, with many well-kept ornamental plants, fishing tackle, enormous hand-woven baskets, and other exotic decoration, but above all because of the homogeneous nature of the unmistakably Cuban Sunday clientele. The men wore their hair close cropped and were clean shaven, with scrupulously trimmed moustaches, many of them in expensive light-colored guayabera or *filipina* shirts, and well-pressed trousers tight around their bulky midriffs, as if trying to hold in the excess fat around their bellies. The señoras were over perfumed, exquisitely glittering, resplendent smartly squeezed into their sky-blue, emerald-green or pale pink dresses, some in combination with beige, with their two-tone designer half-heel shoes and decked out in pearl necklaces that looked all the more false at that hour of the warm evening. They would check the time of their early dinner reservations on their wristwatches that were completely out of fashion, but to a certain extent were some sort of demonstration that they laid claim to a lineage that hadn't died out as many believed. They were evidently not commonplace, forming a distinct group, much more like that of the Cuba they never tired talking about and she'd never had the opportunity of knowing because she hadn't been born, and she asked herself how it was possible that this Cuban community could affect such economic well-being, which they showed off above all in their cars, parked in the enormous open-air car park. You could recognize those Cuban *señoronas* at a distance from the intensity of their make-up and their identically styled hair, with the same grey hair concealed with the same mahogany dye, as well as from the tone and theme of the conversations. Gracielita had the impression of being in a contradictory world that was at once both familiar and alien.

'You're the first Cuban woman I've felt absolutely able to chat comfortably with, Gracielita. Maybe it's because we're so similar in character, and even physically, and maybe in other aspects of our lives. Like you, I didn't have a father figure to help me in difficult times, and I learned to manage by myself, on my own merits and not those of any man, whoever he might be – and that I owe to my mother. I don't know! I have few female friends: most are Central Americans, Hispanics and some Afro-North-Americans. I just don't get on with the Anglos, or the Cuban Americans. I feel out of place in this society. On the one hand I have no clear memories of Cuba, a country I love dearly, though I don't understand what's going on over there. On the other hand, I can't bear to identify with the politics of exiled Cubans, because their mentality is so backward and goes against all the values I believe in. It's as if they'd robbed me of the art of being Cuban, as if that concept belongs only to a small group that's chasing I don't know what, persisting in wanting the island to sink into discord and misery, at whatever price. That's why I talk to you like this.'

That day Gracielita learned, among other things, how Yamila's mother had raised her practically alone; how she'd struggled so that her daughter, and now her new friend, could achieve an education that would at least enable her to escape a little from the ugly things of life. A very familiar theme. She even managed to present a pretty complete, sincere and even justifiable picture of her position on political issues.

'So, you're not against me or the Mariel people?

'No, no way. That's not it. Don't forget I don't know Cuba like you, I'm not as familiar with the problems that you and Jorge – forgive me for mentioning him – and even Reinerio have been through. My point of view is different: it's that of someone searching for her roots and suddenly discovers the tree is burning. No, I'm not against you, or anybody – perhaps myself for not being able to reason better. It's just that it makes me mad thinking about the naivety with which, not just Cubans, but people from many other countries, come to the United States hoping to solve all their problems without taking on board that there are also millions of men and women, children and old people living badly here, and who've lived for generations in this gigantic wealthy country but have been cast aside by the system and trapped in this complicated, exploitative, deculturizing and constantly humiliating machinery of appearances and competition. And nobody can tell me different, because I've traveled from coast to coast, and I've worked for years with that type of immigrant and with the African-American community. Can you imagine that a city like Oakland, right next to San Francisco in California, one of the richest states in the nation, has one of the highest rates of infant mortality in the whole continent? Of course, that's among the blacks. And people don't realize, or don't want to realize, what's going on. They see a beggar and may throw him a crust, but they don't ask why he's hungry. And this goes on under our very noses, in the richest and most powerful country in the world. My country, about which I'm supposed to feel proud! The Mexicans risk their lives crossing the border to harvest fruit and vegetables for the big corporations who pay them a pittance precisely because they're illegal; and '*la migra*', as they call the border patrol, find them and send them back. The US Immigration Service annually expels more undocumented Mexicans than immigrants from the rest of the world put together. Ah, but with Cubans it's different. Whoever they may be, they're received in this country with fanfare. And if it has anything to do with democracy, well, Cuba and Mexico are level, because both have a one-party government. The case of the Haitians is newer but just as scandalous, if not more than that of the Mexicans, because the gringos robbed them of their land. Those poor blacks, totally out of place in this country, constitute the lowest rung of the immigration ladder. They are really persecuted, tortured and assassinated by paramilitary groups in Haiti, yet according to the US Immigration and Naturalization Service those poor people don't meet the requirements to be accepted as political refugees. It's shameful, and my friends at the Haitian Refugees Center are fighting it. They know full well that what they're dealing with is a multiple injustice against the refugees, who, as well as being black, have little public support in Florida. And all in the name of democracy and liberty, because don't ever forget that you live in the freest country in the world; so free that you have every freedom you want to destroy yourself, or for someone to take it upon himself to destroy you. I don't know...excuse the irony, but I'm tired of so much cynicism.'

Gracielita's and Yamila's eyes met again, but only for an instant, each questioning the other in silence and for different motives. Then she continued her monologue.

'Two years after starting to work with the new refugees, and after the riots and all that, I came to the conclusion that among the variety of individuals I myself processed, you can distinguish two distinct groups. In the first are the enterprising, ambitious (in the best sense) and sincere people, who want a different life and to better themselves. The other group is completely the opposite; at times it seems they want everything and nothing. I include you, along with Jorge, in the first group, whatever your motives. It isn't easy, but you both arrived in this country in the middle of a terrible economic recession, and I don't believe the Cubans from Cuba have the least idea what that means for ordinary men and women. It means that work opportunities are limited, the budget for social spending, health and education is cut, including vocational training, student loans, housing, employment and subsidized programs; but there is money there for people like you. For the others, no money comes from anywhere, even though their great, great-grandparents helped build this country, and they continue to live in absolute poverty. And the vast majority are people of color. So, of course, they ask themselves, because they're not stupid:

"Hell, what's happening to us, are we really third-class citizens?" Meanwhile, some honest politicians (and there are some) begin to question why privileges are given to some immigrants more than others, who arrive in their numbers every day, many of them seeking true political asylum and yet are lumped with the ordinary immigrants looking for work. One of the big contradictions of this country's immigration policies is the asylum program. It's really designed to protect refugees fearing persecution in their own countries. But the system is saturated with requests from people with no valid reason to seek political asylum, yet who ask for it so as to get a work permit or to stay a bit longer in the United States. While the Africans, the Dominicans, the Haitians, the Asians, and the Central Americans do absolutely anything to reach the coasts of this country, many of them fleeing hunger, torture and death – or a combination of all three calamities, a mix – the Cubans arrive fresh, healthy and educated, to take advantage of all the bounties of the system. Of course, racism and racist politicking play a fundamental part in all this, and that's what I want you to understand. It's not in any way personal, Gracielita. Quite the opposite. My frustration is more with myself, I told you. I confess I'm confused. All my problems revolve around our identity, because in order to define ourselves we have to begin with the circumstances surrounding us. I feel Cuban, without really knowing Cuba, and I speak Cuban, almost like a Cuban, but my only passport says I'm North-American, from Tampa. I don't identify with that generation of Cuban-American university students, with their skin and minds just a bit too rosy, who, while seeking to give advice on what the internal and external policies of Cuba should be, aspire to swell the ranks of the elite that will decide the future of Cuban exiles in this country, just as their parents did when they came fleeing Cuba. They'll be the ones to get the best posts in the universities, the companies and above all the government, through which they'll be able to influence the power structures of this country. When I was a high-school student, and later at college, I identified more with the Afro-North-Americans than with those Cuban-American students who cared more about fashion and discos than anything else. Mostly they are the children of well-to-do families, privileged by the system. Of course, the blacks among them can be counted on the fingers of one hand. That's why I consider myself a dissident, now that the word has become fashionable again. We have to work hard to pay for our higher education, and I envy you, all that you've been telling me, because your studies didn't cost you a cent. Not even the air fare! Many of these young exiled Cubans have accepted North-American culture more easily because their parents or relatives persuaded them to. They come to consider themselves more American than Cuban, even though they may keep certain strong traditions, such as their ties with family and with the Catholic Church. But I have nothing to do with that either. Not that I don't enjoy a good Cuban dinner from time to time, but the implications go far beyond culinary art. And now I meet you., the two of you. And before that, Reinerio, who's been something of a catalyst, because he has the same confusion in his head as we all have, only multiplied. I want answers, even if they aren't easy ones, to what I'm going through, and I don't know if I'm going to find them. So I want to look for other paths, and I invite you to join me, so that we can help each other.'

'What do you mean?'

'I'm leaving Miami. I've arranged everything. I've managed to get a good job in a community center in Boston.'

'I'm not suited to that, Yamila. You know that. What I'm good at is laboratory work, formulas, tests, and all that. I can't deny how much I'm missing it. And I'm afraid, very afraid that the future awaiting me will be in a pharmacy selling prescription medicines and such. And then, I'd like to be as close as possible to my mother.'

GRACIELITA ON THE KEY

Gracielita felt the separation keenly, although it helped a lot to comfort her that Yamila had asked her to look after her little house in a Cuban neighborhood to the west of Miami, with two bedrooms, living room, bathroom and even a porch with a front garden, in which there were lots of plants and creepers, just like in Cuba; and a large back patio, with some citrus bushes and a couple of areca trees. Yamila had also left her in charge of all her belongings, with the exception of the car, which had been leased for three years and she returned to the agency after winding up her affairs.

The move was made in one go just a few days before Yamila had to hand the car over. Yamila explained all the basics for running the house, and told her that the telephone would continue to be in her name until the end of May, but from then on the company she subscribed to would cut the service if she didn't renew it. Gracielita still couldn't drive, and although Yamila repeatedly tried to persuade her that she should, since it was so difficult to get about Miami on public transport, Gracielita kept saying she was terrified of driving on the highways crossing the city.

'You're going to be very limited in your movements. A car in this country isn't a luxury, it's an absolute necessity. It even comes to be your second home, and at the very least means you avoid having to walk in all those dangerous places of Dade County, which has become so infamous.'

Even so, Gracielita couldn't make up her mind. Besides, the course was expensive and she didn't have the money for it, at least at present – as she let Yamila know when she was explaining the advantages of being able to control her movements about the city.

165

Finally the eve of her departure came. That was the first night that Gracielita spent in Yamila's house, preparing a delicious farewell dinner of mashed potato and seasoned mince, from a recipe of her German friend Helga. The atmosphere was set with music from one of the many radio stations that broadcast day and night in Spanish, or rather, Cuban. News programs, calls from listeners in dialogue and even fighting with the announcers, and the announcers with the listeners, on problems relating to the Cuban community in South Florida, and the government here in Cuba, like, for example, whether sending money and other things to family in Cuba was giving aid to Fidel's government; that you should train in the South Florida everglades to fight for Cuba's freedom; that those who travelled to Cuba weren't patriots, and deserved all they got for helping the 'tyranny'; and all this interspersed with musical groups based in the United States and other parts of Latin America, playing Cuban rhythms. In the spacious kitchen-dining room, Gracielita and Yamila sang along to the occasional chorus, while drinking a glass of the beer they'd been enjoying since nightfall.

After the meal, and when it was already past midnight, Gracielita took note of the long list of details, explanations and recommendations about the house and neighborhood that Yamila had typed up for her. They barely slept, talking late into the night about life and the next steps they were both going to take, in places so far apart. It was Yamila in the end who decided not to sleep, and made herself a cup of American coffee, that's to say, quite weak, before taking a long shower. When she came out, Gracielita had fallen asleep among the cushions on the long, comfortable wicker sofa, and it wasn't until two hours later that Yamila woke her up so she could get ready, because Reinerio would be arriving a bit later to take them to Miami International Airport.

The goodbye was without a doubt very emotional for both of them. The whole time they were waiting, before Yamila went through the flight gate, Reinerio stood to one side, in silence, as the two friends hugged and comforted each other.

'I'll call you as soon as I arrive, and if you've changed your mind by then, don't hesitate to tell me. Reinerio already knows what to do, and so do you. Do you promise?'

'You're too good, Yamila! I don't know what I'd have done without you. I hope everything turns out just as you want....'

'And you too, sister. Take care.'

With these last words, Yamila gave her a big hug, they looked each other in the eyes once more, and hugged each other again. When she separated from Gracielita, Yamila took the enormous check coat, of thick soft wool, which Reinerio had been holding, and she stepped back a bit from Gracielita. Yamila spoke a few words with Reinerio, and they gave each other a brief but moist kiss, and an affectionate embrace. Then she raised her arm, and waved goodbye again to Gracielita, with a lovely smile. Gracielita followed her with her eyes until her hand luggage had gone through the x-ray machine, and Yamila melted into the crowd of men, women and children of all colors and nationalities, laden with bags of all sizes, constantly entering and leaving those labyrinths of automatic barriers. Gracielita had seen many airports – well, some at least – but even if you put them all together they couldn't compare with Miami International Airport. While she couldn't really describe it, it was like a completely carpeted gigantic space station. Half bemused by the spectacle, which reminded her of the circus fairs in the GDR, Gracielita didn't realize Reinerio was at her side asking her something.

'I'm sorry, Reinerio, what were you saying?'

'Let's go. I'll drop you off at the house.'

'*Okei.*'

From when they left the airport terminal, and then the fourth-floor car park where they'd left the car, and on the two other occasions when he tried to get some kind of conversation out of her, Reinerio failed in face of the absolute indifference of Gracielita's answers. It was really nothing personal to do with the poor boy, who did all he could for Gracielita to like him, but with no positive outcome, and suspecting what was wrong, he didn't insist. When they reached Yamila's house, Reinerio got out of the car, and even opened her door for her, like a charming beau. He held out his hand by way of a goodbye, and gave her his work card, after writing his home address and telephone number on the back.

'Just in case you need me. Yamila told me to help you in any way I can... But even if she hadn't, I would be at your command.'

'Thank you, Reinerio. Really, thank you so much! Forgive me if I don't invite you in, but I was up all last night. See you soon, and really, thank you for everything.'

***

During the first few weeks, Gracielita decided to occupy herself with domestic chores, which included a general cleaning, particularly of the bathroom; laundering the bedclothes from both bedrooms; polishing the wooden floor; and finally cutting the lawn and the plants, by which time she was totally exhausted. When she told Yamila on the phone one night all she'd done, from the other end of the line came a peal of laughter, which was the preamble for an exchange of jokes between the two friends about that being a good job to look for, because in some areas it was very well paid. However, from her end, Gracielita couldn't say whether it was really a joke, because if it was, she thought it in very poor taste, or else a veiled suggestion that at any moment she'd have to take it seriously. But that moment hadn't arrived yet. Besides, it was evident that she liked Yamila's little house a lot; it was so cosy, almost made to measure and the whim of its owner, and now of its new tenant. So much so that the enchantment allowed her to relax for almost a month after Yamila's departure, without feeling the need to venture further afield than the supermarket, from which she brought back two or three of the county daily newspapers and then pored over them for hours: not for the international news or the national and regional current affairs, but to pick out the jobs that were advertised there in the classified pages.

It so happened that on a day when she had found absolutely nothing suitable, the following advertisement caught her eye:

> **HOUSEKEEPER WITH EXPERIENCE** Man or woman. Must be competent, efficient, clean and hard working. Polite. Florida State driving licence necessary. Non-smoker. Tasks: take care of laundry, cooking, ironing, cleaning, shopping. Six days a week. From 7.45am to 6.45pm. Reference required. Tel: 792-2829 only between 7.30 and 9.30 pm.

In the first few months, Yamila stayed in regular telephone contact with Gracielita, since she could call her from her office, which was on the outskirts of Boston, and she'd speak wonders about the possibilities for developing an excellent business project, with bank credits for small businesses orientated towards what in the United States are called small ethnic 'minorities'. Which is to say all those who have the luck or misfortune not to have the right color skin, that is, white.

According to her letters, Gracielita was learning quickly. She told how Yamila's backlog of work had obliged her to be absent from Cambridge, the twin city of Boston where she was. This put an end to them continuing their regular and extensive phone dialogues, which, as a result, were limited to two or three a month. Nevertheless, that was enough for them to keep up to date with the details of their parallel lives, and helped fight the loneliness.

Encouraged by Yamila, and after persuading herself to put into practice her decision to go to a couple of addresses, she first responded to a call for applications to teach biology in a county community college. Gracielita had convinced herself it was time to get over her stage fright and take the plunge and look for work, since she couldn't carry on any longer in that limbo and dependency on the Social Welfare office. Even Yamila's recommendations on the phone seemed too maternal: 'Wear your best clothes, and if you haven't got anything suitable, look in the trunks in my room – there are some things there that are good for the Miami climate and would suit you well. Remember your appearance: it's the first impression that decides the outcome of the interview.'

Gracielita didn't recognize herself of late, she'd been so lacking in energy. She'd always been so bright and active, but something had been inhibiting her till that moment, when she decided to fulfill the formal requirements to attend another interview, where they were looking to fill two places for local government environmentalists. The appointment was in a public office building situated on Biscayne Boulevard. The following extract from Gracielita's letter to her mother is self-explanatory, and I'll let it speak for itself:

Well, it's true, Mima, I should have listened to Yamila, because that day I crossed nearly the whole of Miami to get to the college, and by bus – and the heat's unbearable. It's just as well I was dressed lightly, but elegantly. Some really interesting things happened to me. While I was waiting in a very smart room, along with twenty or thirty women from various countries, most of them my age, more or less, by coincidence I sat next to another black Cuban woman, quite thick-lipped, but who seemed to be very well educated. We ended up chatting, and in half an hour we'd told each other the gist of our life stories. It turns out that Rosita Balmaseda, as she's called, came by another route, having married a political prisoner, and so was able to leave the country. And this woman says to me: 'The decision to marry a man I hardly knew wasn't born of desperation, because my ideas were always the same. For years I couldn't stand living in Cuba, not just because of the economic situation, but because I realized I had no future there. I graduated in Information Technology and Library Sciences from the University of Havana, and I'd studied teaching before, but I wanted to get out of that environment of the kids and education that was killing me. That's why I fixed it to come over here believing that would solve everything, but no such luck. Because everything here is down to luck! I arrived in this country with great hopes, as does everyone. To begin with I met a number of people who were very pleasant, but after a while I felt the same as I had in Cuba, without any possibility of making progress. I thought maybe it was because of my age, because I'm a little older than you are; but no, it's not that. Imagine, with the qualifications I have...? I didn't have time to finish my doctoral thesis before a friend who'd done the same told me that a political prisoner friend of her husband was prepared to get married, and that's how I left for here. But I've studied a lot here, and haven't managed to get anything permanent, despite having such excellent qualifications. I've been through interviews like this one, and I haven't been able to get anything. I've hardly any hope left, you know. I live with my husband, the one I left Cuba with, and we've two children, because fortunately we get along well together. We live in a neighborhood of almost entirely Cubans. But they're all white, and it's funny, girl, because when you're new to the area and you go to the markets, those white folks, just like in Cuba, or worse, are scared by your presence, but then when they talk to you and get to know you, it's a great relief to them, because I'm Cuban and because evidently they realize that I'm just as educated as they are. I don't know if you've realized it yet, but we blacks feel like satellites, worse still since the people from Mariel came – don't take it personally. We don't have the support of the black Americans, nor the support of the white Cubans. Sometimes when they hear me speaking Spanish they ask if I'm Dominican or Puerto Rican. Anything, because they've convinced themselves we black Cubans don't exist. How can you fight it if for those people we don't exist? I've had some very bad experiences here.' It was so funny, Mima, because when this Rosita Balmaseda came out of her interview, which had taken place four people ahead of me, the woman came back and sat next to me, and said with a little smile of resignation: 'You see? Just as I told you. Although she didn't say so in as many words, she led me to understand that what they need is a twenty-something-year-old girl. Where the hell are they going to find a girl that age with the experience and qualifications I have? I wish you luck, honey!' With that, she disappeared as if we'd never met. Then it was my turn. The lady, who was obviously Cuban, must have had many years of experience as a secretary, because when she spoke with her assistant over the intercom, she sounded almost exactly like a North-American. She asked me a lot of questions about what I'd been doing in East Germany and Cuba, how much my degree had cost, what projects we'd had in the Center where I worked in Cuba, where the laboratory equipment had come from, and the number of people working there... Mima, I swear she spent almost forty-five minutes with me. And to each of my answers, all she kept repeating was: 'Very

*interesting, very interesting.' In the end, she
said she couldn't promise anything, but I might
be a good acquisition for Dade County, though
it didn't depend on her, but on her superiors,
and the department would let me know if I'd
been successful. Of course, I left feeling very
hopeful. On the other hand, my application to
the college failed. Long before getting there,
I'd lost interest anyway. The college is in a
really bad neighborhood, and the students are
of Hispanic background and black Americans, all
of them, and look bad. So I did all I could to
fail the interview, and I'm not sorry.*

GUESS WHAT?

That midday Monday when Inesita passed by the house to ask Julia and me for our advice on a number of things to do with Gracielita, I'd decided to make tamales with the corncobs I'd bought on Saturday at the peasant market in Virgen del Camino. Julia had gone in the early hours of the morning to the Marianao Bus Station, to see if she could get a ticket to San Cristóbal, to go to look after her mother who had caught a cold. Her mother was very old, and Julia was always running to Pinar del Río, where she lived, for any little thing. Since it was *Eleggua's* day, I wasn't doing anyone's hair unless it was a client with a particular need, because I always respected that day. So, Inesita and I were able to spend a long time together, while I was going about my chores, trying to decipher what was hidden between the lines of Gracielita's letters and work out how things were going for her.

'I know what she's like, Marta, and even if things were going hard for her she won't go into service like us.'

Inesita had been thinking of suggesting to her daughter that she should try to find the Robledo family, for whom she had worked for many years, to see if they could help her in some way. I helped her out there and then with some clean sheets of paper from the notebooks that I scribbled in, and she got down to writing a letter that took her almost three hours, what with one thing and another, since she consulted me on every paragraph.

'But, Inesita, even if she is your daughter, don't forget that she's a grown woman!'

In the midst of all my housework that Monday – which apart from making tamales included washing and boiling the week's sheets and pillowcases, and even the old pink satin bedcover – Inesita wrote her letter, which bit by bit she had finished reading to me by the time the washing I'd hung out in the yard had dried in the afternoon sun.

Among many other things, Inesita told her that she was in good health, 'Thank God and all the santos!' She still had the strength to go on struggling and that things were going well for her at work, with no problems. She also told her that in the last four years she'd spoken a couple of times with her father, Octavio, and that he didn't seem too concerned about her being in the United States, 'because, when all's said and done, he's never concerned himself with you.' She put in the letter that she'd never heard from any of her old *compañeros* from work, but that she'd done nothing to stay in touch with those who had once been her friends. She told her something about how the food problem had improved a bit with the Free Peasant Market, where, although it was expensive, you could buy pork, lamb and poultry, and all kinds of vegetables, fruits, flowers and even medicinal herbs, and that people would go really early in the day to buy the best things the peasants brought from the countryside. And it was true, because I'd go with my nephew before six in the morning to the Virgen del Camino market, to buy fresh tender corncobs to make tamales, which at times I sold for a peso each, without Guillermo finding out, although he guessed, but acted as though he didn't know. I still can't understand why the peasants are criticized so much: for getting rich, for having a house in the countryside and another in the city, for exploiting people by selling garlic at a peso a head and being able to buy themselves two cars, and all that. The thing is that ever since they opened those markets, you could manage to put food on the table, and much more varied, because you couldn't get by only with what was on the ration book. So much fear and suspicion about the peasants and their intermediaries, when everyone is on the take. If we're going to take a clear look at things, absolutely everything in this country functions illegally, so if it wasn't for the black market... That's just how things are. Look what happened with those two sisters at the back of our *solar*. Because they have money, a good house with a garden, and relatives up North who help them out, they managed to get a telephone line installed. Nobody questioned how that could be, since the answer would have been, 'You know how things are...' A contact, two or three gifts to the line engineers of the phone company, and things were arranged. That's why you need to have *FE*, a lot of faith, 'Family in Exile', as Eneida, Baba's woman, used to say. Well, at that time I didn't have family abroad to solve anything for me, so I got by in my own way with my tamales, selling *durofríos*, and fixing hair. When I'd buy the cobs, I'd give five pesos to one of my nephews, and he'd bring me a sack full from Virgen del Camino in his little cart he'd made from a big wooden box and four old roller-skate wheels. People in the *solar* always knew when I was going to make tamales, because they'd see me getting down to brass tacks, as they say. It's a hard job, because you have to strip the corn and hand grind, which I'd already done by Sunday midday. I did that so as not to have to pay more buying the corn already ground, because sometimes they mix all kinds of stuff into the cornmeal to increase the quantity, and it gives it a bitter taste. I prefer to choose the cobs myself and go through the whole process, even if it takes me longer. Then you have to prepare the sauce, with tomato, garlic, onion and other seasonings when you can get them, and, of course, some good pork fat! Then I cook all that thick purée with the cornmeal, and little pieces of pork crackling, when there is any, until the mixture is just right for putting it into the little parcel made out of the leaves from the cob, and tie it tight so that it doesn't spill out during the hours of boiling, depending on the consistency you want when cooked. In eastern Cuba they use banana leaves for wrapping what they call *hayaca*, but I make my tamales different. Each to her own. The smell is delicious, and just one bite of this special dish – which I in fact didn't learn from my mother but from my first mother-in-law, Orlando's mother – is something not to be forgotten! It's not for nothing that my cooking is always praised. Anyway, when Inesita arrived and took almost the whole afternoon to tell me all she could about Gracielita, I just had to invite her to taste a couple of my tamales, the smell of which announced them right round the block.

Although she only had the old address that señora Robledo y Albemar had sent her from a city called Atlanta at the end of the sixties, Inesita, who had kept it like gold, put it into the letter to her daughter, and after sealing the envelope kissed it as if it were the cheek of her darling Gracielita.

'I do hope she can arrange something, Marta!'

Gracielita didn't make it very clear in her letters, in which she was always saying that she had things more or less under control, but quite a time had gone by, and the girl still had nothing secure, just a few jobs here and there, and studying and more studying. It was then, in early January, that Inesita, who had come down with the flu that had hit everyone in a bad way, brought me two letters from her daughter, telling her lots of things.

First, the various attempts Gracielita had made to get a good job had come to nothing, and only through the recommendation of her loyal friend Yamila was she able to get a job teaching Spanish at a night school for the children of Latin American parents who had been born in the United States and couldn't speak their mother tongue. Although she didn't like the work much, she could more or less get by. She didn't say if she had a boyfriend, and her mother hadn't asked. But one of the letters contained a lot of information about Inesita's suggestion of contacting the Robledo family. Fortunately for Gracielita, señora Robledo y Albemar had been living for some years in a sumptious neighborhood to the south of Miami Beach – a kind of semi-private island for the really wealthy. She had been widowed during the time they were in Atlanta, a city she could never stand, because, according to what she had told Inesita in the only letter she wrote to her, shortly before the death of señor Robledo, Atlanta was too American and too cold for her. So as soon as she had completed the formalities for transferring her deceased husband's remains to Miami, she moved to that city, where one of her two sons, who were now married and with children, had studied.

Señora Robledo y Albemar, who had inherited quite a lot of money from her husband, as well as a good pension from the Coca-Cola soft drinks company, for which he had also worked all his life in Cuba, was obsessed with burying her husband in a cemetery in Little Havana. Maybe this was because that's where the remains of two Cuban presidents are, Fulgencio Batista and Carlos Prío Socarrás, along with many other Cubans, including those who took part in the Bay of Pigs invasion in 1961 and who died years later; or maybe because she had a special relationship with the owners of the famous Caballero funeral parlor in the area, because she remembered her grandparents were laid out in Havana by the old funeral parlor that had been founded over a hundred years ago. The owners had left Cuba soon after the triumph of the Revolution and established themselves in Miami, which people say is the city that runs a close second to Havana for the numbers of Cubans living there, and perhaps has even more.

Having tracked down señora Robledo y Albemar and introduced herself over the phone, Gracielita received a warm invitation, as she described it, to visit her one Sunday afternoon, on the day she turned 27. It was that very day that Gracielita decided to learn to drive, and until she managed to buy herself a used car a year later, she didn't stop thinking about how her dear friend Yamila had so often told her that in Miami you couldn't live without a car. She had a hard time of it getting out of Hialeah, having called a taxi to pick her up from home to take her to the bus station she was by then very familiar with, to catch the bus which crossed the whole northeast of the district, running between Liberty City and Overtown, and going as far as Miami Beach. There she caught another taxi, so as not to arrive with her clothes crumpled. But in the end what really made her decide to get a car was the distaste she felt, constantly brushing up against Hispanics, black North-Americans and Haitians, poor working people in their majority, who were the ones who always used the public buses.

Just as she had imagined, it would have been too ridiculous to turn up at señora Robledo y Albemar's apartment in anything other than a taxi, since she still didn't have a car of her own. When the taxi driver arrived at the address, Gracielita held her breath without realizing it, until she was forced to give her name and that of the family she was visiting to the security guard who sat indifferently in a little white stone hut, behind a thick, concave, tinted glass window, to protect him from the rays of the sun, which beat down on his little tower for several hours each day. For her, it was the most exclusive place she had known up to that moment. It was the same security guard, a smartly uniformed middle-aged, dark-skinned man, though from his tone of voice you could tell he wasn't Cuban, who, using an electronic device, opened the two gigantic cast-iron gates, decorated with Spanish colonial-style arabesques. The taxi-driver followed the security guard's instructions to one of the buildings, which had something like twenty floors, and left her at the entrance. She paid him, took the change and, though it hurt her deeply, gave him two dollars in tip.

Whatever Gracielita wore, no matter how simple, looked good on her. Her mother would have felt proud if she had seen her in that very fashionable, light olive green, tailored suit her friend Yamila had given her. The trousers hung comfortably on her, as did the two-buttoned jacket; and she wore a mauve silk blouse, with a bow in the form of a tie, and brown moccasins. As the taxi driver headed back out of the residential gated community, Gracielita took out her address book and entered the code señora Robledo y Albemar had given her over the phone, which was just letters and numbers, since the only list of tenants who lived in the building was on the security guard's computer. When she had finished entering the code, she realized that a closed-circuit camera had been watching all her movements. After some seconds, she heard the buzz of the electronic mechanism and gently pushed the solid glass and bronze door. She crossed the wooden-floored reception area and glanced quickly at the enormous wall mirrors that were flanked by several casually arranged pots of ornamental plants. Before going up the four steps that led to the two elevators, one of which was open, as if waiting for her, she spotted another video camera following her movements. Gracielita entered and pushed the button for the fifteenth floor. Inside, she again looked at herself in the mirror, but in an uncomfortable position, because the only one in the cubicle, which seemed more like a funeral chapel than an elevator, was the one on the ceiling, and it wasn't the glass of a mirror, but a shiny plate of metal, and she wondered whether there wasn't another camera spying from behind her own reflection.

Gracielita didn't have the faintest idea what señora Robledo y Albemar looked like, since the description her mother had given her was from before she'd been born. Inesita had told her that in those days she'd had the body of a princess. When the elevator door opened, without even the slightest sound, she found no difficulty in locating the apartment, since there were only four on the floor, which made her think immediately that they must be enormous, judging by the exterior of the building. She walked looking for 15-B, which from its position had to have a view of the open sea rather than the waters of the bay. And she was right, because when señora Robledo y Albemar opened the door, the first thing that struck her was not the healthy, robust figure of a mature woman who had always paid great attention to her appearance, but the panorama of the serene blue sea, softly lit by tropical glimmers of amber and silvery grey tones. Somewhere the other side was Cuba, Gracielita thought, while holding out her hand to the owner and señora, about whom she'd heard so much.

'What a surprise, Gracielita! I never thought I would come to know you, let alone on this Miami stage. Come, sit down over here, on the sofa, which is my favorite place, looking south, to our beloved Havana.'

Señora Robledo y Albemar offered her a cool lemonade that she herself served, giving Gracielita time to confirm that this really was someone with a lot of money. The enormous living room was not particularly pretentious in its decor, but with touches of luxury and good taste. Where she sat was an enormous, very soft white leather sofa. In one corner was an antique secretaire, which even if it was a reproduction must have been expensive since it was well made, like those in the antique museums. Two big paintings hung on the walls opposite the balcony, one of her alone, sitting sideways, wearing a pink and white outfit, which looked like a cross between a natural portrait painting and a photo of when she was young, and the other of them as a couple, with señor Robledo standing behind señora Robledo, who was leaning on her husband, holding one of his hands that was resting on her shoulders. In another corner of the living room, with its light, mahogany-colored wood flooring, was a black grand piano. Several armchairs, some standard lamps and two croton plants in beautiful black ceramic pots were the only other decoration in that lovely room.

'Well, my child, tell me what you're doing in this country, you who, according to your good mother, had everything in Cuba. I don't know what your mother told you about us, but it was very hard for us to leave Cuba. It wasn't easy. But Caballero Robledo had already said we would when they nationalized, and that measure really was a barbarity. You can't take on the Americans. But things went well for us here, much better than in Puerto Rico. As you can see, islands pursue me and fascinate me, even if they are small like this one. My sons are doing very well. They are both lawyers. Ricardo Lugo, the older one, is a partner in a law firm that works for a Cuban-American construction company, and is president of the Association of Cuban-American Lawyers. He lives right here, in the building behind this one. The younger, Nestor Alejandro, teaches at DePaul University, in Chicago. He never liked Miami, he says it's too hot here. After my husband died, my older son bought me this apartment in this paradise they finished building only a short time ago. He takes good care of me. You don't know what boys are like! He dearly loved his father, who never recovered after a kidney operation. It was Ricardo Lugo who took care of everything to bring his remains here to Miami. My late husband's grandfather, an Asturian by birth, is buried here in Woodlawn cemetery. It was the illness that forced him to retire from the company, which treated him so well for the forty years he worked for them, but he deserved it, because he brought them a lot of profit, opening up markets in Latin America and the Caribbean. For my part, I've kept up with my civic activities, though I've retired as well now. I was treasurer of our Cuban Women's Club, then I was co-founder of the Hispanic-American Association Against Discrimination, which strives for just and equitable work among Hispanic women, always seeking racial and ethnic harmony. Miami has many problems like that, my girl, many problems. But, well, don't let me go on talking, because I'll never stop. Tell me about yourself, what you've heard from your mother, who is so good! She must have suffered a lot when you left Cuba. You look a lot like her... do you take after your father at all? What did you say his name was? You were born some time after we left, isn't that right? You know, we never thought the wait would be so long. You're so pretty and so young.'

Poor Gracielita had questions fired at her after this introduction by señora Robledo y Albemar, who her mother had served for many years. She didn't mention her father's name, nor was she thinking of going into any details, because that wasn't why she'd come, and she had no interest in exposing her feelings.

'I've had no news of my father since he divorced *mima*, and that was a long time ago, señora. And as it happens, today's my birthday.'

'Ah, happy birthday! Let's celebrate with a little drink, shall we?'

Señora Robledo y Albemar's enthusiasm seemed sincere, so much so that Gracielita was quite moved. She was soon to realize all that her mother had said about her, above all how exaggeratedly attentive she was, was well founded. Unusually light-footed, considering the volume of her body and years (she must have been around sixty, although she didn't look it), señora Robledo y Albemar got up off the comfortable sofa, and soon returned from the dining room with a small bottle and two fine glasses.

'It isn't champagne, but it's an excellent sparkling wine from California. They send it direct from the vineyards to my son Ricardo Lugo, since one of his best clients with properties in Miami is also in wine production. Let's drink a toast, for everything to turn out just as you'd like. After all, this is a country of many opportunities for all.'

'Thank you, thank you so much! Things haven't been easy, señora...'

'You can call me señora Robledo y Albemar, like your mother... Everyone calls me that.'

'Well, I was saying that things haven't been very easy, señora Robledo y Albemar..."

And so, little by little, Gracielita told her briefly how things had been in those first years in the United States, working at many minor jobs. Yet she hadn't succeeded in what she most desired, which was to return to her career. When she explained what her profession was, señora Robledo y Albemar's surprise was echoed by Gracielita, but for different reasons.

'Well, it's not surprising, my girl... That kind of career isn't worth much in this country, and less so for someone like you. In the first place, you shouldn't be ashamed; quite the contrary, but you must know that in this country you have the wrong skin color to aspire to anything like that; and you're a woman, which is another disadvantage, and add the fact that you came in the last wave of Cuban immigrants, which has become notorious for the atrocities that have been committed and for the way the press talks about you all. There isn't a truer saying than the one that goes: if you make your bed, you'd better lie in it. It's not that everyone's the same, as we know that only too well, but remember what country you're living in. The youth of today only think about making money in the world of law, finance and investment, real estate and construction. Look at this residential complex... The lawyer's firm where my son Ricardo Lugo is a partner is the one that looks after it, has done ever since this multi-million project began, and he's an intimate friend of one of the principal contractors of the company. They even studied together, and now they are partners. My late husband was right in that respect; those are the careers that bring money and prestige quickly and forever. But the sciences, humanities and those things: no way! They're good for those who work in the laboratories of big companies and in private universities, but to get there you have to be part of that world, and to have been born of good stock or have come already famous from outside, especially fleeing from the communist dictatorships of Eastern Europe – I don't know why they produce so many good scientists.'

Gracielita thanked señora Robledo y Albemar for the sincerity with which she had been speaking, and she didn't need much encouragement to continue in the same vein:

'Look at the case of my daughter-in-law Ileana, Ricardo Lugo's wife. She has a degree in anthropology, but you wouldn't guess what she's working in. Well, she's working for ZETA business consultants, a company worth seventy million dollars. Because there's something else, let me tell you: slowly but surely, we Cuban women are achieving strategic positions, where our power and influence are significant. Ah, but there isn't a single colored woman, not that there are many of them. In this country things are different from how they were in the Cuba of my youth. Although not that much, really, because though they're always going on about how there was never racial discrimination in Cuba, that's not true, and nobody can pull the wool over my eyes. That's just how life is. When talking about Cuban women in exile, that clearly doesn't mean talking about colored women, why fool ourselves? We were never satisfied with being housewives. We've progressed a lot. We had to work hard in hotels and factories, though I never needed to – thank God! – and from there we moved up into executive positions. Now we're ready to exchange our offices for political positions, that's where we're heading. You'll see in a few years where we are. But I repeat, there aren't any colored women like you there. Quite simply, there are none! And nobody bothers to ask why, because quite simply nobody cares; it's not our problem. I'm very glad that in the end your mother decided not to come to be with us, because, although we loved her and needed her, it would have been very difficult for her, with so little schooling and in this world that's so unequal and where things are so hard. That was one of the reasons I retired from my civic activities. There are too many injustices in this world in which we live. And it's not only the communists. Here as well, here above all! We were lucky, both in Cuba and here. My late husband's grandparents came to the United States before the Spanish-American War at the end of the last century. Their only grandson, the one who is up there with me in the picture, studied here, just as our sons did... That's to say there's a tradition, a surname that backs us up, but most people who came to seek their fortune here had little more than the clothes on their backs. But the good thing is that they succeeded, these so-called new rich, who all their lives have never been anything but "Johnny-come-latelies". I'm not saying this about people like you... My son Ricardo Lugo doesn't like me talking like this, because he says the foundations of this country are precisely for that, for everyone having the same opportunity. And maybe he's right, but underneath it's a lie. In our Cuban Women's Club, we try to be like that, though we don't let everyone in, only people from good families. No, I'm not saying this for your good, because I know it wouldn't for one moment occur to you to try, because it's not your world, but for that of others who try to pretend they're fine ladies, when they've not and never have been, neither here nor there. I'm retired now, but from time to time they invite me to give one of my lectures on the history of our exalted Cuban women, and I help out a lot in religious and charitable matters. I wish you could have been here when we inaugurated the chapel of *Nuestra Señora de la Caridad del Cobre*, our patron saint, I imagine you've already seen it on one side of Biscayne Bay. It was very moving. Well, I give way to the younger generations, who I've always given advice to, encouraging them to love their *patria*. That's why the main entrance of the chapel faces south, to Cuba. Many of today's youth think only about making money, money and more money, and don't have the slightest concern for the future of their parents' country, which after all is theirs as well, because, although many have been born here, that doesn't mean they're to stop being Cuban. Sometimes they don't even think about ever visiting Cuba. Oh, if only I could have the chance to return to Havana before joining my late husband in heaven!'

Gracielita didn't have the faintest idea how to break into this monologue, which was unburdening a torrent of words, just as señora

Robledo y Albemar had been used to doing with Inesita when she was working for the family in the old days. In the end she decided to try, so as to animate the dialogue a little:

'And do you think that it's fair, I don't mean you but people in general, thinking about colored people in that way, as you say?'

'Of course not! But where do you think you're living? Take a look and see how many colored people are in the Cuban-American National Foundation, which was founded three or four years ago, or in any of the other patriotic organizations. That's how things are! But well, changing the subject, it's time I asked how I can help you, because according to what you said on the phone, that was the purpose of your visit, apart from it being very pleasant to have you here. Don't be embarrassed, I've always been like this. I like to share ideas.'

From then, Gracielita went on the offensive. She told some parts of her story, disguising it a bit, for example, not mentioning her fiancé, and referring only in passing to her conflicts with the Party committee and the administration of her old work center here in Havana. But it was enough to evince a sharp reaction from Mrs. Robledo y Albemar:

'But, of course! What did you expect from such people, who don't know how to deal with educated people like you? Talent, my girl, talent is something you have to know how to appreciate and respect.'

As Gracielita talked and she became more and more interested in the tale, señora Robledo y Albemar let slip certain observations of that kind. It was half an hour later, after relating ten years of her life, when Gracielita finished by saying:

'That's why my mother thought of you, that you might be able to help me in some way, although I was reluctant to ask you because, as you yourself recognize, we're not all the same, and the fame that we *Marielitos* have earned for ourselves, thanks to a few bad eggs, isn't something that can be easily erased.'

Señora Robledo y Albemar had no need to beat around the bush, and Gracielita was again thankful for her frankness:

'I'm glad you've come to me first, and I'm going to be honest, as if I were talking to your mother, who I respect with all my heart. If you want to continue living in this country and prosper, forget your scientific career and make use of your physical appearance, your intelligence and your youth, doing something that will bring you more reward. Another piece of advice: if you can, leave Florida, the further the better. You have the great advantage of living in an enormous and very diverse country. Though don't forget that Florida is unique, and there's nowhere like Miami. Here at least you have little bits of Cuba all over. Within a few years, this city will be more Cuban than Havana itself. You'll see! But if you do insist on staying here, I can recommend you for some little jobs. If you have money problems, my daughter-in-law is looking for someone to help her with her daughter, and I would be delighted if you could be my two-year-old granddaughter's nanny. Ileana has a job with a lot of responsibility and is always very busy, which is why she needs a nanny, and, if I'm not mistaken, I think you'd be ideal, because you're Cuban and very gentle. You would be paid well, and you could even live with them, since they have a lot of space. Otherwise, I'll see if some of my friends can find you something else. But as the saying goes, the light beside you shines brightest. It has to be said, there's no shortage of work here, you just have to go out and look for it, and be ready to take it when the occasion arises, and not be fussy, like many people in this country who want to have a good job from the start with no sacrifice. Here you have to work hard, very hard, and start from the bottom if you want to rise, unless you have any capital, and even then, you have to work even harder, because the competition is so fierce.'

Although Gracielita didn't reject outright señora Robledo y Albemar's suggestions, neither did she commit herself immediately, and agreed to contact that lady and señora in the near future. Señora Robledo y Albemar didn't give the matter any more attention, and so the visit ended, but not before inviting Gracielita to taka a stroll round the residential estate, which she found delightful. It was so peaceful, with such spacious green areas, where there were two or three people jogging in sports clothes, and others entertaining their pampered dogs. Near the main entrance, Gracielita said goodbye with a brushing of cheeks and a simulated kiss. On the other side of the huge iron gate, a taxi was waiting for her. Crossing the enormous bridge, she looked across the bay to take in the beautiful view and an immense feeling of nostalgia came over her. She spent the rest of that Sunday feeling really homesick, as she said in her letter, very sad and lonely, celebrating her birthday wrapped up in her many thoughts until at around nine at night, while she was pretending to watch a movie, her best and only friend, who never forgot the date, phoned from Boston.

Yamila was envious, since she missed the Florida climate. For several weeks it had been snowing in much of the country. In the capital, as well as in New York and other cities, a state of emergency had been declared because of the persistent snow. The two friends talked for about forty minutes, swapping their latest experiences and giving each other advice, just as they used to. After recommending that she not let herself get drawn into domestic service, which might frustrate her plans, Yamila said she had a big surprise for her.

'Guess what?'

'You're getting married?'

'You must be kidding, girl!'

'Well, you'd better tell me, because I haven't the faintest idea.'

'Think. What's been the dream of my life?"

Gracielita went silent, forcing Yamila to ask her if she was still on the phone. When she was about to say that she was, she shouted:

'No!'

'Yes! I'm finally going to Cuba!'

Yamila had a lot of work on in Boston, and was part of a Cuban friendship association, which among its many other activities organized specialist study visits, since that was the only way American citizens could visit Cuba. The group in question was preparing a journey for the summer, and Yamila was the coordinator of the program. The news didn't come as a surprise to Gracielita, but she took it as a surprise, since the last thing she'd been thinking was that anyone so close to her might travel to Havana; and Yamila would, of course, go to see her mother, and could give her first-hand news, and at the same time take her a whole heap of things. From that moment on, she began making her plans. But what would she tell her mother? There was time to think about it, but for the moment she was happy knowing that, as soon as the preparations for the trip were well advanced, Yamila would let her know, although they would speak before then, of course, and she would try to travel down to Miami a couple of days before, to talk before catching the plane to Havana.

'That's the best gift I've had in a long time, and on my birthday!'

The two friends said their goodbyes, and Gracielita returned to her world.

Yamila in Havana

Summer hadn't ended that year in South Florida, but for Yamila the winter in Boston had been too long. Temperatures were below zero until mid-May in that part of the northeastern United States. Over the last few months, Yamila and Gracielita had been keeping each other up to date with everything that was happening. Yamila was happy that the work project she had submitted to the directors of the cooperative had been accepted. Gracielita, for her part, could no longer hide how depressed she was, because she was doing nothing, or practically nothing, that she liked. The only good news was that she'd received her driving license, and she was thinking seriously of buying a small used car, if she could find one. Her English had improved considerably, and Yamila congratulated her because she could tell, when, for the first time since they'd met, they didn't speak at all in Spanish. Yamila's journey was to be at the end of July, not in August as she had thought. Gracielita, who'd been thinking much more about her mother than she had in previous years, couldn't help but be happy about the great news, almost as if she were the one going to Havana. Yamila's group was made up of men and women involved in social work in different communities in the state of Massachusetts. Until that moment, Gracielita hadn't told Yamila that she was working three days a week as a nanny in the apartment of señora Robledo y Albemar's daughter-in-law, Ileana. Although she couldn't complain, because they treated her well, and she didn't have to pay taxes, Gracielita considered it a very temporary job, a first step towards making contacts; as she kept telling herself, she hadn't studied for so many years only to have the same career as her mother. What was interesting was that she got on relatively well with Ileana, who was more or less her own age and was very considerate; she was always giving her good clothes, preferring it a thousand times to give them to somebody she knew and trusted, rather than fill a box and leave it in one of the many charity shops where they would afterwards be sold on cheap. They were quality clothes, which Ileana would wear a couple of times and then pass on, and her husband's, too. What Yamila used to say to Gracielita made sense, that the only new clothes she bought were shoes and underwear, everything else came from the thrift shops. Ileana had told her the first time they spoke that she didn't like having a maid or nanny, and preferred to be called by her first name. She was the daughter of an architect who was already famous when living in Cuba, and had done some very good work in Miami and other cities in Florida, including a convention center, for which he had won a prize from the College of Cuban Architects in Exile, and was highly esteemed. She worked from home on those days when Gracielita didn't look after the girl. She had arrived in Miami with her parents before she could talk, but she could now speak the two languages fluently, although Gracielita had noticed she was more comfortable in English. While Ileana's mother was always reminiscing about the past, Ileana and her husband Ricardo Lugo didn't speak of Cuba if they could help it, and on a couple of occasions Gracielita witnessed arguments with Ileana's mother, because the young couple repeated constantly that they weren't interested in Cuba and had no intention of moving to the island even if the regime were to change. So the few conversations they had with their first nanny were limited to how the little baby girl had behaved – according to what Gracielita told Yamila a couple of months later, she was 'very bright and good, surprisingly good, enough to encourage you to have one of your own'. As it was, instead of telling Yamila the details of the process she went through to convince herself to work for señora Robledo y Albemar's daughter-in-law, Gracielita let her believe that she was doing fine, giving Spanish classes as always. But, as she explained to her friend a long time later, it wasn't such a big deal. She was almost all the time on her own, the two or three times a week that she went to the couple's apartment, and besides, she didn't have enough money to cover her costs and, what with the imminence of Yamila's journey to Havana, the least she could do was save a little money to send to Inesita and to buy her some things. On the other hand, having begun her second little job in Ileana's house, her correspondence with her mother became limited to a brief monthly letter in which she repeated the same things, giving no clue about her friend's planned journey.

On one occasion Inesita had brought me the two letters that arrived just before Yamila's journey on the eve of July 26th. Her appearance hadn't improved much of late. Quite the opposite. She herself recognized that she was tired of her work and every time she received a letter from her daughter, instead of it making her happy and energizing her, she became more distressed. Gracielita's only fresh news was that she had bought a used Japanese car, which drove well, and that she would soon have some real news.

For my part, I had slackened doing hair somewhat, on the doctor's advice, since I was developing, or rather had already developed bursitis, a kind of rheumatism in my right shoulder, which was getting worse and worse, limiting what I could do. That year something happened that I never thought would happen to me again, although I'd had a premonition it might. But life's like that. It all began little by little. Guillermo's drinking had been getting worse in recent years, to the extent that the GP recommended he see a specialist, since he was drinking so much that he'd be drunk on just a couple of drinks. Of course, this brought many fights, since what with my character and tired of working every day, with hardly any rest, and him having no desire ever to take me out anywhere, the arguments were inevitable. His brothers, who loved me a lot, talked to him, and he promised he was going to change. But he didn't. It reached the point that one night, for the first time since we'd been together, he didn't come home. When he came back on the Sunday afternoon, he told me he'd been on guard duty at work. It was a lie, because a few days later a *compañero* of his from work, who came looking for him, commited an indiscretion, and I found him out. I said nothing to him at the time, but from my indifference he realized that I wasn't happy or convinced by his justifications. He then did the same again and gave me another lame excuse, and so it went on until he became accustomed to disappearing every weekend with the same excuses – that he was on militia duty, or at a Party meeting, and things like that, that not even he'd believe. Foxy lady that I was, I could smell that he was up to something that wasn't exactly what he was telling me. He then disappeared for a whole week without saying absolutely anything. When that happened, even Emilio, another foreman, his friend and *compañero* in Angola, a member of the same Party cell, told me one afternoon that he'd had a long talk with him, and that the only reason he'd given for not going home was that I argued with him about everything. They were very good buddies, and Emilio respected me a lot. I trusted him so much that I asked him to sit facing me and look me in the eyes, and, almost with tears in his eyes, he felt he had to confirm that it was true, Guillermo was with another woman, who didn't compare in the slightest to a woman like me. To begin with, I didn't say anything to anybody, or rather I did, because apart from Emilio, Julia knew, too. But then nobody would have imagined Guillermo was living with a woman in Marianao, and I didn't even want to know her name or what she looked like. My grandchildren, who were now growing up, asked after him, because they loved him a lot, and my answer was always that he was working and working and working; until one day I spoke to my two children, and my son- and daughter-in-law, telling them what they, without asking me, had already thought was happening.

Although for a long time it hurt, like a thorn in my soul, I didn't let it get the better of me and I devoted myself even more to the whims of my grandchildren, who love me to bits. I kept myself busy, as usual, writing, going to the spiritualist sessions in Clarita's house, and the hairdressing once in a while, without putting in too much effort, because I didn't need the money, with what Guillermo would send me from time to time, and the money the kids gave me each month, so I didn't lack anything material, on the contrary. But I can't deny I couldn't get over the emptiness the break up of that more than thirty-year relationship had left in me, especially at my age. And I still wonder how I managed to find the strength to look ahead. But that's why I kept up my writing, which I still hadn't shown anybody; what's more, after I went to the optician and started wearing glasses, I was much more interested in reading. With my children's help, I got hold of good novels and magazines, and always kept myself occupied. I also started to have a social life I hadn't had before and going to the theater and the ballet, which I've always loved; and I'd go more often to help out in the homes of my daughter-in-law and my daughter, who now had five growing children and was working in a special needs school for children who were mentally retarded, like her eldest son, who had meningo-encephalitis when he was two, during the big epidemic in the early 1970s.

That July 26th morning, when Inesita arrived at my place with the biggest smile I'd ever seen on her face, we thought she'd taken the national holiday all for herself, but no, she was bringing the news that Yamila, Gracielita's close friend, had arrived three days before and that Gracielita had sent her all kinds of things, from an envelope with money that she'd left with Yamila for her to buy her some things in the stores for foreigners and Cubans from abroad, to several sets of clothes, shoes, and best of all, an album with lots of photos of her darling daughter. Although the letter wasn't very long, for Gracielita assured her mother that Yamila would be sure to tell her everything, what follows is one of the most interesting fragments:

Mima, I won't deny how envious I am about Yamila's journey to Cuba, but even though I know that it's not the same, it's as if it were me, since she'll be my eyes and ears on this trip. For her it's the realization of her dream of a lifetime, I still don't know what it means for me. Knowing she'll be by your side and hugging you, it's as if I were, and what's more, I asked her to see you again before coming back, and for her not to take off the clothes in which she says goodbye to you. Don't laugh, you know what I'm like. It's now ten at night, and Yamila went out to dinner with her old friend Reinerio, who never got used to her absence. I don't know where all this is leading. I'm taking advantage of a little peace and quiet to finish this letter, which I started almost a month ago, and I've already told you about all my activities. As I said, I'm not going to continue much longer with Ileana, because, as luck has it, she's going to put her daughter in a private nursery that's on the way to her office. I've been keeping myself as far away as possible from the cheap politics of our compatriots here. Apart from it disgusting me, it's a constant prattle that's everywhere, always on about the same subject, of when Fidel falls next year, and when they return to Cuba, and preparations for an invasion by the Freedom Fighters, and all those things. At least I'm meeting people who think a bit different. I've a Cuban friend I go out with sometimes, not often, who's in an organization that isn't warmongering, and I've learned a lot from him. He's not one of those who wants to bring down the government or anything, but rather wants a kind of dialogue with Cubans there, though I don't know how that can be achieved. Don't worry, I'm not thinking

191

about getting involved in any other kind of organization. I know what you're going to say: 'You learn from the blows.' So, Mima, I'm sending you two hundred dollars with this, so Yamila can buy you whatever you need. I'm also sending a bag with drugs and other things, enough for you to share with your close friends, since you need your lifetime friends now more than ever, and this is my way of thanking them for all they do for you. We're not going to sleep tonight, of course, because we have to be at the airport at six, since the charter flight leaves for Havana at ten, and you know how we Cubans always exaggerate things. Since Yamila is one of the organizers of the trip, I'm helping her take calls from the people in her group, who have been arriving on different flights from Boston to meet up with those joining the contingent from other cities, because there are some fifty North-Americans going to the conference. That's all for now. Write to me lots, and talk all you can with Yamila. You know I love her like the sister I never had. I'll be waiting for her at the airport when she gets back, imagining it's you. I'll say goodbye now with a great big hug, your daughter who is the same as ever. Lots of kisses.
Gracielita

During Yamila's visit, Inesita only had the chance to see her twice, because the conference in the Convention Center kept her very occupied, and on two occasions the delegations from several different countries went on excursions to Varadero and Soroa, but it was enough for Inesita to have her first close contact with her daughter's best friend. It was the night before her return to Miami that Yamila took a taxi to Inesita's apartment. Inesita was even more nervous greeting her than when she'd been taken by surprise the first time. Yamila had finally managed to get Inesita to write a list of all the food and other items she needed, and that afternoon, after the farewell reception, she didn't go back to the hotel with the group, but went by one of the special stores and bought not just what Gracielita's mother had asked her for but a lot more. Barely glancing at the two enormous bags filled with all she could buy, Inesita kept hugging her and asked her to tell her again about her daughter. Yamila mixed up memories of how her friendship with Gracielita had begun, and how well they'd got on together from the start. She didn't manage to console her much, since she told her that life wasn't easy in the United States, especially for a relatively young, single woman; and one of the reasons why Gracielita hadn't overcome all her fears was the fact that she hadn't wanted to leave Miami because it was so close to Havana, as if she could take the first plane and return whenever she wanted. Quite apart from the fact that it wasn't easy to return to Cuba for a person like her, who had left through the Mariel boatlift, Gracielita didn't dare even imagine herself in Cuba again, not for the shame she felt about facing her mother, who, being her mother, had forgiven her from the first moment, but because of the possibility of bumping into some of her old work colleagues, or bosses, many of whom were openly hostile to people like her, a feeling that Gracielita shared intensely, though in the opposite direction.

Inesita silently broke into tears, although in a clear voice she told Yamila not to stop talking, to take no notice of her, because she was crying out of happiness for having her there, and at the same time sadness for the imminent parting. Finally, when the time came for the inevitable goodbye, Inesita had calmed down completely, as if to give Yamila that fresh image of her to take back to her daughter in a few hours' time. She hugged her tenderly and accompanied her to the entrance of the passage leading to the street, where the same taxi that had brought her from the hotel was waiting, having come to pick her up at the time she had given.

'Tell her, my dear, tell my Gracielita that I'll always, always be her mother, and give her this hug and this kiss, which are for you as well. You can't imagine the good that your visit has done me. Thank you, and come back one day together.'

***

Yamila's return came at a time when the city of Miami and its most vociferous citizens, were publicly up in arms about another visit, this time of an international character. Although in the end it didn't come to a head, that didn't stop it from being a topic for hot debate on many public and private platforms. To strident protest on the part of leaders of the Afro-North-American community, the Cuban-American mayors of

South Florida refused to give Nelson Mandela, the recently released South African hero, an official welcome. Although Mandela, who was touring several cities in the country, had been invited to a trade union convention, and had never accepted invitations from the city authorities, the reaction of the mayors was taken as a snub and an insult by the African-American community in Miami; and even the Haitians wholly blamed the Cubans, who in their vast majority loudly criticized any kind of relationship with Cuba, her leaders, and above all Fidel. Mandela had publicly expressed his support for the Cuban Revolution for their participation in the war in Angola, and the confrontations with the South African army in which Guillermo had taken part. Gracielita, who was becoming increasingly interested in these problems, which inevitably affected her in one way or another, had saved several newspapers for Yamila, in which there were photos and articles talking about the incident. Among them was a copy of the city's most popular Spanish language newspaper, *El Nuevo Herald*, which carried the photograph of a white Cuban, with the face of a peasant farmer, carrying a placard with the words in English, which Gracielita had translated for us:

> MR MANDELA,
> IF YOU FIGHT FOR FREEDOM
> WHY SUPPORT A DICTATOR LIKE CASTRO?
> THE CUBAN PEOPLE

That was perhaps why the arrival of the first flight from Havana that Friday in early August was much more charged with emotion than usual. On the one hand, the sad goodbyes and uproar of divided families who couldn't possibly carry any more, arguing about paying for excess baggage, doing ridiculous things like putting two, three and even four cowboy hats one on top of the other, to distribute among relatives and friends in the countryside; and the women, many of them fatter than normal, wrapped in half a dozen pairs of trousers, trying to slip through Havana customs, which from time to time would look the other way. On the other hand, the riotous welcome, since the same plane carried passengers to and fro across the Florida Straits, on a journey that barely lasted three-quarters of an hour between Miami and Havana.

Gracielita and Reinerio arrived at the airport separately, for which Gracielita felt very proud of herself, and they met each other in front of one of the terminal entrances where the Marazul travel agency had its assigned dispatch area in Concourse 'D', which, although by alphabetical order one of the first in the semi-circular terminal building, was in an almost abandoned area, apart from the rest. Crossing the wide carpeted corridors of that labyrinth was not easy, because as well as there being far fewer signs than could be found in the other concourses, which clearly indicated where the different airlines were, and gave all the other information needed to board, or to meet passengers, there it was quite the opposite; even the lighting was minimal, as if Special Period began or ended there, turning the journey and the stay into something of a clandestine adventure.

When the first of the passengers began to emerge, the din increased with a mix of shouts of happiness and crying, fainting and all kinds of exclamations, accompanied by not a little swearing, and some insulting the government of the island out loud, along with a smattering of Creole phrases of welcome from the families. Among the crowd, who were jostling to be the first to find their relations, could be seen a few colored Cubans, among them Gracielita, of course, looking all the more mulatta with the intense and prolonged Miami summer, and her new African hairstyle, which was very fashionable, and which Inesita was surprised to see in several photographs in which she appeared with her plentiful hair converted into an enormous mass of pretty little braids. Finally those who from a distance were clearly North-American whites and blacks started to come through. One of the first among them was Yamila, who was very annoyed because customs had confiscated several articles considered communist propaganda, like records, posters and T-shirts, although she'd been able to save a couple of packets of coffee, and even a case of Cuban rum.

After affectionately greeting Gracielita and Reinerio, Yamila said goodbye to the *compañeros* in her group, who were going on to their respective cities, but not before agreeing to file a complaint over the treatment they'd received on returning to the United States, on a journey that had complied with the strict laws of that country's economic blockade against Cuba.

'Good job you got one like this, because in this country they don't make many things on a small scale!'

That was Yamila's comment while putting her bags in the trunk and getting into Gracielita's car, which Gracielita began to drive with ease. Reinerio said goodbye to them both, and promised to visit when he had finished work that evening. During the whole journey, which lasted just over half the flight time between Havana and Miami, Yamila told her she brought lots of love from her mother and, as she had promised, she was wearing the same clothes as when they had hugged the night before in Havana. Gracielita smiled without taking her eyes off the freeway, where cars were flying in all directions, and continued listening to Yamila's report on how she'd found her mother.

Yamila's stay in Miami was shorter then expected, because when she checked long distance, for almost half an hour, the messages on the answer machine in her Boston apartment, among them was a very important work appointment for the following Wednesday and she had to prepare for it over the weekend. But the urgency of her return didn't stop Gracielita satisfying her immense curiosity to know in full detail her reactions to her first trip to Cuba, which she said had been the most overwhelming experience of her life, to the point that she even believed she'd fallen in love with a Cuban and was thinking of returning to Havana as soon as she could. What most impressed her, not only her, but the whole group of North-Americans, was the simplicity of the people, and their humility facing so many problems of every kind they were going through. There had been some setbacks with part of the group, which provoked serious arguments. One of these happened to three of the Afro-North-Americans in the Hotel Capri, where they were staying. It seems the three women, who were also from Boston, were absolutely furious because they said they'd been treated in a racist way. On one occasion there'd been an incident in the dining room, because they complained they didn't eat pork, and the maitre d' said that was all he'd been told to serve them, and to either eat it or leave it, because there was nothing else. Although Yamila had to intervene between the two sides, her *compañeras* and the hotel administration, the incident was just another link in a chain of events that happened to them and other women in the group. One afternoon they decided to take a walk on their own through Old Havana, and a group of youths made fun of their African clothes, and the obesity of one of them. On another occasion, Yamila herself had witnessed how one of the Afro-North-Americans was stopped from entering the hotel, because they thought he was Cuban. Aside from these incidents, which weren't enough to spoil her long-awaited visit, Yamila did comment to Gracielita that there was still a lot to be done in Cuba regarding forms of racism, and that this was a crucial subject that absolutely shouldn't be ignored, above all now that the hateful apartheid system in South Africa was beginning to be dismantled. Yet, according to what Gracielita herself had written to say, Yamila had brought back many hopes and doubts from her trip to Cuba, seeing both its good and its bad sides, all of which had made her reflect and see things from another perspective.

In the following months, every time they spoke on the phone, Yamila always had a new surprise saved up for her, whether about her new Cuban sweetheart, as she described him, or to give her the news that she had been promoted at work and would be in charge of a regional office in Washington, DC, with a salary increase and private funds available to increase the specialist capacity building in the cooperative enterprises initiative. Yamila was to begin her new post at the start of 1991, and she had asked Gracielita to help her to settle in, and so spend Christmas together, an invitation Gracielita immediately accepted.

THE WALL OF WATER

When Gracielita arrived at Washington National Airport, the city was being lashed by a snowstorm that reminded her of her years in the former German Democratic Republic. The first thing she said to Yamila was that in future she would visit her any season but winter. That was her first trip outside Florida since arriving in the United States. She had become so acclimatized that she preferred the hurricanes that from time to time hit the region, to having to protect herself from the cruel winter. The situation was so bad that, in the new car Yamila had hired for two weeks, it was a slow journey home from the National Airport, which is right in the city, and the traffic didn't help.

Yamila had a good apartment, with two bedrooms, two bathrooms, a living-dining area and large kitchen, on 16th Street, in North-East Washington DC. For all Yamila's explanations, Gracielita could not understand why they called it the District of Columbia, nor how you could cross a street and be in another state, yet at the same time Washington DC wasn't a state, but a district, which was the capital of the nation. Such musings kept the two friends up until very late, talking and contemplating the latest snowfall and sipping a reserve rum, saved from Yamila's journey to Cuba. She still didn't have much furniture, because she preferred to have her own, not what was already in the apartment, which she asked to be taken out. She wanted to furnish her new place so as to feel at home. That's why in each of the bedrooms there was just a good mattress on a carpet she'd bought in a store for seconds that hadn't been used and, apart from some small factory defect that you couldn't even see, were in perfect condition. The balcony, which looked out over 16th Street, the one that goes almost to the famous White House, had panoramic glass with a lovely view of the whole avenue. As Gracielita later found out, it was lined on both sides with hundreds of churches, of equal number of denominations and strange cults, 'symbols of the liberty of expression and faith in this country', as Yamila put it, pointing some of them out to her when they went to leave the car in the building's parking lot.

One of the things that most impressed Gracielita was the number Afro-North-Americans in visibly good jobs, something she hadn't seen in Florida – men and women of all shapes and colors, good- and not-so-good-looking, very well dressed, engaged in all kinds of activities. Yet Yamila had warned her that, despite the fact that the population of Washington DC was mainly Black, the real money unfortunately wasn't in the hands of that sector, and race relations were the same as, or worse than, in any other part of the country; and she told her in passing that several blocks away, on the other side of the bridge over the forest, there was one of the most notorious black neighborhoods of the capital, a center for cutting and distributing hard drugs.

One midday, when the storm had passed, Yamila and Gracielita went out to explore the stores that were full of things for the End of Year festivities, and they walked about the city, under a radiant sun tempered by below-zero temperatures. Little by little, as far as the climatic conditions allowed, the two friends did the city tourist circuit: first the museums and government buildings; the monuments to those she'd heard and read so much about, from the White House itself, which she'd imagined to be like an enormous palace and yet is no more than a smallish house painted white, according to her own observations, to the busy corner of 14th Street and U, where the 1968 disturbances exploded in the wake of the assassination of the black leader Martin Luther King, Jr. Another afternoon, shortly before dark, they climbed up the hill to Anacostia, a black neighborhood where there is a museum of Afro-North-American history, where you can look down over the entire city, silvery in the reflection of the new moon on the snow of the previous days. Gracielita was fascinated by the city, which was even more beautiful than she had imagined, perhaps because it was the nerve center of the nation's administrative and political bureaucracy. Since that evening was much more pleasant than the first couple of days after her arrival, and it was Friday, Yamila invited her to dinner at a restaurant in the small city of Richmond, in the state of Virginia, just outside the city, on the other side of the airport, past the famous building of the American military, known as the Pentagon. She'd once been taken there by some friends, who she would later introduce to Gracielita.

'Just look how imposing it is! And to think there's the military brain of the most powerful nation in the world!'

The two women spent a couple of hours enjoying the relaxed, elegant atmosphere of the restaurant, where they lingered over a delicious meal of Italian pasta and meat, accompanied by an exquisite beer. Then they returned to the city, and after some difficulty found parking on a kind of wasteland watched over by two black men, wrapped in an array of dirty, crumpled old clothes that hardly seemed to protect them from the cold.

'It costs a bit more, but we're close and the parking is safe.'

She locked the car, and holding on to each other's arm to stay upright on the snow and ice of the sidewalk, they backtracked towards the club that Yamila had mentioned, though Yamila gave her no clue as to what to expect. The street was very lively, with restaurants, cafés, and even bookstores open late into the night, while cars drove up and down in a fruitless search for a free parking space. Yamila stopped opposite the entrance to the club, and gestured upward with her head. In one of the upper windows, above the entrance, was a Cuban flag, and underneath, in sky-blue neon lights, the name:

HABANA VILLAGE – GALERÍA CAFÉ

Gracielita looked in surprise more than anything else at Yamila, who took advantage of her being taken aback to invite her to push open the thick glass door and go up the stairs, down which came a vapour of humid air, thick with smoke, and a sweet-sounding music that was very much her own.

When they'd managed to settle themselves into a corner at one end of the bar, Yamila signalled to a young-looking man with fun written all over his face, who, microphone in hand, was singing an old *son montuno* of Felix Chappotin, enlivening the party, which had an unmistakably Cuban flavour, because Eduardo, this mulatto with a smile flashing from his lips, radiated Cuba all over. With a wave of his hand, he let Yamila know he'd seen her and would shortly be over. At the entrance to the small cubicle where Eduardo was DJ-ing were several apparently empty record jackets. One had a colored drawing of the famous Puerto Rican singer Daniel Santos, known as *'el inquieto Anacobero'* and really popular in Cuba in the

1950s; another was of Beny Moré, and that famous photo of him in the Jardines de la Tropical... Those were the days!

Yamila and Gracielita, who hadn't been thought of, let alone born, at that time, took refuge in a little corner of the club surrounded by mementos of Cuba, with walls autographed by fleeting visitors and impromptu lovers; decorated with the *íremes* of *abakuá*, maracas, little Cuban and Puerto Rican flags and banners, straw hats, posters and placards from before and after the Revolution. Behind the bar, above the icebox, were countless bottles of spirits, and at the back, covering the entire length of the exposed brick wall, was a panel of mirrors, almost completely covered with bills of different denominations, colors and nationalities, most of them Cuban – a futile attempt to hide the defects in the plasterwork. In another corner, out of reach beside the fire extinguisher, hung one of the simplest of musical instruments so characteristic of Cuban music, a *güiro*. But as if all that wasn't enough, there were the handwritten signs in large lettering, and deliberately misspelled:

PLEEZ NO DWINKS ON THE DANSE FLOOR
EVERY PEOPLE WITH ITS WORLD
ART AND FOLKLORE
MY WORLD IS EVERY PEOPLE

and things like that.

'Where have you brought me, woman?' asked Gracielita, who was enjoying herself immensely, but her question was lost in Eduardo's sudden announcement over the microphone that two new friends of his had just arrived in the club. He immediately left the music department in the hands of one of the barmen who had been looking after the noisy and demanding mixed crowd of mainly Hispanics and North-Americans. When Eduardo reached the two friends, he was effusive in his hugs and kisses for everyone, without waiting for Yamila, even with a minimum of formality, to introduce him to Gracielita. Eduardo was sweating copiously. His hair was shaved off, and his head was shiny. With a quick gesture he called over one of the barmen, who had a lot of straight jet-black hair, contrasting with his small slanting eyes, and the suspicion he was of Asian origin was confirmed when Eduardo presented him as 'my friend from Vietnam-Cuba', and told him to bring them whatever they wanted, on the house. He then excused himself, to return to his role as animator of the party, his party, saying he would be back later.

'This Eduardo is the best I've met in a long time. Tony, a North-American friend who went with us on the trip to Cuba, introduced him to me last week. I haven't known him long, but I feel I can trust him. You'll be surprised to know that he arrived in this country by the same route as you, through Mariel.'

Of all the nightclubs in that half-Bohemian neighborhood of Mont Pleasant, Habana Village was the last to close. Sometime after three in the morning, the volume of music and dancers had dwindled. Messing around with Tony, Richard and Yamila, Gracielita had spent an unforgettable night, dancing as she hadn't danced in years. Now she was chatting with Tony, who was very taken with her. Born and raised in San Francisco, California, he worked in a Latin American investment bank, but his main interest wasn't finance, it was books – aside from his solidarity work, not only with Cuba and other countries of the South, but Cuba held a special place in his heart, as he led Gracielita to understand, speaking to her the whole time in Cuban Spanish, with an amusing North-American accent.

'I love Eduardo, he's a man with a big heart.'

And so saying, he opened his arms like an airplane.

Not being able to avoid raising her voice, Gracielita told Tony a bit too much about her life, perhaps having drunk more than she should have. Eduardo, who had almost completely disappeared with the arrival of Tony and Richard, now returned to the table with an enormous Italian pot of coffee and several small cups, plates with chocolate cake, spoons and a sugar bowl. The group clapped and made space for him. The conversation from then on was in English, so nobody would be left out.

Eduardo talked about about his philosophy of life, and said, in case anyone didn't know it already, that his club was open to all good-hearted people, without distinction, all those who respected others, both physically and intellectually.

'I believe in democracy. There are people who come to our club even from the Cuban Embassy, we celebrate patriotic dates, we read the work of Cuban poets who are still in Cuba, or who live in other countries. Many friends of Cuba come, many who've been to Cuba for a thousand and one reasons, and I don't question them. I just want them to respect me as I respect them, otherwise there's no place for them here. I have no bitterness about the past. My motto is 'live and let live', and things have gone well enough for me that way. Ever since I left through Mariel, I haven't been back to Cuba, but my heart is there, and it always will be. The right moment will come for me to return, even if it's for just a short while!'

Eduardo and Gracielita looked intensely at each other, and their eyes watered.

'Sister, I love you so much and life isn't long enough!'

Eduardo and Gracielita embraced silently in a tight fraternal hug, at which point the 'Vietnamese-Cuban' barman took the opportunity to make a triumphal entrance flourishing a bottle of the famous Paticruzado rum from Santiago de Cuba that Yamila had saved for just such an occasion, and several days ago had given to Eduardo as a gift for Christmas. Only Huang-Troi knew its hiding place beneath the sink, which is why, as he uncorked it and placed it ceremoniously on the table, Eduardo teased him, and the group clapped all together. Before Yamila could serve, Troi himself let spill a few drops of the glorious matured rum on the floor, and in a really Cuban accent defended his action: 'So the the spirits can get drunk as hell, too!'

The group had grown with the late arrival of Sergio, another very likeable black Cuban, judging from Gracielita's comments. He had arrived in the United States by way of several other countries, because he'd been the bo'sun of a Cuban merchant ship and one fine day disappeared in a Canadian port. He now worked in publicity and accounting for a small print business, and his ambition, when the time was right, was to establish himself in Havana. Some of them mixed the hot coffee with the rum, others enjoyed them separately, but nobody missed trying both drinks, toasting each other more than once.

Gracielita was very happy. This was an atmosphere totally unlike the one she'd so far known in Florida, and she wondered how she'd distanced herself from it for so long. When Tony's head began to nod and the whole group was feeling physically exhausted, Yamila was the first to suggest they call an end to the session. They began to kiss each other goodbye, but not without having accepted an invitation Tony had thrown to the group for that same afternoon, to go to the birthday party of a friend who was Cuban-American like Yamila.

The phone ringing was what woke Gracielita some time after two that afternoon. She'd slept very relaxed from the effects of the drink. Yamila came by her bedroom to let her know that at five o'clock Eduardo and Sergio would come by to meet them, and that Tony and Richard would be going under their own steam a bit later.

As she stretched out on the soft mattress, Gracielita had the pleasant sensation that for the first time in years she felt very happy with her new, true friends. Even though she'd met them only the other day, as it were, it seemed she'd always known them, and that in one way or another they belonged to a past in her life she'd neglected.

Eduardo and Sergio finally arrived, very well dressed in wool sweaters and thick leather sports jackets that were much admired by their two hostesses. Neither of them had had the opportunity to visit Yamila's apartment. After taking off their coats, they made themselves comfortable on a pair of thick cushions next to the new flower-print damask sofa, and helped themselves to the white wine and crackers with cheese and salami already laid out on a tray. The two men had met by accident in that very city, and, according to Eduardo, they had both left Miami for the same reasons:

'Sister, you know Miami's no good! It holds you back. We know full well from experience. The only good thing that hamlet has is the climate, and for that, wait till spring and summer to come here in DC. The world's most beautiful flowering cherry trees, after Japan, of course, can be seen here. It's a shame there's no sea, but, well, the Potomac is enough for us.'

Yamila nodded in agreement and looked at her three friends. Almost immediately Eduardo explained a little more:

'For me, the worst of Cuba is concentrated in Miami. I don't mean that only the bad types are there, because there are some very good people, but the envy, the gossip, the greed, the politicking, the racism – all that crap we Cubans know all about – have spread like weeds. The worst of it is that you have to swallow it every day like a laxative, on the radio, in the newspapers, on the street, in the store, everywhere, and you can't complain, or they crucify you in public or assault you in private. And if you're black, you're screwed, sister! Those sons of bitches who want everyone to think exactly the same as them are a worse copy of the ones we left behind in Cuba. Those people wipe their ass on North-American democracy.'

Eduardo laughed at his own witty remarks, and his laughter infected the others, when Sergio took advantage of the moment to make an impression with his own piece of wisdom:

'Here in DC there's something of everything, but the dose of Cubans isn't as much as down there. At least there are many black North-Americans, and not just in the ghettos, which is a big advantage for us. The atmosphere isn't so hostile, though it is a violent city, like all big North-American cities, with the same problems. Here any kid might stop you face-on and empty an easily acquired automatic pistol into you. Since I came here over five years ago – and Eduardo, who's known me from before then, knows this full well – I've changed my way of thinking a great deal, as I've learned things I didn't want to know before. It wouldn't be wrong of me to say I've become more revolutionary than I ever was in Cuba, just as I've become more capitalist, and I'm ready to help our country one day. The United States has been a great school for me. I've learned a lot more than I thought, because you land in this country excited by what they tell you, what you hear and see in the cinema and on television, but the reality is different. In two words, pure propaganda. That's why you can keep Miami with its palm trees, its coconut trees, and its palmettos, and all the rest of the nostalgia.'

With Sergio's final comments, the two couples prepared to leave for Magdalena's birthday party. The afternoon sun was radiant and the snow on the street had melted in part, though the pavements were slippery with ice and everywhere could be seen dirty mounds of snow, of varying sizes, shoveled either by people who could earn a little money by their initiative, or by special machines driven by the city's public service employees.

Magdalena had an apartment in a very cute, chic neighborhood, called Georgetown, just like the university where she worked in the audio-visual department.

'This neighborhood isn't the most exclusive in DC, but not everyone lives here, sister, and very few blacks like us. This is like Vedado in its day. The thing is that Magdalena's one of a kind. Good Cuban that she is, she knows the system inside out. You'll see, she's a great person. We love her. She's done everything, from marrying a very rich Arab then divorcing him, and he left her with plenty of money, to helping Cuba however she can, going and coming whenever she wants with no problem. And best of all is that nobody bothers her, because nobody would want her as an enemy. She's got quite a tongue! All Cubans from other lands passing through Washington have to meet Magdalena, and if they're from Cuba, she throws a reception. She's super, you'll see. She's an institution in her own right.'

The party was very nice and elegant, livened up by more Cubans than Gracielita and Yamila expected. For a moment Gracielita felt uncomfortable in that strange atmosphere, but luck was with her and the feeling passed when Sergio made the formal introductions, and Magdalena gave her personal attention. Eduardo and Sergio stayed talking with Yamila until Tony and Richard arrived, while Magdalena and Gracielita had a brief conversation about the changes in Eastern Europe, and in particular the GDR, once Gracielita mentioned that she'd studied in that part of Germany. 'I was on the other side of that wall they brought down, I was right there,' she told Magdalena, who'd invited her to follow her into the kitchen. Gracielita thought then about one of the last letters from Helga, her friend in Dresden, and the Christmas card she'd received, with a lovely message, saying among other things:

May your Wall of Water dissolve soon, too

Tony and Richard had come over to Magdalena and Gracielita, who were putting the final touches to a wonderful fresh fruit salad, and greeted the two women warmly. Then Tony took Gracielita by the arm and introduced her to the ten or fifteen people who were talking and eating, eating and talking, while a familiar Cuban bolero she couldn't immediately identify erupted into that festive atmosphere that enveloped her that early Christmas Eve. She became more nostalgic than she cared to be, partly because she'd forgotten about white Christmas, especially in certain places where the seasons changed through the year, but also because she was thinking a lot about her mother and the things she didn't have, and what she might be doing at that precise moment. But Tony brought her out of herself:

'I'm sorry last night I couldn't pay you the attention you deserve, but after an exhausting week of work, I was dead tired.'

Although he had no reason to excuse himself, Gracielita took it as a gentlemanly gesture on his part, and told him that it didn't matter. She then mixed with the other guests, and even joined in a spontaneous and improvised chorus that began to sing *With You From Afar*, that lovely bolero of César Portillo de la Luz, which goes:

> *There isn't a moment of the day*
> *When I can be away from you,*
> *The world seems different*
> *When you're not with me.*

In the meantime, two or three couples succumbed to temptation, and Sergio surprised her with a charming invitation, having cut a bud from the red roses Magdalena had in several vases. The two of them joined in the growing chorus and began to dance the way you're supposed to dance a bolero:

Pedro Pérez Sarduy

Far beyond your lips,
The sun and the stars,
Darling, I am there
With you from afar.

Left High and Dry

Since Gracielita left for the North, things had changed a lot in Cuba, especially people who were behaving more aggressively than normal. Sometimes my heart would miss a beat, imagining the cowries turning and life going back to being even worse than it was before. That's what I was thinking as I read Gracielita's letters and because things were continuing to get worse, without being able to see any light at the end of the tunnel, as Eneida, Baba's woman, used to say, 'if you see it, don't get carried away, it won't last', referring to the constant and increasingly frequent power cuts. You couldn't give Eneida the slightest chance to speak, because if you did, you wouldn't hear the end of it:

'Things are getting so bad you can't make ends meet, damn it! You get up, and there's no water in the fucking tap; you try to cook, and you run out of gas; you got hold of an egg, and there's no oil to fry it in; if you switch on the television to watch the soap, there's a power cut; and if you go to bed, you can't switch on the fan and close your eyes... For how long, Blessed *Santa Bárbara!*'

My own life had changed enormously, and though it didn't show, everyone knew.

It had all started when Luisito, one of Guillermo's brothers, turned up at the house one day to give me the news that my ex-husband was very ill with lung cancer and the doctors had given him only six months to live. To be honest, I'm not sure what went through my mind at that moment. I wanted to pull my hair, run out screaming and crying, but I did none of that. I very calmly got up from the rocking chair and went to the kitchen to make some coffee and smoke a cigarette with my brother-in-law, because despite everything, Luisito and Guillermo's other brothers and sisters loved me a lot, and all continued to affectionately call me their 'sis'. I don't know if it was the drinking, the low life, or the smoking that had finished him off. You never know with cancer. Nor could I remember when I'd last seen him. After he left, he turned up some five or six months later, but we didn't speak much, because he didn't dare look me in the face, and didn't even collect his clothes and things, but sent Luisito to do it. Friends who saw him at work, on the street, and later in the hospital when he was undergoing treatment, said I wouldn't have recognized him, he was so thin, and he felt too embarrassed to face me, about which I don't have the slightest doubt.

On the day he finally died, I can't deny I hurt deep in my soul, but I didn't cry. That night, Luisito came to fetch me, and we went together to the funeral parlor, where I spent several hours, not beside the casket where he was lying, but in another room there, with the sisters and the wives of the brothers. The woman who had been his lover didn't show up at all; it seems she had left him after finding out the cancer had progressed so quickly, and the relationship went downhill. When he gave up work, he suddenly found himself alone, abandoned, and with a few months to live. That was what was on my mind when I stopped for a while gazing at his wasted but calm face through the glass of the coffin. I would have liked to have been able to look after him in his final days. I just drew closer to the glass that covered the upper part of the coffin, and I left him with a goodbye kiss across the insuperable abyss that separated us at that moment. Even then I didn't shed a tear.

I was never the same after that. It all seemed to happen at once. On the one hand my daughter finally separated from her husband, since they were fighting so much, and it was affecting the children; and my son, the journalist, had sought permission from his job at ICR-T, and had gone to Europe with his wife, and little boy and girl. What was left of me was wasting away, and only I knew it. Although my two children kept me up to date with what they were doing, it wasn't the same. As time went by, I stopped seeing to my clients and the hairdressing. I was almost at the end of my tether, and to top it all couldn't find consolation with anyone. I knew I wouldn't, because the santos had told me we legitimate daughters of *Yemayá Olokun* have such a destiny. It was then that I took solace in my memories, and went back to writing a bit about the things that had happened to me over the years, perhaps owing in part to the influence of my son, and the long letters we wrote to each other.

Meanwhile, the *solar* more or less went unchanged, except for one scandal that could be seen coming. Katiushka, the oldest daughter of Baba and Eneida, had been arrested for being a professional *jinetera* and going around with foreign currency. Long before she had turned fifteen, the girl had developed an incredible woman's body. I remember that when she was at primary school, Eneida had serious arguments with the headmistress, shouting and everything, because it was difficult to convince her that she was still underage, just a little girl. What I mean is that Katia, as they called her, had more of a woman's body than her sixteen or seventeen years might suggest. Unlike all her brothers, and even the other girl, Katia wasn't interested in studying; her ambition was to be a model, but Eneida, with her big mouth, always criticized her a lot, saying to the girl, her own daughter, whom she without question adored with all her heart: 'Can't you see you've got too much ass and you're too much of a slut to be a model!' It was true, she had more than enough vocation and body. The girl had always liked dessing well and the easy life, with no sacrifice. Always out to impress with her clothes and her ways, Katia attracted men like flies to honey, and since she'd always known this, she took advantage of it. Tall as she was, and with such a slender long neck, the short, fifties' hairstyle really suited her. That fashion of young women wearing their hair close-cut, almost shaven, was not common in Havana, and of course anything strange attracts attention. Another thing was her smooth way of walking, with long steps, and very upright, showing off the almost perfect shape of her shoulders, seemingly always having plenty of time for everything. When she was home, all she did was fix her fingernails and toenails, since she liked to go around in sandals, shorts, or jeans. As she usually got up late, after people had left for school and work, she had free rein in the yard, to go about her business, and tell stories about the mischief she got up to with the foreigners. She even looked like a foreigner, and she exploited this; whatever she threw on, whether simple or extravagant, looked good on her. Some people are just favored by the gods! Strangest of all was how unconcerned she seemed about life, and anything to do with physical exertion. That's how she was.

To begin with, when Katia began to go out at night and come back in the early hours of the morning, Eneida was the last person to hold her to account, saying it was what the young did. To a certain extent this was true, and she did have Cuban friends, though they weren't just any Cubans, but the new young Miramar set, who would all go to one of the most famous discotheques in Havana at the time.

Katia once told me she had a boyfriend, who drove his father's Lada, who she went dancing with at El Johnny, a club on Zero Street, near the Miramar tunnel. But she left him because he was too stuck-up. I told her I didn't know the club, and that it must be new; but no, it turns out I was once in service near there, and in its day the club had been called La Red. Anyway, it was there that this young set went to dance, as if they were in another country. There were few, if any, blacks among them. I wasn't the one to say that, because I didn't go to that type of club, and not even Katia could make it up, it was her own experience, and it came out in that same way of speaking as her mother:

'Ay, no, woman, no way! Blacks don't fit in there at all. The music they play in El Johnny is disco-*miusic*, which is foreign music, with jumping, shaking and all that stupidity. There's no salsa, no Cuban music of the Van Van, or those other vulgar bands the *aseres* dance to. It's like being in Miami there, without leaving Cuba. It's the *pepillo* in-set, and from what I know, blacks aren't *pepillos*, they're tough *guaposos*.'

Katia, who had always had a tongue for saying what she thought, told me that nobody knew she lived in a *solar*, at least, nobody in the *pepillada* that met in the club, and although they would sometimes invite her to a party at one or other of their houses, she had always declined:

'I'm the independent kind, Marta. I don't want to be in with the Cubans, least of all them. They're all machista and right away want to control your life. They're too pretentious, always showing off their Swiss and Japanese watches, or the latest T-shirt *Papá* or *Mamá* brought them back from abroad. And they're very racist, because you'll never see them even with a mulatta like me, just blondes, even if it's dyed. They're all the sons of leaders or intellectuals and buy in the stores for foreigners. They're always throwing it in your face, and I want nothing to do with it. My dear, it's another world! That's why I prefer the foreigners, who know how to appreciate the good things in life.'

Sometimes, almost at dawn and when one or other of us was finishing the CDR night watch, keeping an eye on the block, she'd arrive, in a car with the license plate of a foreign technician, or diplomat, or tourist. When her father found out, all he said was not to get him caught up in problems with foreigners, or anything of the sort, because both she and her mother knew he had a position to maintain, as a member of the Party and of the Armed Forces. Although her 'friends', so Katia said, were decent people, everyone knew that no one came home at that hour of night from church, especially smelling of alcohol and American cigarettes, in a fine car, with a man at the wheel, no matter how old, sunburned from the beach, and, worst of all, foreign – saying goodbye to him with lots of kisses and squeezes. And it was one after another, always someone different. People knew that Katia was also caught up in the *bisneo* that had become fashionable, going around romancing foreigners who could buy in the hard-currency stores, and that helped her mother out a lot with food and her brothers and sisters with T-shirts and trinkets. Nobody bothered. Not only that, what with things as they were, nobody could interfere in anyone else's life, least of all with Katia, who might have been soft-spoken but had a real temper. With her, no man's getting a free fondle, or intimidating her, and least of all cursing her. So her mother said to herself deep down that Katia knew full well how to defend herself, and was safe wherever she might be. 'The problem is she's a real slut, Marta, and you can't go around being such a slut these days,' was what Eneida would say, and Katia herself confirmed it when she told her stories in the passageway about what the men from different countries would do, the Europeans, the South Americans and the Scandinavians, among others, when she climbed on top of them, as if she were mounting a horse, and told them to keep still, that she was the one who was going to do the riding.

'To avoid problems I don't go with Cubans, because if one of those fuckers lifts a hand to me, I'll cut it off, I sure would, and then I'd really be screwed. I don't know what all the mystery is about, when we should be given a medal because our contribution to the economy is making Cuba known and helping the country.'

What a girl! You had to hear her to appreciate who that Katia really was! Well, the thing is that Katiushka passed herself off as a foreigner and stayed for six weeks in the Hotel Riviera. None other than the Hotel Riviera, on the seafront! There she was, enjoying all the privileges in the swimming pool, in the bar, in the restaurant, having massages, in the steam room, having a manicure and having her hair done, and all that, as a millionaire from some Caribbean country or other, Martinique I think, French Martinica, or something like that. The thing is that she even changed her name, and since she'd studied French in a language school, people who know say she spoke it well, and so she fooled the hotel staff. One day, in the restaurant, they brought her a mixed salad, and she pretended she'd never seen an avocado in her life. The whole time, she put everything on the tab, and she'd become very popular because she gave the staff little gifts. She'd get socks and underwear for the children of the lift operators, so that they'd look the other way when she went up with her friends; she gave ballpoint pens and soap to the receptionist and telephone operators so they'd take her messages; and little bottles of rum and batteries for transistor radios to the taxi drivers, so they'd fetch and carry her no matter where and whatever the hour. She became a head of public relations, organizing informal meetings between foreigners who came as tourists or to set up a business in the country and her Cuban friends, men and women, all very beautiful, who like her were into the *jineterío*. Katia had a friend who was almost always with her, like a bodyguard, a handsome black man known as '*Chocolatico*', who was very mysterious because he didn't let himself be seen much, and, according to the stories, even comes highly recommended from abroad and is much sought after, because he always strives to give the European women very personal attention. Yes, there are those who specialize by region. For example, there are those, male and female, who take care of Mexico, Chile, Argentina and Brazil; others look after the Spanish, Germans, Swiss, and so on. According to Katia's stories, whenever she met up with a Frenchman, she gave everything.

'They're the best, Marta, I swear, they're the best!'

I learned all this from her stories, which were told for everyone to hear, right out in the yard.

But, well, when the month passes, and she hasn't paid her bill, the deputy manager of the hotel begins to leave messages in her box for her to settle her tab, since she was over her credit limit of two thousand pesos. She acts all innocent, and starts to invent stories, one after another, until they suspend her credit. Then, that same day, she gets clumsy and really puts her foot in it. She starts to protest to the administrator, and instead of disappearing, since she knows she's already in trouble, the girl begins to complain about and insults the head of reception, who had reported her to the hotel supervisor, for the security guards to investigate the case; and they in turn pass the matter on to the economic police, and then the whole case is uncovered, because they'd searched her room and found banknotes and coins from many countries, which apparently amounted to quite a lot of money. It was just as well she wasn't caught up in anything political. When they finally arrested her that morning, in the swimming pool, the first thing she did was to justify herself saying that her husband is the foreigner, not her, and that in his country the woman takes the husband's surname, and that's why she signed with his name, but that he wasn't in Cuba at that moment; then she came out with the story that her fiancé had promised they were going to get married when he came back from a business trip to another country, and he hadn't come back yet. I don't know how many stories she invented, because she insisted she was a 'pure-blooded' Martinican. But lies are lies, and sooner or later they begin to come out, like a sea surges over the shoreline. At least it happened when her father was away three months, working as an instructor in a military academy outside the capital. Although he tolerated a lot of irregularities in his children, I'm sure she wouldn't have had an easy time of it if he'd found out, for he'd warned her not to complicate his life, since he had no time for her foolishness. So Eneida wasn't surprised when a police patrol car arrived asking for Katiushka's parents, and later we found out in detail what had happened, because there's nothing like a Cuban when it comes to gossip. That day, Eneida acted as if she didn't know anything; she went crazy, and we had to give her water for an attack of nerves, and all the police did was to leave her a paper to go to the police station to see her daughter. But she, Eneida, was to blame, when all's said and done, for having encouraged the girl to go out and look for 'a man with money, and if he's white, better still, because the blacks aren't good for anything except hitting you and making you pregnant.' Or if not that, then she should always look for a man with lighter skin than herself, to 'improve' the race; or that she was going to suggest to Fidel that if he wanted to sort out the country's problems, he should make the mulattas an industry, and include them in the export plans.

'Sugar and mulattas, lots of mulattas, because the mulattas are the fucking future of mankind!'

Of course, she shouted and cursed like this in the yard when her husband wasn't home, and since everyone in that damned *solar* does just what they like, we took no notice. But her eldest daughter did, and the one who was coming up behind was on the same path. Eneida's sons agreed that their mother wasn't right in the head. Without a doubt, Katiushka had an enormous capacity as a man-eater, but I think it was for that very reason that she treated them badly, and wasn't seriously interested in any. What I mean is that never, in all the years that I've known her, has she shown herself to be seriously in love with any man. But she gives them all pleasure, and, according to her, each one is a little box of surprises.

'It's just that I'm naturally hot, Marta, and I get really excited, and they know nothing.'

That's what her comments were like when she was about to confess. In the end they sentenced her to two years in the Bello Amanecer rehabilitation camp for women, out by the Monumental Highway. They didn't give her longer because Eneida pushed Baba, reluctantly, to intervene. Her father would have really liked them to give his daughter five years in prison, to reform her, as he himself said after they announced the sentence at court in Old Havana, 'because otherwise that damned girl's going to end up in the cemetery for being so stupid.' In the end, she served only eighteen months, on a rehabilitation plan that consisted of working on a chicken farm from five in the morning till noon, and then studying in the afternoon, from two to five. They even had her teaching French to the other inmates.

When Katia finally came out of the women's prison with a very good record, the welcome we gave her that day in the *solar*, and even the whole block, was like one big birthday party.

'All that, and we're the real guerrillas, *jineteras mambisas*, and proud of it!'

That was the very first thing she said to me when she came to say hello, give me a kiss, and ask if I'd cut her hair, which had grown a lot.

'Of course, girl, but make sure you take better care next time!' I answered, and she continued on to her own house, if that's how you can describe that small place where I don't know how seven adults fitted, because there's a living room that at night turns into a dining room and then a bedroom, because the rest is a small room with a shower and toilet, right next to the kitchen.

That was the biggest incident in the *solar* during those years. Apart from that, life was harder than ever for us, now that the Soviet Union had become an unexpected corpse, and we'd been left high and dry, as Eneida liked to mouth off constantly. I told Inesita she should be happy that her daughter was outside the country, although this wasn't much consolation, as I can confirm from my own experience. I knew that my son and his family were fine where they were in Europe, yet I couldn't help but miss them a lot. Their situation was different, however, from Gracielita's, since he wasn't one of those who leave the country with permission to travel and when they're out end up staying wherever they can rather than return to Cuba. But you can't have everything. Children grow up, they become independent, and you can't be fussing over them as you did when you were breastfeeding them. The thing is, for a mother, her children never grow up.

It was talking about children with Inesita and Julia one Sunday afternoon, commenting on Katia and how well things were going for her now, that the comparison between their state of mind and mine stood out, and we spoke a lot about how a mother's love will always be selfish. Inesita was much better, although it was a real struggle for a single person to live off the ration book, and almost everyone made sacrifices to tighten their belts with the announcement that a Special Period of economic austerity was coming, and we'd know when it was to begin, but not when it would end. What with first the elimination of the free farmers markets, and then that new Russian transplant that people called *pereztrópika*, it was just as well it never worked or we'd have ended up copying that as well. Anyway, it was all the same to us, because as long as we can remember, we've come out of one Special Period to go into another, foraging all the time. But, as the old folk say, 'after it rains, it clears'.

When it was getting dark and Inesita was preparing to return to Marianao, one of my clients, Olguita, who I hadn't seen for a while, came by my place since she wanted me to do her hair on Tuesday, during the day, because that night she was going to the Carlos Marx Theater, to a concert by the well-known *Nueva Trova* movement singer and composer, Omar, who had a house in the Siboney neighborhood that she was looking after the whole time, because he traveled a lot in Latin America and Spain.

'So, there I am, passing myself off as white, until they find out! With Oscar, things are going better for me than ever before. You know he's quite a celebrity, and he's not up to anything, because he doesn't need to be. He earns a lot of money, and he's got everything he wants. He even had a recording studio built in what was once the library, because it's a real mansion, with marble floors and stairs. When he's in the country he spends the whole time in his studio, composing his songs, and nobody disturbs him. I answer the phone, taking messages from his friends and people from the music company, and he even leaves me messages that I have to send on the fax machine, which is the best little toy I've seen in my whole life. Can you believe it, sending written letters by phone! After his wife left him and he stopped all that fooling around he got up to when he was younger, the people who come to his house are decent folk – well, so far as it goes, because artists are always into all sorts of things. I look after his visitors, who come from all over the world, and every night is like a party, but an organized party, as though it were a wake, singing his songs on the guitar; or sometimes it's the group that accompanies him on his foreign tours, and it all goes on till the next morning, when I make them a decent breakfast, and some of them stay to sleep, especially the foreigners, most of them Brazilians, Mexicans, Argentineans and Spaniards, because the house is enormous and beautiful, with even a swimming pool, and all that. Omar is very good to me, and trusts and respects me a lot. That's why

I promised I'd go to his concert, and I want to look as elegant as possible, because I've a couple of good seats for me and my friend.'

When I asked Olguita how she'd managed to get such a good job, all she said was that since he was a great artist loved by everybody, she felt it her revolutionary duty to help him in his career. But that was just a ploy so as not to have to say any more! Not so much to protect herself, since if you press her just a little she'll talk the hind legs off a donkey, but rather to protect Omar, because everyone knew him and held him in high esteem. To tell the truth, few people knew he had a maid, which is why Olguita acted as though she were his secretary, and although she's pleasant enough, she doesn't look like anybody's secretary. After she'd decided to give up teaching Russian, Olguita had found she liked domestic work and had no intention of giving it up. With her light-hearted attitude to life, she always managed to have things work out well for her. And besides, more and more middle-aged women like her were doing the same.

'You have to take life as it comes, honey, and always be on top of things. Never underneath. Without being an educated person, I've become his private secretary. And it's all very serious, so serious that I don't give the phone number even to my own family, which he appreciates a lot. Anyone who wants to see me has to send me a message by fax, but since almost nobody has a fax... well, you can imagine! And all this has its payback, of course. Each to his own. Well, my dears, see you Tuesday.'

Olguita hadn't changed. She was the most cheerful woman I'd ever known. She always faced the world with a sense of irony, and had a new story each time she came by my place. Her last visit wasn't to have her hair done but to bring me a Mothers' Day gift. It wasn't much, but it's the thought that counts, especially coming from someone who isn't even a relation of yours. And here was Olguita with her stories again. Although she was no longer in the Youth, she somehow managed to find out all the gossip that never reached the street, at least not in all its detail.

'Ay, girl! I tell you, all those whites are the same, even if they swap the Marxist manual for the Bible. They all react alike when you prick them where it most hurts, like everyone does. It turns out that in my half-brother's Party cell, there was a nasty situation because one of the members handed in his Party card at a meeting, because he was completely opposed to his daughter getting married. But the situation wasn't as simple as it seems. It turns out that this man's daughter studied in a boarding school in the countryside, and she fell in love with a classmate, whose father belonged to the same cell. When the girl's father found out her boyfriend was black, he screamed bloody murder, and things became really heated when the two decided to get married, and her father took it out on his Party *compañero*. The boy's father asked him what all the fuss was about: the two had known each other a long time, they were good kids, studious, even members of the Youth, they wouldn't have a problem with housing, since there was space in both their houses, so what on earth was the problem? But the girl's father said no, no way, that each should keep to their own, and it all started, with insults and all. The argument went further and reached the secretary of the Party cell, who called a meeting to discuss the case. There, the girl's father said that the Revolution had demanded that he make all kinds of sacrifices, and that he had never refused, but he wasn't prepared to allow his daughter to date or marry... He couldn't say the word, because he wasn't going to say 'with a black', or 'with a black *compañero*', or 'with the son of a black *compañero*'. In the end he pointed to where his *compañero* was sitting and muttered 'with his son' through his teeth, at the same time taking his membership card from his pocket and handing it over, with tears in his eyes, to the cell secretary, which effectively meant his resignation. Of course they accepted it, although not without first trying to convince him that he was committing a political error that he'd regret. The poor man – I say poor, because he can't be anything else, carrying around such prejudice – well, the poor man even punished his daughter to stop her seeing her fiancé, but they managed to meet in secret, because their school friends found out about what happened and the Youth supported their cause, because they were very good students, like I said. In the end they got married, because they're of age, without the consent of the girl's parents. They had the wedding at the school, with a reception and everything. Now they're living with the boy's parents. So, what do you think about that?'

That was the last story Olguita brought me, along with that Mothers' Day gift, which was a couple of bars of Mirurgia soap, from Spain, which I hadn't smelled for ages.

After that Sunday, which we spent happily gossiping and chatting about when we were young and about the struggle of daily life, Inesita disappeared. She not only stopped attending her spiritualist sessions in Clarita's house, but also stopped paying us her occasional visits. Nobody knew what was up, and, to be honest, I didn't do much to find out, because with so many headaches, I didn't need any more. But one day – I can't remember exactly whether it was a Thursday or a Friday morning – Inesita appeared, really agitated, with a couple of envelopes with two letters from

Gracielita that had arrived through a friend of Yamila who was in Havana with a group of North-American journalists. In the first letter, a little hurried and shorter than the second one, she told her mother she was on the point of moving to Washington, where, with Yamila's help, she'd found a job. In the other, with much more detail and already settled in Washington, she said she was very close to Yamila's apartment and just around the corner from the Cuban Interests Section, and she'd pass it every day on her way to work. One day she decided to find out what the procedure was for traveling to Cuba and began the process to come at a future date, and soon she would tell her when.

Inesita was choked with emotion. She wanted to sort out the letter of invitation that Gracielita needed that very day, to hand it into the Immigration office in Havana. I helped her, of course. From then on Inesita's visits, including the spiritualist sessions, became almost as frequent as they'd been before, and communication between the two of them also became more regular. What with one thing and another, the exchange of letters and the red tape lasted about a year and a half. In all that time, according to the letters Inesita left me to study, her daughter had straightened herself out a bit.

Her first visit to Washington was the turning point. Before saying goodbye to Yamila, she herself had said she was ready to live in Washington. Yamila helped her all she could. First she traveled to Miami at the end of the summer and let her house through a real estate agency. She sold some of the belongings she didn't need, and kept the decent electrical equipment. She even organized the move for Gracielita, who for the first time travelled by train, because she was taking a lot of things with her, but said that it would be the very last time, since, according to her, she was convinced the trains in the United States take even longer than those in Cuba. 'I didn't look back,' she wrote to her mother. In her own words, there was no single reason that led her to take that decision, but an accumulation of incidents:

Mima, I can't take Miami any more. The propaganda here is so contagious I was being contaminated without realizing it. While people in Washington think for themselves, decide what they want to do and who they want to do it with, in Miami I came to live in dread, with strange forebodings, in fear, and I didn't realize it until my true friends in Washington opened my eyes. I felt hounded. As I told you once before, it's not that I'm going to get caught up in the politics, because even my relationship with some good people in Miami got messed up because everyone there wants you to think just like them. And you know you can't change us Cubans, because we're a world unto ourselves. I know that things aren't one hundred per cent good in Cuba, but every time a balsero, a writer or an artist, a plane hijacker, someone from the military or even a former government functionary arrives, they say the worst things about what's going on in Cuba. My conscience is clear. I never took part in those games. Not before, and not after. I left Cuba precisely because of that same kind of opportunism, which hurt the country more than the blockade itself. Things have got really ugly since they passed the Cuban Democracy Act, the so-called Torricelli Bill. There are people who support it and others who are against it, but they don't dare say so in public. A short time ago there was a big debate in the Miami press between a black historian of Cuban origin called Carlos Moore, who has been living for years in one of the French Caribbean islands, and the most right wing of the exiled Cubans. The only thing this Mr Moore said was that it was counterproductive for Cubans who live in Cuba to support the strengthening of the economic blockade against Cuba, and that the people should be left to sort out their own problems. But I believe he also expected that the same thing that happened in the old socialist countries would happen in Cuba. Yet, according to what he said in an interview in El Nuevo Herald, these groups form 'a kind of semi-autonomous republic of white, Spanish-speaking Cuban Americans' who in post-Castro Cuba want to re-establish private militia, paramilitary political organizations, radio stations giving *out disinformation, tabloid press, demagogic politicians and a general climate of intimidation and terror against artists, free thinkers and liberal dissidents. 'If all this materializes,' said Moore, 'it would throw Cuba into decades of political torment, civil war, social tensions and shortages, which would inevitably affect the rest of Latin America and the Caribbean.' Isn't that reason enough to run away from Miami? Even he left like a shot, having been in Miami giving lectures and promoting his book on Cuba. And it never stops, Mima. On the streets, in the stores, in the newspapers, on the radio, in the schools, in the universities, wherever. I no longer had any desire even to go out, or to look for work. I couldn't go on living with that paranoia. What happened in the socialist countries makes me very afraid, and I simply couldn't go on like that. Yamila wasn't surprised by any of what I've been saying to you. She just told me she was very happy with the conclusions I eventually drew, and that it's never too late to make amends. Here in Washington I feel I've come back to life. You can't begin to imagine the anxiety I've been living with all these years.*

I could quite understand why Inesita appeared that day with her heart in her mouth. These letters, along with others Inesita brought from then on, helped to distract me for a while and to plan how I would incorporate all that material into what was already forming into a memoir, which Inesita and Julia were quietly and willingly helping me write, all of which made my son very happy when I told him about it in a letter.

Gracielita established herself in Washington with the help and co-operation of those who were her first real family in the North. She was really happy because Tony and Magdalena between them helped her to find a temporary position as a laboratory assistant in a two-year college for Afro-North-American students. But the biggest news was that she had started going out with Sergio, which Inesita interpreted as being a real summersault, showing how much her daughter had changed.

Gracielita didn't go into much detail, which mortified her mother a bit, making her complain about the lack of explanation. For example, after Inesita had resolved to sort out her part of the papers with Immigration, Gracielita didn't let her know anything about how the preparations for her trip were going, or when she was thinking of coming. She limited herself to saying she'd received notification from the Consulate. Inesita even wanted to know whether she had any intention of marrying some day, to which her daughter replied that when the time came, and if she made that decision, then she'd be the first to know, but for now she had no intention of marrying, much less giving birth. That's where Inesita's obsession came from, since with every letter from her darling daughter, the hope of having grandchildren drew further and further away. Yet, she spoke about the city and how much she liked it. She told her about her first weekend in New York, with her friend Sergio, Yamila and Tony, and what a good time she had. They went in Yamila's car, and stayed in a hotel in the heart of the city. Always together, the four friends visited museums, and they went to Central Park, which according to Gracielita is like Lenin Park multiplied by ten, starting at 23rd and L in Vedado. They even went to a concert by Gonzalo Rubalcaba, a young Cuban pianist who was on tour in the United States, and they had a good time. 'Really swell', she'd written at the end of the letter.

On her return to Washington, Gracielita was already preparing to surprise her mother with the trip she'd been planning for the end of the following July or early August. Her work contract was only for one school year, and when she came back from Cuba she would look for something else. She was breathing a different atmosphere now, because there the people thought more about how to resolve the conflict between Cuba and the United States through means other than the insults, intimidation and violence of Miami. She said there was also hope of an invitation from the government to a meeting in Havana between the Cuban exile community in various countries and Cuban officials, and she hoped things would move faster, for, despite feeling a lot better now, she felt in the air, with nothing to hold on to. Another subject Gracielita didn't go into detail about was what was being said about Cuba, in those days when the Special Period was causing more devastation than Hurricane Flora. Every so often, Gracielita would write something about what was in the newspapers, but there wasn't anything really new, according to her, since everyone agreed that the economic crisis in Cuba was going from bad to worse, and we knew that better than anyone. But she also said that every time more *balseros* arrived on the Florida coast, the stories they told were alarming. Tales about those who drowned and became a feast for the sharks divided everyone in their opinion of what was making people throw themselves into such an adventure so full of danger and uncertainty. They'd even been holding symbolic funerals in Little Havana, which turned into demonstrations against Cuba, real repudiation rallies.

The recent arrivals spoke of the lack of medicine, the lack of food, the lack of freedom, the lack of everything. Inesita, too, told Gracielita the same as I told my son and his family. We were up to our necks in water, but by making little jumps we were still able to breathe.

Although Gracielita didn't refer to it until months later, when she was in Havana, she had a premonition that something like Mariel was being master minded by some. There were too many coincidences, she told her mother during her visit. On the one hand, going into the embassies in Havana, one after the other, then the enormous number of *balseros* and hijacking of boats. There was even a young blond man, very good looking and healthy, who turned up one day on one of the Miami beaches on a surfboard, as if it was nothing. He was on the front page of many papers and earned a lot of money advertising a windsurf board factory, all of this was on the radio abroad.

Gracielita wasn't wrong. In Havana, the country's capital, in particular, there was agitation in summer 1993. Very strange things were happening. People were seeking asylum in the embassies, one after the other, as if it were a kid's game, pressuring the government to let them leave Cuba: just like before Mariel. There were thefts, armed assaults, murders, rapes. People got irritated over everything. Nobody wanted to work, and there was widespread indolence regarding the problems of others, which had never happened before. The lack of gas, kerosene and even charcoal for cooking had the housewives up in arms. Eneida, Baba's woman, was like she'd never been before, cursing the government at the top of her voice, above all every time the electricity went off at night, just when the Brazilian soap was starting. It was really good, but it was impossible to keep up with it because of the power cuts. I'd even stopped making my *durofríos*, because there was no point. Apart from the fact that there wasn't much to make them from, when I'd managed to fill a couple of trays, they'd all melt, and the small amount of food I had stored would go bad. It was the pits!

On the other hand, the *solar* stayed much the same. Katia had gone to live in Miramar with a Spaniard who owned a discotheque in Santa María del Mar. Foreign tourism had gone from strength to strength, and ever since they had decriminalized owning hard currency, people had gone crazy because now the peso wasn't worth even wiping your hands on, and not everyone has family abroad. Katia herself, who had had problems for going around with foreign money, was surprised by the measure. Things had got very expensive, and if it wasn't for those little greenbacks, which people started to call *fulas*, from *fulastre*, you couldn't get hold of much. Contraband had flourished to such an extent that it was the only way you could find anything to eat. Everyone was caught up in it, making millionaires out of crooks, who could get you even an elephant on a bicycle, if you could pay for it.

In the middle of all this day-to-day struggle, halfway through February, Gracielita wrote to her mother saying that at last she had everything in place to travel to Havana in July. She was still waiting for confirmation of the flight, but she wanted to give her the news since she knew how much it would cheer her up. And, of course, it did, and, even though there were still five months of anxious waiting to go, Inesita had already begun to make plans. When she brought me the news, I shared it with her as though Gracielita were my own daughter. Ramoncito and his family didn't intend coming back for now, but we kept in touch by phone almost every month. By comparison, in all those years Inesita had heard her daughter's voice just once, on a cassette she had sent just before her thirtieth birthday, nothing like what she was about to experience in a few months' time.

With You From Afar

The same night, that Monday, 15ᵗʰ of August, after Inesita and I went to the airport in Rancho Boyeros to say goodbye to Gracielita, the radio news was announcing that the hundreds of people who had the day before occupied the tanker *Jussara*, loaded with crude oil in the port of Mariel, had left voluntarily, without the need for any violence. It was a crazy thing to do, because you have to be really desperate to do something like that. Though that's what I thought, I never let Inesita know, let alone her daughter, out of respect. But without question all these things happening wouldn't help her much. Or perhaps I'm wrong.

Inesita had decided to come back to my place to release some of the tension built up during all those days, and to have a bite of something to eat. She was heartbroken. Shut in her own sadness, and me giving her what company I could, we watched the eight o'clock television news, when the presenter read a note from the Ministry of the Interior announcing the end of the dramatic episode that had kept the government in suspense since the day before. The mass boarding had happened on Sunday, just after the rally in Mariel in homage to the 38-year-old naval officer, Roberto Aguilar Reyes, who had been murdered by a recruit during the hijacking of another boat the week before. It seems some people had plotted with the tanker's Greek captain to take it North to the United States. But from the start, MININT let it be known they had taken special measures to prevent the movement of the foreign ship, which was loaded with fuel.

I'd had a couple of opportunities to spend time with Gracielita during the two weeks she was in Havana, and I saw for myself how hard it was for her to disguise how anxious she was, right to the last moment of her visit.

There were too many coincidences. The memories of fourteen years ago pursued her constantly, day and night, from when we welcomed her at the same airport on the morning of Sunday, 31st July, until we said goodbye.

Inesita had decided to stay at my place, to leave very early for Rancho Boyeros. That night I fixed her hair really beautifully, and we chatted with Julia until the early hours. It goes without saying that the poor woman never closed her eyes that night. I did go to bed some time after two, but in my sleep I could sense her tossing and turning in the folding bed Julia had lent me. We were up before six, and I prepared her first an infusion of lime leaves, and then we had some warm rice pudding made with condensed milk for breakfast.

By seven o'clock we were already at the bus stop at the Ciudad Deportiva, and two and a half hours later reached the airport. To be honest I'd done all this because Inesita had been so insistent, but for a while now I hadn't been going out, so as to avoid the whole tragedy of trying to catch a bus, especially to there. The last time I'd been in the airport was when my son and his family left, but then we all went in one of their friends' car. The journey takes less than half an hour by car, but the bus, if it turns up and stops, takes at least three times as long. But with God's help we got there in the end, though we had to hurry because the plane was about to land at the new terminal on Rancho Boyeros Avenue, and we'd by mistake gone to the old one.

Inesita had pulled herself together. The infusion had done her good. She was calm and happy, like most of the people piled behind the two parallel wooden barriers haplessly there to hold back the public. The moment long awaited by both mother and daughter finally came. The screaming of some two or three hundred people – I would think at least three or four per passenger – was unbearable. Almost an hour after the plane landed, Gracielita, looking radiant, appeared through the automatic passenger exit and entry gate. Her mother had gone so cold I thought her blood pressure had dropped and she was going to faint, and if it hadn't been for the tremendous '*Mima!*' that Gracielita shouted out above all the noise, I don't believe the woman would have recovered.

The meeting was so, so emotional, full of hugs and kisses, and more hugs and more kisses, that even my eyes watered.

'Darling, do you remember Marta? She saw you being born. Give her a kiss too, she's your aunt and has helped me so much all these years.'

Half timid, and visibly moved, the girl also gave me a strong embrace, telling me that of course she remembered me and knew how much I'd cared for her dear mother.

'Thank you, Marta, thank you so much! I think if it hadn't been for you...'

'Not a word, girl! You don't have to thank me. Your mother's like another sister to me. I'm so happy as well that you've come, looking so pretty. May you be blessed by the santos! Now, see to your mother, she needs you a lot.'

All the time arm in arm, or holding hands, Gracielita and her mother sorted out the baggage and the plastic bag with the medicines. The taxi Gracielita had hired dropped me at home, and the two of them continued on to the Hotel Comodoro, where they would be staying for two weeks. Gracielita would have liked to stay at her mother's place, but the tourist package for the Cuban community abroad still didn't include that option. Exactly one week after Gracielita left, the government announced a series of modifications to Cuban migration policy, stipulating, among other things, that it would no longer be necessary to have a hotel reservation in order to travel to Cuba, and that those who had left the country legally would no longer need a visa to enter Cuba, for a regulated period, as long as they had done nothing against the Revolution. Although Gracielita had become a North-American citizen, she was obliged to use a Cuban passport to enter the country of her birth, since it didn't recognise what they call dual citizenship.

It was on the Sunday after her arrival that Inesita and her daughter appeared at my place around midday, to invite Julia and me to lunch at the hotel. They also brought us a few things, which we thanked them for a lot. As luck would have it, I'd already cooked some soy empanadas, and I set about fixing them something delicious to eat, which meant we didn't have to go out, since neither Julia nor I really wanted to, at such short notice, without being dressed up for the occasion. Besides, Gracielita didn't have to spend her dollars on us.

The girl was beautiful, as sweet as ever. She had her long, well-groomed braids tied up with a really pretty orange-colored band. Her beautiful hands, with the nails painted magenta, suited her tan from the sun and salt she'd been enjoying in the hotel swimming pool and beach. Those days of rest and good food with her daughter had done Inesita the world of good. Of course they talked a lot, as mother to daughter, and woman to woman, each reflecting on her achievements, her mistakes and life's miracles, but without much fuss on Inesita's part, and with much maturity on Gracielita's, according to what her mother told me much later, after her daughter had left.

That hot, endless summer, it was impossible not to talk about the country's current situation. It so happened that the power cut began early that day, and I'd disconnected the fridge to avoid burning out the motor when the electricity came back on. So I had nothing cold to offer them, and it was the same with everyone around. Gracielita was struck by many things she'd seen in the few days she'd been there, especially the deterioration of Havana. She'd quickly realized people seemed to be waiting for something important to happen, as if they expected the lifting of the US blockade would solve overnight all the problems that had built up over more than thirty years. She also realized that many people were pretending about everything, exaggerating the slightest things, constantly telling lies, much more than she'd known years before. She had the impression that nobody cared about anything.

Gracielita was alarmed by the events of the 5th of August, a few days after her arrival, when hundreds of young people started throwing stones at the tourist shops of the Hotel Deauville, and had a run-in with the police on Escobar, Virtudes, Galiano and San Lázaro Streets, near the Malecón. Nothing like it had ever happened before, not even at the time of Mariel. Days earlier, the ferry that makes the trip across the bay between Casablanca and Havana had been hijacked, under the astonished gaze of the people walking along Avenida del Puerto. That was after the other hijacking of the passenger ferry to Regla, on none other than the 26th of July. Thirty people were on board, including the crew. Half of them returned, and the rest were rescued by the US Coast Guard. But before that the worst incident of all took place, when a tugboat was hijacked in Havana harbour with sixty-three people on board, again with the intention of travelling North. The boat sank in high seas, having been chased and intercepted by three other tugs. When two of the boats crashed, thirty-one people survived and another thirty-two were taken in anger by *Yemayá Olokun*, who lives enchained at the bottom of the sea. You can't play around with her. Gracielita had been aware of events from long before, and had even brought two or three newspapers from Miami and Washington containing articles specifically about that incident, accusing the government of having caused the sinking of the tug *13 de Marzo*.

After we had a better lunch than I'd expected, because it turned out everyone enjoyed my soy empanadas, Gracielita told us lots of stories about how things were in the United States, about her life in Washington, and about her friends.

'Sergio and I got along really well from the first moment, and we love each other, but we're not in any hurry, and enjoying the romance. Look how handsome and elegant he is in this photo we took one night in Eduardo's club.'

Gracielita had taken out a small photo album from her handbag and was showing us one of her and Sergio very close, surrounded by a group of friends who she identified one by one.

Inesita was spellbound contemplating her daughter, and softly stroking her hair, arms and shoulders, as if cleansing her of all the evil eye that might have befallen her, she opened up her mother's heart and voiced her innermost thoughts:

'Isn't my daughter beautiful, Marta? And what do you say, Julia?'

Up until then, Inesita didn't know Gracielita had moved into Sergio's spacious apartment, and that they'd been living together for four months. His business was doing very well. Gracielita told us they were thinking of visiting Cuba together, without waiting for relations between the two countries to improve, and they were convinced that Cuba and the United States couldn't go on being so hostile to one another for much longer, now so many countries that had had serious disputes were sorting out their differences and even making concessions. One of Sergio's dreams was to open a commercial design press, since he was an expert in that area and very skilled in the new technologies.

'But I don't know, *Mima*... I've told you, I don't know if we will get married or have children, or anything, though I don't have much longer to make up my mind – but Sergio and I are into other things. Yes, we're serious about each other, at least up to now. But I can't say for sure if in the future we'd come back here to live, though we want to be able to come and go from our own country whenever we wish and to help out as much and as honestly as we can. Not everyone who lives over there thinks the same way, of course. True, there are a lot of good people, but there are also a lot of bitter and resentful people. I've learned a lot, and I've been able to compare our conflicts with those of that country. You can't imagine what things are like there! There's so much wealth, yet so many very poor and neglected people, who will continue like that to the end of their lives, if some kind of a miracle doesn't happen. And in the United States, people don't believe in miracles like we do, even if they go to the churches and temples every day. My big dilemma continues to be why people feel forced to leave their country when in reality they don't want to. And I've thought about it a lot during all these years. I don't regret the decision I made; nobody forced me. I left out of my own conviction that something was going wrong, and I was in conflict with my other self. For years I was conscious of the indignation of a whole people towards those of us who left through Mariel. But even so, I don't believe I was altogether wrong.'

At this point, I got up from the table and went to make some of the good coffee she had brought. Mmmm… what an aroma! Gracielita had paused, but I told her from the kitchen to continue, I was listening. That girl has a golden tongue. She expresses herself so well! If only I could write as she talks! I could easily understand what she felt. It didn't matter that she wasn't my own daughter, or that I didn't know her as well as her mother did, but I understood her. I'm convinced that even at my age I wouldn't be justified in criticizing her actions, however desperate they were. There's a strange force in human beings that compels us to make decisions that can't always be explained.

After drinking the coffee and lighting a menthol cigarette that looked like a thin little cigar, which Inesita had brought me from the Comodoro, Julia asked Gracielita whether she sometimes had a pain in her neck and forehead, and felt really exhausted. Gracielita had said she did, on repeated occasions, although I don't know whether she said so to please Julia, who immediately set about blessing her, without asking what her beliefs were. With her pretty smile, Gracielita told her it was alright, but that they shouldn't forget she was still a scientist, and commented that every day Miami seemed more and more like Havana, with these customs of magic and religion. I went into the kitchen, and left the three of them alone for a moment, while they joked that even the priests were becoming scientists, and asked Gracielita if she realized that even the Pope was concerning himself more with scientific than religious questions. 'And soon even with *espiritismo* and santeria, you'll see!' Julia told her, half seriously, and half in jest, which provoked some laughs. After that I could only hear the last part of the prayer for the Holy *Virgen de la Caridad del Cobre*:

> *Let this body rise above the vibrations of its lower nature and reach the spiritual mind through which we know you. Bring me peace, strength and life, I beg you, O ever-present spirit, because I am indeed your daughter. Amen.*

Having said the prayer, Julia told her that she didn't have to, but when she got home she should place a glass of fresh water on top of a cupboard or shelf, somewhere high up, and that she should read the prayer from time to time at night, before going to bed, after wetting her fingers with a little of the water, thinking about her, and should then throw the water out into the street, then she'd see how the headaches would stop.

After thanking Julia for the advice and me for the food, mother and daughter made ready to leave in search of a working telephone to call for a taxi, unless they found one on the Calzada del Cerro. But in keeping with her good manners, Gracielita invited us again, this time to go to the theater to see *Santa Camila de La Habana Vieja*, a play that had caused quite a stir in the 1960s. Now it had been put on again at the Bertolt Brecht Café Theater, on the corner of Línea and J Street, in Vedado, and it was packed every weekend, from Friday to Sunday. My son had been a good friend of José Brene, playwright, who died a few years back, apparently from drinking and fast living, and had taken me to the opening, where I met him. Brene was a likeable man, with a down-to-earth wisdom, who had travelled the entire world as a merchant marine and overnight had become a famous scriptwriter for theater and then radio and television.

Julia, for her part, had never in her life set foot in a theater, and neither did she have any intention of making an exception now. So she gave Gracielita a little kiss on the cheek, and thanked her for the invitation. I was certainly going to take her up on it, because I didn't have anything to do and was totally bored. Of course I knew the play. I remember when it first opened in the Musical Theater of Havana, there were a lot of people there who hardly knew what a theater was like on the inside. You could tell from way off that they were people from the barrios who, like me, respected the santos, and who also wanted to make sure they weren't being messed around with. The applause was the best answer imaginable. I couldn't remember the play very well, scene by scene, since a lot of water had flowed under the bridge since then, but I knew it was about our lives, we people of the *solar*.

The theme was similar to *María Antonia*, by Eugenio Hernández, another of my son's friends and a neighbor of ours, from round the corner on Cerezo Street. That play also caused a sensation here in Havana, because it reflected much of our lives, with poverty, trash talking, flashy dressing, and that machismo of ours, all mixed up with the santería. The opening was at the Mella, in 1967, and throughout its run it played to full houses and standing ovations from the audience. The whole of Havana... well, that's a bit of an exaggeration, but on that occasion, many people went to the theater for the first time to see *María Antonia*.

I really enjoyed myself that night, because it had been a long time since I last went out, and it cleared my mind. Gracielita behaved just as a good daughter who loves her mother should behave, very obliging. From the theater we went to the hotel, always by taxi, because there was no way we could catch a bus. The hotel is beautiful. I'd never imagined it would be like that. We went to the café and ordered ham and cheese sandwiches, beer and then ice cream and coffee. It was years since I'd seen anything like that. Then we walked for a while by the swimming pool and the little beach. We went up to the room, watched color television, even with programs from the United States, we chatted; in short, I had a lovely time, it was like a breath of fresh air. At around two in the morning, they went down with me to the hotel entrance, where Gracielita got me a taxi to take me back to the reality of my Cerro *solar*. But, well, I'd been in the Hotel Comodoro.

Meanwhile, Havana continued very agitated. The Youth organized an act of revolutionary reaffirmation for Saturday the 13th, at La Punta del Malecón in Havana, where days earlier there'd been a showdown between the people and the new antisocials. It had been no coincidence that same day Fidel celebrated his 68th birthday, and the young people were going to mark it with songs and patriotic anthems, updated with what was happening. It was good to know not everyone was against the Revolution, which was going through such bad times.

It was later, returning from the airport with Inesita, she told me that Gracielita had said she wanted to take part in the action, so that nobody could lie to her about it, since on her return her people would ask her what had been going on in Havana, and she didn't want to say she had spent the whole time in the hotel swimming pool talking with her mother.

We had gone through two weeks of serious events, with the two murders, and it just so happened the two were black: the 38-year-old sailor and the 19-year-old policeman named Gabriel Lamoth Caballero. The boy was born in Guantánamo, and they held a wake for him there. According to the news, more than 150,000 people turned out for the ceremony in Mariana Grajales Revolution Square, and he was posthumously awarded the Antonio Maceo Order. I thought to myself it was too much of a coincidence that the Order they gave to the young man who had fallen was that of the Bronze Titan, and that the wake took place in the square that bore the name of the mother of the Maceos. I say it was too much of a coincidence, because the only two to fall during those days were from our race, like Mariana and Maceo. The mothers of those who had fallen also behaved like Marianas that day. It was as if the santos were reminding us that there were still many sacrifices to make before we could live with a little more dignity. Ay, God Almighty, how much longer?

Gracielita didn't try to see any of her old friends. She didn't even mention them. The night before her return she left several postcards of pretty Cuban scenes with her mother for her to mail. One was to Helga, who lived and worked in Berlin, which was now a single city, because the country had been reunified. Her mother couldn't read it, because it was in German. She saw that the others were for her friend Yamila, señora Robledo y Albemar, Tony, Eduardo, Magdalena and a special one for Sergio, with a lovely greeting that said:

I love you, and I'll go on loving you. If only we'd been together.
Kisses, Gracielita.

That was the only postcard Inesita read, and she pressed it tight to her chest.

The taxi with Gracielita and her mother came to pick me up mid-morning, since the flight was leaving at two in the afternoon, and the check-in at Boyeros was at least as chaotic as in Miami, if not more so, according to Gracielita. They both looked very sad, as you'd expect, but each for their own reasons. All that mattered to Inesita was her darling daughter, who was leaving again, and nobody knew whether her weak heart could stand another separation, especially if she'd have to wait so long for the next visit. Although many things changed in the weeks and months following her return, the state of mind of these two women depended in large measure on the ironies of politics between the two countries, and for all I've tried to understand, I find it harder and harder to accept that every day I understand less. At that precise moment few people imagined that whole business of makeshift rafts from bits of wood and anything else that might float, and setting out to sea from the beaches or the Malecón itself, heading North, would end so soon, after the United States got the wind up about Fidel's warnings that the pot would be at pressure point again, as they say.

At last came the farewell hugs and more hugs and weeping. There were too many ironies, standing in the middle of the airport, saying goodbye to Gracielita, who was going to Miami. She never told us anything, but I'm sure that from the plane she would have looked down trying to see, from the height of an eagle, a raft or two adrift on the sea.

'Come back soon, girl,' I whispered to her when it was my turn for hugs. Gracielita let two tears fall, which dampened my soul. She didn't speak, her throat was choked up, as were ours. I swallowed back my tears and dried hers. She kissed me on the cheek, and whispered in my ear, with a sigh that came from the depths of her being:

'Ay, Marta, I don't know if I can...!'

GLOSSARY

abakuá – all-male religious society unique to Cuba, and also a member of the society, likewise known as *ñáñigo*.

aguardiente – firewater, a strong, unrefined white rum made from sugar cane, associated with poor rural and urban settings and Afro-Cuban religions.

Antonio Maceo – mulatto general from eastern Cuba, in the 1868-78 and 1895-98 wars of independence fight against Spain, who died in battle in 1896, often referred to in Cuba as the Bronze Titan.

asere – common greeting of friendship among men, originating in abakuá.

balsero – rafter, referring to the 1994 exodus on makeshift rafts.

barbudos – 'bearded ones', referring to those fighting with Fidel Castro in the Sierra Maestra mountains in the 1950s, against the Batista regime.

Batista – Fulgencio Batista, who first came to power in the 1933 Sergeant's Revolt, engineered the 1952 coup, and fled Cuba on 31st of December 1958. A light-skinned black, he was euphemistically called 'Indio' (Indian).

bisneo - Business.

bolita – a form of lottery that before 1959 was illegal but tolerated by the police and other authorities who were given backhanders and after 1959 was prohibited and penalised, but not eliminated. The bets were 'collected' by individuals working as runners on commission.

bolos – slang for the Soviet technicians working in Cuba, who were seen as big and round; literally translates as bowls.

botánica – store selling religious artefacts, and herbs and flowers with medicinal and magical properties.

237

BRAC – Buró de Represión Anti-Comunista (Bureau for Anti-Communist Repression).

brujería – offerings for the gods or spirits, which may be food, flowers or other objects, that might be left by a tree or roadside; associated with witchcraft as the magic of the blacks, as opposed to *hechicería*, the witchcraft magic of the whites.

Carabalí – generic name for African slaves embarked from the West African port of Old Calabar.

carabela - During the slavery period in Cuba, *carabela* was the term of Congo origin, meaning 'from the same place', used to refer to Africans transported on the same slave ship, in the sense of fictive kin and also figuratively 'we're all un the same boat now'. Here it is used as a play on the word *calavera*, which translates as skull or skeleton.

Castro – Fidel Castro, who came to power with the 1959 Revolution and was President of Cuba until 2008.

CDR – Comité de Defensa de la Revolución (Committee for the Defense of the Revolution).

Changó – *sangó, Shangó, xangó,* orisha (*santo*) in the pantheon of the Afro-Cuban religion known as santeria or *lucumí*, god of thunder and war, syncretised with the Catholic saint *Santa Bárbara*.

Chester - Chesterfield cigarettes.

Chow – Show

compañero/a – translates as companion and comrade, widely used in Cuba.

Congo – generic name for African slaves of Central African Bantu origin, in what is today the Congo and Angola, who were reputed to be fearsome and warriors.

criadita – affectionate or pejorative terms for *criada* (maid), depending on the user and the context, literally translates as little maid.

Crusellas – soap and candle company founded in Havana in 1863 by Catalan brothers Juan and José Crusellas, in a 1929 joint marketing venture with Colgate-Palmolive, and as of 1967 operating out of Miami. It was famous for its products and advertising in Cuba in the 1940s and 1950s.

CTC – Central de Trabajadores de Cuba (Central Confederation of Cuban Workers).

danzón – musical genre that evolved in Cuba in the second half of the nineteenth century from a fusion of African and European rhythms, especially the contradanse/*contradanza*, forerunner to the *son*.

Day of the Kings – Epiphany, 6th of January, in Cuba the only day slaves were allowed their festivities in return for small gifts, the origin of Cuban carnival.

Divorciadas – Divorced Women, a hit radio soap in Cuba in the early 1950s.

durofrío – flavoured ice-cube, made in the ice tray of a home refrigerator and often sold in the barrio.

El Derecho de Nacer – The Right to be Born, a famous Cuban radio soap of 1948-9.

Eleggúa – Elegba/Legba, orisha in the pantheon of the Afro-Cuban religion known as santeria, who opens and closes all ceremonies, as also the crossroads for the deities, holding the key to 21 pathways, whose special day is Monday; syncretised with the Catholic *San Antonio* (St Anthony).

escoriados – invented word, which translates as scumbags, to denote the people who left in the 1980 Mariel boatlift and were at the time referred to in Cuba as *escoria* (scum).

espiritismo – spiritism in Cuba, known as *espiritismo de cordón*, with a fundamental belief in good and evil spirits, and considered 'cleaner' than santeria since it does not involve animal sacrifice; as with Alan Kardec's Spiritism, involves belief in a superior infinite intelligence (one God) and spiritual life as eternal.

filipina – long- or short-sleeved shirt for men, with chest and flank pockets, pleats, and sometimes embroidery, made from cotton, silk, linen or synthetic fabric, considered a dress shirt in tropical countries and worn at solemn ceremonies.

Florisén – Florsheim shoes.

FOCSA – a building called that because, when it started being built in the mid-1950s, the main investment came from the company Fomento de Obras y Construcciones Sociedad Anónima (Construction Works Development, Ltd). Situated in the heart of Havana's central Vedado district, it is considered one of the seven wonder of civil engineering. It was built in 3-4 months, and its completion in 1956 caused a sensation in Cuba for its technological innovation, signalling the era of Havana's tall buildings.

free belly – The 'free belly' law was passed in 1870, whereby the children of slaves were, according to law, born free.

fula/fulastre –*fula* was the term popularly given to the US dollar, or greenback, and *fulastre* translates as rotten.

gangá – also *ngangá*, referring to one of the ethnic groupings in Africa.

GDR – German Democratic Republic, East Germany before the fall of the Berlin Wall in 1989 and the break-up of the Soviet Union shortly after.

Granma – official daily newspaper of the Cuban Communist Party.

Guéstinjaus - Westinghouse.

japi-beidi-tuyu – Happy Birthday to You

Guantanamera – literally a woman from Guantánamo, in eastern Cuba; theme tune for a radio programme on crimes of passion taken from the press and police archives, with the *guajiro* or peasant voice of Joseíto Fernández, later to become a signature patriotic song.

guaposo – tough macho kind of man, often associated with blacks, the opposite of *pepillo.*

guapita – roughly made sleeveless shirt, associated with *guapos*, those considered tough on the streets.

guayabera – see *Filipina*.

Guerrita del Negro – Little Black War, also known as the Race War, of 1912, when several thousand blacks were massacred in Cuba's eastern Oriente province.

güije – goblin-type creature in parts like the north of Las Villas province in Cuba, described by some as a little old black man, by others as a black boy with bulging eyes.

güiro – musical instrument made out of a hollow gourd, etched with lines, played by passing a stick over the lines

gusanos – worms, the name given to those who left Cuba after the 1959 revolution, alluding to how they 'wormed' their way into the United States.

ICR-T – Instituto Cubano de Radio y Televisión (Cuban Broadcasting Institute).

indio – term used to characterise Amerindian features, especially in black and mulatto Cubans; euphemistically used to describe Batista (*El Indio*), as it was also widely coined at the time under the Rafael Leonidas Trujillo regime in the Dominican Republic for all Dominican blacks and mulattos, to distinguish them from Haitians.

ireme – *diablito* (little devil) masked figure of *abakuá* on the Day of the Kings.

isleño/a, isleñito/a – islander, commonly used in Cuba to refer to a Canary Islander.

jabao/a, jabaíto/a, jabá – light-skinned person with hair and facial features associated with darker-skinned persons.

jinetero/a – term used for those going with foreigners, usually though not always offering sex, for money or kind, literally translates as jockey, alluding to 'mounting' for the ride.

kilo prieto – Cuban term for the US cent, which circulated in Cuba at the time; cent coins of the US dollar were used in offerings for cleansing or exorcisms in Afro-Cuban religions.

Lechón/lechones – well-seasoned, slow-cooked pork, Cuban-style.

Machado – Gerardo Machado, who came to power in 1925 and was overthrown in the 1933 Revolution.

Malecón – the Havana seafront is a famous spot and hugs the length of the bay.

mambi/mambisa – used pejoratively by the Spaniards for the Cubans fighting their colonial power, signifying rebellious black, which over time has come to symbolise Cubans who are ready to fight and die for their country, as in the 1868-78 and 1895-98 wars of independence.

Mariana Grajales – a revolutionary independence fighter, a *mambisa*, mother of Antonio Maceo, and after whom the 1950s insurrectional platoon of women was named.

Marielito – one who left in the 1980 boatlift from the port of Mariel.

Martica, Martina, Martona, Martucha – diminutive, often affectionate, names for Marta.

micro – short for microbrigade, a group of voluntary workers in construction.

Mima – affectionate contraction of *mi mamá*, my mother.

MININT – Ministerio del Interior (Ministry of the Interior).

MINREX – Ministerio de Relaciones Exteriores (Ministry of Foreign Affairs).

moreno/a – black man/woman, used in slave times in contradistinction to *pardo/a*, for mulatto man/woman, and still used today whereas *pardo/a* has lost currency.

ñáñigo – see *abakuá*

negra, negrita, negrona – affectionate or pejorative terms for a black woman, depending on the user and the context, literally translate as black, little black, big black woman,

Nuestra Señora de la Caridad del Cobre – Our Lady of Charity of El Cobre. See *Virgen de la Caridad del Cobre.*

Nueva Trova – movement in Cuban music that emerged in the late 1960s, with its roots in the traditional trova, with often policitized lyrics, linked to the Latin American new song movement of the time.

palero/a – practitioner of the Afro-Cuban religion known as Regla de Congo, Mayombe or Palo Monte, from the Kongo/Congo nation, another of the main ethnic groupings to arrive in Cuba during the slave trade.

patria – homeland, watchword for the late nineteenth century independence struggles and late twentieth century revolution.

pepillada – a group of *pepillos.*

pepillo – fashionably dressed young man, mostly associated with whites.

peseta – basic unit of Spanish currency; in Cuba a twenty-cent coin.

peso/pesito – old Spanish silver coin; basic unit of Cuban currency, used in the diminutive form to refer to few of little value.

postigo – a small opening, usually in long wooden doors in older houses in Cuba, often the front door opening onto the main living room, which can be rectangular, square or oval in shape, serves as ventilation, and can be used to check on visitors and also to watch the world outside go by.

quince – fifteenth birthday/party, <u>the</u> party for girls in Hispanic tradition.

quinceañera – fifteenth birthday girl.

Radio Bemba – slang for word of mouth, *bemba* being a reference to the thick lips of black people.

real – a coin worth ten cents, a dime.

Reina por un día – Queen for a Day, a popular Cuban TV program of the 1950s, which was also an American TV radio and then TV programme, precursor to 'reality TV', versions of which were to be found throughout the Americas.

Rompe Saragüey – wild plant, scientific name Eupatorium odoratum, used for cleansing in santeria.

sagüero/a – person from the town of Sagua la Grande in what used to be Las Villas province.

San Lázaro – St Lazarus, in Cuba the revered saint of the poor and the needy and the sick, for whom pilgrimages are made on 17th of December to the altar in El Rincón, just outside Havana, to give offerings and make penitence; syncretised with the orisha *Babalú Ayé*.

Santa Bárbara – St Barbara, celebrated on 4th of December, syncretised with the orisha *Changó*.

santeria – Cuban religious belief system derived from Yoruba belief systems, also known as *regla de ocha* and *lucumí,* whose orishas or gods are syncretised with Catholic saints, to whom offerings are made in the form of food, plants, and animal sacrifice, for spiritual cleansing and other purposes.

santero/a – practitioner of santeria.

santo – orisha or god in santeria, deriving from the orishas of the Yoruba nation, one of the main ethnic groupings to arrive in Cuba during the slave trade, and syncretised with a catholic saint.

señorona – superlative of señora.

Siguaraya – popular name in Cuba for the Trichilla havanensis jacq, a tree which in Afro-Cuban religions is considered as sacred and is used to open roads and luck to whom invokes them, but closes them to the enemy, associated with the orisha *Changó*. There are also known medicinal properties. Cuba has been called *siguaraya* country (*país de la siguaraya*), figuratively meaning unbelievable things can happening there. Here also used as a play on *Alice in Wonderland*.